# WINGER

Also by Andrew Smith

*100 Sideways Miles*

# WINGER

ANDREW SMITH

SIMON & SCHUSTER BFYR

*New York   London   Toronto   Sydney   New Delhi*

*This is for my son, Trevin Smith,*
*who played rugby for me.*
*Until I broke his collarbone.*

*Now he writes.*

SIMON & SCHUSTER BFYR

An imprint of Simon & Schuster Children's Publishing Division

1230 Avenue of the Americas, New York, New York 10020

Text copyright © 2013 by Andrew Smith

Cover photograph copyright © 2013 by Meredith Jenks

Illustrations copyright © 2013 by Sam Bosma

SIMON & SCHUSTER BFYR is a trademark of Simon & Schuster, Inc.

For information about special discounts for bulk purchases, please contact Simon & Schuster Special Sales at 1-866-506-1949 or business@simonandschuster.com.

The Simon & Schuster Speakers Bureau can bring authors to your live event. For more information or to book an event, contact the Simon & Schuster Speakers Bureau at 1-866-248-3049 or visit our website at www.simonspeakers.com.

Also available in a SIMON & SCHUSTER BFYR hardcover edition

Book design by Lucy Ruth Cummins

The text for this book is set in Adobe Garamond.

The illustrations for this book were rendered in charcoal and ink washes.

Manufactured in the United States of America

First SIMON & SCHUSTER BFYR paperback edition September 2014

10  9  8  7  6

The Library of Congress has cataloged the hardcover edition as follows:

Smith, Andrew (Andrew Anselmo), 1959–

Winger / Andrew Smith. — 1st ed.

p. cm.

Summary: Two years younger than his classmates at a prestigious boarding school, fourteen-year-old Ryan Dean West grapples with living in the dorm for troublemakers, falling for his female best friend who thinks of him as just a kid, and playing wing on the Varsity rugby team with some of his frightening new dorm-mates.

ISBN 978-1-4424-4492-8 (hardcover) — ISBN 978-1-4424-4494-2 (eBook)

[1. Boarding schools—Fiction. 2. High schools—Fiction. 3. Schools—Fiction. 4. Interpersonal relations—Fiction. 5. Rugby football—Fiction.] I. Title.

PZ7.S64257Wi 2013

[Fic]—dc23

2011052750

ISBN 978-1-4424-4493-5 (paperback)

# ACKNOWLEDGMENTS

TO PLAY RUGBY AND TO BE A RUGBY player are inextricably enmeshed. There is something about the sport that attaches to character. Some of the greatest people I will ever know are ruggers. This book would never have worked its way out of me and onto the page without them. Davis Russ, a fly half, and Kyle Alvarez, a lock, had the bravest and most honorable makeup of anyone I've ever known, on and off the pitch. They were the models for all the good, selfless things the kids in *Winger* do. Landon Drake Alexsander Veis, a center, and Beau Mitchell Donohoe, a scrum half, made me laugh so many times, and I apologize if any of the funny things in *Winger* are an embarrassment to them. My friend and fellow author Joe Lunievicz, a fullback, was the first "real" person who got to read this manuscript. He is, after all, a rugger, and I had to be certain that I did the sport justice. And to Amy—the author A. S. King—thanks for keeping me from going as crazy as I likely would have gone.

And what a great team *Winger* has. Many thanks to my editor, David Gale, and Navah Wolfe, for their faith and persistence in making this story come to life; and to Sam Bosma for his amazing and spot-on artwork.

I have endless appreciation and love for my wife and kids who put up with me. Writing is every bit as hard on them as it is on me, and it's just as tough as rugby.

*crede quod habes, et habes*

# THE TOILET WORLD

I SAID A SILENT PRAYER.

Actually, *silent* is probably the only type of prayer a guy should attempt when his head's in a toilet.

And, in my prayer, I made sure to include specific thanks for the fact that the school year hadn't started yet, so the porcelain was impeccably white—as soothing to the eye as freshly fallen snow—and the water smelled like lemons and a heated swimming pool in summertime, all rolled into one.

Except it was a fucking toilet.

And my head was in it.

My feet, elevated in Nick Matthews's apelike paws while Casey Palmer tried to drive my face down past the surface of the pleasant-smelling water, were somewhere between my skinny ass and Saturn, pointing toward the plane my parents were currently heading back to Boston in, and whatever else is up there.

I hate football players.

And I gave thanks, too, or I thought about it while grunting and grimacing, for the weights I'd lifted over the summer, because even though they were about to snap like pencils, my locked elbows kept my actual face about three inches away from actual toilet fucking water.

But then I felt bad, because I was convinced that cussing during a prayer—even a silent one—meant that I would make my rookie debut in hell as soon as Casey and Nick succeeded at drowning me in a goddamned school-issue community toilet.

And I realized that all those movies and stories about how clearly a guy's thoughts and perceptions materialize in the expanding moments just before death were actually true, because I couldn't help but notice the nearly transparent and unperforated one-ply toilet paper that curled downward from the shiny chrome toilet-paper-cover-thing-that-looks-like-an-eighteen-wheeler's-mudflap-but-I-don't-know-what-the-hell-those-devices-are-called, and I thought to myself, *God! They make us use THAT kind of toilet paper here?*

And all this happened in the span of maybe three seconds, now that I think about it.

Oh, yeah. And I had spent the previous five weeks or so chanting a near-constant antiwimp, inner tantric mantra as an attempt to convince my brain that I was going to reinvent myself this year, that I wasn't going to be the little kid everyone ignored or, worse, paid attention to for the purpose of constructing cruel survival experiments involving toilets and the tensile strength of my skinny-bitch arms.

My mom and dad—Dad especially—were always getting on me about paying better attention to stuff. It kind of choked me up to think how proud he'd be of his boy at that moment for all the minute details I was taking in about my new, upside-down toilet world.

But I guess I should have paid more attention earlier to the fact that room two, which was my dorm room, wasn't the second fucking door down from the stairwell.

So when I walked in on Casey and Nick's room—room six, whose location made absolutely no mathematical sense to me at all—carrying my suitcase and duffel bag, and they were somewhere near what I could only guess were the completion stages of rolling a joint (some kids, especially kids like Casey and Nick, do that here because the woods are like one big, giant pot party to them), they not only warned me, in a very creepy Greek-chorus-in-a-tragedy-that-you-know-is-not-going-to-end-well-for-our-hero kind of way, to not ever step foot in their fucking room again, they came up with this spontaneous welcoming ritual that involved a toilet, the elevation of my feet (one of which had detached itself from a shoe, the same way a lizard loses its tail to distract potential predators) . . . and me.

That was a really long sentence, wasn't it?

I should probably stick to drawing pictures, which I do sometimes.

Okay. So there I was, in Upside-Down Toilet Land, about to collapse, wondering how bad toilet water could possibly taste, and I gritted my teeth and recited the convince-yourself mantra I'd been using: *"Crede quod habes, et habes,"* which means something like, if you believe in what you have, you'll have it.

At that moment, I believed I'd have the ability to hold my breath for a really long time.

Grunt.

Big inhale.

And maybe some cosmic forces happened to perfectly converge in the Universe of the Upside-Down Toilet. Maybe O-Hall had some kind of spell on it; or maybe things really *were* going to be different for me this year, because just at the precise limit of my endurance, a voice called out from the hallway.

"Mr. Palmer! Mr. Matthews!"

And they let me go.

Feet and head reoriented themselves.

The universe, which smelled pretty nice and lemony, was right again.

Nick Matthews started giggling like an idiot. Come to think of it, he did just about everything that way.

And Casey said, "Fuck. It's Farrow."

The boys ran out of the bathroom and left me there, alone, kind of like the last clueless guy at a party who just doesn't know when to go home.

But I wasn't going home.

I had stuff to do.

PART ONE:

# the overlap of everyone

# prologue

JOEY TOLD ME NOTHING EVER GOES back exactly the way it was, that things expand and contract—like breathing, but you could never fill your lungs up with the same air twice. He said some of the smartest things I ever heard, and he's the only one of my friends who really tried to keep me on track too.

And I'll be honest. I know exactly how hard that was.

# CHAPTER ONE

NOTHING COULD POSSIBLY SUCK WORSE than being a junior in high school, alone at the top of your class, and fourteen years old all at the same time. So the only way I braced up for those agonizing first weeks of the semester, and made myself feel any better about my situation, was by telling myself that it had to be better than being a senior at fifteen.

Didn't it?

My name is Ryan Dean West.

Ryan Dean is my first name.

You don't usually think a single name can have a space and two capitals in it, but mine does. Not a dash, a space. And I don't really like talking about my middle name.

I also never cuss, except in writing, and occasionally during silent prayer, so excuse me up front, because I can already tell I'm going to use the entire dictionary of cusswords when I tell the story of what happened to me and my friends during my eleventh-grade year at Pine Mountain.

PM is a *rich kids'* school. But it's not only a prestigious rich kids' school; it's also for rich kids who get in too much trouble because they're alone and ignored while their parents are off being congressmen or investment bankers or professional athletes. And I know I wasn't actually out of control, but somehow Pine Mountain decided to move me into Opportunity Hall, the dorm where they stuck the really bad kids, after they caught me hacking a cell phone account so I could make undetected, untraceable free calls.

They nearly kicked me out for that, but my grades saved me.

I like school, anyway, which increases the loser quotient above and beyond what most other kids would calculate, simply based on the whole two-years-younger-than-my-classmates thing.

The phone was a teacher's. I stole it, and my parents freaked out, but only for about fifteen minutes. That was all they had time for. But even in that short amount of time, I did count the phrase "You know better than that, Ryan Dean" forty-seven times.

To be honest, I'm just estimating, because I didn't think to count until about halfway through the lecture.

We're not allowed to have cell phones here, or iPods, or anything else that might distract us from "our program." And most of the kids at PM completely buy in to the discipline, but then again, most of them get to go home to those things every weekend. Like junkies who save their fixes for when there's no cops around.

I can understand why things are so strict here, because it is the best school around for the rich deviants of tomorrow. As far as the phone thing went, I just wanted to call Annie, who was home for the weekend. I was lonely, and it was her birthday.

I already knew that my O-Hall roommate was going to be Chas Becker, a senior who played second row on the school's rugby team.

Chas was as big as a tree, and every bit as smart, too. I hated him, and it had nothing to do with the age-old, traditional rivalry between backs and forwards in rugby. Chas was a friendless jerk who navigated the seas of high school with his rudder fixed on a steady course of intimidation and cruelty. And even though I'd grown about four inches since the end of last year and liked to tell myself that I finally—*finally!*—didn't look like a prepubescent minnow stuck in a pond of hammerheads like Chas, I knew that my reformative dorm assignment with Chas Becker in the role of bunk-bed mate was probably nothing more than an "opportunity" to go home in a plastic bag.

But I knew Chas from the team, even though I never talked to him at practice.

I might have been smaller and younger than the other boys, but I was the fastest runner in the whole school for anything up to a hundred meters, so by the end of the season last year, as a thirteen-year-old sophomore, I was playing wing for the varsity first fifteen (that's first string in rugby talk).

Besides wearing ties and uniforms, all students were required to play sports at PM. I kind of fell into rugby because running track was so boring, and rugby's a sport that even small guys can play—if you're fast enough and don't care about getting hit once in a while.

So I figured I could always outrun Chas if he ever went over the edge and came after me. But even now, as I write this, I can still remember the feeling of sitting on the bottom bunk, there in our quiet room, just staring in dread at the door, waiting for my room-mate to show up for first-semester check-in on that first Sunday morning in September.

All I had to do was make it through the first semester of eleventh grade without getting into any more trouble, and I'd get a chance to file my appeal to move back into my room with Seanie and JP in the boys' dorm. But staying out of trouble, like not getting killed while living with Chas Becker, was going to be a full-time job, and I knew that before I even set eyes on him.

# CHAPTER TWO

NO ONE HAD TO KNOCK IN O-HALL.

The knobless doors couldn't be locked, anyway.

That's the biggest part of the reason why my day started off upside down in a toilet.

So when I heard the door creak inward, it felt like all my guts knotted down to the size of a grape.

It was only Mr. Farrow, O-Hall's resident counselor, pushing his mousy face into the room, scanning the surroundings through thick wire glasses and looking disappointedly at my unopened suitcase, the duffel bag full of rugby gear stuffed and leaning beside it, a barrier in front of me, while I slumped down in the shadows of the lower bunk like I was hiding in a foxhole, preparing for Chas Becker's entrance.

"Ryan Dean," he said, "you'll have time to unpack your things before picking up your schedule, but I'm afraid you'll need to hurry."

I looked past Farrow's head, into the dark hallway, to see if he was alone.

I was still missing one shoe.

"I can do it this afternoon, Mr. Farrow," I said. "Or maybe after dinner."

I leaned forward and put my hands on my suitcase. "Should I go to the registrar?"

"Not yet." Mr. Farrow looked at a folder of schedules in his hands. "Your appointment is at one fifteen. You have time."

A shadow moved behind him.

"Excuse me, Mr. Farrow."

And there was Chas Becker, pushing the door wide and squeezing past Farrow as he hefted two canvas duffels that looked like the things a coroner would use to cart away bodies, and dropped them with a *thud!* in the middle of the floor.

Then Chas noticed me, and I could see the confused astonishment on his face.

"I'm rooming with *Winger*?" He turned to look at Farrow, like he didn't know if he was in the right place. Then he leered at me again. "How'd Winger end up in O-Hall?"

I didn't know if I should answer. And I didn't know if Chas even knew my actual name, because, like a lot of the guys on the team, he just called me Winger or Eleven (which was the number on my jersey), or the couple times when I'd dorked a kick, he called me Chicken Wing, or something worse that included the French word for "shower."

I glanced at Farrow, who shrugged like he was waiting for me to say something. Oh, and besides the sports, no cell phones, and the neckties and uniforms, PM had a very strict ethics policy about telling the truth, especially in front of officers of the Truth Police like Mr. Farrow.

"I stole a cell phone." I swallowed. "From a teacher."

"Winger's a boost?" Chas smiled. "How cool is that? Or is it dorky? I don't get it."

I felt embarrassed. I looked at my hands resting on my suitcase.

And then Chas, all six-foot-four inches and Mohawk-stripe of hair pointing him forward, stepped toward the bed, loomed over me like some giant animated tree, and said, "But you're sitting on my bed, Winger. Don't ever sit on my bed. You get tops."

"Okay."

I wasn't about to argue the Pine Mountain first-come-first-served tradition. Anyway, I thought he was going to hit me, so I was happy that Mr. Farrow was watching our heartwarming get-acquainted moment. Even though I'd always liked school, I suddenly realized how shitty this particular Sunday-before-the-school-year-begins was turning out after the simple addition of one Chas Becker. That, and the whole head-in-a-toilet thing.

And Mr. Farrow cleared his throat, mousylike, saying, "You're going to need to reinvent the haircut, Chas."

Nothing that bordered on the undisciplined or unorthodox was tolerated at PM. Not even facial hair, not that I had anything to worry about as far as that rule was concerned. I'd seen some girls at PM who came closer to getting into trouble over that rule than me. The only thing I'd ever shaved was maybe a few points off a Calculus test so my friends wouldn't hate me if I set the curve too high.

"I'll shave it off after schedules," Chas said.

"You'll need to do it before," Farrow answered. He explained, "You know that ID pictures are today, and you're not going in looking like that."

I waited until Chas backed up a step, and then I stood up, hitting my head squarely on the metal frame beneath my new sleeping spot.

And as I rubbed my scalp I thought Chas was probably just waiting for Farrow to leave so he could reassign me to the floor.

"You need to wear a scrum cap when you go to bed, too, Winger?" Scrum caps are things that some players wear to protect their heads in rugby. But wings don't wear them, and all they really are good for is keeping your ears from getting torn off, so second-row guys like Chas *had* to wear them. In fact, I clearly saw one on top of his kit bag when he came in and I felt like—*really* felt like—giving him a clever comeback so Farrow could see the new, eleventh-grade version of me, but I couldn't think of anything witty because my head hurt so bad.

INSERT HEAD HERE

BREATHING HOLES FOR THE FUCKING SQUIRREL THAT RUNS AROUND ON THE WHEEL INSIDE HIS CRANIAL CAVITY.

CHAS BECKER'S SCRUM CAP.
HAVE YOU EVER SEEN ANYTHING DORKIER IN *YOUR* LIFE???

I fucking hated Chas Becker.

There were chairs at each of the desks in the room, but I knew better than to pull one out, because Chas would just say that was his too. And as I fumbled with climbing up onto the top bunk, wondering how I was ever going to get in and out of bed if I needed to pee in the middle of the night, already mentally rigging the Ryan Dean West Emergency Gatorade Bottle Nighttime Urinal I would have to invent, Farrow slipped backward out the door and pulled it shut behind him.

So it was me and Chas.

Pure joy.

Bonding time.

And I couldn't help but wonder how much blood could actually be contained by the 160-pound sack of skin I walked around in.

Well, to be honest, it's 142.

Yeah . . . I am a skinny-ass loser.

And I'd had a talk with my very best friend, Annie, just that morning when we showed up at school. Annie Altman was at Pine Mountain because she *chose* to enroll at the school. Go figure.

Annie Altman was going into eleventh grade too, which meant she was two full years older than me, so, most people would think there couldn't possibly be anything between us beyond a noticeable degree of friendship, even if I did think she was smoking hot in an alluring and mature, "naughty babysitter" kind of way. I was convinced, though, that as far as Annie was concerned, I was more or less a substitute for a favored pet while she had to be here at PM, probably a red-eared turtle or something. At least she usually got to go home on weekends and see the pets she really loved.

I had hoped that she'd get over it, but there's no balancing act between fourteen-year-old boys and girls who are sixteen, even if I did grow taller over the summer, even if I didn't sound or look like such a little kid anymore.

Even if Annie knew everything in the world about me.

Well, I didn't tell her about the toilet thing.

Anyway, Annie told me that this was going to be my make-it-or-break-it year, and that I was going to have to suck it up if I was going to survive in O-Hall, which is about the same as a state pen as far as we were concerned.

It kind of made me feel all flustered and choked up when she told me that I might have to take a few lumps in order to gain the respect of the other inmates so they'd learn right away not to mess with Ryan Dean West.

She said she'd learned that particular strategy by watching a documentary about guys who get killed in jail.

So now that Chas and I were alone, I closed my eyes and tried to relax, wondering if I was taking my final breaths or taking the first steps toward standing up to Chas Becker and becoming someone new.

Or something.

There weren't any lights on in our room. That was bad, I thought. People like to do terrible things to other people when the lights are out, even if it's daytime.

In the unvoiced and universal language of psychopaths, a flipped-down light switch is like one of those symbol-sign thingies that would show a silhouette stick figure strangling the skinny silhouette stick figure of a fourteen-year-old.

I could see the swath of Chas's Mohawk pointing at me, and the whites of his eyes looking straight across at me, where I sat on the bunk bed.

Chas began unpacking, stuffing his folded clothes into the cubbies stacked like a ladder along one side of our shared closet.

"You got any money?" he asked.

And I thought, *God, he's already going to start with the extortion.* I tried to remember what Annie told me, but the toughest, most stand-up-for-yourself thing that wasn't in Latin I could think of was "Why?"

Chas folded his empty bags and kicked them under the bed. He turned around, and I could practically feel him breathing on me. He put both of his hands on the edge of my bed, and at that moment I felt like a parakeet—but a tough, stand-up-for-yourself variety of parakeet—in a stare-down with a saltwater crocodile.

"After lights-out, a couple of the guys are going to sneak in here for a poker game. That's why. We always play poker here on Sundays. Twenty-dollar buy-in. Do you know how to play poker?"

"Count me in."

I don't know if the choking or unconsciousness urge was stronger at that point, but I survived my first private, witness-free encounter with the one guy who I was convinced would end up trying his hardest to thoroughly ruin my life just before killing me sometime during my eleventh-grade year at Pine Mountain.

THIS IS ME —

**WINGER.**

I LIKE TO DRAW.

I COULD DRAW THE HAND THAT MADE THE CARTOON, BUT THAT WOULD BE A BIT META-COMICAL.

TO BE HONEST, I DREW THIS PICTURE WHEN I WAS WRITING PAGE 104, SO I COULD DRAW THE PAGE 104 RYAN WHO WAS DRAWING THIS COMIC AT THE BEGINNING OF THE STORY.

LOOK, EVERYONE IS AWARE THE CARTOONIST KNOWS THE ENDING OF THE STORY BEFORE HE DRAWS THE FIRST FRAME.

JUST LIKE I DO NOW, WHEN I TELL YOU THIS STORY ABOUT ME AND MY FRIENDS AND MY JUNIOR YEAR AT PINE MOUNTAIN ACADEMY.

BUT YOU'LL JUST HAVE TO HANG IN THERE AND RIDE THE RIDE.

OH, AND DON'T SKIP AHEAD TO PAGE 115.

THAT'S THE SCARY PART.
—RDW

# CHAPTER THREE

AFTER CHAS TRIMMED HIS MOHAWK down to a buzz cut, we put on our shirts and ties and went to the registrar to get our schedules and ID photos taken—not that we actually walked there together.

I saw my former roommates, Seanie and JP, waiting in line for pictures, and it made me feel good to see my old friends, but sad, too, because I missed rooming with them. We all three shared a room for our first two years at PM.

In the regular boys' dorm, the rooms were big and comfortable and usually had three or four guys per room, not like O-Hall, where the rooms were like tiny cells with those dreaded metal bunk beds.

Seanie and JP played rugby too. We hung out and got along because they weren't forwards either. Seanie played scrum half, even though he was really tall and skinny, but he had a wicked pass and flawless hands; and JP played fullback, which is the position usually given to the all-around fittest, most-confident guy on the team, and with the highest tolerance for pain. This year, they'd both be moving up to the varsity team since about half the starters from last year had graduated.

One of the things about rugby that's an inescapable tradition is that everyone on the team has to sing, and everyone also gets a nickname. It's not conscious or thought out, it just happens. Like salmon swimming upstream, or the universe expanding . . . or contracting . . . or whatever it does, I guess. And, when someone finally settles on calling you by a nickname, you're stuck.

Forever.

So, no matter what happened to me in life, as far as the guys on the team were concerned, my name was always going to be Winger. JP's nickname was Sartre. His real name was John-Paul, so, naturally when I started calling him Sartre, the name just stuck even though most of the guys on the team didn't get it and they just assumed that since I was so smart it probably meant something ultraperverted in French (which I hinted it did). Seanie was lucky. He inherited the most nontoxic kind of nickname; his real name was just Sean.

Chas Becker's nickname was Betch, a nonaccidental shortening of "Becker" combined with what a lot of guys didn't have the guts to call Chas to his face.

But there's no arguing nicknames once a rugby team tattoos yours in their heads. You just have to forget about it and smile.

"The Winger's still alive," Seanie said as we shook hands.

"God, Seanie. What've you been doing?"

"Nothing. I played two-and-a-half straight months of video games since school let out. This is the first time I've seen the sky since last June. It's so bright, I think I'm going to have a seizure."

Seanie was kind of a geek, and I completely believed what he said was true.

"They didn't put anyone new in our room with us yet," JP said. "So maybe that's a good sign that you're going to be coming back. How's the O-Hall, anyway?"

I almost said, *The toilets smell real nice!*

But I didn't.

"I'm sharing bunk beds with Betch."

I saw a horrified look of grief wash over my friends' faces.

"He's going to turn you into an asshole," JP said.

"Or kill you," Seanie added. "You'll never get out of that shithole."

We moved a step forward in line, toward the beacon of flashes at the photographer's booth. Each of us clutched a class schedule in our hands. After the pictures, we'd be free for the rest of the day to mourn the final moments of our unstructured summer.

"He actually did something kind of nice, kind of weird," I said. "He asked me to play poker with some of the guys tonight after lights-out."

"Winger, you know he's going to end up getting you in so much trouble this year," JP said.

And Seanie added, "Why do you think so many of the first fifteen are permanently assigned to O-Hall, anyway? And everyone knows about those games. You just better look out for the *consequence*."

The consequence was what they'd assign to the first guy who lost his way out of the game. It was usually innocuous and embarrassing stuff, like the time they made Joey Cosentino run around the rugby pitch naked in the middle of the night, and then, when he snuck back into the room, they made him do it again because he accidentally ran counterclockwise, something the team never allowed; or the time they made Kevin Cantrell swim across Pine Mountain Lake in his boxers (also in the middle of the night). Of course, all the consequences had to be performed in the middle of the night since just playing the poker game after lights-out would get the guys into a lot of trouble. And getting caught by anyone from school during the commission of the consequences was sure to be even worse.

And anyway, I considered myself to be a pretty good poker player, so I wasn't too concerned about the consequence. No sweat.

After our pictures were taken, and fresh, chemical-smelling laminated ID cards were spit out into our hands, we agreed to catch up to each other again at dinner. JP and Seanie left to finish unpacking, taking off in one direction and leaving me sad and envious of their start of our junior year in the nice dorm room I used to live in.

So I set off, alone, already feeling weak and small and sorry for myself when I swore I wasn't going to be any of those things this year, on the narrow and kind-of-Ansel-Adamsish trail along the lake toward Opportunity Hall, the leaking, dilapidated, and lonely two-story log building that at one time was the only housing structure on this entire campus.

"Hey! West! Did you get everything taken care of?"

Annie came running up on the path behind me.

She called me *West*. I liked it, I guess. Nobody else called me that.

I stopped and turned around and quietly held my breath so I could get the full impact of watching Annie Altman coming toward me like it was some kind of movie where she actually *wanted* me to throw my arms around her or something.

I held up my schedule and ID card to answer her question.

"How'd it go? This morning, with Chas?"

"Not a mark on me," I said. "I was scared about nothing. He was kind of nice to me, in an edgy and predatory sort of way."

"He probably is counting on banking up frequent disappear-for-half-an-hour-so-he-can-have-sex-with-Megan favors from you," she said.

Megan Renshaw was Chas's girlfriend.

Smoking hot, too.

"Or my money. We're supposed to play poker tonight."

Annie Altman went on, in a scolding tone. I'll admit that I had fantasies involving Annie. And scolding. "You haven't even been to one day of classes and you're already doing something idiotic that could get you into trouble."

We began walking toward O-Hall.

"Yeah. I know."

I tried to swallow the dry and hairy tennis ball in my throat.

Annie did that to me.

Especially when she used the *scolding* tone.

I looked at my feet as we walked.

This was actually a beautiful place, especially with Annie walking beside me. The lake was about a mile and a half long, half a mile wide, and surrounded by tall pines that stood like an army of giants stretching all the way up to the tops of the mountains surrounding us.

Of course, Annie stayed in the girls' dorm, which was a good walk in the opposite direction down the lake from the secluded O-Hall. It was built near the mess hall, class and office buildings, the sports complex, and the boys' dorm.

The top floor of O-Hall was for the boys, with the ground floor segregated for girls. But, girls being girls, it almost never had any residents. It was perfectly clean and unoccupied now, except for the resident girls' counselor, a frightening mummy of an old woman named Mrs. Singer.

"Well, what classes do you have this semester, West?"

Annie and I sat on an iron bench facing the lake and exchanged schedules. I looked at her ID card. Her picture was so perfectly radiant, it burned my eyes. She just had this faint, closed-mouth, typically Annie smile, like she knew something embarrassing about the photographer. And she looked so confident, too, staring straight ahead with her dark blue eyes and the most perfect-looking black eyebrows, her hair hanging down across her forehead. I could never tell if she wore lipstick and makeup; her skin and lips always looked so flawless and, well, Annie-like.

"West. You're just staring at my ID. The schedule's on the bottom."

"Oh. Sorry. Nice picture, Annie."

I saw her thumb my ID card over. And there I was, staring out from behind the lamination, necktied and looking all lost between my goofy ears, mouth half-open in a not-really-a-smile smile, short-cropped dirty blond hair that never sat even, and that pale skin of mine that looked like it would never, *ever* so much as sprout a stray strand of peach fuzz.

"Aww," she said. "What a cute boy."

Okay, I'll be honest. I think she actually said "little boy," but it was so traumatizing to hear that I may have blocked it out.

She might as well have kicked me square in the nuts.

I am such a loser.

I had two PE classes—Conditioning in the morning and Team Athletics at the end of the day—but at least Annie and I had one class together, American Literature, just before lunch break. Annie's sports were cross country in the fall and track in the spring. Rugby season started in November, so playing on the team was a year-round commitment since it didn't end until May.

"Cool. We got Lit together," I said. "I better go."

I stood up abruptly and handed Annie her stuff.

"Are you mad or something, West?"

"No. I gotta go and get my stuff unpacked, or Farrow's going to get after me. O-Hall. You know," I lied.

"If you're sure you're okay," she said. She stood up.

"Yeah."

I took my schedule and ID from her and started off toward my new home.

"Look," she said, "I'm going on a trail run before dinner. You want to come with me?"

"I can't," I said.

And without turning back I went straight for the O-Hall doorway.

*Little boy.*

What a bunch of crap.

# CHAPTER FOUR

IT TOOK ABOUT FIVE MINUTES FOR
me to unpack. That's all. I didn't have anything. Of course Chas wasn't
there. He'd be out goofing around with his friends, or sneaking off
somewhere with Megan Renshaw, who I also thought was unendur-
ably sexy, but not in a mature, Annie kind of way; it was more like an
intimidating and scary female-cop-that-arrested-me-in-Boston way.
But she was still hot. And, yes, I *did* get arrested in Boston when I was
twelve. It's what inspired my parents to enroll me in Pine Mountain
Academy in the first place.

I know you're going to ask, so I might as well tell you: It was for
breaking into and trying to drive a T train.

I was twelve.

Boys like trains.

Back to unpacking.

Chas had left the bottom cubbies open and bared enough of the
closet rod for me to hang up my school jacket and sweater, as well as
the uniform pants and shirts that would supply me from wash day to
wash day. After I did that I was alone, so I just stared out the window
at the lake and sat there in the dark room on a chair that I wasn't really
sure I'd be allowed to sit on.

I sighed.

My parents had dropped me off that morning, along with my bags, a supply of cash, adequate stereophonic warnings about my behavior and what they expected from me now that I was a full-fledged "young man," and instructions to phone them at the usual time every Saturday afternoon. They didn't even get out of the rental car; they had to hurry back to the airport to catch their flight to Boston, where I lived for the few unfrozen months out of the year.

When I saw Annie run by, alone, out on the trail around the lake, I immediately tore off all my clothes, pulled on my running shorts, and dug around in my formerly organized cubbies for my running shoes. I had been so busy sitting there moping and feeling lonely that I'd nearly forgotten my commitment—well, plan, at least—to try reinventing myself this year, to not be such an outcast. I took off out the door, leaving it open wide, displaying the wreckage of scattered clothing and footwear I'd left behind in my hurry to catch up to Annie Altman.

I knew where she was going. It was a trail we'd run together many times, winding to the north side of the lake and then along a rock-lined switchback path through the forest to the highest point around, a lookout post called Buzzard's Roost where you could see out in every direction—the entire valley where our school had been built on one side, and, on the other, a faint and hazy flatness that was the Pacific Ocean.

I estimated that by the time I got my shoes on and was out on the trail, Annie would be nearly a mile ahead of me, so as I ran along the lake I tried to script the innocent-sounding lies I'd say to her when she caught me on her way back down from the top. Because of course I really *did* want to take the run with Annie when she asked, and if it wasn't for that kick-Ryan-Dean-in-the-balls comment she'd made, I'd be up there with her right now, and we'd be talking about all kinds of things that just naturally come out of your head when you run.

The trail cut away from the lake through the densest part of the forest. Last year, in a clearing cut by loggers, Annie and my then-roommates and I built a circle of stones. We called it Stonehenge.

I stopped there to shake the twigs from my shoes.

Although some ferns had overgrown the outer ring of rocks, our monument was still standing. I didn't have any socks on, or a shirt, either. Just my running shorts, because I had been in too much of a hurry once I saw Annie run past O-Hall. My ankles were streaked with dirt from the combination of dust and sweat. It was hot and muggy, and I was slick and dripping as I started up the switchback trail, following Annie's shoeprints.

Anyway, I thought maybe she'd notice that I'd been lifting weights over the summer, that I was taller, that I really wasn't a *little boy*.

Yeah, right.

Just before the summit, the trees gave way to nothing but scrub brush and grasses, and the trail wound around the point of the mountain. I was almost to the top when Annie rounded the corner in front of me on her way down. And I could tell I startled her, too; that she wasn't expecting to run into anyone up here. She tensed and froze up when she saw me, but I could see her shoulders relax when she realized it was just me.

I put my head down and kept running, only stopping when I came up right next to her.

"I thought you couldn't run today," she said.

"I finished early. I had some energy. I didn't think you'd come up here." It wasn't really a lie, but then I added, "I'm sorry."

"Oh. No big deal," she said. Then she started running, going downhill again. Without me.

"See ya, West."

"Hey, wait!"

She stopped about twenty feet down the trail.

"Did you go to the top?"

She gave me a "duh" look, hands on her hips.

"Well, could you see the ocean?"

"Yeah. It's really clear today."

"You want to go back up?" I asked.

"No," she said, so matter-of-factly, like she was singing a song in grade school, like nothing at all mattered to her. The way she always sounded. "I'm going back."

I quickly calculated my alternatives. If I just stopped there, turned around, and followed along with her, that would make me look pathetic and wimpy. And, after all, she was the one who told me just this morning that I was going to have to get tough this year. I said the same thing to myself, even if I had serious doubts about my ability to pull off the transition from *little boy* to something else, something less insignificant—if "less insignificant" is actually a combination of descriptors that doesn't cause some kind of literary black hole. Plan B meant sprinting like hell to the top, taking a quick three-sixty just so I could say I saw the ocean too, then running like hell again back down the trail to catch up to her before she got to Stonehenge. That would work, but I'd have to burn it, because Annie was a damn fast runner, and I had this feeling that she was going to try to not let me catch up to her.

So I took off for Buzzard's Roost as fast as I could. My legs burned, but I *had* to get even with her somehow, to try and salvage the last day of summer, and the last wimpy shreds of my *little-boy* ego.

There.

I made it to the top. I was dizzy and dripping with sweat. My hair lay plastered, flat and dark against my scalp, and when I rubbed it, a misty spray of soothing droplets rained down on me. I lifted my arms to let the faint breeze blow a cooling breath under my arms and across my aching ribs. I looked down at the school, the narrow black strip of lake that cut a gash through the dark green points of the trees, and turned around to see where the sky faded down to a grainy fog-gray over the distant line of the Pacific.

Did it. I took off back down the trail after Annie as fast as I could.

I almost fell three times sprinting down that trail when my feet shot out in front of me, rolling over loose rocks. But after I came around the corner of the final switchback, before the trail flattened out through the forest, I saw Annie ahead of me.

And part of me wanted to just stay back and watch her, seeing her legs and arms move so smoothly while her black hair swung from shoulder to shoulder like a pendulum. She was one of those girls who never seemed to sweat. Everything about Annie Altman was perfection.

The shade beneath the pines was cool and fresh, and the air smelled like summer and freedom, the smell of never having to go home.

"Hey!" I called out.

She turned back, looking over her tan shoulder as her hair brushed across the line of her jaw. I couldn't tell if she smiled, but she did slow down to a jog so I could catch up to her.

"You're hard to catch," I said between gasps.

"Did you go to the top?"

"Yeah. It was awesome." We slowed our pace even more. "Look, Annie, I'm sorry about not running with you. I was mad, I guess."

"I know," she said. "You think I couldn't tell?"

"It's nothing." And then I told a major lie. "I'm just mad about being in O-Hall. Away from my friends."

Our eyes met. She had that same look she had in her picture, like she knew the truth.

"You know what we're going to do this year?" Annie said, and my heart just about stopped cold, because I was really scared she was going to say something, well . . . scary. "I'm going to find you a girl-friend."

I stopped running, and Annie took about three more strides and stopped too, but she kept on talking. "What freshman girl wouldn't just *die* to go out with you? I mean, it's the best of both worlds: You're the same age, plus you're an upperclassman *and* a varsity rugby player. Don't worry, West, I'll find you the best one."

"What if I don't want a girlfriend?" I said.

Then she got this smirky look and said, "You want a *boyfriend*?"

And I know she was just teasing me, but I turned away and walked off the path and into the trees.

I heard her following. "Come on, West. Don't get all I-can't-take-a-joke on me. I'm just looking out for you."

"Don't do me any favors, Annie."

I stopped, knee deep in ferns, sweating, at the edge of the circle of stones.

"Hey, it's still here," she said.

"I looked for it on the way up."

I wouldn't look at her. I was still mad. But I felt her heat; she was standing so close to me.

Stonehenge wasn't much like Stonehenge. The rocks were small enough to position with just the four of us working on it. Sure, some of the outer rocks were fairly heavy—they were the ones stacked in threes, a ring of doorways like the monument on Salisbury Plain—but it wasn't, like, an amazing feat of engineering to get them there. It was more a feat of boredom last spring as we all got ready to go off in separate directions for a break from school.

In the middle of the circle was a spiral path; two lines of evenly spaced smaller stones that wound around and around, coiling in on themselves until the path ended right in the center of the ring. That was the part of our Stonehenge that took the longest time to create. We started in the center and worked our way out, and when we finished, I think the path might have been a quarter-mile long if you could stretch it out straight.

Annie proclaimed it a wishing circle and told us if you walked it all the way in and then all the way out without saying anything, you'd get your wish. Of course I knew she had just made that up, because I'd only ever wished for *one thing* whenever I walked in and out on that path, and that one thing never came true.

"I don't want you to do it, Annie," I said. "I don't want you to look for a girlfriend for me."

"Suit yourself," she said, shrugging. "I was just trying to help."

"Like you said, things are going to be different this year. But I'm going to do it for myself."

"Okay."

We stood at the opening to the spiral path.

"You want to do it?" she said.

You know, there have been times when I would have just about cut a finger off to hear Annie, or any girl for that matter, but especially Annie, ask me that question. *Do you want to do it?* Of course I knew she was only asking if I wanted to walk the pathway with her, but on that Sunday just before the school year started, I guess I was feeling pretty down about things. And I almost said *no*, but then I decided to do the usual Ryan Dean West retreat from reality and try to make her laugh, just so I could take my mind off of things, off of how I felt.

I noticed she was looking at me. She was staring at me.

"Oh, yeah," I said, holding my arms out and turning my open palms upward. "It's not easy getting all this going. Every day, all over the world, countless men endure the pain and humiliation of laser treatments and waxing to achieve a body like this. It really *is* a burden."

I flexed.

Annie laughed. I liked the way I could so easily see the water building in her eyes when she laughed. It was a real laugh.

"You know, that's the only thing I even like about this craphole school," she said.

"What?"

"Having you as a friend."

"Shut the fuck up, Annie."

Okay, well . . . yeah, I didn't really say "Shut the fuck up," because I honestly don't cuss. But I wanted to. I think, in reality, I raised my finger to my lips and said, "Shhhhh," so she wouldn't say anything else as we spiraled into the center of that wish circle.

# CHAPTER FIVE

"OKAY, DOUCHE BAG." CHAS SHOVED me, sending me back against the doorjamb as soon as I crossed the threshold into our room.

Now, *this* was the Chas Becker I had been expecting earlier that morning.

"I had to pick *your* shit up off the floor—*your* stinky socks, *your* sweaty underwear—and put them away all nice and folded like your mommy, or we'd be restricted by Farrow. And, not only did you leave *your* shit all over the floor, you left the door wide-fucking open too, so he could see how *WE* left it. This is O-Hall, Winger. You don't get caught doing stupid shit like that."

That doorjamb really hurt between my shoulder blades. And Chas was standing so close, the only thing I could do besides watch his fist clenching just at the bottom of my field of vision was offer him a semiwheezing but fully sincere, "Uh. God. I'm sorry, Chas."

Chas pushed me again, his hand pinning me against the jamb. And I estimated, hand, door frame . . . *I am about three and a half inches thick right now. Maybe less.*

"Yeah, well, this is the one time. The *one time*, Winger. If you were someone not on the team, I would probably kill you right now. But Coach would get pissed."

He slackened his pressure on my sternum. I thought about saying thanks, but I just kept my mouth shut and my eyes down. I went over to my cubbies and pulled out some clean clothes and a towel and disappeared down the hall for the showers.

It was time for dinner, and I missed my friends.

# CHAPTER SIX

I FOUND SEANIE AND JP SEATED together in the mess hall. They were already on dessert, or maybe their entire meal consisted exclusively of desserts.

One of the only good things about PM was the food, because nobody stopped you from making poor choices. Our rugby team had a "physio," which is what we call a nutritionist-slash-doctor, though, and during season, there were only certain things we were allowed to eat and drink, and he'd keep watch on the mess hall from November until May.

I had been having such an all-around crappy day, and seeing JP and Seanie didn't make me feel too much better. I felt isolated, even though we were right there together. I felt like I couldn't tell them how frustrated I was about this whole Annie thing. Even though we were all juniors and going through reasonably the same kinds of crap, Seanie and JP both had two years of extra confidence on me. So I always struggled with pretending that maybe my friends could overlook that I was only fourteen, even if I couldn't.

"Hey. I made it," I said.

"It's about time, Winger," JP said. "I don't think I'm liking this new living arrangement. Seanie and I were just talking about leaving after dessert."

I sat down across from them with my tray of tacos and salad. I scanned the hall for Annie. She wasn't there. Among the hundred or so students who were having dinner, I saw Chas sitting with Megan, over where all the seniors hung out. I didn't get the Megan thing. She was so smart; she was going to be in the Advanced Calculus class with me, and Chas could barely count.

Megan Renshaw played Chas Becker like he was a pair of pocket aces. She knew what his alpha status was worth in social settings, but all the kids in the smart classes saw the obvious softness Megan Renshaw had for intelligent and sensitive boys who would never have breeding rights in the wolf packs run by the Chas Beckers of the world.

That was just another reason why I thought Megan Renshaw was so untouchably hot. She gave hope to losers like me.

JP was wearing his ever-present striped beanie, pulled down over his ears so that just the last inch or two of his wavy light hair curled out over his eyes. He was so popular and smart, and seemed to just go from girl to girl without ever taking it the slightest bit seriously.

"I'm going back for more, anyway," Seanie said. "So don't worry about being late, Ryan Dean."

"Dudes," I said, "I do honestly believe Betch was just about to kill me before dinner."

I told them about my run up to Buzzard's Roost, but I also told them Annie and I ran the whole way together. They listened quietly to my story about our walk in the circle at Stonehenge. I knew they were kind of jealous, too. Not one of us had a girlfriend, and we all recognized how unattainable—and hot—Annie Altman was. Then, of course, I ended the story with my return to O-Hall and a very pissed off Chas Becker.

"You're not going to make it to the end of the semester alive," JP concluded.

"You ever seen Betch's MySite?" Seanie said.

We both looked at him. Seanie was such a video-game-Internet geek with a strong stalker flavor to his personality. I guess he could see what we were both thinking, because Seanie said, in a surprised kind of tone, "What? Well, haven't you seen Betch's MySite?"

"I haven't," I said.

"Me neither," JP added.

"Well, it's creepy, that's all," Seanie said. "It's nothing but pictures of Betch. Almost every one is Betch without a shirt on. Betch wallpaper. Betch in front of a bathroom mirror. A downloadable Betch calendar, which, by the way, I downloaded and printed out and have right now in our room . . . just in case a perfect opportunity should ever arise. And then there's all these comments about what a stud Betch is. I made up a fake account with a picture of a hot girl just so I could get him to friend me."

"You're really kind of sick, Seanie," I said.

"I know." Seanie smiled, like he was letting us in on a dark secret.

Then JP said, "Sometimes I lie awake at night thinking about how horrible my life could be if you hated me," and he added, "stalker."

I took a bite of taco. "Maybe that should be his new nickname."

Seanie just stared at us both with his unblinking stalker eyes. He had one of the strangest senses of humor of anyone I ever knew, because it was always so hard to tell whether he was joking around or if you should really be afraid of him. Either way, I guess it was a good thing Seanie was our friend.

"And, dude, anyway, you gotta tell us what happens at the poker game," JP said.

"Hey," Seanie said, "I could loan you my deck of Betch playing cards."

And he said it so straight-faced, but he *had* to be joking.

Seanie, expressionless, with his unblinking dead eyes, exhaled and stood, saying, "I'm going for more ice cream."

I watched Seanie get up and walk across the mess hall, stopping for a moment to say something undoubtedly creepy and demented to a group of freshmen, and JP just smiled and shook his head. That's when I saw Annie come in. She was with her roommate, Isabel Reyes, who was also kind of hot in a faintly mustached kind of way. Annie smiled and waved at me, and I waved back as JP just sat there, watching me watch her.

# CHAPTER SEVEN

LIGHTS—OUT CAME AT TEN O'CLOCK every night, except for Fridays and Saturdays, when they'd let us stay up until midnight. Usually, guys would hang out in the common areas, where we didn't have to wear uniforms—we could just wear T-shirts if we wanted to—watching television until bedtime. In the regular dorms, there was a common area for every two or three bedrooms, but in O-Hall, there was only one TV room for the entire floor, and we currently had twelve guys living here, along with Mr. Farrow and Mrs. Singer, who got the first-floor living room all to herself since there were currently no girls in O-Hall.

So when the TV went off at ten, we all went back to our rooms. As I closed our door behind us, I saw that Chas had already set out a deck of cards (regular, not "Betch" cards, which I highly doubt ever existed unless Seanie made them himself, which is something Seanie would actually take the time to do) and a case of thirteen-gram poker chips on top of one of the desks.

I'll admit I was kind of scared about Chas's poker game. I really didn't want to get into trouble on day negative-one of my junior year at Pine Mountain.

I pointed at the empty desk, nervously trying to make conversation.

"Is that one going to be my desk?" I asked.

"Yeah, sure," Chas said, obvious in his lack of enthusiasm at engaging his new roomie in conversation. "Whatever. Turn off the lights and get in bed."

"Oh. Okay."

I turned off the light and began taking off my pants.

"What are you doing, you idiot?" Chas whispered. "Keep your clothes on. We're going to play poker, asswipe."

I honestly thought we were going to bed.

I pulled my pants up.

"Oh. Yeah. Sorry."

I really didn't get it, but I knew if Chas said keep my clothes on, I was keeping them on. I climbed up onto the top bunk and instantly fell asleep.

I woke up to a burning flashlight beam stabbing my eyes as Joey Cosentino thumbed one of my eyelids up and whispered, "Nah, he's alive."

It took me a minute to register where I was and what was going on. I looked at the red numbers on the digital alarm clock. It was midnight. Actually, 12:04.

*They start their games at midnight when there is going to be school in the morning?*

"Wake up, kid. I thought you wanted to play," Chas said.

I sat up.

There were four of us: me, Chas, Joey, and Kevin Cantrell. The three guys I was playing with were all seniors. There was something especially scary about that. I swung my feet over the edge of the bed, and, rubber-legged, hopped down onto the floor.

Chas collected twenty dollars from everyone and put the money in the chip box. He handed out stacks of chips and explained the blinds. The game was Hold 'Em. I rubbed my eyes. The other guys looked perfectly awake, like it was lunchtime or something. I tried to straighten my hair, but it always did whatever it wanted to do, anyway.

There was a towel stuffed along the floor at the bottom of the door, and another covering the creepy tilting-window thing on top, so no one would see the light from our room.

None of us wore shoes. Kevin and Joey obviously had to keep it as stealth as possible, sneaking through the hallway past Farrow's door. I was wearing my school uniform pants, my belt, unbuckled and twisted halfway around to my back, and a wrinkled T-shirt. Chas was still in his uniform shirt from dinner, but without the tie, and Joey and Kevin wore loose sweatpants and T-shirts. And the funny thing is, I noticed they were wearing their black and blue hoop rugby socks, too, and I thought, *God, either these guys are really dorks, or they just can't wait for the season to begin.*

We sat on the cool linoleum floor, all facing each other, Chas with his back resting against the bottom bunk. The floor space was barely big enough for us, and those three other guys were monsters, anyway. Kevin played lock alongside Chas, so he was exactly Chas's height; and Joey, who was six-one, played fly half, number ten, which is kind of the equivalent to quarterback in American football. So I had more dealings with Joey in practice and during games, since we were both in the back line, and I got along with him and trusted him, too, and I wasn't creeped out or anything about Joey being gay.

Everyone on the team knew that Joey was gay, but no one ever had a problem with it, either. He was honest about it with the guys, and they accepted him because of it, plus he never acted or talked like the stereotypical gay guys that people think are caricatures of the entire population. I mean, who does that, anyway?

That's one of the other things about rugby too: I think that because it is such a fringe kind of sport that practically borders on the insane, rugby guys stick up for and tolerate one another more than boys tend to do in other sports. Sure, sometimes the guys would make teasing jokes behind Joey's back and even to his face, but they did that to every single player on the team, and being gay, or uncoordinated, or only fourteen and in eleventh grade for that matter, didn't really have anything to do with it, because there was absolute equality of opportunity in being picked on in a good-natured kind of way. But no one on our team ever took it too seriously.

Chas was kind of the exception on the team, and maybe he was always overcompensating through his bullying because he recognized that he didn't fit in very well; and maybe, too, the guys and the coach just put up with his being such a colossal asshole because he was a great athlete.

I yawned and folded my legs, Indian style, as we put in the first blinds and Chas shuffled the non-Betch cards.

Chas looked across at Joey and Kevin and said, "Did you bring the refreshments?"

"Sure did." Kevin smiled, and then he and Joey stretched their legs out straight, so their socks were practically in my face, and pulled up their sweats from the bottom. That was when I could see why they wore their rugby socks. Both of them had two tall cans of beer on each of their legs, snugged down tightly inside our team hoops.

So when they rolled their socks down and made a little shrine from eight twenty-four-ounce cans of beer on the floor beside us, I really felt scared . . . because three didn't divide evenly into eight, and I had never, *never*, taken a drink of alcohol in my life.

What if it stunted my growth?

"And they're still pretty cold," Joey said. He obviously was the designated beer-passer-outer. He handed a can to Chas, then Kevin, and then he grabbed one from the shrine and tilted it toward me, a calm and serious look in his steady, fly half eyes.

"I never had a drink before in my life," I said.

"It's okay, Winger," Joey said. "I was just offering. I understand."

I was so relieved, and I liked Joey even more at that moment, but I mean that in a totally non-gay way, because I felt like he was sticking up for me.

Chas and Kevin had already opened their beers and were drinking before the first deal, and Joey took the beer he'd offered me and popped it open for himself. Then Chas reached across our little poker circle and grabbed a can of beer away from Joey's arrangement, pulled the tab forward so I could hear and smell that beer trying to find a way out of the can, and placed it on the floor beside my knee.

"It's time for you to lose your beer virginity, Winger," he said. Then he raised his can to the center and said, "Cheers."

And we all tapped cans. Six eyes watched me, and I closed mine as tight as I could and took my first-ever swallow of beer.

As Chas began dealing the cards out, all these things kind of occurred to me at once:

1. The taste. Who ever drinks this piss when they're thirsty? Are you kidding me? Seriously . . . you've got to be kidding.

2. Little bit of vomit in the back of my throat. It gets into my nasal passages. It burns like hell, and now everything also smells exactly like barf. Nice. Real nice.

3. I am really scared. I am convinced something horrible is going to happen to me now. I picture my mom and dad and Annie (she is so smoking hot in black) at my funeral.

4. Mom and Dad? I feel so terrible that I let them down and became

a dead virgin alcoholic at fourteen.

5. For some reason, Chas, Joey, and Kevin are all looking at me and laughing as quietly as they can manage.

6. Woo-hoo! Chas dealt me pocket Jacks.

An hour later, I had finished an entire beer. I needed to pee so bad, there were tears pooling in my eyes. I forgot what my home phone number was—I don't know why it mattered, I don't even know why I silently asked myself the question *Hey, Ryan Dean West . . . what's your home phone number?*, but I was emotionally devastated, crushed, that *I forgot my home phone number*—and I was the first player to lose all his chips, too.

By two in the morning, the game was finished. Joey won everyone's money, which gave him the right to determine the *consequence*.

Oh, yeah . . . the consequence.

# CHAPTER EIGHT

THANK GOD IT HAD NOTHING TO DO with getting naked.

Thank God, again, it had something to do with peeing.

I needed to pee so bad, I sat rocking back and forth in a near-catatonic state, with my hand jammed down between my legs.

Then Joey told me, "Here's all you gotta do, Ryan Dean. This is an easy one. All you gotta do is go downstairs and take a pee in the downstairs girls' bathroom."

"But Mrs. Thinger is down there."

(I couldn't remember her name.)

"Singer," Chas corrected.

I rocked. I thought he was telling me I had to sing, too. Oh, well. I kind of felt like singing.

Yeah, 142 pounds gets pretty stupid when you add twenty-four ounces of beer to it.

"Hey," I said, continuing my journey into stupidity, "Do any of you guys know my home phone number? I think it's got a twenty-four in it, too."

At that moment, I think everything in my universe had a twenty-four in it.

"Come on, retard, before you piss in your pants," Kevin said, pulling me up by my armpits. It felt like I was standing on ice skates, and I nearly fell down, but Chas was right there behind me, holding me steady.

"Hey, thanks," I said. "You guys are really awesome."

I would have shaken hands with them, but I didn't dare let go of my dick.

They turned out the flashlight and pushed me toward the door.

"You remember what you gotta do?" Chas said.

"Yeah," I said, confidently. "What?"

"Go pee in the girls' bathroom downstairs," Joey reminded.

"Oh, yeah," I said, "And sing, too."

I don't know exactly where I got the singing part from, but Chas, Joey, and Kevin weren't about to stand in the way of my willingness to compound my idiocy.

"Come on," Chas whispered, pushing me out the door. "And you better do it, 'cause we're going to be following."

"You guys are the best," I said, and they all three whispered "Shhh!" as we made our way down the lightless hall to the stairwell.

And every step I took made me feel like a water balloon filled to the bursting point. I was convinced I would explode in a shower of pee and guts right there on the stairs. It hurt so much to move, but each foot forward brought me closer to relief.

I was sweating like a heroin smuggler at a border crossing when we cracked the door open onto the girl-less girls' floor. I ice-skated in

my socks down the dustless linoleum hallway. It felt n[...]
feet, so nice I almost began laughing, but I wasn't stup[...]
do that, yet. Chas, Joey, and Kevin made their way arou[...]
of the building. They instructed me to pull open the wi[...]
gotten into the bathroom so they could help me get away if I needed
to.

And I thought, no wonder I couldn't remember my home phone
number (but it still choked me up, nevertheless), because I drew a
mental Ryan Dean West Brain-Capacity-Allocation Pie Chart, and it
came out like this:

## RYAN DEAN WEST BRAIN CAPACITY ALLOCATION

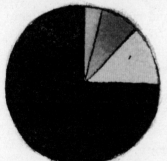

2% REMEMBERING TO OPEN THE WINDOW FOR THE GUYS

5% DECIDING ON WHAT SONG TO SING

13% FINDING A TOILET IN THE DARK

80% CONCENTRATING ON NOT PEEING IN MY PANTS

So there you go. It's a miracle I didn't forget to breathe.

I am such a loser.

I found the bathroom. When I got inside and shut the door, I
reached over to flick on the lights, but the switch was on the opposite
side of the door from the boys' bathroom, and this gave me time to

...lize how stupid turning on the lights would actually have been.

But, drunk or not, at least I was smart enough to latch the door behind me.

And then I thought, *Wow, this is a really nice bathroom, so clean and spotless, with nice clean curtains hanging across the row of shower stalls.* It was so nice, I almost wanted to lie down on the cool, clean floor and take a nap. But I had to pee too bad. So I turned toward the wall opposite the showers and hurriedly unzipped.

The urinals were gone!

Oh, yeah.

So, standing there as I was, pulled halfway out of my pants, made me want to pee even worse. I literally almost began to cry. Then I heard a scraping at the window and ran over and unfastened the catches.

Chas lifted up the window and stuck his head inside.

My pants fell down around my ankles.

I pushed open a stall.

The goddamned toilet seat was down!

Too bad. I couldn't slow down for such genteel considerations as raising a toilet seat (something for which I hadn't been yelled at since I was about seven).

Sweet mother of God, it felt good to pee. And it wasn't just peeing, it was something more: It was the God of Peeing, it was Zen archery, but with a stream of piss rather than a bow and arrow.

And it was so loud and musical sounding, which reminded me to start singing. Heck, I figured the stream wouldn't likely slow down before dawn, anyway. So, while I am sure that the natural sound of Zen Peeing was, in itself, loud enough to roust Mrs. Singer, the girls' floor resident counselor, from her sleep, my choice of song ensured the fact.

I began singing a rugby song called "Proper Ranger," whose lyrics include some of the most tasteless imaginable descriptions of sex acts. And it doesn't even rhyme very well, either, but some of those words just don't have good rhyming matches, anyway. The thing about the song, though, is that if you are a rugby player and are present when another rugby player begins to sing it, you have to sing along . . . so, Chas, Joey, and Kevin all joined in at the appropriate time while I continued the liberation of my unstoppable torrent of pee.

And, Zen-like, everything came together at the end. I shook off, pulled my pants up (failing with the complexities of my zipper), the song finished (with words I won't repeat here), and the very unhot Mrs. Singer began rattling the doorknob and trying to pound her way in.

"What are you doing in there?" she demanded through the door.

And I giggled, because I thought, *That's a dumb question.* Who, within a hundred feet, door or not, couldn't tell what I was doing in there?

*Pound pound pound.*

"Who's in there?"

And Chas said, "Come on, Winger!"

And just as Chas and Kevin grabbed my wrists and pulled me through the window, I heard the exceedingly never-spent-a-fraction-of-a-minute-in-her-life-being-hot Mrs. Singer say through the door, "I am going to put a diarrhea spell on you."

Well, I can't be sure exactly, but it sounded like that was what she said to me.

I fell down, giggling, in a clump of ferns beneath the windowsill.

"Hey. Where are my shoes?" I asked. I studied my feet, where I had propped them up on the outside of the log-constructed O-Hall.

Yeah, I was ultrastupid.

"You weren't wearing any, retard," Chas whispered.

"Then why'd I come outside if I wasn't wearing shoes?"

It was like I'd forgotten everything that had taken place in the past two hours and was willing to have a conversation about it so I could fill in the holes. I realized then that the Ryan Dean West Pie Chart of Brain Activity was an empty tin. Not even a crumb of crust left in that skull.

Thank God I had my teammates there to look after me.

Well, at least I had Chas, because Joey and Kevin had already climbed up the outer wall of O-Hall and squeezed back inside their window.

"Come on, Winger. We gotta go," Chas said. He began climbing up the corner logs on the bottom floor and whispered over his shoulder, "I am *not* carrying you, so you better get moving now or your ass is toast."

# CHAPTER NINE

THE NEXT THING I CAN REMEMBER

is thinking, *What is that fucking noise?*

Somehow, I had managed to get out of my clothes and under the sheets. So much for memory. And for a brief instant, a thought flashed of all those cheesy and predictable crime dramas where someone kills another someone and then doesn't remember doing it. I thought I should check my hands for blood or something, but it felt like I'd left my arms in another room, in another state, or maybe on another planet.

*Please make that goddamned noise go away.*

The alarm clock was blaring. It was seven o'clock, the first day of school, and I was lying there twisted up in my bedding on the top bunk, alone in my O-Hall cell.

Chas was gone.

Maybe I killed Chas Becker.

The alarm clock *would not* shut up.

And when I sat up and tried to get my feet down off the bed, it felt like I left the inside part of my head, the invisible Ryan Dean West part, on the pillow next to me.

This wasn't good.

I was almost about to start crying because the alarm clock wouldn't leave me alone. I tried to remember what happened the night before, but everything seemed disjointed and out of sequence. I felt horrible. I somehow had convinced myself that everyone in the world had woken up to the news that Ryan Dean West had gotten drunk off one giant beer and had ruined his entire life in the span of about three hours.

By the time I could stand, it was 7:04. The alarm clock and my head were still buzzing.

Classes began in fifty-six minutes.

I finally got the alarm turned off, opened the door, and stumbled down the hallway toward the bathroom, wearing only my boxer shorts and one dirty pulled-down sock with bits of what looked like ferns on it, pie chart still empty, with no idea how I ended up like this. If I could have thought clearly enough at that moment to formulate a plan of action, I would certainly have killed myself on the spot.

I did not kill Chas Becker.

Chas was in the bathroom, wrapped in a towel, shaving. I saw him smirk at me in the mirror when I staggered through the door. I stood at the sink beside him, turned the water on cold, and held my face in front of the mirror with both of my hands propped on the tile countertop, elbows locked, like I was steadying myself on one of those godforsaken crab boats in the Bering Sea. And I don't know why I turned the water on either, because I just stood there, looking horrified at my reflection in the mirror as Chas smirked and shaved and smirked and shaved.

"I think you can skip a shave today, Winger," he said, and wiped some menthol-smelling shaving cream on my never-so-much-as-fuzzed cheek. And Chas just looked so normal, too, like he could do shit like that every night and it didn't even affect him.

I suddenly felt very sick.

"Oooh, Winger partied too hard last night," Chas said, and I heard some other voices laughing, but I really can't say for sure who else was in there. Ghosts of dead teenage alcoholic former O-Hall inmates, probably. I pushed away from the sink, leaving the water running, and I thought, *Why did I forget to put my face under that flow and drown myself?* And then I thought, *Oh yeah, because . . . I . . . need . . . a . . . toilet.*

I stumbled past the row of shower stalls with their torn and moldy plastic curtains, and the bank of urinals opposite them, and I began to remember being in this place, but it was different, too.

God! I was sick.

I made it to a toilet stall and slammed the door shut. I hardly had time to pull my boxers down and sit, and that's when it all came back to me, and I remembered Mrs. Singer's cursing me.

A diarrhea spell.

*You have got to be kidding me.*

I knew it was just a weird coincidence—it had to be—but this really, *really*, sucked.

Welcome to the eleventh grade, loser.

As I stumbled out of the stall, my skin cold and sweaty, feeling like one of those eyeless white cave salamanders, Chas was there, still smirking, wiping his face, and watching me.

"Hey, asswing, you better hurry up if you want to have time to eat," he said.

*Asswing?* That was a new one. Clever.

*"Eat?"*

"Yeah. You know. Breakfast. Eggs. Milk. Yogurt."

Bastard. The yogurt part did it. Why the hell did he have to say *yogurt?*

I went back into the stall.

# CHAPTER TEN

ALL THE BOYS IN O-HALL LEFT before me. I'm sure they were enjoying their yogurt and talking about their classes, or about how Ryan Dean West got drunk last night and ruined his life.

Somehow, I managed to get myself dressed: gray socks, tan pants, white long-sleeved shirt, black and royal blue striped school tie, dark navy sweater vest, black shoes. And I thought, what a stupid waste of energy since period one was Conditioning 11M (that meant it was for eleventh-grade boys), and I'd just have to take all these stupid clothes off right away, but at PM you couldn't walk anywhere on campus during the school day without being in the proper uniform.

I thought about going to see the doctor, because I had to make two more trips to the toilet before I was fully dressed, but I was afraid that the doctor would discover that I was a fourteen-year-old with booze in his system, and that was too scary for me to deal with. So I decided I'd have to be tough, like Annie told me, and suck it up, even if it felt like I was dying.

I made certain this time that our room was entirely clean and the beds were made before I grabbed my schedule and backpack. It was seven forty-five. I wondered what Chas had done with those beers, and then, just thinking about it made me realize another stop at the bathroom was required.

And as I went downstairs and pushed through the double doors that opened on O-Hall's large mudroom, I saw the so-not-hot-you-should-never-look-at-her-when-you-have-a-hangover Mrs. Singer, just standing on the other side of the window in the door that opened onto the hallway of the girl-less girls' floor, with her arms folded across her withered breasts, breathing on the glass, watching me as I left for school.

Nothing in the world could convince me at that moment that she *didn't* know I was the sick and guilty sonofabitch who woke her up five hours earlier.

*How could she not know?*

I practically ran out of O-Hall, which was a mistake, because the speed at which I was moving made me feel sick again.

I kept my head down as I walked through the crowds of uniformed kids clustered around the main campus, smelling all the nauseating smells of brand new clothes, brand new backpacks, brand new shoes, and hair gel. It was like I was a bug trapped inside a Macy's bag. I felt like every one of the eight hundred students at PM knew about what I'd done the night before, and what a loser I was, so I just concentrated on the path that would lead me to the locker room at the sports complex.

I ran through my schedule in my mind as I staggered to first period:

1. Conditioning 11M. Seanie and JP would be in that class with me.
2. Advanced Calculus. Scary-hot Megan Renshaw and Joey Cosentino, who knew what an "asswing" I was, were both in that class.

3. AP Macroeconomics. Megan and Joey, hour two of two.

4. American Lit. Ultrahot Annie. Oh, and JP, too.

5. Lunch. I could find a shady spot away from my friends to die.

6. Team Athletics. The first day of rugby, a possible reason for rising from the grave of lunch.


"Hey! West! Wait up!"

It was too late to just put my head down and pretend I didn't notice her. Annie came running up behind me, fantastically perfect in her school skirt. I knew I looked so guilty, too, like I had done something *wrong* to her. I felt sick. And I almost wanted to cry when I saw her, but I didn't have any idea exactly why.

"Where were you? I was looking for you this morning," she said. Then I noticed her expression change when she got close enough to see my eyes.

"I'm sorry, Annie. I am really sick."

"Oh my God, Ryan Dean, you look terrible!"

And it was so wonderful to hear her actually say my first name like that.

I sighed. "Gee, thanks."

I looked at my watch. There were no bells at PM. You just had to be where you had to be, when you had to be there. It was 7:55.

"Maybe you should go see the doctor," she said. "What's wrong with you?"

"I'll be okay," I said. "I didn't want to miss first day. I'm going to be late for PE. I'll see you in Lit, okay?"

I turned away, and she brushed my hair with her hand and said, "I hope you feel better."

# CHAPTER ELEVEN

ON THE FIRST DAY OF CONDITIONING, we had to go out on a three-mile run to the north shore of the lake and back. I knew Seanie and JP could tell something was wrong with me. We all stayed in the back of the pack, jogging slow so we could talk.

"What happened last night?" JP asked it first.

"The game got started at midnight," I said.

"That's when it *started*?" Seanie said.

"A little bit after midnight," I said. "Kevin Cantrell, Joey Cosentino, me, and Chas. And they brought beer with them."

Just saying it made me feel sick again.

"God, Ryan Dean, you could get so thrown out of school for that," JP said.

"Did you drink?" Seanie asked.

"They kind of made me." We ran a few steps in silence. I thought I could tell what they were thinking, and I said, "I got drunk. And I lost out first, too."

"Oh, God," JP said.

And Seanie, always the cheerful one, added, "So . . . what's it feel like to be a *fucking alcoholic*?" Then he pushed me, and I almost fell into the lake. I knew he was just joking around, but Seanie was always so creepy about how he said things.

"Man, Seanie, I am so fucking sick."

Well, I didn't actually say "fucking," because I really never do cuss, but I was *fucking sick*. I sure thought the word, even if I didn't say it. And then I wondered, does cussing count in the general scheme of things if you only cuss in your head and not out loud? And I added, "I am *never* going to do that again."

"That's what all *fucking alcoholics* say," Seanie deadpanned. "Then they go home, get shitfaced, and shoot their wife in the fucking forehead while she's cooking a meatloaf and green beans."

I had to laugh. I also had to get back to the toilets in the locker room.

"What did they do to you when you lost?" JP asked.

I tried to remember, but it seemed so grainy and unclear, like those films of Neil Armstrong walking on the moon.

"Wait," Seanie said. "If Joey was there, maybe it's something you should talk about, like, with your dad."

"You're a freak, Seanie," I said. "They made me go downstairs and pee in the girls' floor bathroom. And sing. And there's no girls there, except for that—eew—Mrs. Singer."

"She is so freakin' hot," Seanie said. "Did she look at your wiener?"

I had to stop. I doubled over laughing. And Seanie still didn't even crack a smile.

"I locked her out. She was pissed off. The guys pulled me out the window."

"So then," Seanie said, emotionless, "did Joey look at your wiener?"

"That's messed up," I said. "I like Joey. And he's a hell of a fly half."

"Joey's cool," JP added.

And Seanie yelled up to the sky, "Universal takeback! I am sorry, Joey! I will never, ever make fun of your gayness again!"

Of course Joey, who was a senior, wouldn't have been anywhere near the class, anyway.

We had reached the turnaround spot and were heading back to the gym.

JP asked, "What song did you sing?"

"Proper Ranger."

"Oh. Nice."

Then Seanie and JP started singing it, and I *had* to join in, and some of the guys ahead of us heard it too, and the ones on the rugby team were singing up there right with us. But I didn't tell Seanie and JP about the diarrhea spell, because I didn't believe it was anything more than a sick coincidence—karma, kind of. It served me right for being stupid enough to get drunk in the first place.

And I didn't tell them about seeing Mrs. Singer staring at me from behind the door when I left for school, either.

# CHAPTER TWELVE

BY THE TIME I MADE IT TO CALCULUS, I felt like the hangover/diarrhea spell was losing strength, but now I realized that I desperately needed to go back to sleep too. The only real sleep I had gotten the night before was when I dozed off before the game even started.

I have never slept during a class, though, and I was honestly afraid that if I did, two horrible things would happen. First, I would have a dream about that witch downstairs (I had now convinced myself, after two more stops at the toilet—*I must be caving in! I must have lost 30 percent of my skinny-bitch-ass body weight*—that Mrs. Singer was an honest-to-God witch); and, second, I would get an extension on my sentence in O-Hall. After the night before, I realized that I needed to get out of there before Chas succeeded, as my friends warned me, at turning me into an asshole.

When I thought about it, as inevitably I did, stumbling down the corridor toward the mind-numbing experience of Calculus, I figured out that most of the guys in O-Hall except for me (the cell-phone hacker), and three compulsive class ditchers, were in Opportunity Hall for fighting. Eight of twelve of us were fighters: five football players, and Kevin, Chas, and Joey.

Of all the guys you'd think would *never* get into a fight, you'd have to pick Joey. I never asked him about it, but I figured it had to have something to do with him sticking up for himself when another guy was trying to start some shit. Probably.

And, because Advanced Calculus was pretty much the end of the math highway (unless you took Statistics, which I planned to take in twelfth grade), the class had only eight students in it. I was the last one through the door.

There were so many empty desks. I was overwhelmed by the pressure of choosing where to sit. And every single person in the goddamned room, even Mrs. Kurtz, the teacher, who was actually kind of hot in a bespectacled-Lois-Lane kind of way, seemed to be watching the *Ryan Dean West Show*, aware of the internal dialogue taking place in my headachey-hangovery-diarrhea-dehydrated head:

RYAN DEAN WEST 1: Sit in the very back of the room. Close to the door.

(*Ryan Dean West glances at the solitary desk beside the door.*)

RYAN DEAN WEST 2: Dude, that is entirely . . . three . . . four . . . five empty desks away from the closest other person. They will think we're a pathetic fourteen-year-old loser with no social skills.

RYAN DEAN WEST 1: Uh. So? We *are*.

(*Ryan Dean West drops his Calculus book. It weighs almost as much as he does. Suppressed laughter among the students in the room. He turns red.*)

RYAN DEAN WEST 2: Are you turning red? You are such a fucking loser.

(*Ryan Dean West picks up the book.*)

MRS. KURTZ: Why don't you come up front and sit close to everyone else?

RYAN DEAN WEST 1: How the fuck did *she* get in the play?

RYAN DEAN WEST 2: I don't know, but she's kind of hot.

(*Ryan Dean West looks at the seats in the front of the room.*)

RYAN DEAN WEST 2 (*cont.*): If you sit next to Joey, the other kids might think you're gay.

RYAN DEAN WEST 1: They might just think I'm confident, and comfortable with my own sexuality.

RYAN DEAN WEST 2: Dude, "Ryan Dean West," "Confident," and "Sexuality" are entirely distinct concepts which cannot exist simultaneously in the same universe. It could cause a black hole or something.

RYAN DEAN WEST 1: Fuck you. I'm sitting next to Joey.

RYAN DEAN WEST 2: Is it because you feel guilty 'cause Seanie the Stalker made fun of him being gay?

RYAN DEAN WEST 1: I don't feel guilty. And I'm going to sit next to him. And I don't care what you or anyone else thinks, 'cause you know I'm not gay.

RYAN DEAN WEST 2: Score! That's right behind Megan Renshaw (five out of five chicken potpies on the Ryan Dean West Heat Index). Maybe her hair will accidentally brush against your hand.

RYAN DEAN WEST 1: *Chicken potpies?*

RYAN DEAN WEST 2: Whatever.

(*Ryan Dean West takes seat next to Joey.*)

"Hey, Ryan Dean."

"Hey, Joey." I cleared my throat. "Hi, Megan."

"Hi, Ryan Dean!" She smiled and turned around in her desk. Her soft blond hair swept across my desktop and over my hand. It felt so cool.

*Score.*

Then she even put her hand on top of mine and said, "Look at you! You must have grown a foot. You look totally hot! How was your summer?"

I almost lost consciousness; I could feel all the blood in my dehydrated skinny-bitch-ass body surging downward to some useless region below my belt.

"Amazing."

"What did you do?"

"I can't remember."

"I heard about you last night." Megan patted my hand. "Sounds like you had a little fun."

I looked at Joey.

"I didn't tell her," he said. "Are you okay?"

"God. I am so sick. Don't ever let me do that again."

"I tried to stop you. You know. Chas wouldn't let me."

"I know."

We all sat in the same arrangement in Macroeconomics, too:

Megan in front of me, Joey on my right. I wondered why teenagers do that sort of thing, but I've seen it happening in classes ever since I can remember. I guess it's like an unconscious way of making the universe consistent and uniform, even if your anchors to reality happen to be (1) extremely hot and unattainable, and (2) gay.

After Econ, we had a twenty-minute break. I just looked around for a bench in the shade and stretched out on it. I put my backpack over my face so I wouldn't have to see anyone and, maybe, no one would see me either. I could have stayed that way forever, but I heard Seanie and JP standing over me, laughing about something.

"Hey, hangoverboy, we've been looking all over for you," JP said. "Come on. Get up. It's time for Lit class. We're almost through to lunch."

Oh, yeah—another thing about the charms of PM. Since nobody can have cell phones and stuff, the kids here actually *talk* to each other. And they write notes, too. I know these are both ridiculously primitive human behaviors, but what else can you do when your school forces you to live like the fucking Donner Party?

The reason I mention this is that as I lifted the backpack away from my sweaty face, Seanie slipped me a folded square of paper with flowers and hearts drawn on it, and said, "Here. Read this. I wrote you a haiku about how gay you are for sitting next to Joey for two classes in a row."

"I also sat right behind Megan Renshaw."

"That's called compensation."

I slipped my hand inside my vest and put Seanie's note in my front pocket.

"Nice," I said. "In Lit class I'm going to write you a sonnet about how nothing could possibly be gayer than writing your friend a haiku."

# CHAPTER THIRTEEN

IT JUST PROVED THAT EVERYONE
was right about Seanie being a stalker.

Why would he be so obsessed as to find out exactly where I sat in my classes? He probably kept little stalker charts and notebooks on everyone he knew.

I had been feeling so sick that day that I wasn't even thinking about Annie until I saw her in our American Literature class.

Just seeing her made me feel momentarily healed.

I walked down the aisle beside her desk and sat in the empty seat next to hers. She just glanced at me and then refocused on a paperback she was reading.

"Hi. Can I sit next to you?"

"I don't care."

Whoa. The very last time I had seen her, she actually touched me; she rubbed her hand through my hair, she called me Ryan Dean, and she said she hoped I'd feel better.

And *now*?

All of a sudden she was so obviously pissed off at me. JP sat down on the other side of her. I saw him look at me. He had watched our little exchange. I could tell he saw something was up too. But, before I could ask her about it, Mr. Wellins began blathering away about

American Literature and Nathaniel Hawthorne (an author I honestly *do* like, but how was I supposed to pay attention to him when I felt like crap *and* Annie Altman had just about slapped me across my face with her "I don't care"?).

*Note to self: Now, that last paragraph ended with a cluster of punctuation marks I have never seen together—in that order—in my life.*

I took Seanie's note out and unfolded it. He actually did write me a haiku (and there was no way I was going to waste my time responding with a sonnet). The top of the page had been decorated with a rainbow. Beneath it were two crudely drawn stick figures holding hands. Arrows pointed to each of them from identifying names: "Winger" on one side and "Joey" on the other.

Winger and Joey
Beside each other in class
"Let's be study buddies."

And I wrote underneath it:

YOUAREAFUCKINGMORONWHOCAN'TEVENCOUNT
SYLLABLESSEANIE!!!
Is something wrong, Annie?

I wrote it on the edge of Seanie's note. I put a smiley face next to the question mark.

She leaned over and scrawled:

*I heard you got drunk last night.*
*You're an ASSHOLE!*

I'm sorry. I didn't mean to.

You're an asshole just like Chas.

Don't even talk to me.

See ya.

And that was that. She ignored me for the rest of that endless lecture on Hawthorne, which I couldn't listen to. My ears were ringing.

I sat there, wishing I could just die.

And, underneath the note I had left for Seanie, I wrote one more line:

ANDFUCKYOUFORTELLINGANNIEIGOTDRUNK LASTNIGHTTOO!!! GOODFRIEND.

When Mr. Wellins dismissed us for lunch, Annie sprang out of her chair and rushed out the door.

"Annie, wait."

But I knew I wouldn't catch her.

"What's going on?" JP asked.

"Nothing. She's pissed off at me."

"You think?" JP tried to smile. "Let's go get lunch."

"I'm not feeling good," I said. "I'll see you at rugby."

JP just shrugged and packed up his stuff.

# CHAPTER FOURTEEN

NOW I REALLY FELT TERRIBLE. I
wanted to give up, and I wanted to kick Chas Becker in the teeth too.

Just about everyone was crowding into the mess hall, all buzzing
with first-day-back stories. Those who didn't hang out inside sat in
segregated groups on the grass between the mess hall and the stadium.

I followed the path along the lake, alone, and found a bench near
O-Hall. I put my pack down as a pillow and kicked off my hot, brand
new shoes that turned my socks black in spots. I lay down, staring up
into the branches on the pines that towered over me.

This was the worst day of my life.

Scarcely twenty-four hours had passed since my parents had abandoned me here, and already my life was spiraling out of control. I got
drunk with Chas Becker, the ultra-unhot Mrs. Singer downstairs did
*something* weird to me, my best friend hated me, which made me realize that I would never have any chance with her or any other girl for
that matter because I was a fourteen-year-old-skinny-ass-loser-bitch,
and I felt like steaming hot dog crap.

Other than that, things were just swell.

Then I did something I actually, honestly, have not done since I
was in, like, fourth grade. I actually, honestly, started to cry.

I am such a loser. I really didn't belong here.

I folded my arm across my eyes. I think only about two tears came out before I got hold of myself and stopped feeling so stupid and useless. Well, maybe I got hold of myself; maybe those two tears drained all the fluid I had left in me. And I just lay there like that until I began hearing the motion of kids on their way to afternoon classes, so I straightened up, put my shoes on, and headed back to the locker room for the last class of the day.

# CHAPTER FIFTEEN

IT MADE ME FEEL ALIVE TO LACE up my rugby boots. As long as they were on me, I could forget about everything else that swirled around inside this 142-pound sack of dehydrated failure.

I love the sound of all those metal cleats moving around on the cold concrete floor in the locker room. There was something ancient in that noise, the music of a coordinated herd. I sat on the bench between Seanie and JP while we changed. I pulled the folded haiku from my pocket and gave it back to Seanie.

"You suck at poetry," I said.

Seanie was tying up the drawstring inside his shorts.

"You pissed off Annie, too," JP said.

Sometimes, just sometimes, Seanie could be sincere about things. He said, "I'm sorry I told her about you, Ryan Dean. I thought she'd think it was funny too. Really. I'm sorry."

JP sat on the bench and pulled his long socks up to his knees.

"God," he said, "I've been dying to play all summer. I need to hit someone."

"Me too," I said.

"You want to hit me, Ryan Dean?" Seanie asked.

"Get a ball in front of me on the field and you're going the other way, yeah," I said. "Other than that, I don't think I'd ever hit anyone off the field."

"Me too," JP said.

And that was all we needed to say to let Seanie know it was okay.

I couldn't wait to see Coach McAuliffe—Coach M, we called him—again. He was a little guy, a former winger too, and he was a transplant from England who could talk the most civilized-sounding shit you would ever hear, and he could cuss you out with the most vicious obscenities and it would sound like he was reading from Shakespeare. But Coach M was a die-hard traditionalist as far as the sport was concerned, and everything had to be perfectly maintained that way, from the words we used (and didn't use, because on the pitch *nobody* could cuss except for Coach M) when we were around him, to the clothes we wore during practice. He'd make us wear the shortest rugby shorts anyone ever saw. Now, inexperienced observers do not understand why the shorts in rugby have to be the way they are, but just trust me, that's how they need to be.

Nowadays, pretty much all the guys wore compression shorts under them anyway, and those would just about go down to our knees, but compression shorts were crucial because you'd almost never make it through a game without getting a square hit, punch, elbow, grab, or sometimes even the bottom of a foot, right in your balls.

One of the funniest things I ever saw happened when Seanie first started playing after he'd quit the basketball team. Since Seanie was so tall and skinny, Coach M wanted us to try to lift him in lineout practice. A lineout is when the ball gets thrown in from out of bounds and players can lift up a teammate (by his shorts, usually) so he can reach the ball. Well, Seanie, at the time, was just wearing boxers under his shorts, rather than compression shorts, and when the forwards lifted him, he said it felt like his balls ended up in back of his nipples. His eyes bugged out, his hands both went right down to his crotch, and he said, "Ohmyfuckinggod!" Of course, the ball just sailed past him. He had other things on his mind.

And he never came back to the pitch without some tight compression shorts on under everything.

We shook hands with the other guys (the team always had to do that) when we passed through the locker room, and the three of us walked together up the hill path that cut between the other practice fields to the rugby pitch. This, of course, took us right beside the fields where the soccer and football teams practiced.

We always got along well with the soccer team; they tended to be pretty clever with the jokes they'd play on us and were always appreciative of what we'd do to them. But, for whatever reasons, the football team just absolutely hated us. I don't even think "hate" is a strong enough word for the emotions we stirred in them, which is why two of them had no problem whatever in deciding to put my face in a toilet the day before.

I figured there was a sort of predictable pattern to a football-player-versus-rugby-player exchange that went something like this: The football player fires a put-down he'd probably been thinking about all day; then the rugby player comes up with an even more-scathing comeback and laughs; then the football player, who can only think of one thing to say and nothing else, says something about wanting to fight and walks away.

So, as I fully expected, when JP, Seanie, and I passed the football field, Casey Palmer, the quarterback and practically my next-door neighbor in O-Hall, and Nick Matthews, his roommate and coconspirator in the give-Ryan-Dean-a-welcoming-bath-in-the-toilet plot, were standing by the fountain trough at the edge of the sideline, and Casey shouted to us: "Oooh! Rugby players! Nice shorts, gayboys!"

Good one. What a predictable dipshit.

And Seanie, as stoic as ever, said, "You wanna know how I know you're gay, Palmer? 'Cause you got a picture of some guy's ballsack on your MySite, that's how! Ha ha!"

"Are you the one who did that, Flaherty? If you are, I'll fucking kill you!" Casey yelled back.

JP and I just looked at each other, and then at Seanie.

"Does he have a picture of some guy's balls on his MySite?" I asked.

"Sure," Seanie said. "Haven't you seen it?"

"No."

"No," JP added.

Then Seanie just looked at us with his cold reptilian eyes and said,

"Okay. It took me about ten straight hours on Friday to hack his password and put that picture on. I guess he hasn't been able to resolve the issue yet. Maybe he'll figure it out if he goes home this weekend. I sent a mass e-mail out to everyone on the football team, saying, 'I wonder why there is a picture of some guy's nutsack on Casey Palmer's MySite.'"

JP and I began laughing, staring right at Casey, who looked at that moment like he could kill someone.

"The best part is, they're my balls," Seanie said, absolutely straight-faced. "I have a printout, if you guys want to see it."

"Sean Russell Flaherty," I said. "You are so disturbed."

"That's fucking demented," JP agreed. "In an elegant way, though. And, no, you don't have to show me the printout of your balls, Seanie."

"Dude, Seanie," I said. "You put a picture of *your own balls* on the Internet."

"I know." Seanie actually laughed. Twice. Monotone. Weird.

"This is probably the best reason I have right now for why I don't have a MySite," I said.

"Oh, but you do have a MySite, my friend," Seanie said in an incredibly creepy voice. "I've seen it. You friended me. And JP's got one too."

"You are fucking kidding me," JP said. He sounded pissed.

"Ha ha!" Seanie said, "Yeah. I'm just kidding."

And again, that was what was so fucking creepy about Seanie. Who could tell if he really was kidding?

And then, as we were about halfway up the hill toward the pitch, as if Casey Palmer's inflated sense of masculinity hadn't been assailed enough, we all heard a soft, familiar voice with an English accent say, "Why are you boys staring at my players' asses?" Because I guess Casey and Nick just kept watching us as we walked up the hill.

Coach M knew what was up. He'd never let the football team get away with any shit on us.

Not ever.

# CHAPTER SIXTEEN

PRACTICE WAS LIGHT. COACH M SAID we weren't going to start hitting until he could see what he had; and I was okay with that because I was weak and felt so shitty after what I'd gone through.

We ran through a usual warm-up: a slow jog, some stretches, a few quick-hands passing drills, then we ran some forties and suicides, and that's when Coach M noticed that I was definitely *not* the fastest guy out there.

He said, "Did you slow down over the summer, Winger? You're going to need to put on some speed if you expect to keep your job."

And that made me feel even worse, because not only did I screw things up for myself and Annie, but I let Coach M down too. So, before we broke up into teams for a little touch sevens, I asked Coach M if I could talk to him.

"I'm sorry, Coach, I'm just really sick today. I'll be back up to speed tomorrow."

"What's the matter, Ryan Dean?"

"I just . . ." And then, "Last night was my first night in Opportunity Hall. And I couldn't sleep at all. I feel horrible." It wasn't really a lie.

He put his hand on my shoulder and said, "I understand, Ryan

Dean. Let's hope you can get your shit straightened out this year and get out of O-Hall."

See? That's just how he talks, but it sounds so musical and soothing with that English accent. And then he added, "Before Chas Becker turns you into an asshole."

Coach M picked four guys to be team captains, and then we had a little sevens tournament. Sevens is a scaled-down version of rugby where there are only seven, as opposed to fifteen, players on a team. And we were playing touch instead of tackle, so the entire game was really based on speed and ball handling.

I was still surprised, though, when Joey, who is our regular Backs Captain, picked me first to be on his team. JP was also on our team, along with a couple centers and some of the second-string loose forwards.

Seanie actually ended up on a team with Chas and Kevin, so I knew the games would be really competitive, and, when it came down to the end, it was our two teams in the final match. I scored first off a sweet fake-loop pass from Joey, because as soon as I had that ball in my hands I was gone. But that was all we managed to put up, and Chas's team came back with three unanswered scores to win the tournament.

Sometimes, losing in rugby is more fun than winning. On that day, at the end of practice, Coach M made the three losing squads jog down to the practice fields and sing a song to the football team.

Joey led us, and we all decided to sing "Oh! Susanna," but we changed "Susanna" to "Casey." And we are horrible singers, but we sing really loud, so Casey and the other football players couldn't do anything about it. They tried to ignore us, but they were helpless, and all they could manage to do was fire out comments like "What a bunch of faggots."

When we were finished, some of the football players actually clapped. At least they got it, that it was all in fun and that if you messed with the rugby team, we were going to mess right back. But it wasn't a threatening or intimidating "messing with"—it was always meant to show that we could take a joke, and joke back, too.

Casey started it with his "nice shorts" comment at the start of practice, and now he had to endure being the object of our serenading. When we finished the first verse and one chorus, we jogged down to the locker room.

The day had finally ended, and as I sat down on the bench and took off my cleats, the horrible day I'd had came back to me, and I thought again about what a loser I was already turning out to be on the first day of my eleventh-grade year.

# CHAPTER SEVENTEEN

I THREW MY CLOTHES ON WITHOUT showering. I could do that back at O-Hall, even though the showers here in the locker room were so much cleaner and more private. But all I wanted to do was get away from school and deposit myself into bed. So I just wadded up my gear and stuffed it into my locker. I put my sweater inside my backpack and sloppily hung my tie over my shoulders without even buttoning or tucking in my shirt. The day was over, and now it didn't matter if we were dressed properly or not.

I didn't even wait for Seanie and JP to get out of the showers. I shook hands with a few of the guys as I left the locker room.

I guess it was about four thirty when I made my way down the hill on the path toward the lake. I could see some people walking around the campus below, but most kids at that time of day were either back in their dorms or finishing up whatever team sports were being practiced in September.

I noticed Joey walking on the path, maybe about a hundred yards ahead of me, obviously heading back to O-Hall too. But when he got down to the football field, I saw Casey and Nick step out of a crowd of players who were standing around doing nothing (which is what most football players do all practice) and run over to Joey. And I could tell just by the way they were moving that they were looking to start shit with Joey, so I turned around, but no one else from the rugby team was walking down from the locker room yet.

Great.

Me and Joey versus the entire steroid-crazed-dumbass football team.

I started walking faster. Casey and Nick didn't even notice I was coming. They looked up the hill toward the locker room as Joey got closer, but who would notice my skinny-bitch-ass body coming down that way? Or, if they did notice me, what would it matter to them, anyway?

Then I saw Casey, puffing his chest out, walk right up to Joey and push him hard, knocking Joey back. And Casey said, "You think you're funny with your song, queer?"

I threw my backpack down and ran as fast as I could.

I knew Joey would fight. He wasn't afraid of anyone. You had to be like that to be a fly half, and I'm sure that Joey had been hit square against his unpadded body at least a thousand times more than Casey ever had. But I wasn't going to let him get gang-jumped by those assholes.

So I ran faster than I did in practice. I had to. And just as Joey was making a fist, Nick was circling behind him, and Casey was in the process of throwing the first punch, I launched myself, head up and shoulder down, right into Casey's knees and wrapped my arms around his legs, driving him, crashing, to the ground.

I sprang up off Casey.

Casey said, "What the fuck?" and he punched me in the face just as I got to my feet, knocking me down into Joey.

And just then, one of the football coaches saw what was happening and yelled at us to cut it out. The coach just stood there, down the field, holding a clipboard and spitting tobacco, watching us like he was too lazy to come over and see if this was really a fight or not.

All I can say is that if Coach M had seen what I did, my ass would be done. Over. Off the team. Kicked out of school.

"What the fuck you think you're doing, you little piece of shit?"

I could only assume Casey Palmer was talking to me.

Then I noticed my chest was covered in blood and my unbuttoned, once-white school uniform shirt was splattered with red. My knees buckled. I had to sit down.

Okay, I thought, this was it. I had done as much to my body as it could take in the last twenty-four hours. Now I was surely dying. I prepared myself to look into the tunnel of light and see my great-grandma and the little Chihuahua dog I had when I was four that got run over by a UPS van.

Well, they didn't *both* get run over by the UPS van, but you know what I mean.

Then I heard a whistle, and the football coach screamed at Casey and Nick to get back over to their standing-around drill, and I knew I wasn't dead, but my nose was bleeding pretty good.

"God. I am such an idiot," I said.

"Why the fuck did you do that?" Joey sounded pissed off.

"Overlap. Two on one."

I slipped my shirt off and held it over my face. I pulled it back and looked. I wasn't bleeding so bad anymore.

Maybe I was empty.

"You better get cleaned up, or you're going to be in a lot of trouble."

I wiped off the blood as much as I could with my ruined shirt and stood up.

"I'll just say it happened in practice," I said. "Tackling a guy. It's the truth."

I'd gotten more bloody noses playing rugby than I could count.

Well, actually, I only have one nose that's been bloodied, but it has happened dozens of times.

"God. I am so done for today."

I balled up my shirt and stuffed it into my backpack. I took off for O-Hall just as I saw the guys from our team coming out from the locker room and making their way down the hill.

Joey just stood there at the edge of the football field, looking at those assholes practice, waiting for our teammates to catch up to him.

# CHAPTER EIGHTEEN

THE WATER ON THE TILES IN THE shower stall turned pink around my feet where the dried blood washed down from my body. When it was finally clear, I turned the water to full cold and stood there for thirty seconds. It almost made me scream. I toweled off and went to bed.

It was five o'clock.

I lay there with my books, finishing the small amount of homework I'd been assigned—just a couple review problems in Calculus. Then I opened a paperback and began reading. We were supposed to read "Rappaccini's Daughter" and write a response paper on it, but I had until Wednesday. So I read the first page, then put it down beside my pillow and stared up at the ceiling.

I love the way Hawthorne said things. I wished that I could also find "no better occupation than to look down into the garden" beneath my window, but I had, in such a short time, gotten myself so occupied with crap that I lay there convinced there was no way I would make it through my eleventh-grade year.

I opened my notebook and wrote a letter to Annie. Even if I never gave it to her, at least I felt like I could write down what I wished I could tell her. In true Ryan Dean West fashion, I drew a Venn diagram on the note, trying to explain to her something about myself, the *little boy*, hoping that maybe she would realize what I thought was so obvious about the people we deal with, who are all around us, everywhere and every day. And as soon as I'd written the first couple of sentences, I reread them and they sounded so pathetic and lost that I just tore the page from my notebook and threw it away.

I was so tired.

I climbed down from the bed, undressed, and turned off the light.

# CHAPTER NINETEEN

"WHAT THE FUCK IS WRONG WITH you?" Seanie said.

The light came on and I woke up.

My books were scattered around my head, and I was lying, face up, on top of the covers.

Seanie, JP, and Joey were standing just inside the door, dressed in their shirts and ties, like they had just come from dinner at the mess hall.

I propped myself up on my elbows and looked at them.

I rubbed my hair and sat up. My head nearly touched the ceiling, but not quite.

"I just needed to sleep," I said. "What time is it?"

I looked at the clock. It was eight fifteen.

"Everyone was looking for you," JP said. "You missed dinner."

Yeah. I bet Casey Palmer was looking for me too.

"I wasn't hungry." But now that they mentioned it, I felt like I was starving.

"Well," Seanie kind of whispered, glancing around, "we smuggled you some food, just in case you were."

Taking food from the mess hall was a definite violation. But as far as rule breaking was concerned, having visitors from the regular dorms in O-Hall was probably just as bad.

Seanie placed a wadded napkin and a paper coffee cup on top of the Calculus book next to my pillow. "It's a ham sandwich and some tomato soup."

Now, that was *awesome*. It sounded so good.

"Thanks, Seanie," I said. "And thanks for not wrapping it up in your printout from Casey's MySite."

JP laughed.

"Have you ever seen Casey's MySite, Joey?" I asked.

Seanie had a sick and pissed-off expression on his face.

"No. Why?"

"Well, when you go home this weekend, look it up," I said.

"Okay."

Joey's parents were ultrarich. They lived in San Mateo and flew him home every Friday after school. I saw how Seanie was looking at me, so I just fired him back a Ha-Ha-I-just-got-Joey-to-look-at-your-balls-so-write-a-haiku-about-that, fucker expression, if there is such a thing.

But whether or not there actually is such a look, Seanie and I just had an intense and wordless conversation about Japanese poetry, his balls, and our gay friend, Joey Cosentino.

"I got you something to drink," Joey said.

I looked at him. Maybe I still had the balls/haiku expression on my face, so I guess Joey thought I didn't trust his evening beverage selection.

"*Not* beer," he added, and smiled. He pulled a bottle of water and another of Gatorade from his school pack.

Now, *that* was a miracle. I was so thirsty, I opened the Gatorade and emptied the bottle without even taking a breath.

"Joey told everyone what happened," JP said.

"Dude, you're like a superhero, laying out Casey Palmer, sticking up for your fly half," Seanie said.

"I wasn't sticking up for Joey," I said. "I was sticking up for me. I have to walk up and down that hill every day too. We can't let them start off with crap like that on the first day of practice. So I just kind of closed my eyes and took him out. I was so pissed off about everything anyway, so I did something really stupid that I'm lucky didn't end up with me being killed. Like we said in the locker room, I wanted to hit someone, and a game of touch rugby didn't quite do it for me today."

"How's your nose?" Joey asked.

I hadn't even thought about it since seeing that blood in the bottom of the shower stall. I took a bite of the sandwich—it tasted better than anything I could possibly imagine—then touched my nose.

"It's not broken or nothing," I said, inhaling. "I think. Just stuffed up. Man, thanks so much for the food. I think I actually feel *normal* again."

But feeling normal meant I immediately thought about Annie, too.

"Did any of you guys see Annie tonight?"

"I talked to her," JP said. "She is really pissed off at you, Ryan Dean."

Maybe my head was still a little off, but I kind of got the feeling that JP was glad about Annie feeling that way.

"Dude, her being pissed just shows how much she cares about you," Seanie said.

That sounded like something you'd tell your kid before giving him a spanking.

"I think she feels like you didn't tell her the truth," JP explained.

"I never had the chance to. I never had a minute to talk to her about it." I guess I sounded pretty whiney.

Then the door pushed open. I expected it would be Chas coming in, and that he'd tell my friends to get the hell out, but it was Mr. Farrow. And he looked pissed, too, because *he* was going to be the one to tell them that.

"What are you two boys doing here?" he said. He fired a displeased look at me as I sat on my bunk, eating my dinner. I pulled the sheet over my legs. Mr. Farrow had a way of making me feel so uncomfortable.

JP said, "Ryan Dean was sick. We just brought him something to eat."

Mr. Farrow took a step toward the bed and looked more closely at me, which, like I said, creeped me out because he was practically exhaling on my chest and I was only wearing boxers.

"Are you sick, Ryan Dean?"

"I'm feeling better now. I just woke up."

"Maybe we should have the doctor take a look at you in the morning."

"No. Really. I'm okay," I said.

Then Farrow pulled a scrap of paper and a pen from his pocket and looked sternly at JP.

"You boys are obviously not new students. You know the rules," he said. "What are your names?"

JP swallowed one time and answered, "John-Paul Tureau and Sean Flaherty."

"Mr. Farrow, please don't get them in trouble," I said. "Really, they were just looking out for me."

"Ryan Dean, sometimes when boys take it upon themselves to look out for one another, there are unpleasant consequences."

Holy shit if that wasn't the recap of my first day here. Then I thought, they must have picked him and Mrs. Singer to run this place because they're like Satan's minions or something.

And Mr. Farrow continued, "But, Mr. Tureau and Mr. Flaherty, I do appreciate your apparent concern for Ryan Dean. However, I expect you to leave immediately, and that you won't do this again without asking me ahead of time."

Then Farrow tucked his slip of paper back into his pocket and stepped out into the hallway, leaving my door standing open.

"Because we have plenty of room here in Opportunity Hall," he added, then disappeared down the corridor in the direction of our common room.

"I guess that means we're leaving," Seanie said.

"Hey. Thanks, guys," I said as Seanie and JP turned to go. Out in the hallway, Seanie swung around and flipped me a middle finger with a smile and a fuck-you-for-getting-Joey-to-look-at-my-balls expression on his face, if there is such a thing.

I finished my sandwich. I didn't say anything, but I suddenly felt really awkward being here, in my bed, alone in my room, with a gay guy. And then I immediately got pissed off at myself for even thinking shit like that, for doing the same kind of crap to Joey that everyone else did, 'cause I knew what it felt like too, being so not-like-all-the-other-guys-here. And I don't mean I know what it felt like to be gay, because I don't, but I do know what it felt like to be the "only" one of something. Heck, as far as I know, there's just got to be more gay eleventh graders than fourteen-year-old eleven graders, anyway.

I wondered if it bothered Kevin Cantrell, though. Joey and Kevin had been roommates for two years, and no one ever talked shit about Kevin or wondered if he was gay, because everyone knew he just wasn't.

I am such a loser.

"I feel so much better," I said. "You want this water, Joey?"

I held the bottle out for Joey.

"No, thanks. I'm going to go watch TV with the guys until lights-out. You want to watch some too?"

"No," I said. "I really think I just need to sleep. And anyway, aren't Casey and Nick going to be there?"

"So what?" Joey said. "I'm not afraid of them."

"I didn't say you were."

"They can fuck off," Joey said. "They're not going to do anything else. Trust me. You're not afraid of them, are you?"

I thought about it.

"Yes. I honestly am."

"Don't worry about it," Joey said. "That was a fucking awesome tackle. But don't ever do shit like that again. Do you want the light off?" He was halfway out the door.

"Yeah. Thanks. See you in Math."

# CHAPTER TWENTY

I HEARD CHAS COME IN THAT NIGHT, but it didn't fully wake me up. I was in that kind of sleep that just feels so paralyzingly restful and deep, like my body had become the mattress. So when I woke up around two o'clock, needing to pee, I actually did consider using the empty Gatorade bottle I had saved from my dinner in bed. But I decided it was a good opportunity, early on in our life together, for me to see if I could actually climb out of bed without inspiring Chas to beat the crap out of me. I thought I'd go ahead and save the Gatorade bottle for the future, though. Just in case.

And I was like some kind of ninja climbing out of bed, only my invisible and silent mission dealt with peeing, as opposed to murder.

O-Hall was completely still and dark when I stepped out into the hallway. Every part of my body felt so alive and healed; I had finally recovered from the idiocy of the previous night, and my bare feet felt so good on the slick and cool linoleum floor as I made my way down the hall toward the bathroom.

I stretched and yawned. I was actually looking forward to the morning, to the opportunity to find Annie at breakfast and try to make things right again. I had to try. It was making me crazy. After not seeing her for two-and-a-half months over the summer, we'd

already had two I'm-pissed-off-and-don't-want-to-talk-to-you episodes, and that sucked.

After I finished peeing, I switched off the light in the bathroom
and headed down the hallway to bed. That's when I saw a flash of
light through the window on the door to the stairwell. It was one of
those things that you just catch in the corner of an eye, but it stopped
me cold and I stood there in the middle of the dark hallway, silently
watching that door to see if it would flash again.

It did, but only for a second, maybe less.

It was a pale green light, the kind you see from one of those snap-
activated glow sticks; it lit the stairwell, and then everything was suddenly dark again.

I thought that maybe Chas and Joey and Kevin were doing something they shouldn't for the second night in a row, but that didn't
seem right, because I was certain I'd seen Chas sleeping in his bunk.
And I was kind of scared, too, but there was something about that
light that made me want to go see what the person responsible for it
was doing there.

I know. Pretty stupid. And I wasn't even drunk.

And as I padded in my bare feet to the end of the boys' floor, I kept
thinking about all the horror movies I'd ever seen where you just sit there
yelling inside your head, "Don't open that door, you fucking idiot!"

So what did I do? I opened the door.

Then I almost screamed like a little girl, but I was too scared to do that, and if I hadn't just done what I did a minute earlier, I would have peed myself too, because when I opened the door, I was standing there, in nothing but my underwear, face to face with the so-unhot-she-is-quite-likely-the-only-two-legged-female-besides-his-mom-no-wait-including-his-mom-Ryan-Dean-West-wouldn't-want-to-run-into-at-night-when-he-is-only-wearing-boxers-and-nothing-else Mrs. Singer from downstairs.

And I thought, *I am never going to not-have diarrhea for the rest of my life.*

I am such a loser.

And she was standing right there, inches away from me, in a black robe and her black hair tied back in a black scarf, looking like some kind of child-sacrificing Druid, or a bad illustration from an endless volume of Dickens; and for a moment, I was so startled, I just froze.

I should have used the Gatorade bottle.

When my knees thawed, I spun around and ran back down the hallway without saying anything or turning around, my feet frantically slapping their way back to my bedroom.

I felt something cool on my chest. My nose was bleeding again.

*Okay,* I thought, *she's not a witch. Casey Palmer made your nose bleed; it wasn't that creepy Mrs. Singer.* I pressed my hand to my nose, and it was immediately covered in blood.

When I got back to my room, I pulled the bloodstained shirt I was wearing when Casey punched me from my school pack and held it to my face. That shirt was beyond salvation at this point anyway. Then I attempted to one-handedly maneuver my way back to the upper bunk.

To make matters worse, I kicked Chas in the head when I climbed back up onto my bunk, not that there wasn't a pretty big part of me that was deeply satisfied by kicking him in the head after he forced me to get drunk and caused Annie to hate me. It probably would have been more satisfying if he woke up, but he just grunted and rolled over as I pulled myself up onto my bed.

My heart was pounding. I panted. I rubbed my hair as I stared up at the ceiling, pressing the wadded-up shirt against my nose to stop the bleeding. I was actually sweating. I couldn't get comfortable, and I guess I was fidgeting a bit, convinced that Mrs. Singer had it in for me and was just slowly working on some weird method of killing me. Then Chas punched the mattress from below; I felt the thud of a fist in my kidney.

"Please tell me you're *not* doing what I think you're doing up there, you fucking homo."

What was he thinking? What an absolute moron Chas Becker was.

"I'm not doing nothing," I said, my voice muffled in my ruined shirt. "I got a bloody nose. Sorry."

He went back to sleep.

I tried to relax, but I kept thinking about that weird woman downstairs, imagining the horrible crap she was going to put me through in the morning. What could possibly be worse than day one?

I sighed, and drifted off to sleep again.

# CHAPTER TWENTY-ONE

WE BOTH WOKE UP AT THE SAME time to the buzzing jangle of the alarm clock.

I felt so rested and ready for a real, and hopefully normal, day of school. When I got down from the bed, Chas saw the bloody shirt and said, "Is that from Casey Palmer?"

I said, "Yeah."

"I heard about that. You want me to fuck him up?"

And I thought, wow, I could almost fool myself into thinking Chas Becker cared about me or something.

"Naw."

I threw the shirt down onto the floor of our closet; then I picked it up and put it into the laundry bag marked WEST as Chas glared at me.

"He's a puss, anyway," Chas said. "And I heard you laid him out pretty good."

"I guess."

"You got some balls for a little kid."

And I thought, *Screw you, Betch.*

*Little kid.*

# CHAPTER TWENTY-TWO

I COULD FEEL MYSELF GET LIGHTER; my heart beat faster, and my scalp kind of tingled when I saw her. Maybe it was just the dandruff shampoo I used that someone had left in the shower that morning.

I'll be honest. If someone asked me am I in love with Annie Altman, I'd have to say I don't know, because I really *don't* know. I have nothing to compare with how I feel about her. But I do know that I feel this kind of a need where she is concerned; I need her to notice me more than she does; I need to think that I make her feel lighter when she sees me. And there's no way I could ever believe that was possible, because it was just little me, Ryan Dean West, fourteen years old, walking around in the exact same clothes and tie as four hundred other guys here at Pine Mountain, every one of us so much the same, except for me, except for that one thing she noticed that she couldn't get over, that made me so unattractively different from every other eleventh-grade boy in this shithole.

It's what I tried to tell her in the note I threw away the night before.

It was a waste, anyway, because I knew I'd given her enough of a good reason for not ever talking to me again: I had crossed over, tried to make myself so much the same as a guy like Chas Becker by breaking the rules and playing poker and getting drunk, as if those stupid behaviors could ever incite some magical evolution in the ape of Ryan Dean West and cause him to shed his tail and walk upright in Annie's eyes.

But I could hope, even if I was such a loser.

She sat across from Isabel Reyes at breakfast, eating a bagel and sipping from a carton of orange juice. And despite JP calling out "Hey, Ryan Dean," and Seanie trying to wave me over to where they sat by the door so they could see every girl who came and went, I ignored them, but not in an unfriendly, stuck-up way, because I was kind of scared and had this jumping-off-the-highest-ever-high-dive feeling as I kept my eyes focused forward and walked right to where Annie sat.

She saw me coming up, but I couldn't tell from her expression whether or not she was happy to see me. As always, Annie looked totally hot, but so did Isabel in her rustic, more-facial-hair-than-Ryan-Dean-West-will-have-in-college kind of way (God! Why do I think that's hot?). And then I saw Annie lean over and whisper something to Isabel, and I could only imagine what they were saying.

## What the Girls Probably Said: A Play by Ryan Dean West

ANNIE: Here comes that fucking alcoholic Ryan Dean West. Observe how I treat him like he's some kind of pathetic red-eared slider turtle.

ISABEL: His ears look kind of pink to me. I think he's cute.

ANNIE: You think he's *cute*? He's just a *little boy*. I'll probably just ignore his skinny-bitch ass, pretend like he isn't here.

ISABEL: You always told me how much you liked him.

ANNIE: He acted like an asshole as soon as we got to school on Sunday. First he wouldn't talk to me, he lied about wanting to go for a run with me, and then he got drunk with Chas Becker. Definitely so *not-cute*.


And then I thought, *Would you really ignore me, Annie? Do I really want to keep walking toward you just so you can kick me in the nuts again?*

I glanced back and saw that JP and Seanie were watching me.

Crap!

Something happens when guys watch guys doing things like this. They knew what was going on, and they got to watch the Ryan Dean West suicide mission from the front row. It's like jumping out of a plane. There's no time-outs or do-overs, there's just gravity. That, and lots of witnesses to see your chute collapse as your body plummets helplessly toward certain death.

All I could do now was hope I didn't cry like a little girl in front of the hundreds of kids having breakfast.

It was a surreal comic of my life, and I pictured the worst possible outcome:

"Annie. Would it be okay if I sat down with you for a minute?" I said in the sweetest, most injured tone of voice I could manage. (It's not like my voice hadn't changed last year, though. I was no candidate for a position in one of those churchy boys' choirs.)

Then she looked at me square in the eyes, and at that moment I knew everything was going to be okay. There's just ways friends can see things in each others' faces, kind of like the ha-ha-I-made-Joey-look-at-your-balls/haiku conversation I'd had with Seanie the night before, except, of course, the way Annie looked at me was really nice.

"Hi, West. Sure," she said.

Score.

Except I really wished she'd call me Ryan Dean.

And I lucked out again, because Isabel was sitting right across from her, which meant I had to sit beside Annie, which gave me the opportunity to ever-so-gently brush my thigh against hers, which caused a very dizzying and embarrassing migration of otherwise fully employed red blood cells to a highly depressed and underemployed (as my Econ professor might speculate) region of Ryan Dean West Land.

"Hi, Isabel." My voice cracked when I said it. I felt like an idiot. I don't think there was any blood left in the northern provinces. "Did you have a good summer?"

"Yeah," Isabel said.

*Okay, now go away, moustache-girl (not that your moustache isn't kind of hot). Ugh. I think I'm passing out.*

I cleared my throat. I looked at Isabel. God! I wanted her to leave, because I knew exactly what they'd do after this whole uncomfortable scene ended: They would replay and reinterpret everything that happened, and they would make stuff up, too—things they thought I'd said that never came out of my mouth.

"Annie," I began.

After that, I didn't have any idea what to say. I just sat there staring at her. I was so lost, I even thought about the Preamble to the Constitution.

I, the people, am such a loser.

And then, thank God, Annie saved me.

"Are you feeling better this morning?" she asked.

Okay. That's when I knew, *knew*, I was totally, *totally*, in love with her. And that realization made me instantly sad, too, because I'm a smart kid; I knew I had absolutely no chance at all.

I looked at my hands where they rested on the table next to a mustard stain. And I thought I actually *did* feel pretty good, relieved that Mrs. Singer hadn't coincidentally caused me to come down with a fit of projectile vomiting or something.

"Yeah. I feel a lot better. How about you?"

"Good. I started reading that Hawthorne story."

"So did I. It's weird."

"Yeah."

I squeezed my fists as tight as I could. They turned white.

Time to jump.

"Annie, I am really sorry about how stupid I was. I didn't know what I was getting myself into, but now I'm smarter, but I'm also worse off because I made you mad and I would never do anything, ever, to purposely make you mad, 'cause you're my best friend in this whole pathetic place, so I'm really sorry and I guess I'll go now, but I just had to tell you."

Zen archery of run-on-sentence apologies.

And I almost looked up to see if my chute would catch air or just flutter around up there like a giant dirty sock.

I pressed my hands on the table and started to stand.

Then she put her hand on top of mine and said, "It's okay, West. I don't want you to go. And I'm not mad anymore either. You were just temporarily stupid. What boy doesn't hit that mark at least ten times a day?"

I sighed and relaxed in my seat. My leg touched hers again.

*Please don't move your hand, Annie.*

When she started to pull her hand away, I covered it with mine and squeezed. And she squeezed back.

Ryan Dean West was actually holding hands with a girl who wasn't his mom.

People began moving around us, hefting their books and packs. The day's first class would be starting in five minutes, but I didn't want to move. Besides, I probably would have collapsed if I tried to stand up.

Then Isabel got up from her seat and said, "Bye, Ryan Dean. See you later, Annie."

And, still holding on to Annie's hand, I said, "Can we just talk later? Alone?"

"Sure."

"Will you meet me at Stonehenge after practice?"

"You want to go for a run?"

"No."

"Okay."

"Okay."

# CHAPTER TWENTY-THREE

FOR CONDITIONING CLASS, WE DID tear-offs in weight lifting on Tuesdays. Tear-offs can make a guy scream if you do them right. Seanie and JP were spotting the bar and pulling off weights until I was just down to the bar and nothing else, until I couldn't even lift the bar anymore and they had to help me just to get it back on the braces.

"Damn. Winger's been lifting weights," JP said.

I just lay there on the bench and rubbed my shoulders. I felt so good.

"Winger's pumped," Seanie said. "What'd Annie say?"

"If I told you, you'd probably make a MySite about it."

"I already did make an Annie and Ryan Dean MySite," Seanie said.

"Yeah, right."

I wasn't buying his shit anymore.

"Yeah. I did," Seanie said. "And nothing ever happens on it."

"Annie's pretty hot, dude. You really not going to tell us?" JP asked. I grabbed his hand, and he lifted me up so we could trade places.

"She's not mad at me," I said. I matched the weights on my side to Seanie's. Of course, at his size, JP was almost twice as strong as me. And then I added, "And we held hands, too."

"No way!" Seanie said. "You are such a fucking loser, Ryan Dean. You're in eleventh grade, not kinderfuckinggarten."

I flipped Seanie off and then had to pull one of JP's weights from the bar.

"Just remember, Seanie. I made Joey look at your balls."

"Dude, Joey's gay. You can't *make* him look at my balls. But you could charge him to. And he hasn't actually seen them yet."

Yeah . . . in the weight room, we often have deep, philosophical conversations.

We pulled off another round of weights, but JP was struggling because he started laughing.

When it was Seanie's turn, JP and I got him all loaded up, and just when he raised the barbell and locked out over his chest, we walked away and left him there as he yelled, "Hey! Fuck you guys! Assholes!"

Of course we didn't leave him like that. We were just messing with him. But Seanie always had a way of obsessing about things like they were the greatest trespasses ever committed against his pitiful soul. Maybe that's one of the things I found so funny about Sean Russell Flaherty.

And when we were changing back into our school clothes for the second class of the day, JP asked if I thought there was going to be any trouble about them coming to visit me in O-Hall the night before.

"As weird as he is, I think Farrow understands that you guys were just trying to help me," I said. "I wouldn't expect he'll turn you in to the headmaster, and even if he does, you guys won't get into trouble for what you did."

"I hope you're right," JP said.

"I'd kind of like to get put in O-Hall," Seanie said. "So I could kick your ass at poker."

"No you wouldn't. It sucks. And I think that woman who lives downstairs, Mrs. Singer, is a witch or something."

"You're fucking crazy, Winger," JP said.

"Yeah," Seanie agreed.

But they didn't see what I'd seen.

# CHAPTER TWENTY-FOUR

MEGAN RENSHAW WAS A STRESS case. When we went over the Calculus review problems Mrs. Kurtz had assigned from day one, Megan got every one of them wrong. She spun sideways in her desk (her hair brushed across my hand again—yes!), and she practically had tears in her eyes as she complained to Joey and me, "I think I became completely stupid over the summer!"

And then Joey said what I didn't have the guts to say: "I think hanging out with Betch would lower anyone's I.Q."

"Look," I said, moving my pencil over her paper, just near enough to her hand that I could feel her warmth and smell the ginger lotion on her skin, "here's where you got this step backward."

Megan swept her hair back from her face and propped her head on an elbow, resting on my desk. She sighed in defeat.

She was definitely the hottest defeated multivariate calculus student I'd ever seen.

Megan said, "You guys who get this stuff . . . ," and she looked from Joey to me. When our eyes locked, I had to look away. Megan Renshaw was *looking at me like she liked me or something*. And she said, "Smart guys are such a turn-on."

Joey cleared his throat.

Chas Becker must have been a genius in at least one thing Megan Renshaw liked.

Mrs. Kurtz had been looming over us, watching Megan's frustration, and she said, "Why don't the three of you form a study group to work on tonight's assignment?"

And I thought it was just like Seanie's haiku coming true, except for the Megan part. And the Megan part practically gave me an aneurysm when she put her ginger-lotion hand on my arm and said, with pleading and helpless eyes, "Will you help me, Ryan Dean? Please?"

I wasn't sure if I could physically tolerate all the up-and-down surging of blood I'd been experiencing that morning. I swear I could actually see my heart thumping in my chest beneath my sweater.

"Sure." And I was kind of scared—no, terrified—so I said, "Joey can, too."

And, just like that, the three of us agreed to meet in the library after dinner that night, with Mrs. Kurtz's approval. Students were allowed to do homework in the library until lights-out, but O-Hall kids had to have a teacher's consent. So, thanks to Mrs. Kurtz's facilitation, I had scored my second smoking-hot-girl date on just my second day of eleventh grade.

Things were definitely looking up.

The day before, the day after the poker game, postconsequence, I felt like I had been stuffed with a combination of cement and sleeping pills; but that Tuesday I practically floated through the entire school day.

# CHAPTER TWENTY-FIVE

NOTE TO ANNIE DURING LIT CLASS:

*Don't forget.*

Then I drew a picture on the bottom:

And, yeah, she did think I was a pervert.

# CHAPTER TWENTY-SIX

THIS TIME, I SHOWERED AFTER RUGBY. I put my school clothes back on and tied my necktie as neatly as I could. I even borrowed some cologne from Joey. I got some gel from Kevin Cantrell and put it in my hair and tried to comb it.

Everyone knew something was up.

This time, Casey Palmer and Nick Matthews weren't waiting at the side of the football field as the guys came streaming down from the locker room.

I would have run on my way to O-Hall, but I didn't want to get all sweaty before seeing Annie. I planned to just drop off my school books in my room so I wouldn't have to carry my pack with me all the way to our stone circle.

O-Hall looked deserted when I got there. I guess I must have been the first boy back from school. Despite all the attention I'd paid to my clothes and hair, I'd still rushed to get out of the locker room and managed to make it back to O-Hall before anyone else. So when I opened the outer door to the mudroom and stairwell, I wasn't expecting to see anyone; and this time, I did kind of squeal more than a little bit when I ran straight into the not-even-hot-on-Pluto Mrs. Singer.

And I don't know why I was so terrified, but after that diarrhea spell I was convinced she'd laid on me, and the spontaneous bloody nose of the night before, I completely believed that she was determined to do something horrible to me, like turn me into her eunuch slave former-boy, or breathe poison into me.

Maybe that Hawthorne story was getting to me, I don't know.

Our eyes met as I stood, petrified, at the bottom of the stairwell. And I don't know where all my blood went, but I know it didn't go anywhere I particularly cared about.

Then she said, "I am going to suck your fucking soul out through your eye sockets with my lampreylike tongue."

Well, to be absolutely honest, she actually just said, "Oh, hello. It's you again," but I wasn't about to stand there and listen to her demonic incantations. I was on a mission. I ran upstairs, wondering whether or not I should jump out the window so I wouldn't have to see her again on my way down.

Damn! I was starting to sweat.

I threw my door open and tossed the book pack up onto my bunk.

I looked out the window, and I could see Chas, Joey, and Kevin returning from practice. At least I knew I wouldn't have to jump, because Chas and Kevin's souls were way more suckable than mine; they had to be much more liquefied, since they were forward-pack guys. But what sucked most of all was that just as I was about to leave so I could go meet Annie, Mr. Farrow appeared, blocking the doorway out of my room.

"Ryan Dean," he said, "it looks as though you're feeling much better today. Let's have a chat, shall we?"

On second thought, I would rather have had my soul lamprey-sucked from my skull.

Mr. Farrow stood in the open doorway, just watching me like he was waiting for some kind of confession. My head spun, because there sure was a lot of crap I could potentially be confessing to, pulled from the Ryan Dean West record of the past forty-eight hours. So all I could do was try my best to look and sound innocent, and of course my voice cracked like a Cub Scout's when I said, "Mr. Farrow, I'm supposed to meet someone before dinner. It's about a homework assignment, and I'm afraid I'm going to be late."

I heard the sound of the guys coming up the stairs.

"I'm concerned you may have gotten off to the wrong kind of start this semester, Ryan Dean."

Oh, God. It sounded like he knew everything.

Now there'd be the inevitable call home; and next thing you knew, Ryan Dean West would be an ex-PM junior on a plane to Boston with a goddamned unaccompanied-minor-smiley-airplane-name-tag-that-says-hi-my-name-is-fucking-loser stuck to his skinny-bitch-ass-fourteen-year-old collar in the morning. I could only hope the stewardess in charge of feeding and toweling me off would be, well . . . five out of five steaming bowls of chowder on the Ryan Dean West

In-Flight-Entertainment-Things-You-Don't-Mind-Burning-Your-Tongue-On Heat Index.

"I'm sorry, Mr. Farrow. I can do better."

"I expect you can, Ryan Dean, especially if we've set a goal of getting you placed back in the boys' dorm by the semester break."

It sounded like there was hope after all.

*Now, careful, Ryan Dean. Don't say too much.*

"But as far as the food in the room and your two visitors last night are concerned," Farrow said, "I think I'm going to have to put you on in-room detention."

Which was even worse than being kicked out. It meant no Annie. No Megan Renshaw.

What a cruel deal it is to have been born with testicles, and to have to carry them around along with me on my miserable path through life. They may just as well have been the size of Volkswagens for the burden they had become.

I tried my hardest to make some tears pool in my eyes. Thinking about peeing usually does it for me; at least, it works on my parents.

"Please, Mr. Farrow," I said. "I was really sick, but I forced myself to go through the entire . . ."

*Think about peeing. Think about peeing.*

". . . first day of classes because I want to try so hard . . ."

*Think about peeing. Think about peeing.*

". . . this year to show I can be better. But then I fell asleep . . ."

*Think about peeing. Think about peeing.*

". . . and my friends were concerned, so they woke me up and brought some . . ."

*Think about peeing. Think about peeing.*

". . . food."

To kind-of quote Ovid: "Tears at times have the weight of speech."

Just as the guys spilled noisily out from the stairwell, one perfect tear streaked down from the corner of my eye. And I quickly wiped it away, pretending I'd be embarrassed if the other guys had seen I was crying.

And I could see by Farrow's pained expression that the time-tested and sparingly applied Ryan Dean West pee-tear scam worked beautifully.

Ryan Dean West, performance fucking artist.

"Please," I added, so sweetly, like a bullfighter inserting the final *estoque*. I imagined the ultrahot and impassioned Annie and Megan throwing a shower of blooms at my feet, and I'd pick one up, smell it, and clench it between my teeth; and the impaled Mr. Farrow looked at the boys coming down the hall, then leaned close as though he were protecting my vulnerability, and whispered, "I'll let it go this time, Ryan Dean. You just take care. Now run along."

Yes!

And when I sailed through the hallway, past Joey, I raised my hand and slapped him with the hardest and loudest high five ever executed in the history of gay-straight high fivery, and said, "Thanks for the hair gel, Kevin. Thanks for the smells-good, Joey."

And I flew down the stairs, not even slightly concerned that I'd run into that soul-sucking-and-so-unhot Mrs. Singer.

# CHAPTER TWENTY-SEVEN

ANNIE LAUGHED WHEN SHE SAW me. Her eyes squinted, full of water like they get when she laughs. She held the note I gave her in Lit class and waved it at me like a surrender flag.

"You are such a pervert, West. Babysit? Bathe?"

"'Here, Beatrice,'" I said, quoting our Hawthorne story, "'see how many needful offices require to be done to our chief treasure.'" And I swept my hand downward along my body and pointed.

To me.

She giggled. "Per-vert!"

"You would not believe the bullet I just dodged, Annie."

We sat on a mossy and black tree trunk that had fallen down in some storm years before I'd ever entered Pine Mountain. I told Annie all about my run-in with Mr. Farrow, and how hard I worked, thinking about peeing, to make myself get a tear from one eye, and she laughed and leaned close to me, so close that we were almost touching. And, unfortunately, at that moment I realized that all my pee-mantra meditations with Mr. Farrow and the recounting of the story actually *did* make me want to pee, but I wasn't about to move, either.

"I've never seen you with gel in your hair, West," she said. And she leaned her face really close to my neck (I tipped just a little closer toward her, hoping her lips would touch me), and she inhaled and said, "And you smell like cologne."

"I always wear this stuff," I said, trying to sound as confident and masculine as possible, considering the magnitude of my certain and fourteen-year-old wimposity.

"Well, you look absolutely adorable," she said.

I just stared at her soft knees, where they peeked out from beneath the perfect hem of her skirt.

I hate that word. "Adorable." Especially the way Annie said it. Because it sounded like something any girl might say about a pink hoodie sweatshirt in a Hollister catalog, not something she'd say about a boy. Unless he was wearing diapers or drop-seat pajamas with feet on them and had a pacifier in his mouth, which kind of gave me a semiperverted idea for a Halloween costume I'd like to wear just for Annie. Okay . . . I'll be honest. It wasn't semi-, it was *totally perverted*.

I sighed.

"Thanks, Annie," I said. "You look totally hot yourself. Want to make out now?"

Well, I didn't actually say the "want to make out" part, but I sure wanted to say it. But just thinking it was a mistake, because I suddenly couldn't think of anything else and found that, once again, Ryan Dean West's brain was strained to its capacity with thinking of . . . well, sex. And, as usual, I couldn't get my mind off of it, so I quickly drew up a brain-function chart in my bloodless head:

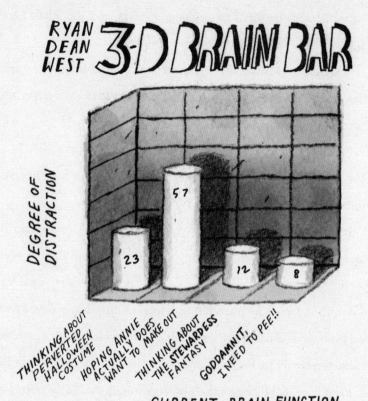

RYAN DEAN WEST **3-D BRAIN BAR**

DEGREE OF DISTRACTION

57

23

12

8

THINKING ABOUT PERVERTED HALLOWEEN COSTUME

HOPING ANNIE ACTUALLY DOES WANT TO MAKE OUT

THINKING ABOUT THE STEWARDESS FANTASY

GODDAMNIT, I NEED TO PEE!!

CURRENT BRAIN FUNCTION

I am such a loser.

"Hey, Annie, did you really mean what you said when you told me that having me as a friend was the only thing you like about this school?"

"Well, I did like the smoothie I had at lunch today, but, yes. I do mean it."

"Thanks."

And I wanted to hold her hand so bad right then, but I was afraid.

Can you imagine that? Yesterday I took down Casey Palmer, and today I was scared of touching a girl's hand.

And I said, "Are you going back home this weekend?"

Annie's parents lived near Seattle, so it was an easy trip.

"Yeah."

"It sucks being here alone on the weekend. All my friends are gone," I said. "Maybe one weekend you could stay, so we could do something together."

She stood up, and we walked into the center of our Stonehenge, toward the spiral path.

"I know," she said, "I'll ask my parents if you can come home with me one weekend. That would be fun. They've been dying to meet you."

Score!

"Have you told them about me?"

"Of course."

I wondered what she'd said. If she made me sound like a pitiful little boy to them.

"Do you promise to ask them? This weekend, ask them, okay?"

"Okay."

Suddenly, my brain was at 100 percent imagining spending a weekend with Annie at her house. I could have peed in my pants right then and not even known it.

We started following the spiral wish path toward the center.

I gulped.

I reached over and held her hand.

She held mine back.

We stopped walking, and Annie said, "Hey, West, are we *holding hands*?"

"Uh. Yeah."

"Weird."

"I know."

"Want to let go?"

"No."

"Okay."

And that's all she said. Okay. In that singing, relaxed kind of voice she had that made everything sound painless, like it didn't matter, like there were no big deals anywhere in the universe.

When we walked back out of the path, she said, "What did you wish for?"

And I said, "I didn't think you were supposed to tell."

"Tell this one time."

"Okay," I said, "come here."

And I led her over to where we'd been sitting on that log. I brushed the dirt on the ground flat with my brand new shoes and kneeled down. I drew two overlapping circles: a Venn diagram.

"That's what I wished for, Annie."

"It looks like a Venn diagram, West."

"It is." I put my finger in one of the circles. "These are all the boys here at Pine Mountain. We're all almost totally the same. We dress the same, we all pretty much like the same stuff, we all play sports, and every one of us thinks you, Annie Altman, are totally hot."

"Shut up." She laughed.

I put my finger in the narrow crescent of the other circle, the outside part.

"And here's Ryan Dean West. Well, at least, it's the one tiny part of Ryan Dean West that makes him stand out as being so different, the only thing that everyone notices about him. The number fourteen. And you think that makes me so different, like I'm a little kid. But the thing is, everyone has that little part that's outside the overlap of everyone else. And a lot of people zero in on that one little thing they can't get over. Like for Joey, 'cause he's gay, I guess. Some people are better than others about not getting that outside-the-overlap part so noticed, but not me. So that was my wish. What do you think?"

"I don't know," she said. She looked suddenly serious.

"I didn't mean to make you feel bad," I said. "Sorry. What was your wish?"

"Maybe I shouldn't say."

"No fair, Annie."

"Seriously?"

"Serious."

"I wished for you to get your wish."

# CHAPTER TWENTY-EIGHT

AFTER DINNER, JOEY AND I WALKED
to the library with our Calculus books to meet Megan. I guess I didn't
feel right after seeing Annie out in the woods, like maybe I'd said too
much and it was going to ruin our friendship now, so I was a little
depressed and didn't say anything to Joey.

I kept picturing those circles in my head. I hoped I'd made
sense to Annie, that I didn't sound like a whiny little crybaby.
And I thought about Joey too, and how bad and terribly lonely
he must feel sometimes; and that's why I tried to always go out
of my way to not notice the thing about him you couldn't notice
anyway.

We stayed in the library until they kicked us out, at nine forty-five.
Megan looked so deliciously good, and she smiled so broadly when it
finally all started coming back to her. I guess Joey and I counteracted
the brain-loss effect caused by Chas Becker's brilliance.

Megan walked us back to O-Hall, between Joey and me, with her
arms locked inside each of ours. I will admit that twice I feigned trip-
ping on a rock just so my right arm would brush against her breast,
and that was awesome.

The performance artist was on the mark that day.

When we got back to O-Hall, Joey and I said good night to Megan and started for the door.

"Thank you boys so much for helping me," Megan said. "You are such good friends, and I love you both."

"No problem," Joey said.

"Yeah."

Then Megan stepped up to Joey and kissed him on the cheek, and I could see he kissed her back too, all suave and mannered, like he did that kind of stuff all the time. He pulled open the door to the mud-room, and Megan turned to me.

I thought I was actually going to die. Megan Renshaw, in all her smoking five-out-of-five-habanero hotness, was going to kiss me, Ryan Dean Never-Been-Kissed-by-Anyone-Who-Wasn't-Alive-When-Sputnik-Got-Launched West.

I closed my eyes.

She put her hands on the sides of my jaw.

She kissed me right on the mouth.

AND SHE STAYED THERE.

I think she actually had to hold me up when she slipped her tongue past my lips.

Then she put her face to my ear and whispered, "I think you are really adorable."

Okay . . . I'll admit I no longer hated that word.

Then she whirled around and left us there.

In the stairwell, I gave Joey the all-time-record-breaking gay-straight high five.

And he said, "You don't have to worry about me. I won't tell Chas about you making out with Megan. He's a douche bag, anyway, and you know he'd kill you for it."

PART TWO:
# the sawmill

# CHAPTER TWENTY-NINE

BY THE FIRST WEEK OF OCTOBER,
it was freezing cold up there in the Cascades at Pine Mountain Academy.
And things just continued along from day to day in their usual way.

We'd played poker a couple more times, always on Sunday nights,
because that's when the guys got back from their weekends. But I never
drank beer again after that first time. Chas tried to make me do it, and I
thought I was actually going to get into a certain-death-for-Ryan-Dean-
West fistfight over it, but Joey got between us and let Chas know that he
was ready to fight him about it too. I even lost again, the second time
we played, and that time the guys made me swim across the lake in the
middle of the night wearing only my boxers. It was so cold, I could hardly
breathe, and I was convinced as I paddled through that liquid hell that
Mrs. Singer was going to turn herself into a multitentacled monster and
drag me down to her icy black lair.

In Lit class, we had finished reading *Billy Budd, Foretopman*, and I
was convinced by that time that Mr. Wellins was some sort of pervert,
because he believed that everything we read had something to do with
sex. According to him, "Rappaccini's Daughter" was about incest, and,
he argued, *Billy Budd* was about homosexuality. Mr. Wellins said it didn't
matter what a writer intended his work to mean, that the only thing
that mattered was what it meant to the reader, and I guess I could see

his point, but I still thought he was a creepy old pervert. Anyway, I just thought Melville wrote a good story, but what do I know?

And by mid-October, Coach M had pretty much named the first fifteen on the rugby team. I kept my spot and my nickname, at number eleven, JP made fullback, Seanie made scrum half, and the rest of the team were the returning seniors from last year, including Chas, Kevin, and Joey. We were also getting ready to play our first preseason friendly match against Sacred Heart Catholic School in Salem. So, with that game coming up, we were all pretty damned excited and nervous.

And, on the topic of being excited and nervous, that night during the first week of school—the night I'd made out with Megan Renshaw—I remember that when I got back to my room, I could hardly face Chas. I felt like I had stolen something, but I felt damned good about it too. And after that, anytime Chas laid it on thick with his put-downs and threats, I'd just smirk and think to myself, *Your girlfriend puts her tongue in my mouth and she likes it*, and my smirk would piss off Chas even more because he had no idea why I had suddenly become so confident around him.

Megan Renshaw and I flirted constantly in Calc and Econ, and sometimes we'd get kind of perverted about it. Joey just watched it and laughed at us, and he never said anything to anyone, because that was the kind of guy Joey Cosentino was. But I was still kind of afraid of Megan, and had no misconceptions as to who was holding the power in our quirky relationship.

One time, she even followed me out of class when I left for the bathroom, and we made out for about thirty nonstop and frenzied seconds in a drinking fountain alcove, and then she just left me there, completely unable to walk to the bathroom, much less back to class.

I felt really weird about the whole fooling-around-with-steaming-hot-Megan-Renshaw thing. First of all, and I'll be honest, I felt really guilty before and afterward. It was during, though, that I didn't feel anything even close to guilt—when Megan had her mouth all over mine and let me slip my hand up inside her sweater. When that was going on, it definitely was *not* guilt that occupied my mind.

When I was away from her—and could think sanely, that is—if I wasn't having any perverted fantasies about airline stewardesses or Halloween costumes, I felt terrible, because I knew I was being the same kind of asshole to Chas Becker that he was to everyone else; and I tried to do anything I could to *not* think about how Annie would feel if she found out about us.

It tore me up, except for the couple minutes here and there when Megan would sneak off and get that nasty-policewoman-who-wants-to-arrest-bad-Ryan-Dean look in her eyes, but I felt like there was nobody I could talk to about it. If I talked to JP and Seanie, everyone else would know. Shit, Seanie would make a website about it. I definitely couldn't talk to Annie, because I knew I was being bad and doing something that was just plain wrong (even if I liked the occasional chance to play Bad Ryan Dean). The only person I could talk to about it, of course, was Joey, who was gay.

I tried asking Megan about it, but she played me off. I got the impression she really *did* like me, which made me feel worse about Annie. In the end, it just seemed to me that Megan Renshaw was the kind of girl who only wanted a Chas Becker trophy mate because all the other girls at Pine Mountain wanted him. It was a game to Megan, and I felt sorry for how sad and lonely she was going to end up.

## the DULL POINT on the LOVE TRIANGLE

●●●

The Monday before the team took the bus to Salem to play, Joey and I walked back to O-Hall together after practice.

"Oh. I've been meaning to ask you, Ryan Dean," Joey began, "what's the deal with that Casey Palmer website? I didn't think he was so . . . extroverted, I guess, but I could be wrong."

Score. I had succeeded in making Joey look at Seanie's balls.

This was, indeed, the stuff of future epic sonnets.

"I only heard about it," I said. "I haven't seen it."

"Oh, sure," he said, and laughed, like he didn't believe me. "Then why are there so many comments posted by *you* on there about how gay Casey is?"

Seanie. Even when you think you've caught up with him, you realize he's always pushing it a step further.

"Seanie Flaherty's a dick," I said.

Joey laughed.

I sighed.

And Joey said, "You guys shouldn't mess around with Casey Palmer's ego. I've seen that guy do some pretty crazy shit."

"Like what?" I said.

"He flips out. He can hurt guys," Joey said.

"Oh." I shrugged. "I'll tell Seanie to lay off. He won't listen, though."

"Seanie never does."

"Joey, I need to ask you. You're the only guy I can talk to about this, and it's really bugging me. What do *you* think I should do about Megan?"

"You're going to do whatever you want to do, it looks like. Or, whatever *she* wants you to do," Joey said.

"Someone's going to find out."

"Bound to," he agreed.

"Really. I don't care what Chas does to me if he finds out, 'cause I do deserve it. I just think it's unfair to treat a guy like that, even if it's Chas, but especially if we're on the same team. But I really do like Megan. She's supersmart. And she is so freakin' hot."

"Ryan Dean, I know you'd feel terrible if someone you care about ended up getting hurt over this."

"Like Annie."

"Exactly. And, anyway, don't you love Annie or something?" Joey asked.

"Dude, I am so insanely in love with Annie Altman that I can't even think straight. No gay pun intended."

Joey smiled.

"Well, obviously you can't think, straight or otherwise," Joey said. "That's why you're messing around with Megan."

Then Joey stopped walking, and he looked directly at me. He looked pissed off, too. "It's one thing to be an asshole to Betch. He deserves it. But why would you hurt Annie? Why don't you fucking grow up, Ryan Dean? At the very least, you have to talk to Annie about it. She is your best friend, isn't she?"

I stopped in my tracks.

I had never been told off like that by Joey.

It stung.

And he said, "Sorry."

"No, Joe. You're right." I sighed.

We started walking again. "How come *you* don't have these problems?"

"Are you *fucking stupid*, Ryan Dean?"

I pushed him. "Just kidding, Joey."

Joey smiled, and I said, "But you know, I really don't get this liking-boys-better-than-girls thing. No offense, 'cause you know I'd like you the same, no matter what. I just don't get it."

"Ryan Dean?"

"What?"

"Shut the fuck up."

"Okay."

I am such a loser.

No matter what Megan offered, or tempted me with, I never got over being totally crazy for the totally hot Annie Altman. And playing with Megan was like playing with a rattlesnake. Well, a smoking-hot rattlesnake. With incredible boobs. That Ryan Dean West had actually touched.

I knew Joey was right.

I had to stop.

# CHAPTER THIRTY

ANNIE KEPT THE PROMISE SHE'D made that day we told each other our wishes at Stonehenge. Her parents had spoken to mine, so Annie and I got tickets to fly up to Seattle together on Friday after school. I was going to spend the weekend at my best friend's house. And every time I'd almost get up enough courage to ask where I'd be sleeping (and what I should wear, since I don't have any drop-seat pajamas with feet on them—in fact, I don't have any pajamas at all), hoping she'd say something ultrahot like, "On the couch in my room," to which she might add, parenthetically, "And I believe that sleep is something that should only be done while completely naked," my throat knotted up and my ears turned red. God! What a dork I am.

It was blissful and it was terrifying at the same time. And as I made my way through the week, I just stumbled around in the stupidest kind of daze.

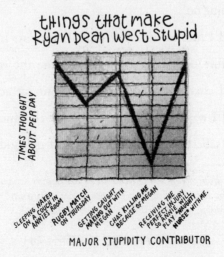

things that make
Ryan Dean West stupid

TIMES THOUGHT ABOUT PER DAY

SLEEPING NAKED ON A COUCH IN ANNIE'S ROOM

RUGBY MATCH ON THURSDAY

GETTING CAUGHT MAKING OUT WITH MEGAN

CHAS KILLING ME BECAUSE OF MEGAN

RECEIVING THE PERFECT INJURY SO ANNIE WILL PLAY NAUGHTY NURSE WITH ME.

MAJOR STUPIDITY CONTRIBUTOR

I fantasized about our first game and the prospect of receiving just the perfect degree of injury so Annie would want to play the naughty nurse all weekend long as I lay on her couch, naked, in constant need of sponge baths and hernia exams. At 1,492 total thought episodes per day, it was my Columbus-discovers-perversion fantasy.

So of course it was next to impossible to concentrate at all on schoolwork while keeping meticulous tallies of my impure thoughts, much less for me to listen to Mr. Wellins blather on and on about sex, because, now that I look at it, every single thought in my head—Annie, Megan, Chas, the game—all, in some way, had something to do with sex. So maybe Wellins was right after all, that *everything* does have something to do with sex, even though I found his argument about the underlying sexual themes in *A Connecticut Yankee in King Arthur's Court* to be a bit of a stretch, and totally perverted, too.

Hello, Central![1]

I mean, come on!

Annie and I met for lunch at school that day. It was Tuesday; two days before the game, three days before the weekend that I hoped would change my life. JP and Seanie sat across the table from us, and I was between Annie and Isabel, which was kind of hot because Isabel kept brushing up against me, and, even though

---

[1] Okay. If you haven't read *A Connecticut Yankee in King Arthur's Court*, you should. Because it is fucking hilarious, and there's no way you'd understand "Hello, Central" unless you read the book.

there wasn't really room for it in my head, I imagined Annie and her having a warrior-princess-fight-to-the-death for breeding rights with me. I noticed Seanie was particularly fascinated by Isabel's faint fuzzy moustache. Joey, who almost never sat with the other seniors, was with us too.

"Do you guys know that this weekend West is coming to my house for two days?" Annie announced.

I hadn't told anyone. I noticed Joey glanced at me with a have-you-told-Megan-yet look on his face.

Seanie kicked me under the table and raised his hand.

"High five, Winger," he said. He slapped my hand over our burritos, and I watched Annie's expression to see if that was the wrong thing to do. Seanie added, "Why does this remind me of salmon swimming upstream to spawn and die?"

I thought about my white, bloated corpse floating in Puget Sound. At least I imagined I had a contented smile on my face. Fins and gills, too.

"Probably because you're a sick freak," Annie answered.

"You know, Annie, Ryan Dean doesn't wear pajamas. So . . . where's he going to sleep?" Seanie asked.

"Probably on the couch," she said.

*OH MY GOD! YES!*

I know . . . she didn't say which couch, but I figured I was halfway home. Just hearing her answer, so comfortably and honestly, caused yet another of my chronic blood-and-attention-migration episodes, and I nearly jerked my hand skyward for another high five with Seanie, but controlled the urge.

"Stop being such a pervert, Seanie," JP said.

"You're just in denial that you weren't thinking the same thing, even if it *was* about permavirgin Ryan Dean," Seanie said.

*Permavirgin?*

The moment had come to strike swiftly. I kicked Seanie's shin and brushed up against Annie's thigh in the process. Two scores at once.

"Speaking of perverts, what did you think about Casey Palmer's MySite, Joey?" I asked. My voice cracked again. I am such a dork.

"Pretty sick," Joey said.

"It's nasty," Annie added.

"*You've* seen it too?" I said.

I saw Seanie turning red. He also looked really pissed off at me. Oh, well, that's what he gets.

And Annie said, "*You* told me to check it out, West, so I did. And it's gross. What do you expect from a football player, anyway? It's probably the only way he can get someone to look at those small, pitiful things."

Despite Seanie's tortured expression, I found myself suddenly thinking about the deeper meaning of the last statement Annie had made there.

Yeah. I know. I'm such a loser.

"Are you okay, Ryan Dean?" JP asked.

"Huh?"

"Dude, you looked like you were sleeping with your eyes open for the last five minutes," he said. "Didn't you hear anything I said?"

"About what?"

"Halloween."

"Oh," I said, "what did you say?"

And I thought, did I accidentally babble something about what I'd like to wear for Annie?

"About the dance," Seanie said.

Halloween was coming up on the Thursday after our game.

Whenever Halloween fell during the week, since we were so isolated, Pine Mountain would have a dinner dance. I hadn't even thought about it, beyond my perverted fantasy about Annie, but it suddenly dawned on me that I couldn't go. Pine Mountain's rules did not allow O-Hall boys to attend such events.

"Me and Annie are going together," JP said.

Okay. I really wanted to cuss. But I didn't.

I felt my eyes get big, and a little watery. I looked at Annie with a what-the-fuck-is-he-talking-about look on my face, but she just looked perfectly normal; perfectly, hotly, matter-of-fact Annie.

I looked at JP. *"What?"*

"Dude. You don't want her going alone, do you?"

I looked at Annie again.

"No. You're right."

I stood up. My head was spinning, and I felt like I was going to end up on my face. I needed to get out of there. Now I knew what it meant, all those times I noticed JP looking at her, watching me, too. I wanted to kick his fucking head in right there, so I just left. I went for the doors and stepped out into the cold afternoon.

And I could hear her calling, in her I'm-singing-a-song voice, all relaxed and sweet, "West? West? What's wrong *now*?" But I didn't even turn around.

Joey came after me.

"Hey," he said. "Are you okay?"

"I cannot believe that crap, Joey."

"It's just Annie and JP. It's no big deal," Joey said.

I was practically crying, but there was no way I was going to cry in front of a gay guy, even if he was my friend.

"I can't believe he'd do that to me," I said. "We're supposed to be friends. Why would he do that?"

"You know what, Ryan Dean? You're a fucking hypocrite. So now what are you going to do?"

And Joey turned around and walked back into the mess hall.

# CHAPTER THIRTY-ONE

RUGBY PRACTICE CAME. IT WOULD be our last hard practice before the game.

I wanted to hit someone. I wanted to get hurt, too.

After two hours of running drills, backline plays, and conditioning, we were all of us covered in sweat and grass and mud. It was the toughest practice we'd had all year, and Coach M told us he wasn't going to let us play a game, which is how we usually ended, because he didn't want to see us making any mistakes.

Instead we ended with a resistance drill we called Sumo, a one-on-one drill where a ball carrier had to drive the ball in and touch it down to a very small circle in the grass against one tackler. And the drill would not stop until the ball got there, no matter what; so there have been times when I've actually seen guys collapse from exhaustion if they couldn't get the ball in against a very tough tackler.

After we'd gone about halfway through the team, Kevin ended up in the middle, as the tackler against Chas. It was an intense fight. They were equal in size and strength, and Kevin just kept taking Chas down, inches before he could touch the ball into the circle, taunting Chas and pissing him off.

Finally, I think Kevin either got tired or felt sorry for Chas, because Chas slipped his arm through and got the ball down into the circle, diving onto his belly as he did and saying, "Fuck you, Kevin."

Then Kevin helped him up to his feet, and I looked at Coach M, who seemed to be pretending he didn't hear Chas cuss.

Now Chas was in the middle, and the way we play is that the guy in the middle gets to call out whoever he wants to have run against him.

I already knew who I'd call when I got a chance.

Chas looked around the circle of our dirty and tired teammates, and he bullet passed the ball to me and said, "Winger."

What a jerk.

I smiled.

Chas stood in front of the small circle in the grass and crouched in a hitting position, just staring at me. I took two steps toward him and stopped. He was so flat on his feet, I knew he wouldn't be able to touch me. I head-faked, then cut back the other way and sailed around him, touching the ball down without Chas even wiping a finger's width of sweat off me.

The guys on the team laughed at Chas, murmuring "Betch," and he turned to me and mouthed, "Fuck you," in a whisper so Coach couldn't hear.

Now I had the ball. Normally, I'd call out Bags, one of our other wings, because we were about the same size, even though he was older, but I'd made my mind up ahead of time that if I got the ball, there was one guy who'd have to run against me.

"Sartre," I said.

Everyone had to figure this would be no contest, that a guy who was built with JP's strength and drive would be able to stay low and plow right through me, that I had to be insane for calling out our fullback.

I heard a bunch of low-toned "oooh"s from the guys, and I threw the ball at JP, low, at his knees, so he had to bend down to catch it. It was a dick move; I'll admit it. Because I took off as fast as the ball, and as soon as it was in his hands, I flew, shoulder first, into JP's legs and twisted my body as I wrapped him up and drove him into the ground.

"Fuck," JP grunted as I hit him.

Springing to my feet, I pushed myself up by putting my left hand firmly down into his nuts, and JP groaned and doubled up, letting go of the ball. When he tried to scoop the ball back in, I hacked it out of his hand, kicking his fingers as I did. I know this was dirty, but I was pissed off at JP and now, I'm sure, he knew it too; because he had to get up and chase after the ball and try to run it in again.

JP broke through the circled boys who stood watching us. When he ran to get the ball I'd kicked, I followed right behind him. I noticed that Coach M was moving toward us on the outside of the Sumo ring. He looked amused.

As soon as JP had his fingers on the ball, I took him down again, this time pulling his jersey up out of his shorts and dragging him with it until it was fully inside out and covering his head. We were about ten feet out of the ring now, and the guys opened a gateway for JP to run through so he could get to the score. If he could make it past me.

JP stood up, leaving the ball at his feet as he tucked his jersey back into his shorts.

There were streaks of grass and black mud on his face.

"What the fuck, Ryan Dean?"

"Watch your mouth, JP," Coach M warned. He added, "Nice job, Eleven."

I don't think I'd ever been so physically aggressive in my life, but all I could think about was JP and his smug I'm-taking-your-girlfriend-out announcement over lunch, and how Annie told me to get tough this year. So I was sick of this shit, of being treated like a little kid, especially by my best friends, and I wasn't going to let it keep on happening to me.

"Trick or treat, assbreath," I said.

I'm certain Coach M had to think about that one, and, since he didn't say anything, he must have concurred with me that "assbreath" is not a true cuss word.

JP smiled. "Oh. I get it. Okay, Winger. Happy Halloween to you, too."

Now it was clear to everyone. JP and I were in a full-scale fight, the only kind you could possibly get away with at PM.

He ran at me again, but this time he slipped my tackle and I fell, managing only to wrap the crook of my arm tightly around his left ankle. I rolled, and JP fell on top of me, dropping his knees (on purpose, I'm sure, but it was totally fair for him to do it) right into my back. It felt like he broke my ribs, but as he went down JP dropped the ball, and his left cleat came right off his foot and into my hands.

I got to my feet. I was sweating and in pain. I could feel my heart drumming against the bones inside my chest. I knew I was just about finished, that I couldn't keep JP out of the circle much longer and he was getting really pissed off about it.

I think what probably pushed him over the edge was that, as he was getting up again, I threw his cleat as far as I could down the pitch and some of the guys laughed.

I could hear Seanie saying, "JP's Winger's bitch," and the guys laughed even more.

JP stood there, panting, the ball tucked into his arms. He looked to where I'd thrown his cleat, then he looked back at me, not even a hint of friendship in his expression, then he got low, put his head down, and wearing only one shoe, came at me full speed.

When I hit him from the front, JP went straight into my tackle and landed squarely on top of me. He went down, too, but he brought his knee up into my face and I heard something pop—like stepping on a grape—when he hit my eye. I remember hearing the "ooh"s from the guys when I sat up, and as I tried to get to my feet I saw a blurry red image of JP scoring behind me, and the next thing I knew, Seanie and Joey were there, putting their hands against my shoulders and telling me not to stand up.

Everyone began crowding around me.

I looked down at my lap. I was covered in blood, could feel it pulsing down my face and onto my jersey, splattering my muddy legs.

Coach M kneeled beside me. "Let's have a look," he said. I realized my left eye was closed for some reason, so I turned my head to look at him.

"That's going to need stitches," he said.

And then Seanie was right in my face, saying, "You can see his skull! You can see his skull!"

Which is probably just about the last thing you want to hear at a time like that, even if Seanie did sound overjoyed by the discovery.

I started to lie down, but they wouldn't let me. The physio was there, wrapping gauze and tape like a headband tightly around my pulsing head, over my left eye. Then Seanie and Joey each took an arm and helped me to my feet.

I was sore and dizzy, but I willed myself not to collapse.

I remember Coach M telling them to put me in the cart and drive me down the hill to the doctor's, and I saw JP standing in front of me, holding the cleat I'd thrown.

"Hey. Sorry, Ryan Dean."

"Yeah. Whatever."

# CHAPTER THIRTY-TWO

IT TOOK EIGHTEEN STITCHES TO close the cut across my eyebrow, some inside the skin, and some outside. But the cut itself wasn't that big. The doctor let me look at the stitches in a mirror when he was finished, but I mostly paid attention to how horrible the rest of me looked. I was filthy and damp and covered with blackened crusty blood that clotted on my skin and in my hair.

Seanie and Joey stayed there with me while the doctor stitched me up, but he wouldn't let them stand too close when he was doing the actual sewing part. I didn't say a word the whole time I was there; all I could do was think about JP and Annie and how mad I was.

Then the doctor left the room, and his exceedingly five-out-of-five-possible-fruit-arrangements-on-your-head-in-a-Brazilian-dancer-kind-of-way-on-the-Ryan-Dean-West-Samba-mometer nurse came in and asked me to lay my head back on the pillow.

"Let's take off that bloody shirt," she said, so sweetly. "Here. Raise your arms."

*And—oh my God—she had a stainless-steel basin of warm damp towels with her!*

She pulled my jersey up out of my shorts and lifted it, so gently, over my head. When it was all the way off, I quickly looked around the room to see if my great-grandma and that run-over Chihuahua were present. I was convinced I had died and gone to a much, much better place.

Thank God for compression shorts.

"Boiiing!" Seanie said.

I had to laugh. "Shut up."

You know, I sometimes disappoint myself. Because at that moment, if anyone had asked me about Annie, I know I would have said, "Who is that?"

"Does it hurt?" she asked. She softly swiped a warm towel around my face and began rubbing my hair clean with a second wet towel.

I tried to look extra sad. "Just a little."

I lied. I couldn't feel it at all.

"Aww," she said.

If I was a cat, I would have purred.

If I was an alligator, I would have been hypnotized.

But since I was only me, all I could do was lie there and contemplate everything perverted I had ever dreamed about since I was, like, seven years old.

She dropped the first blood-rusted towels onto a tray by the bed and grabbed two more. She wiped off my neck and shoulders. She sponge bathed me where blood had dried on my chest and belly, right down to the waistband of my shorts. She even toweled off the thin hair in my armpits, which kind of tickled, but there was no way I was about to giggle. And I wanted to close my eyes, but I couldn't stop staring at her extreme hotness. Then she gently wiped the blood from my knees and up my thighs, all the way to where my compression shorts ended, and at that point I got so flustered, I began hiccupping.

I am such a loser.

She put all the dirty towels in a pile beside the bed and said, "Now you look perfectly handsome again. There's no concussion, so you won't have to stay here tonight. . . ."

*Damn. Uh . . . you look pretty good yourself.*

". . . but you'll need to take it easy . . ."

*I can't move right now anyway.*

"We'll call your parents and let them know. Would you like to speak with them?"

*NO!*

"Uh." *Hiccup.* Crap. "Just tell them"—*hic!*—"I'm okay."

"Do you have any clothes you can put on?"

*No, you better take the rest of these dirty things off me. I don't mind.*

"We can get his stuff from the locker room," Joey said.

*Shut up!!!*

"That's so sweet of you. Thank you," she said, then she bundled up the towels and threw them into a hamper by the door as she left. "I'll be right back, boys."

"Dude," Seanie said. "That was like watching a porn flick. *Nurses Gone Wild.*"

"Ugh." I closed my eyes and dropped my arms out from the sides of my bed. "I thought I was going to lose"—*hic*—"con . . . consciousness. Please tell me that really happened just now."

"All I can say is, no matter what, I'm cracking my skull open tomorrow," Seanie said. "And if you want me to, Ryan Dean, I can go get her and tell her she missed a spot."

"Oh my God. Would you do that for me, Seanie?"

"Dude, you are such a perv for a little guy."

I laughed.

The door opened again and Coach M came in, carrying my clothes from the locker room on a hanger he held over his shoulder. He had my shoes and book bag in his other hand.

"I brought these for you, Ryan Dean," he said. "Save you an unnecessary trip."

"Thank you, Coach." I sat up, dangling my feet over the side of the bed. Before the door swung shut, I could see that there were a number of guys from the team, showered and changed back into their school clothes, waiting outside. Knowing they had come made me feel really good, but not as good as that warm-towel session did.

"And thanks to you two for looking after your mate," Coach M said to Joey and Seanie. "Here, let's see that."

I tilted my chin back so Coach could have a good look at my stitches.

"Welcome to the Zipper Club, Ryan Dean," he said. That's what rugby guys said when they got stitches.

"Flaherty," Coach M said, "why don't you go back to the showers and get dressed. I want to speak with Ryan Dean and his captain."

"Will you be able to make it to dinner?" Seanie asked me.

"I'll be there."

Seanie left. I could hear him talking to the guys outside as his metal cleats clacked against the shiny infirmary floor.

I began changing into my clothes. I pulled off my shorts. Right about now, I thought, it would be really cool if that nurse came back.

"You can't get those sutures wet," Coach said.

"They told me," I answered. "Eighteen stitches. But no concussion."

I knew where this was going. If I'd gotten a concussion, I'd be off the roster for a long time.

"I've never seen you hit like that before, Ryan Dean," Coach said. "That was inspired, to say the least. Is there something going on between you and Tureau you'd like to tell me about?"

I was stuck. I'd have to tell the truth, especially in front of Joey. And Coach M did not tolerate fighting among the team. He'd probably have to kick me off, and I probably deserved it. I changed my socks and began buttoning my dress shirt, avoiding their eyes, trying to think of how I'd say it.

I felt sick. Maybe it showed in my eyes.

I said, "Coach, JP and I . . ."

Joey interrupted. "Were just seeing how hard they could go. And

Ryan Dean proved why he belongs in the first fifteen, Coach."

"Oh. I thought I picked up on something else going on there."

"Ryan Dean and JP are best friends, Coach."

Now, that was going a little too far, I thought. I looked at Joey and then at Coach. I pulled my pants on and began knotting my necktie.

Coach M turned to Joey. "Who can play left wing on Thursday?"

"I can," I interrupted before Joey could answer.

"I can't let you play like that, Ryan Dean. What would I tell your parents if you hurt yourself again?"

"You'd tell them what they already know. It's part of the game. Please, Coach. I don't have a concussion. I'll prewrap it and tape it up. Guys do it all the time. It's no big deal. I really want to play, sir."

I wasn't going to do the fake-tears thing. I could bring real ones up at the thought of being benched for our first game.

"I want Ryan Dean in my line, sir. He's our best wing. You know that," Joey said.

*Note to self: In your prayers tonight, be sure to thank God for making (a) that unbelievably hot nurse, (b) compression shorts, and (c) Joey Cosentino.*

"I'll have to think about it," Coach said. Then he went to the door, cracked it open, and called out, "JP?"

JP came in, walking slowly, looking down. I could tell he felt bad, but I didn't care about his feelings, anyway. Why would I? He didn't care enough about mine. He held his hand out, and we shook. Coach wouldn't have made him do that if he didn't already know we'd been fighting.

"I'm sorry, Ryan Dean."

"You already said that on the field, JP," I said. I slipped my feet into my school shoes. "I'll see you tomorrow, Coach."

I grabbed my cleats and the rest of my bloody practice clothes, threw my pack over my shoulder, and quietly walked out without turning back once.

# CHAPTER THIRTY-THREE

I WAS ALMOST BACK TO O-HALL when I heard someone running up toward me from behind. I didn't care who it was. Because once again, now that I was alone in the quiet beside the lake, all the anger and frustration over Annie and JP, and my possibly sitting out of the game, came swirling back through my aching head.

It felt like JP was trying to ruin my life in every way possible.

"What's your fucking problem, Ryan Dean?"

I should have known it was JP behind me.

I thought about just going on into Opportunity Hall. He wouldn't follow me there, not after getting in trouble for it the first week of school. But I stopped and turned to face him.

He was out of breath, panting fog in the cold as he caught up to where I stood.

"You know what this is about, JP," I said. And then I really did cuss. "Fuck off."

I turned around, thinking how stupid those words actually sounded coming from my mouth. It almost made me want to laugh, hearing myself say something like that, which is kind of hard for me to understand, because I don't have a problem writing words like that.

I started walking toward the door again.

"You want to have it out right now?" JP said. "No one's around. You want to fight again?"

I just kept walking and ignored him.

"Fuck you, Ryan Dean."

I opened the door.

I went inside.

# CHAPTER THIRTY-FOUR

AT DINNER, I SAT ALONE AT A TABLE full of kids I didn't even know. They were freshmen. They were all my age. And I didn't understand them at all. It was like they were from a different planet entirely.

This is how much of a loser I am: I am such a loser that I don't even fit in with other kids who are exactly my age.

Annie, JP, Seanie, Joey, along with everyone else, were sitting where we all usually sit, the way teenagers do, but I didn't go over there. I was tired, sore, and pissed off, and I wanted to be left alone, exiled to this other world I didn't know. As far as I could tell, my friends didn't even know I was there, anyway.

I just kept my head down and ate my dinner. The freshmen around me probably thought I was a new kid or something. I could hear, a couple times, one of them say, "Who's that kid?"

"Hey."

I felt a hand on my shoulder. I lifted my head and saw Megan standing behind me.

"I heard you got hurt," she said.

"I did."

It felt so good just to look at her, to feel the way her hand rested on my shoulder.

I glanced around to see if Chas was anywhere in sight. And, of course, I saw Joey, across the room, watching us. I looked away. I didn't want to hear it, what I knew he was thinking.

"Let me see."

Megan sat down beside me. I felt all the eyes of the freshman boys on us, like they were wondering if she was my older sister, or maybe a teacher, or a cop coming to arrest me, because there was no way a girl who looked like Megan Renshaw should be sitting there next to someone like me.

"I think stitches are sexy," she said when I turned my face to her.

I almost choked on a crouton.

She had that look in her eyes like she was going to pin me down on the table and make out with me right there in front of the whole school. She touched the stitches over my eye.

"Are you okay?"

"You shouldn't be doing this, Megan," I whispered.

"What? Making sure my friend's okay?"

"Come on, Megan. No girl here at Pine Mountain cares about me. I'm not a prize like Chas Becker. You can stop being nice now."

"Is that what you think, Ryan Dean?"

She dropped her hand down onto my knee and rubbed my leg.

*Stop looking at me, Joey!*

"Hey, Meg. Where you been?"

Chas appeared out of nowhere, standing right next to me like the tree I was about to be lynched from. And Megan just left her hand on my leg, and I know Chas saw it, but she innocently said, "Did you see Ryan Dean's eye?"

Chas lowered his face so that it was mere inches from my nose. He looked real serious. He looked like he could kill me and not even think twice about it.

"How many stitches, Winger?" he asked.

"Eighteen."

"Looks like you won't be playing." He said it like he wasn't just talking about the game.

"I can still play." My voice cracked. Loser. What was I doing? I felt like I was facing off in a gunfight.

Chas didn't move. He stayed there, staring at me.

"Everyone says you're in a fight with Sartre."

"I am."

"You really do got big balls, kid. You better watch it."

"It doesn't matter."

Chas straightened. "C'mon, Meg. Let's go sit at the big kids' table."

Megan patted my leg and stood. "Don't forget, Ryan Dean. Tomorrow. Calculus in the library. You and Joey. Okay?"

I tried to say "okay," but nothing would come out. I squeaked like a doggie chew toy in Megan Renshaw's unyielding pit bull teeth.

And Chas practically pulled Megan away, leading her off to where the seniors were sitting. But I saw him turn his face over his shoulder and look at me once, and I'll be honest, it scared me. I considered scrawling a makeshift will on the back of a napkin, but as I took mental inventory of my life's possessions, I realized no one would want them anyway.

I was as good as dead now.

Images of my funeral again: both Annie *and* Megan looking so hot in black; Joey shaking his head woefully and thinking how he told me so; JP and Chas high-fiving each other in the back pew; Seanie installing a live-feed webcam in my undersize casket; and Mom and Dad disappointed, as always, that I left this world a loser alcoholic virgin with eighteen stitches over my left eye.

"What the fuck are you doing all alone over here in loserland, Ryan Dean? How hard did you hit your head?"

Seanie pulled the chair out across from me and sat down. Annie stood behind him. No one else.

"I didn't want to talk to anyone."

I could see by the way Annie tilted her head that she was trying to look at the cut or trying to look at my eyes, but I didn't really want her to. As much as I wanted to just see her and nothing else on this whole weird planet, I felt so terrible about everything that had happened to me and the shitty things I had done to myself that I just couldn't bring myself to face her.

Seanie tapped the shoulder of the freshman boy who was sitting beside him. "Hey. Kid. Move so she can sit down."

The boy picked up his tray and moved farther down the length of the table.

"By the way," Seanie said as Annie took the vacated seat, "I forgot to tell you, I liked the 'Trick or treat, assbreath' comment at practice."

I sighed.

Sometimes I just wanted to grab Seanie by the neck and shake him.

I was finished eating. I really wanted to leave. Then Annie reached across the table and lifted my chin with her soft hand. I know that Annie had touched me before—how could it be avoided? Friends touch. But it never felt like that. And she held my head there and looked at the cut above my eye, then she just looked right into my eyes and we didn't blink or anything. I don't know what I looked like to her, because I don't think there was any expression on my face at all, and it didn't matter. All we could see were each other's eyes.

"Wow," Seanie said. "This is one heavy moment. Are you two getting ready to make out or something? 'Cause if you are, it's about time."

Annie pulled her hand away, and I looked down.

"Are you okay, West?" she asked.

"Yeah. I'm fine."

"You still planning on coming to my house this weekend?"

Nothing, especially not John-Paul Tureau, could stop me.

"Is it okay if I do?"

I was scared she'd say no.

"Best friends," she said. "It's going to be fun."

"Best friends."

Then she stood and left us there. It was getting late, and most of the students were making their way back to the dorms. I was so glad she didn't say anything else, anything about JP.

She didn't have to.

"Damn," Seanie said. "Why don't you just get it over with and fucking kiss her, Ryan Dean?"

"Shut up, Seanie. Annie knows what's going on."

"Everyone on the planet knows what's going on. Except you."

"Seanie?"

"What?"

"Thanks for not saying nothing about JP and me."

"There's nothing to say."

# CHAPTER THIRTY-FIVE

I WAS AFRAID THAT JOEY WOULD be waiting outside when I headed back to O-Hall. I didn't want to hear him lecture me about Megan again. But there wasn't anyone there, and I walked along the trail by the lake in the dark alone.

I got lectured anyway.

I stopped by the shore so I could just stare out at the blackness of the lake, and that's where I got that arguing and taunting voice in my head that went something like this:

RYAN DEAN WEST 2: *Now* what are you going to do about Megan?

RYAN DEAN WEST 1: What are *you* going to do about Megan—times infinity?

RYAN DEAN WEST 2: You are such a loser.

RYAN DEAN WEST 1: And she's so five out of five Space Needles on the Ryan Dean West Reasons-Why-Male-Architects-Design-Structures-Shaped-Like-That-in-the-First-Place Hall of Fame.

RYAN DEAN WEST 2: You must spend a lot of time thinking up perverted stuff.

MR. WELLINS: Proof that sex actually does motivate everything.

RYAN DEAN WEST 2: Sex doesn't even exist in Ryan Dean West's universe. Not even in the architecture. Everything is skinny-ass-bitch flat and flabby.

MR. WELLINS: Good point. Maybe I need to go fine-tune my theory.

RYAN DEAN WEST 1: Hey! How did an old pervert end up in my play?

RYAN DEAN WEST 2: Your head is a freaking watering hole in the desert of purity for all things perverted. So . . . back to the issue at hand: You know what you got to do about Megan. So do it.

MRS. KURTZ: Don't forget your study group tomorrow night, Ryan Dean!

RYAN DEAN WEST 1: Ugh.

(*Ryan Dean West throws a rock out into the lake.*)

ANNIE: What are you doing, Ryan Dean?

Oh, wait . . . that was real.

"What are you doing, Ryan Dean?"

*And she called me Ryan Dean.*

"Nothing. I was just thinking."

I turned around and looked at her.

She was so beautiful, standing there in the dark. I kept thinking about what Seanie had said—about why I didn't just get it over with and kiss her. I mean, what's the worst that could happen, right? We've known each other for more than two years, and I've only held her hand a couple times. God! I wanted to kiss her so bad, but I didn't have the guts.

I am such a loser.

"What are you thinking about?"

I smiled. "God, Annie. Don't you know me by now?"

She laughed. "Oh, yeah. You are so perverted, Ryan Dean."

*Wow. She called me that twice.*

And I could see the real smile in her eyes. I loved that about her.

She touched her fingers to her eyebrow, like I was a mirror or something. "Does that hurt?"

"Not really."

"You're mad at me, aren't you?"

"Kind of." I sighed. "It's stupid. There's nothing I can do about it."

"Seanie said you and JP were really in a fight."

I looked out at the lake. I didn't want to talk about this with Annie.

"I'm going to be in trouble if I don't check in at O-Hall in, like, two minutes, Annie."

"Come on," she said. Then she held my hand and walked me to my dorm.

We stopped in the dark outside the mudroom door.

"Good night, Annie."

She didn't let go of my hand.

"Wait," she said. "Don't be mad at me, Ryan Dean. I'm so looking forward to this weekend. Please don't be mad at me."

And I thought, *Crafty girl almost sounds like I did when I fake-cried for Mr. Farrow.*

"Okay, Annie."

Then she got real close to me. Her unbuttoned jacket even tickled, brushing against the zipper on my pants, and I suddenly forgot everything in the world about JP and stitches, or anything else that existed at an altitude higher than my waist besides Annie Altman. Our lips were just inches apart, and I could feel her heat and smell that awesome stuff she uses on her hair, and I thought, *Oh my God, she is finally going to kiss me. We are finally going to kiss, and this is going to be the best thing I've ever felt and tasted in my entire pathetic life*, and I *knew* we were going to kiss; and just then the door opened and the glacially unhot Mrs. Singer stuck her head out and said, "Young man, you are going to be late if you do not check in with your resident counselor immediately!"

And that was like a Niagara Falls of razor-sharp ice cubes pouring right through the fly on my pants. Oh . . . and some of those ice cubes were shaped like rusty bear traps and triple fishhooks, too.

She had to be a witch.

Annie released my hand and turned away.

"See you, West," she said.

I sighed. The biggest part of me wanted to go after her and just get it over with, like Seanie told me, but my only chance was gone, and Mrs. Singer stood there watching me, unblinking, holding the door propped open against the cold and dark.

*Do not look into her eyes.*

As I passed Mrs. Singer, I kept my eyes on the floor, unwilling to battle the soul-sucking-diarrhea-spell-casting witch that she was. Then I felt her arctic fingers on my shoulder, and she said, "Your head would happen to look nice on a serving platter."

And I squeaked like a frightened baby mouse and hurried for the stairs.

Well, to be perfectly honest, I am pretty sure she said, "What happened to your head? Is something the matter?" But that could just have been part of the spell-thing-whatever-it-is she'd been working on me ever since she caught me peeing in the girls' bathroom. And as I made my way up the darkened stairway, she said either "You better be afraid" or "Why are you afraid?" But, again, I can't be sure which it was, to be totally honest. But I swear, *I swear*, I really do think I heard her say something about "a catastrophic injury to your penis" just as I slammed shut the door to the boys' floor behind me.

Diarrhea I can handle, but the catastrophic-penis-injury thing strikes the deepest imaginable chord of fear in any boy's mind.

I was sweating, stitched-up, panting, and terrified. But at least I wasn't late.

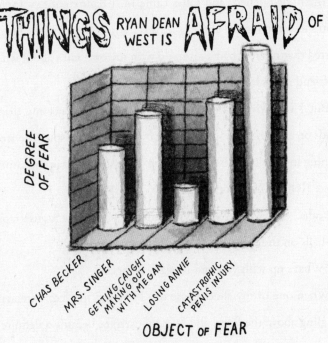

THINGS RYAN DEAN WEST IS AFRAID OF

DEGREE OF FEAR

CHAS BECKER · MRS. SINGER · GETTING CAUGHT MAKING OUT WITH MEGAN · LOSING ANNIE · CATASTROPHIC PENIS INJURY

OBJECT OF FEAR

•••

I am. You know.

Such a loser.

I made it to the common room just in time to sign off on our check-in sheet with Mr. Farrow. The TV had just gone dark, and most of the guys from O-Hall were sluggishly making their way to their rooms. After I signed in, I went down the hall to the bathroom.

I stood in front of the mirror for a few minutes, looking at the stitches closing the cut over my eye. As I stared, the cut seemed to get bigger, blacker, worse than it was. I was tired and wanted to go to bed. I ran the water and washed my hands and face.

The door opened, and Chas came in. I hadn't entirely forgotten about how he'd looked at me as he was leading Megan away, but I also figured that my fear had a lot to do with my own guilt about what his girlfriend and I were doing behind his back.

But I was wrong, because before I could even get my dripping hands on a towel, Chas grabbed me by the neck and spun me around, pinning my back against a hand-soap dispenser, right in the same spot where JP had knee-dropped me.

Yeah . . . it was definitely a four out of five possible mousetraps-on-the-balls on the Ryan Dean West Pain-ometer.

"What's up with you and Megan, Winger?"

When one of my shoes came off, I realized my feet were actually dangling above the floor, and four mousetraps became a definite five.

"I saw how you two were looking at each other tonight," he said. "Everyone says you flirt with her all the time."

"Chas, who *wouldn't* look at Megan like that? She's smoking hot," I gurgled.

I was sure he was about to hit me. And, like I said, I deserved it. So . . . ouch.

There was nothing else I could do. I had to hit him. I balled my right hand into a fist and drove an uppercut just below his sternum. I'll be honest. I have punched guys before, but punching Chas Becker hurt my hand. Chas loosened his grip, and I was standing again, but he held on to my necktie with his left hand as he raised a fist with his right.

Whoever invented neckties must have never gotten into fistfights.

Okay. This was really going to be ugly, because I could quickly calculate the trajectory of his intended punch, and I estimated the point of impact would be somewhere between my tenth and eleventh stitches. All I could do was hope my saddest possible stitched-up-lost-puppy-injury look might earn me some sympathy.

Chas froze midswing when the door opened. He released my tie and dropped his fist. He turned around to see that Joey had followed him into the bathroom.

"What the fuck are you doing, Chas?" Joey said. "Can't you see Ryan Dean's hurt?"

And Joey was a fighter. He looked really pissed off, and stormed over to Chas and shoved him down the entire length of the bathroom, practically into a shower stall.

Then Joey yelled, "Don't ever touch him! I'll fucking kill you, Betch!"

I slipped my foot back into my shoe.

"It's nothing, Joey," Chas said calmly. "It's no big deal. I wouldn't hurt him. I just don't like the way he looks at my girlfriend. No big deal. I just wanted him to know."

And then Chas walked out of the bathroom, but as he pulled the door open, he grumbled, "You guys are fucking queers."

Joey just stood there, leaning against the pale green tiles of the wall, his arms folded, staring at me. I could tell he was mad.

"You should have just let him punch me, Joe."

Joey didn't say anything.

I left and went to bed.

# CHAPTER THIRTY-SIX

WEDNESDAY MORNING BROUGHT ONE of those cold Pacific rains that makes you feel like the gray of the sky has worked its way inside your skin.

When the alarm sounded, Chas and I both sat up. Usually, when we woke up, we would say things to each other—stupid things, the kind that Chas could understand. I never really minded sharing a room with him, either, to be absolutely honest. But that morning, our silence was ominous. Like a funeral. I kind of felt like telling him I was sorry for punching him, but then I thought it would just remind him that he was in the middle of returning the favor when we got interrupted by Joey, so I thought I'd better just leave the whole thing alone.

I lowered myself from the bunk bed to the cold floor, grabbed my towel, and headed down the hallway. The doctor told me I'd be able to take a shower that morning, as much as I'd have liked that nurse to help me out again.

I was really sore. My head, my back, my shoulders—I felt like a 142-pound sack of broken shards of glass. Actually, I was 152 now. I'd put on some weight since school started, and my skinny-bitch-ass pants were getting too short in the leg for me, too, which made me look like even more of a dork. Annie told me she'd let them down for me when we went to her house, which, of course, made me think of the perfect oh-I-didn't-know-I'd-need-to-actually-take-my-pants-all-the-way-off-for-you-to-do-that plan.

When I got out of the shower, I saw Chas standing at the same spot where I'd punched him the night before, bent over the sink, shaving. He stopped and watched me as I padded, barefoot and wrapped in my towel, behind him.

I didn't say anything to him.

He didn't say anything to me, either.

Annie wasn't in the mess hall for breakfast. I saw Isabel, though. She told me that Annie was sick and staying in bed. At first, I thought Mrs. Singer had put a diarrhea spell on Annie, but I shrugged off the idea. I was mostly disappointed because there was no way I'd be able to see Annie now until Friday. Boys were not allowed inside the girls' dorm, and the team would be leaving early the next morning to drive down to Salem for our game.

I felt like I desperately needed to find out something from her. And I knew I could tell the truth by just looking at her, that I wouldn't have to actually ask her if we'd really been about to kiss, because I don't think I'd ever have the guts to say it.

But Isabel did give me a folded note from Annie, so I thanked her and told her I'd give her one later to take back.

I couldn't go sit in my usual place; JP was there with Seanie. I knew I couldn't keep avoiding JP forever, but I wasn't ready to be around him yet, either, because I still wanted to fight him, and I believed I would if we were forced to be too close together. I knew that now, after punching Chas the night before, and I still really felt like JP and I needed to have it out some more.

So I took Annie's note and tucked it inside my heavy coat and headed up to the locker room, half an hour early for Conditioning.

I straddled the bench by my locker and looked at the paper.

It wasn't folded fancy, like some girls do. It was just in half, and then in half again.

On the outside, she'd written Ryan Dean West.

I opened it.

Hey, West.

I am really sick today and I'm just going to stay in bed, so I'm sorry I'll miss seeing you today at school. Because you always make my day. And I'm bummed because I won't see you tomorrow, either, so I have to tell you good luck in your game and have fun. And I hope your dumb coach lets you play, because you deserve to play more than most of the jerks on your team. So, do good, and score lots of whatever you call scores in rugby, and I will be thinking about you.

I don't mind missing classes today, though. Mr. Wellins is a creepy, dirty man, and I don't care what he says—everything in the world is not a symbol of penises and vaginas, except for maybe the Space Needle, which you will see when we go to Seattle on Friday.

I am excited you get to come to my house this weekend. You will like my mom and dad, but probably not my dog. It's a pug named Pedro who likes to hump people, especially boys. Oh . . . if I forgot to tell you, I hope you're not allergic to horny dogs (ha ha). I'm sure you and Pedro will get along just fine. You are kindred spirits (ha ha). The horny part, I mean, not the gay part. Trust me, I KNOW you are not gay, but my dog is, I think. No, yeah, he REALLY is gay.

I am sorry you got your head cracked open by GP, and I hope you are feeling better today. Everyone says you were beating the crap out of him before that happened, and that you were both really mad, so everyone says you deserved it and that you cheap-shotted him in the balls and stuff. Why are you mad at GP? Is it because he asked me out? You don't have to answer that, because I know that's why. Whatever, West. Okay. One more thing. Last night, were we about to kiss or something? That is too weird to handle,

West, and I'm not saying it was your fault or anything. I think it was mine. Maybe I felt so sorry for you sitting over with the little kids all alone with those stitches in your head. But it won't happen again.

Oh, and make sure you bring some running stuff with you this weekend. I have some really nice runs down by the beach and the woods on Bainbridge Island, which is where we live. And I'll tell my mom to make sure and pick up some doggie breath mints, because my gay pug can't wait to meet you in person (ha ha).

Well, I'm going to go vomit now. Play good tomorrow. I will see you at school on Friday, okay?

Bye,

Love,

AA

So I *knew* she really did want to kiss me. And, as far as I was concerned, her it-won't-happen-again was nothing more than a challenge. I had a perfect plan, thanks to her confession, and I had to get it down on paper before I forgot it. I tore open my backpack and began writing.

Dear Annie,

Wow. I really hope you are feeling better. And thanks for wishing me luck for the game. I promise I will score a try (that's what they're called in rugby) just for you, but if not, I will play my best, and I'm pretty sure Coach M will have me in the lineup, because Joey said he wants me there, and Joey is the captain. So I will be thinking about you tomorrow too.

To me, honestly, it sounds like BOTH you AND Mr. Wellins need to get your minds off of sex and think about something else. I never knew you thought the Space Needle looks like a penis (ha ha).

I can't wait to see you on Friday. I am so excited about flying to Seattle with you. I have already packed, and I am bringing all three of my school pants so you can fix them like you said you would. Sorry, but you're going to have to see me in my boxers, so try to control yourself when you do (ha ha ha). I am not allergic to dogs, but I think I will also bring doggie tranquilizers, because I don't think I can handle getting humped by your gay pug dog. I think he AND Mr. Wellins need to deal with some issues, but not at my expense.

Oh, and about my head: It hurts worse today, but I'll be okay. And, yeah, JP and I were going at it pretty good up until that happened. And we almost fought again after practice, too. We are definitely NOT friends anymore. And I don't think we should talk about JP with each other, either. Okay?

I already packed my running stuff. It will be fun to run on the beach with you, so I hope you can push me pretty hard.

Now, one more thing: about last night Man! I had no idea you were going to kiss me, Annie! Yuck!!!! I guess I was groggy from the stitches, but I didn't ever think you'd try to do something like that! 'Cause, damn! Why would you want to kiss a LITTLE KID??? And, anyway, let me tell you that if I ever wanted to kiss you, I would have already done it. I am a guy, and that's what guys do. That's why we have BALLS No big deal, but if I am not afraid to get in a fight with JP or Chas (who I punched last night), I wouldn't be afraid to kiss you, believe me. I would have done it a long time ago. Here's some calculus for you:

$2 \times BALLS = $ YOU DO WHAT YOU WANT, WHEN YOU WANT TO DO IT.

I think the best thing for you to do to make yourself stronger and test your resolve is to make sure that we sleep as close to each other as possible this weekend. Like, maybe if you have a couch in your room or something (keep the gay dog out of there). That is the only way you can prove to yourself that you are really strong enough to keep yourself from ever trying to kiss me again. I will even sleep naked if I have to. But, man, am I surprised at you!

Remember, I am only thinking about you, and I need to help you get over this need you have to kiss me, no matter how much work is involved, so I am willing to make this huge sacrifice just for you.

I will play good tomorrow.

See you Friday.

Love,

Ryan Dean

PS—I drew a picture of the Space Needle for you . . .

Perfect.

Now we'll see about it-won't-happen-again.

I folded the note just as the guys began coming in to the locker room. I wanted to change and get out of there before something else happened between JP and me.

# CHAPTER THIRTY-SEVEN

WE TOOK A SLOW THREE-MILE RUN in the rain for our conditioning, but I wasn't about to lag back with Seanie and JP. I felt bad about it, because I missed Seanie, but since they were roommates, I couldn't expect him to ditch JP just so he could talk to me. At least I was relieved that I'd only have to sit through one class, Lit, with JP; and Annie's empty desk would be between us.

There aren't many things I like more than running in the rain, even if I wasn't supposed to get my stitches too wet. I stayed right at the front of the pack, and I was completely drenched by the time I made it back to the locker room.

# CHAPTER THIRTY-EIGHT

JOEY WATCHED ME WALK THROUGH the doorway to Calculus class. We hadn't said anything at all to each other since practice, not even after the fight in the bathroom with Chas, but he didn't need to say anything. His pissed-off look was enough. I know what he would have said, without the words.

As soon as I stumbled to my seat, Megan spun around, her amber hair sweeping silently across my desktop and over my fingers—*damn!*—and, smiling at me, she said, "Hi, Ryan Dean!" like nothing ever happened.

And then Joey intervened, looking as serious as he did the night before, after Chas backed down. Joey leaned over between Megan and me and grabbed my chin firmly and said, "Let me see that."

He tilted my head like an unskilled barber and looked quickly over my stitches. My hair was still wet from the run.

"You going to be good to play tomorrow?" Joey said flatly, still holding my head steady.

"Uh-huh. You know I will."

Then he kind-of whispered, even though I know Megan heard the whole thing, "Get your shit together, Ryan Dean."

I didn't know if he was talking about JP or Megan or Annie or just me. No . . . I guess I did know.

Then, birdlike, and in a hot-therapist kind of way, Mrs. Kurtz was looming over us, chirping, "Oh my goodness, Ryan Dean! What happened to you?"

Joey let go of my face.

"I play rugby," I said. "I got eighteen stitches."

"What a stud!" Mrs. Kurtz said. She always said the dorkiest things, but I never met a student who didn't love her. Then she tousled my wet hair, which, due to her mysterious, my-best-friend's-mom-kind-of-hotness, made me feel weak and flustered and convinced that I was destined to keep making the same kinds of stupid mistakes with girls over and over, no matter how spectacular my 2 x BALLS argument to Annie was, and she said, "Maybe you should take it easy today, Ryan Dean."

"I think Ryan Dean should skip our study group tonight," Joey said. "So he can rest. We have our first game tomorrow."

I fired a look at Joey, then at Megan.

I sighed.

Joey was right, and I realized then that I was still just making excuses to avoid dealing with my out-of-control Megan thing.

Megan said, "I'll miss you tonight, Ryan Dean." Then she put her hand over mine.

*Ugh!*

"You should definitely stay in bed tonight," Mrs. Kurtz said. I, of course, thought this was a very hot thing to say.

"Thanks, Mrs. Kurtz," I said. "Thanks, Joe. Sorry, Megan."

But to me, my voice sounded so pathetic, almost like I was crying.

# CHAPTER THIRTY-NINE

IT HAPPENED AT PRACTICE.

The worst thing imaginable.

Practice is always relaxed and fun the day before a game, especially in the rain. Coach would usually just talk about a game plan, then we'd play a fun little scrimmage, just so we could get all muddy. Nothing serious.

My head was taped up, so I was okay, and I was glad Coach could see that I was ready for the game. We were all just having fun.

Seanie and I ended up on opposite teams, playing sevens, which, like I said, is a much more wide-open and fast game with fewer pile-ups. I had the ball and was running downfield when I got caught up in a tackle from a flanker who was playing on Seanie's team.

In rugby, when you're tackled, you have to let go of the ball. Usually, you do it in a way that makes it easy for your own teammates to pick it up. But when I released the ball, no one was there to get it, so Seanie stepped right over me and poached the ball away for his team.

And the terrible thing is, right when he stepped through, he planted his foot between my legs.

Yeah.

Like the world wasn't big enough for Seanie to find somewhere else to put his fucking foot.

And that's how Sean Russell Flaherty, my good friend, the same guy who contrived so many Internet hoaxes about so many people, the same guy who'd told Annie Altman, the girl I am insanely in love with, that I got drunk with Chas Becker the night before school began, that same guy, wearing size twelve metal cleats, stepped right onto my balls.

I became a black hole.

Let me explain the physics of having your balls stepped on.

The entire Ryan Dean West universe instantly collapsed to the size of a five-eighths-inch metal cleat stud, and everything I knew, everything I *would ever know*, got sucked into that pinpoint of agony.

Newton obviously skipped that one crucial law.

When my hearing came back, I heard Seanie saying, "Uh-oh."

And I'm pretty sure that everyone in the Pacific Northwest heard Ryan Dean West shout, "YOUSTEPPEDONMYFUCKINGNUTS YOUSONOFABITCH!"

Yes, I will admit to cussing that time.

My universe gradually began expanding, but so did the agony. I could think again, and the thinking led to a heightened sensation of pain, if there could be such a thing, and a frightening realization, too.

Mrs. Singer.

*Catastrophic penis injury.*

*You have got to be fucking kidding me.*

*I must be out of my mind.*

And as I lay on my side, in the fetal position, hands clutching for what I could only imagine in my most horrific visions had been damaged beyond salvation, my teammates formed, for the second time in the past twenty-four hours, a mournful and morbidly fascinated circle around me.

"He's dead," one of them said.

"If he isn't dead, he should kill himself immediately," another added.

"Did you really step on his nuts?" A third one.

I tried to answer them, but the only sound I could make sounded something like *ehhhhrrrrrrrrrrrrrrrrrrrrrrgggh*, and, shuddering, lying there with my face in an expanding puddle of mud, I realized I couldn't unclench my jaw.

Coach M blew his whistle to break practice.

I rolled onto my back in the mud, my face turned up into the rain, eyes blurred, scanning the darkness of the clouds for the giant face of a mocking God who might be up there laughing at my stitched-and-stomped-on-skinny-bitch-ass.

"Not exactly the best two days of your life, eh, Ryan Dean?" Coach tried to smile, looking down at me, rain dripping from the brim of his hat. "Can you move?"

And Seanie fell beside me, trying to help sit me up.

But he was kind of laughing when he said, "Dude, my bad, Ryan Dean. And I know you've probably waited all your life to hear another guy say this to you, but, dude, how are your balls?"

And, all at once, I somehow instantly composed a haiku in my mind about how much I hated Seanie Flaherty, and, in a simultaneous flash of inspiration, derived a kind of mathematical, tautological formula about reality, that I could easily envision as a Venn diagram:

Finding Humor in Getting Hit in the Balls = The
Universe Minus One

Seanie helped me to my feet. My head was groggy, my eyes swirled with tears of pain, and I felt like throwing up. The other guys were already making their way into the locker room and the warmth of the showers.

I slipped my hand down inside my compression shorts, just to make sure everything was still attached properly. Something stung, and when I pulled my hand out and looked at my fingers, there was blood on them.

Crap.

# CHAPTER FORTY

Seanie Flaherty,

Asshole, you stepped on my nuts.

Please. Someone kill me.

"Here," I said, dropping the folded paper beside Seanie where he sat eating dinner. "I wrote a haiku about how much I hate your stinking guts, Seanie."

"Dude, how gay are *you*?" Seanie said in his usual deadpan, focusing on his food and opening the note. "You wrote me a haiku about your balls."

JP was just sitting down across the table. I didn't care. I wasn't talking to him, and he wasn't going to keep me away from my friends.

And then Joey asked, "What did the doctor say, Ryan Dean?"

Yeah. Here's another thing I realized: You'd think that receiving an injury to your balls is probably the worst thing that can possibly happen to any guy, but it's not.

Going to the doctor for an injury to your balls is much, much worse.

So here I was, sitting down to eat among friends and enemies alike, with the alluringly hot and faintly moustached Isabel, wide-eyed in rapt attentiveness, no doubt taking it all down so she could get right back to the recuperating Annie Altman and deliver an update on the status of Ryan Dean West's testicles.

"Was that hot nurse there?" Seanie practically drooled.

"No," I said. "Just Doctor No-gloves."

"Eww," Seanie said. "Did he touch your little Westicles?"

I took a bite of chicken, pretending that was all I was going to say about the matter. I looked over at JP, and he looked away.

"Are you going to tell us, or what?" Seanie said impatiently.

I paused to gather my thoughts.

"Do you believe in witches?" I asked.

"I give up," Seanie said, and took a drink of milk.

I looked at Isabel. It was kind of embarrassing, but not as embarrassing as telling *everyone* in the infirmary why I showed up, scared pale and covered in mud with my hand thrust down my shorts, holding onto my balls. Even my friends were too embarrassed to go there with me, afraid they might have to face their own fears and watch in that cold examination room while I sat naked on a rustling paper sheet and the doctor looked me over. Head wounds were one thing, but, like I said, no boy *ever* wants to come face to face with a catastrophic penis injury.

"It's just a cut," I said. "On my balls. He put a Band-Aid on it."

"Was it a SpongeBob Band-Aid?" Seanie asked, almost spitting out his milk when he said it.

Even Joey laughed.

I am such a loser.

"Dude," Seanie announced, "how awesome is that? You are the

only guy I've ever known in my *entire fucking life* who had to have a doctor put a Band-Aid on his ballsack. That's the kind of thing you just can't make up. Ryan Dean West, you are going to be a fucking legend!"

"Seanie," I said, "I can't even begin to put into words how much I hate you right now."

"Aww . . . I love you too, Ryan Dean," he said.

# CHAPTER FORTY-ONE

I NEVER COULD SLEEP THE NIGHT before a game, especially a first game.

After dinner, Joey kept his appointment for our Calculus study group with Megan at the library, and I came back to O-Hall alone and tried to relax in bed. But it was absolutely impossible to get comfortable, considering the locations of my injuries. And I know I'm a pig for thinking it, but I really wanted to make out with Megan again.

So I just lay there, staring up at the ceiling with my knees bent, listening to Chas's breathing, wondering if Annie had read my note, and what she was thinking about at that moment, if she was awake like me.

And I knew that if you could keep score for such a thing, and, of course, I did keep that score, my Degree of Loserdom would be nothing short of godlike.

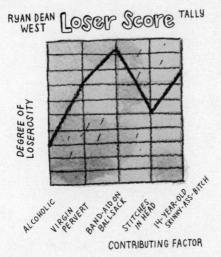

RYAN DEAN WEST Loser Score TALLY

DEGREE OF LOSEROSITY

ALCOHOLIC · VIRGIN PERVERT · BAND-AID ON BALLSACK · STITCHES IN HEAD · 14-YEAR-OLD SKINNY-ASS-BITCH

CONTRIBUTING FACTOR

To make matters even worse, by midnight I had to pee. But there was no way in hell I was going to go down that hallway on the night before a game and run the risk of a face-to-face with Mrs. Singer again. So I held it as long as I could, but that just made my Band-Aided wound hurt more. When I couldn't stand it any more, I fumbled around the side of the mattress where I stored that Gatorade bottle Joey brought me when I was sick. I unscrewed the top—*Mmm! It still smelled like lemon*—and, kneeling on the top bunk, I filled it to within half an inch of overflowing.

The Ryan Dean West Emergency Gatorade Bottle Nighttime Urinal was an invention of depraved genius. After a quick check on the snugness of my Band-Aid, and, pausing momentarily to wonder how many days it might take to fall off, since—sweet mother of God—there was no way I was going to yank it and all the hairs affixed to it off, I screwed the lid back on as tightly as possible, tucked the bottle down by my feet, where I noticed it produced a very pleasant warmth, pulled the covers back over me, and finally went to sleep.

# CHAPTER FORTY-TWO

AT SIX IN THE MORNING, WE WERE all on the bus heading down from Pine Mountain to play our first rugby match of the year. It had stopped raining during the night, so it was going to be a perfect and soggy day for rugby. Twenty-five players rode on the bus, most of us stretched out in our own seats, along with the coach and a couple other adults, and I swear I had to go from seat to seat and personally tell the story of the Band-Aid on my balls to every one of the boys who hadn't been there at dinner the night before.

It was a four-hour bus ride to Sacred Heart. Our kickoff was scheduled for one o'clock; and, as always after the game, in a rugby tradition called a social, we would sit down with the opposing team and have dinner before our ride back to Pine Mountain. We always had to wear our school uniforms and ties whenever we showed up for a rugby match; that was just the way things were done. So every one of us knew it was going to be a long and tiring day.

But we didn't know just how tough, and unexpected, things would actually turn out to be.

We sang almost the entire way there. I don't know how Coach M put up with it. It was like he was deaf or something, because he never showed the slightest expression even when the songs got completely vulgar. It was like singing was the only time he'd tolerate our cussing, and he'd just keep his attention pinned on his notebook, where he'd organize rosters, medical forms, and notes on plays. But I could tell the singing was making the driver of our chartered bus really agitated. He started looking so frustrated and mad, but I could hear Coach M explain to him in his Henry Higgins tone of voice, "They are a rugby team. They sing. There's nothing I, you, or God can do about it beyond hope that they eventually tire."

And just before we got to the field, someone got into our first-aid kit and secretly passed around Band-Aids to everyone on the team except me. So when we arrived at the locker rooms at Sacred Heart, and the headmaster, who was dressed in his full priestly attire, and a couple nuns from the school greeted us, every one of our players with the exception of me came down the steps at the front of the bus wearing a black and blue school tie, white dress shirt, and khaki pants with a Band-Aid stuck across his fly.

Nice.

We changed into our uniforms and took the field to warm up. I had my head taped up, and I felt like I was completely ready to go. When Sacred Heart came out to begin stretching, we ran around them on the field, singing "She Wore a Yellow Ribbon," which was the only song we were allowed to sing at a Catholic school because it wasn't really dirty, it was just about a guy who fathers an illegitimate child and then gets his balls shotgunned off by the girl's father. Tame by our standards, and as Coach said, it wasn't likely to incite a religious war or anything since it contained a moral lesson.

But the Sacred Heart boys didn't think it was very funny, and instead of singing something back at us, which is what any decent and proper rugby team would do, they just scowled and prayed.

I am not religious at all. Some of the kids at PM are, though, and we do have a nondenominational chapel on the grounds for kids who don't go home on weekends. But we always prayed before games, and praying with the team was the only kind of praying I ever felt good about. So, a few minutes before kickoff, we would all take to our knees in a circle and put our arms around each other, and Kevin Cantrell would stand over us and give thanks for the day and for the other team that was there to play with us, and for being able to play the greatest sport that was ever created, and hope that everyone, even our opponents, would be safe and have fun.

Then, just a few minutes before the game, Coach M pulled me aside and told me that he wasn't going to let me start, that he was putting in Mike Bagnuolo, a sophomore winger who was actually older than me, because he wanted to see how Bags could handle himself.

Of course I was crushed, but I knew better than to say anything or try to plead with Coach. That's just something you never do on the sideline of a game. At least Bags was wearing number sixteen and I got to keep the eleven, so everyone knew who the real left wing was. That's how numbers work in rugby: a player doesn't pick his number, his position on the team determines that, and it's something that never gets messed with. So all I could do was watch the game start from the sideline and just hope that by some miracle I'd get a chance to sub in.

Joey was standing there with us when Coach M made his decision, and I could see he was upset about the call, because he looked like he felt sorry for me too. But he shook Bags's hand and said, "I'll be looking for you out there," and then he said, "Sorry, Ryan Dean, Coach is just being careful," and he tapped the bandage on my head.

"I know that, Joey, but I still totally hate JP."

"You remember how I told you to get your shit together? Well, Megan couldn't stop talking about you last night. So when's it going to happen, Ryan Dean?"

Then Joey ran off to his spot on the field, and all I could do was watch the game begin.

The worst part of it, worse than Joey's scolding—because I knew he was right—was that it was the kind of game I love to play in. Our teams were so evenly matched, and every time it looked like a score was about to happen, the other team would crank up its defense and force a turnover. So it went that way, scoreless, for almost the entire thirty-five-minute half, and then finally JP got called on a dangerous tackle and Sacred Heart scored a penalty kick just as the half ended, to go up 3–0. And I was kind of glad that JP was the one who gave up those points, because everyone could see how terrible he felt about it.

Bastard.

In rugby, halftime only lasts five minutes and the players are not allowed to leave the field. And unlike other sports, there are no substitutions where a player can go out and come back in, which, I think, is one of the reasons the football team hated us so much—because rugby players had to be in such better condition than players in just about any other sport. During halftime, though, Coach brought the team in and said, "Bags is coming out. Ryan Dean, mind your head," and that absolutely made my day.

Joey shook my hand, and I pulled him close to me and whispered, "Look, I swear I will take care of the Megan thing as soon as I can. Just get me the ball."

"Okay," he said.

And he did. About five minutes into the half, Joey skipped the ball past both of our centers, right into my hands, and all I had to do was beat the opposing winger, who had no chance of catching me. I centered the ball right between the posts and put it down to score a try, and I did think about Annie as soon as I got to my feet.

Seanie was our team's kicker, and he scored the conversion, so PM went up 7–3. We chest bumped each other after his kick, and Seanie laughed, saying, "I think that's the gayest thing I've ever done."

And I said, "No, it's not even close. You wrote me a haiku *and* you asked me how my balls were yesterday, remember?"

The score stayed locked at 7–3, and we ended up winning the game.

We had to shower and change back into our ties before the postgame social. The food was great, and the best part of the afternoon was that the Sacred Heart boys all had cell phones and Coach let us borrow them to call our parents and tell them about the game.

I borrowed the phone from the number fourteen winger, the boy I outran to score my try, and he was real nice about it too, but he did promise they'd even it up against us when we played them during the regular season.

And yes, cell phones apparently can be used to dial directly into hell, because my call went something like this:


MOM: Hello?

RYAN DEAN WEST: Hi, Mom. It's me, Ryan Dean.

I always said that on the phone, like there was someone else who might call her "Mom," even though I don't have any brothers or sisters.

MOM: Oh my God, baby. Are you hurt again? How's your head?

I was never allowed to call during the week. PM rules.

RYAN DEAN WEST: I'm fine, Mom.

I wasn't about to say anything about the Band-Aid-on-the-balls thing. God! Who would ever have the guts to talk about something like that with *their mom*?

RYAN DEAN WEST (*cont.*): I'm calling from our game. We won. I scored
a try.

MOM: Your dad's going to be so happy to hear about that.

RYAN DEAN WEST: Is Dad there?

MOM: No, sweetie. He's in New York.

Then she sounded really serious.

MOM (*cont.*): Ryan Dean, how did you get a phone?

RYAN DEAN WEST: Well, I just wanted to tell you, Mom, 'cause Coach is letting us use the other boys' phones today since we're not at school. But I wanted to let you know, and to say thanks to you and Dad for letting me go stay with Annie this weekend.

MOM: Oh. Ryan Dean?

RYAN DEAN WEST: What?

MOM: Is that why you wanted to talk to Dad?

Awkward silence.

MOM (*cont.*): Do you need to ask him . . . about . . . *girl things?* Because I spoke with your father in New York, and so yesterday I FedExed you a box of condoms and a pamphlet about, you know, how to have sex the first time. You should be getting it this afternoon, sweetie.

You know . . . I have lived my entire life and never once, *not one time*, have I ever talked to my mother about "condoms" and "how to have sex the first time." I felt my ears turning red. I am such a fucking loser. My life is hell. No—worse than that. My life is a Band-Aid on my ballsack.

RYAN DEAN WEST: No! Please, God. . . . Tell me you did not do that. . . . Mom? FUCK!!!

Okay. I'll be honest. I do not say "fuck" to my mom. During the ensuing and second awkward silence, I spend a moment seriously thinking about killing myself.

MOM: Well, you should ask your friend if she would like to visit Boston sometime.

*"Your friend." Ugh. Oh, yeah, Mom, just stock up on the rubbers and porn.*

RYAN DEAN WEST: Okay, Mom.

I realized how deeply I hated talking to my mom ever since I became a teenager. And if there's a more potent deterrent to perversion than the Niagara Falls of razor-sharp ice shards poured down your pants, it has got to be talking to my mom about "condoms" and "how to have sex the first time."

RYAN DEAN WEST (*cont.*): Well, tell Dad I said hi. I should probably go now, Mom.

MOM: I love you, Ryan Dean.

RYAN DEAN WEST: (*Garbled, so hopefully the boy next to him doesn't understand*) Iloveyatoomom. Bye.

Click.

I suddenly felt so *dirty*.

# CHAPTER FORTY-THREE

THE SOCIAL BEGAN WINDING DOWN a little after four o'clock, and we moved through the cafeteria shaking hands and migrating out toward the bus for our long ride back to Pine Mountain.

Seanie and I were among the first to leave. I don't think either of us really paid much attention to the group of four boys who were waiting around for us by the bus. If we had, we surely would have noticed that they were not Sacred Heart kids, because they weren't dressed in ties and slacks.

They were just scrub kids from Salem, out to watch a rugby game, I guessed.

As Seanie stepped ahead of me onto the bus, one of the boys said, "Congratulations. Good game."

"Thanks," I said. I put my foot up on the first step into the bus.

"I'm waiting to say hi to my cousin," the boy said. "He's on your team. Joey Cosentino. Is he coming out?"

I turned around and saw Joey and Kevin leaving the cafeteria.

"He's right back there." I hitchhiked a thumb over my shoulder.

Then the four boys walked back to where Joey was, and I watched them, but it didn't look like Joey was expecting them at all. In fact, Joey looked startled when he saw them. And the next thing I knew, all hell broke loose and someone yelled to look out because the kid had a knife in his hand.

I've seen people do some pretty stupid things in my life, but trying to jump a rugby player in front of his whole team has to be about the stupidest. One of the boys ran off right away. I saw Chas going after him, but the punk had too much of a lead on Chas, so I thought I'd help him out, which was also pretty stupid considering my stitches and that other injury I'd been trying to forget, but couldn't, because I felt the sting of pain every time I moved my right leg.

I caught the kid and took him down right on the wet black asphalt of the Sacred Heart driveway. I didn't get hurt, because he was wearing a down jacket and I landed on top of him, but he scraped up his face pretty good when he hit the pavement. I just pinned him down and tried to not get his blood all over my dwindling supply of school shirts, and Chas caught up to us and kicked the kid twice in the ribs. I know he broke something when he did it, too, because Chas was never one to go soft on anyone if he decided to actually go that far.

"What the fuck are you thinking?" Chas said, but the kid didn't answer, he just gasped and bled. A lot. And Chas continued, "You're hardly bigger than Winger. I should just piss on you, you stupid dumb fucker."

Well, that really didn't do much for my self-esteem, but I said, "Let me get off him first if you do, Chas."

When I stood up, I heard sirens. Someone had called the police.

I looked back to the crowd where Joey and Kevin had been standing, and I saw that Coach M and some other adults were holding on to the other three boys.

"Let's take him back to the others," I said.

And Chas grabbed the bleeding kid in a wristlock and forced him back toward the cafeteria. As we got closer, we both saw that several people were kneeling. Kevin was down on the ground, lying on his back. A nun had her hand on his forehead. Joey was saying something to him. He was holding Kevin's hand. The front of Kevin's shirt was covered in blood, and he was coughing and staring straight up into the sky.

Kevin Cantrell had been stabbed.

A knife lay on the ground beside his shoulder.

The sirens grew painfully loud, and the first cop car screeched up right alongside where Kevin was lying.

# CHAPTER FORTY-FOUR

COACH MCAULIFFE RODE WITH KEVIN to the hospital in an ambulance.

The boy who pulled the knife was taken, handcuffed, in another.

Kevin had been stabbed in the shoulder when he tried to take down the guy with the knife. He wasn't badly cut, and Coach assured us he was going to be okay. Not so good for the guy who stabbed him, though, because Joey broke that boy's arm and jaw when he slammed him into the pavement. I honestly think that kid might have died if there haven't been so many grown-ups around.

By the time the cops had arrested the four boys and gotten us all to write out our statements, it was almost seven o'clock and a cold rain was falling. Coach called from the hospital and told the bus driver to take us back to Pine Mountain.

It was a quiet and dark ride home.

No singing.

I don't think any of us could stop thinking about Kevin and why something like this happened to someone as easygoing as him. It hurt us all because Kevin could accept anyone and anything, which is why, we all knew, he didn't mind rooming with Joey—something that would be social death to most guys.

But Kevin was just Kevin.

I hoped it didn't ruin him.

JP was still upset about the penalty he'd given up. Every fullback I'd ever known was like that; they had the toughest job on the team, and when they made mistakes, it was usually costly, so they tended not to let go of things very easily. That was probably the biggest reason why I believed our fight was far from over—the fullback psychology. But I knew I'd have my opportunity over the weekend to ruin his chances with Annie once and for all.

Seanie sat beside JP, but JP wasn't talking. He just stared out the window, brooding, until he fell to sleep.

I sat stretched out in a bench seat by myself. I looked back the length of the bus and saw that Joey was alone too. So I got up and stumbled down the aisle to sit with him. Joey put his arm across the back of the seat in front of him and lay his head down on it. He had to be hurting about Kevin, but who wasn't? It wasn't Joey's fault.

"Hey," I said.

Joey didn't answer.

I never saw anyone on the team cry before, but just then I thought Joey might have been. And I felt really awkward, but I put my arm around Joey's shoulders. And then I thought how stupid I was for feeling like that because I wouldn't feel weird about putting an arm around Seanie or Kevin or any other guy friend of mine who was hurting.

Seanie turned around from where he was sitting up near the front of the bus, and he looked at me and mouthed "homo," then smiled. That was just Seanie being Seanie. So I flipped him off.

"Everything's going to be okay, Joe," I said. "You want to talk or something?"

Then I patted his head and put my hand down so I could push myself up to stand.

"Oh, and hey, I never did say thanks for that pass, Joe. So, thanks. Oh, and I'm breaking up with Megan tomorrow. I swear. As soon as we make out one more time, that's it. Well, maybe twice more. Okay, three more times. But that is *it*."

I laughed. Joey looked at me.

He looked pissed.

"I'm just kidding, Joey."

I stood up and looked out the window.

"How stupid was that, anyway, trying to jump a guy in front of his whole rugby team?" I said.

Joey didn't say anything.

"Okay. I'll go now. I guess you don't want to talk. Sorry, I just thought this fucking ride was getting boring."

"Since when do you cuss?" Joey said.

"I cussed when Seanie stepped on my balls yesterday."

"That doesn't count."

"In that case, I take back what I just said about the bus ride, just to keep my record clean."

"Sit down," Joey said.

"Okay." I sat next to Joey.

"And, yeah, it was a pretty stupid thing to do," Joey said.

"The one guy said he was your cousin. That's why I pointed you out. I'm really sorry, Joe."

"He isn't my cousin. And it wasn't your fault."

"At least Kevin's going to be okay," I said. "He might have saved your life."

"Yeah."

"Do you know what it was about, Joey?"

"Yeah, I do."

"Okay," I said. "Well, you know I totally trust you, Joey. I know you can keep a secret for me. So if you want to tell me anything about it, it's okay, and if you don't want to talk about it, I understand too."

Joey took a deep breath. He glanced around. The bus was dead. Nearly everyone was asleep.

He said, "The kid with the knife. His name's Mike. His brother and I used to see each other. When his folks found out, they flipped. They sent him away to a hospital for crazy kids."

"Oh."

Joey said, "It fucked him up worse than anything. Mike told me he was going to come after me one day. I never believed him."

"Oh."

"Yeah." Joey cleared his throat. "I never tell anyone this shit, Ryan Dean."

"I won't say anything, Joe."

"I know."

"Did you tell the cops?" I asked.

Joey nodded his head. "I wrote it all down, Ryan Dean."

"Oh. Okay." I drummed my fingers against my leg. That Band-Aid, which had become a symbol of my life, was really starting to bug me. "Hey, Joey? Can I tell you about how stupid my mom is?"

He looked at me. In the dark, I could see he looked really serious and tired, but his eyes were kind of smiling.

"Sure."

Then I told him the whole thing about the phone call and the condoms and the "how to have sex the first time" pamphlet, and Joey actually laughed out loud.

"Oh, your mom just cares about you, Ryan Dean, and sometimes parents don't really understand the best way to show it. But that *is* fucking funny."

"I swear to God, Joe. My life is a nightmare."

"I don't think so. Not compared with most guys'."

"And I haven't even talked to you since the other night, but thanks for getting in Chas's face too."

"Did you actually punch him?" Joey asked.

"As hard as I could. And I am pretty sure he would have killed me if you didn't stop him."

"Damn."

"Hey, Joey? What would you do if, let's say hypothetically, you had to sleep in a bunk bed over Betch and you had a giant Gatorade bottle filled with your own, foamy, day-old piss just sitting there getting cold in your bed?"

And Joey laughed again, like he didn't believe I was telling him the truth.

On that bus ride home, I believe Joey Cosentino and I became best friends.

# CHAPTER FORTY-FIVE

BY THE TIME WE GOT BACK TO O-HALL, it was almost midnight.

Joey and I followed behind Chas, up the stairwell and down the hall. I hoped he'd run into Mrs. Singer, but, when I thought about it, it seemed like I was the only boy in the whole building who'd ever had any run-ins with her.

Maybe she didn't even really exist.

I decided that sometime before Halloween, I'd have to design a Ryan Dean West is-the-permafrost-eye-poison-known-as-the-unhot-Mrs.-Singer-actually-of-this-universe? experiment, fully controlling, of course, for all unexpected variables.

We checked in with Farrow and said good night to Joey, and I envied him for having a room to himself, even under the circumstances. Then I went to the bathroom-slash-execution-chamber to pee, and Chas headed off to our room alone.

When I got to the room, Chas was already in his bed, but the lights were on.

"What's in the package?" Chas said.

I groaned.

A white FedEx mailer was sitting on my bunk.

I am such a loser.

"Some porn and a box of rubbers," I said. "From my mom."

"Whatever. You're a fucking dick, Winger." And Chas rolled over and covered his head, mumbling something about kicking my ass one day.

Confronting Chas Becker with the truth was the surest way to get him to think I was lying.

I turned off the lights and climbed up onto my bunk. I stuffed the package down between the wall and my mattress, right next to the Ryan Dean West Emergency Gatorade Bottle Nighttime Urinal repository full of pee.

I thought, pretty soon I'm going to run out of sleeping space.

I slipped out of my clothes and listened to the rain until I fell asleep.

# CHAPTER FORTY-SIX

I SAW ANNIE AT BREAKFAST IN THE morning.

Everything seemed to click back into place and get better on the spot. The whole school was buzzing with the rumors of the "Rugby Riot," and I heard all kinds of bullshit stories from people who weren't even there, about Kevin Cantrell almost dying, and how "the gay kid" started a fight.

But Mr. Farrow had already told us before we left for school that Kevin was fine and would be back in O-Hall on Monday, so I just shut up when I heard the ridiculous versions circulating, except I did push one boy and call him an asswipe for saying Joey started the fight.

I sat down across from Annie. We held hands on top of the table. Isabel, the constant, fuzzy-lipped-flying-monkey companion, sat beside her. Seanie, Joey, and JP were there too.

JP noticed we were holding hands, gave me a dirty look, and then turned his face away.

"Hey," I said. "Are you feeling good today?"

"I was back at school yesterday," Annie said.

"I scored a try for you, like I said I would."

"I heard all about everything from Sean," she said. "Are you ready for today?"

"Oh my God, Annie. I've been ready for a week." I fired a look at JP. He wasn't watching, but I *knew* he was listening.

"Let's meet at the front of the office at the start of lunch," Joey said.

Kids who flew home usually rode to the airport together, since seniors were allowed to leave their cars at PM. I didn't even find out until after the arrangements had been made that Joey would be driving Chas Becker's SUV and taking me, Annie, Chas, and Megan to the airport with him.

Chas Becker's driver's license had been suspended. Go figure.

Joey was going home to the Bay Area, Megan lived in Los Angeles, and Chas, I assumed, would be going with her, but I didn't care and wasn't going to ask him. I just wanted to get out of there, even though I dreaded the awkwardness of the long drive to the airport and sitting in the same car with Annie and Megan. But I did come up with a couple perverted fantasies involving getting stuck in a snowdrift and sending Chas and Joey out into the cold to search for help. Unfortunately, the first snow hadn't fallen yet.

"Did Isabel give you my note?" I asked.

"Nice Space Needle cartoon," Annie said. "But you are a total liar about not knowing what was going on the other night, Ryan Dean West, and you know it."

I stared right into her eyes, giving her my most innocent look. I even leaned forward over the table, just like she did to me that night outside O-Hall when Madam-Frosty Mrs. Singer caught us as we were about to kiss.

But, God! I really wanted to kiss her so bad.

"Oh, really?" I said.

"Yeah," she said. "Two times balls equals *they* do the thinking. Oh, which reminds me . . . How's the SpongeBob Band-Aid?"

Then Isabel laughed.

"Score," I said. "Made you talk about my balls. And, anyway, Seanie's making that up. It's a Princess Barbie Band-Aid."

Then I gave Seanie a dirty look and nonchalantly scratched the bridge of my nose with my middle finger. I stood up. It was time to go to Conditioning.

# CHAPTER FORTY-SEVEN

ANNIE AND I PASSED NOTES TO
each other all during Mr. Wellins's American Literature-slash-Sex-Ed
class; and I could tell JP was getting pretty ticked about it. Oh, well, I
thought, I've got all weekend, buddy, and by the time we get back to
Pine Mountain she won't even know you exist.

Less than forty-five more minutes of sex talk about how
gay Henry David Thoreau was and we're out of here.

Yeah, but then, with you, it's going to be
Friday to Sunday of nonstop sex talk.

We don't have to just talk (wink).

You are so perverted.

Try to be nice around my parents.

And your gay dog. Just remember, I am here to
help you through this Intense-Need-to-Kiss-Ryan-Dean
obsession you have.

Like I said: LIAR. And you know it.

Want me to draw you a picture?

I dunno. Is it perverted?

You want perverted? I can do.

Ugh! get me an airsick bag. Freak!

Here you go. Love, Ryan Dean West (fifteen more minutes!!!).

# CHAPTER FORTY-EIGHT

I KNEW THE DRIVE TO THE AIRPORT would be awkward. Chas went out of his way to make it even worse than it had to be.

After we'd loaded our suitcases in the back of his SUV, Chas informed me that I would ride shotgun—front passenger seat. And, as Chas explained, that meant the gay guys could sit up front so Chas could be in the backseat with what he called "the two hotties."

Chas Becker was such a tool.

Not that I wouldn't have called them that, much less given just about anything to sit between them. I even tried to argue that it would be more comfortable for Annie and Megan if I did, because I was smaller than Chas, but Chas just looked at Megan one time, then gave me a look like he was about to punch me and said, "Shut the fuck up, Winger."

And, when we were on the road, I turned back and saw that Chas was sitting in the middle with his arms stretched over the seat backs, pretending he was holding on to both girls, just looking at me like he was the king of the world or something, which, for whatever reason, made me think about that bottle of piss I still hadn't gotten rid of.

"What are your plans for the weekend, Ryan Dean?" Joey asked, paying attention to the road but flickering his eyes to the mirror once in a while to watch Chas and the girls. Normally, they would have been in Kevin's car, which was bigger than Chas's SUV; Joey's car was out of the question, since it only carried two people.

"Nothing boring," I said. "No TV watching. Me and Annie are going to do some running on the beach, I guess. I don't know. Maybe go fishing if it's not too rainy."

"Sounds thrilling," Chas said. "When are you two going to actually start fooling around? Or are Annie's parents going to play watchdog all weekend?"

"Shut up, Chas," I said. "Annie's not like that."

I looked at Annie, and she smiled at me. And then I saw Chas scoot himself closer to her.

"I bet she could be like that," he said.

"Maybe I should sit up front," Annie said.

Then Megan tried to change the subject but chose the worst imaginable direction to steer the conversation: "I bet Ryan Dean's a real good kisser, Annie. Is he?"

As soon as she said it, all kinds of things happened at once:

1. I felt my balls actually retract up inside my body cavity. I don't know if I turned white or red, but I definitely felt something turning.
2. Megan got this testy and challenging look on her face—definitely the very, very bad policewoman look.
3. Joey coughed like he was choking on something, then fired me the get-your-shit-together-Ryan-Dean look.

4. Chas took his arms away from both girls and folded his hands on his lap, pouting, with a look on his face that said he wanted to snap my skinny-bitch-ass neck. He had to know what was going on with me and Megan. I was convinced.

5. And Annie said, "Oh, yeah. He's a great kisser. And he has puppy breath."

Then Chas said, "Do you guys want to pull over and play Spin the Bottle, or should we just get to the airport in time to catch our flights?"

Megan straightened up and winked at me. I didn't even want to look at Annie to see if she'd caught it. This could easily ruin what I was convinced would be the best weekend of my life.

I cleared my throat and said, "Annie's just messing around. We've never kissed. Not even close." And I looked directly at her and said, "Even though I've asked her to hundreds of times."

So I let her off the hook. For now.

I knew she'd think about that. I knew Annie. She wasn't going to let a statement like that go unresponded to all weekend long, so I turned back around, faced the road, and tried to will my nuts back down from behind my belly button, smiling, confident that I'd get Annie Altman to cave in to her weakness before too long.

# CHAPTER FORTY-NINE

GOD! WAS I GLAD TO SEE OUR GROUP split up once we got to the airport.

We all agreed on a meeting time and place in the terminal after our return flights Sunday evening, then we headed off to our gates.

Annie and I checked our bags and took off our shoes to pass through the security line. And, of course, as these things happen to losers such as myself, when I was walking through the metal detector, an alarm sounded because I'd left my belt on. And just when the Transportation Security officer was waving me to stop, my Band-Aid conveniently came unglued after its two-day vacation on my balls. It fell out the bottom of my dorky, too-short school pants.

This, of course, made the guard think that I was some kind of black-tar-heroin-cakes-or-whatever-the-fuck-you-call-them-Band-Aided-to-my-ballsack-smuggler, and he and another very unhappy-looking man in a white shirt escorted me behind a thin screen, the kind you'd see in a run-down clinic.

That was where they told me to strip down to my underwear.

Nice.

Annie laughed at me.

Well, I think she was laughing at me. I couldn't tell, because I couldn't see her since I was standing in my boxers behind a goddamned hospital-cloth screen while one of the TSA guys turned my socks inside out and shook them.

At the same time, the other agent actually grabbed my now Band-Aid-free balls (and it was probably not in good judgment for me to ask him if he wanted me to turn my head and cough, because he just kind of nodded and said something about me being a "smart ass," and then he pulled out the waistband on my underwear and gave my actual-not-so-smart-skinny-white-ass a glimpse of airport-terminal fluorescent light).

Annie was doing her best, I am sure, to pretend she didn't know heroin-ballsack-boy.

Yeah.

I'm a loser.

Not just a loser, a loser who was still standing behind a screen, bare-foot and in his boxers, when he heard the final boarding announcement for his flight to Seattle. The TSA guy just placed my boarding pass on top of my thoroughly ransacked and inside-out school clothes and said, "Sorry, Mr. West. You're free to go."

I quickly pulled on my now-beltless pants and slid into my shirt. I grabbed my shoes and the rest of my clothes and boarding pass in a bundle under one arm and walked out from behind the screen.

Annie stood there, laughing, her eyes all wet.

"Why do these things always happen to you?" she asked.

"Because I'm a fucking loser," I answered.

Yeah, well . . . I didn't say "fucking," of course, because you know I never cuss, especially not in front of Annie, but to say that I *wanted* to say "fucking" is a fucking understatement.

"Here," she said, "let me help you," and she grabbed my shoes and belt as I hopped along to the gate, my unbuttoned and untucked shirt fluttering behind me as I tried to pull on one sock and my pants slipped down toward my knees. I dropped my tie and had to stop to pick it up.

I gave up.

I followed Annie to the boarding gate half-undressed and barefoot, with one hand holding up the waist of my pants.

And the attendant at the gate, who, I will say, was pretty damn hot in a paramilitary-Andrews-Sisters kind of way, raised her very disciplined-looking eyebrow as I pinched my boarding pass to her with the same hand I was using to try and keep my pants up.

"Oh, yeah," I said, dropping my tie and one of my inside-out socks at her feet, "I plan on being completely naked by the time we get to our seats."

# CHAPTER FIFTY

"I REALLY *DO* WANT TO HOLD HANDS on takeoff," Annie said.

I slipped my hand into hers.

"Oh, yeah?" I said. "Well, considering I get naked *before* takeoff, I'd say that exactly nine months from the moment we fly over the Columbia River, you'll probably be giving birth."

She laughed. "Pervert."

I buttoned my shirt.

I couldn't help myself now:

RYAN DEAN WEST 2: So . . . loser, did you pack the condoms?

RYAN DEAN WEST 1: Don't be ridiculous. Annie is not like that.

RYAN DEAN WEST 2: I bet five out of five Buffalo wings on the Ryan Dean West Spice Matrix Megan Renshaw is.

RYAN DEAN WEST 1: Hmmm . . . I haven't been keeping up with that particular scale, but that stewardess up the aisle has got to be a four-and-a-half . . . I wonder if I could swing a trip to LA next weekend. . . . Just a thought.

JOEY COSENTINO: Goddamnit, Ryan Dean. I am going to stop sticking up for you if you don't grow the fuck up. You are finally getting to go somewhere with the girl of your dreams, and you can't stop thinking about every other female on the planet.

RYAN DEAN WEST 1: I'm sorry, Joey. Hey, how could *you* be on this plane?

JOEY COSENTINO: I'm not. I'm the part of your subconscious that actually (a) knows the right thing to do and (b) is not perverted.

RYAN DEAN WEST 2: You mean there is a part of my brain that doesn't think about sex? You're making that up!

RYAN DEAN WEST 1: Go away, Joe. The stewardess is about to come around to check if my seat belt is snug enough.

I actually managed to get dressed, shirt tucked, necktie knotted, one sock still inside out but at least in my shoes, before the plane was on the runway, and all this despite the fact that I was wedged into a middle seat between Annie and a drunk-bald-fat guy who fell asleep, sitting on my seat belt buckle, with his head on my shoulder.

We were still holding hands when the plane began its descent into Seattle. Me and Annie . . . not me and the drunk guy.

"This is going to be so great," Annie said.

"What's the best thing you've ever done in your life?" I asked.

"I don't know. What about you?"

"Top three," I said—my shoulder leaned against hers, and it felt so good—"were those last two times you and I were alone at Stonehenge, and being here right now, holding your hand."

I looked right at her.

"You're trying to see if you can make me do it, aren't you, West?"

"I wouldn't dream of it," I said.

"Sure." Then she said, "It is not going to happen."

"Stay strong, Annie."

"You too, Ryan Dean."

Crap.

She was playing the same game.

# CHAPTER FIFTY-ONE

ANNIE'S MOTHER AND FATHER WERE waiting for us when we came through the arrival gate. I had never even seen a photograph of them, but they both looked so Annie-like that I would have known them anyway. They were doctors, and they looked so young and healthy. When they saw us, their eyes smiled the same way that Annie's did.

Annie's father kissed her, then he held his hand out to me.

"You must be Ryan Dean," he said. "Annie thinks the world of you."

I looked at her; and she actually blushed. I couldn't believe it—Annie Altman turning red; and I wondered if she had that same inner-voice thing where she was currently calling herself a loser, even if I did think it looked totally hot when it happened to her. Blushing, I mean.

"Thank you," I said, and then I thought, *What a stupid thing to say,* so I added, "Doctor Altman." Which sounded even stupider.

Then Annie's mom hugged me, which kind of flustered me for two reasons: first, because she was a doctor, it made me immediately think she was going to ask me to take my pants off; and, second, I have to admit it, being Annie's mom, she was really hot.

And she said, "'Doctor Altman' won't work in our house. We won't know who you're talking to. But you are so polite, Ryan Dean."

Now *I* was blushing. Loser.

"You should just call me Rachel, and the other Doctor Altman is Keith."

I hated calling grown-ups by their first names. It seemed so flower-child-nineteen-seventies to me. So I decided I'd try to not use their names at all, or if I had to, I'd call them "Doc Dad" and "Doc Mom."

Annie's father had to drive us to the docks in Seattle to catch the ferry; it was a thirty-five-minute ride to their home on Bainbridge Island. I had never been to Seattle before, and I thought it was one of the most intense-looking cities I'd ever seen, built right up against the tree-lined coast, in the shadow of a giant volcano.

On the way to the docks, we talked about school and sports. Doc Dad was one of the only adults in America I'd ever met who had actually played rugby when he was in college, so we hit it off right away, even though he had been a loose forward. Loose forwards are usually not the most evolved primates on the planet. Still, I knew I was going to fit in just fine with Annie's family.

Hand-holding in the backseat with Annie was definitely off, though. It took only one look from her to quietly get that message to me. And I could feel her getting a little embarrassed again too when her father and mother began talking about her.

"This is what Annie's told us about you, Ryan Dean," her mother said. "Tell us if we're right. She says you are the smartest boy in the school, you're a great athlete, and you made the varsity rugby team when you were in tenth grade. And she told us you are the best-looking boy at school too."

Annie coughed.

My ears turned red.

"You're Annie's first real boyfriend," her father said.

"Okay, that's enough of that," Annie said. "Ryan Dean and I are just really good friends. That's all."

I guess that whole "boyfriend" label did kind of make it sound like salmon spawning, as Seanie might have noticed.

"Tell us about where you live, Ryan Dean," Doc Mom said, turning sideways to look at me.

"O-Hall," I said, and then I thought, why am I such a fucking idiot? I wasn't even listening to her; I was too caught up in thinking about being Annie's "boyfriend."

Annie coughed again, no doubt choking on the thought of bringing a delinquent to Bainbridge Island for the weekend.

"I mean . . . I live in Weston," I corrected. "I don't get home much."

"That's a shame," Doc Mom said. "Well, you are welcome to visit us anytime you'd like."

I looked at Annie and smiled, and she mouthed "pervert" to me.

We were paused in a line of cars making their way onto the ferry.

"Well, what brought you two together?" Doc Dad asked me.

"Annie was the first person I met at Pine Mountain," I said. "I was really lost and out of place when I started." I slid my hand over so I touched Annie's fingers, and she pulled her hand away. "But Annie came right up and introduced herself and helped show me around. She's been my best friend ever since that day, and I'd do anything for her."

"You are such a sweet boy!" Doc Mom chirped. "Have you ever been to Seattle before, Ryan Dean?"

"No, ma'am," I said, laying it on as thick as possible, momentarily fantasizing about that dreamed-of couch in Annie's bedroom. "But it really is beautiful here."

"Wait till you see the house," she said. "We are right on the waterfront, and we look across the sound to the Seattle skyline and Mount Rainier. It's a perfect spot."

Yeah, I thought, how could it *not* be? As long as it's got Annie in it—and you keep her gay dog off my leg—you could live in a fucking plywood lean-to.

"Oh, I forgot to tell you," Annie said. "Did you bring any swim trunks? We have an indoor pool and Jacuzzi."

"Wow," I said. "No. I didn't."

I looked down, then shrugged and looked over at Annie and whispered, "I'll go without."

Annie rolled her eyes.

"We can pick some up for you on the island, Ryan Dean," Doc Mom said.

Score.

Even if it rained all weekend, I'd still get to be Annie Altman's pool boy.

# CHAPTER FIFTY-TWO

OKAY.

I realized why my dad refuses to shop for anything, even golf clubs and fishing gear, with my mom.

For most women, I think shopping becomes something like a model of the expanding universe, only rather than relating to the Big Bang, Ryan Dean West's Law of Shopping deals with the expansion of time, and "adorable stuff" to look at. Kind of like a supernova rather than a black hole—the opposite of having your balls stepped on, as similar as the experiences may actually be.

I can only imagine, not that I thought for even a fleeting instant about opening that goddamned package, that my mother had spent all day long asking all kinds of questions before deciding on just the right condoms and "how to have sex the first time" booklet, which she later undoubtedly exchanged for a cute pair of socks with sailboats on them before ultimately leaving the store and going to a different goddamned condom and "how to have sex the first time" emporium.

This is shopping.

And this was the Ryan-Dean-West-swim-trunk-shopping expedition with Annie and Doc Mom.

At first, Annie was messing around and tried to make a case that I was on the Pine Mountain swim team, so she told Doc Mom to look in the Speedo section.

Her mistake. I completely went along with her. What was she thinking? I actually thought it would be kind of hot to wear Speedos in front of Annie and her mom. But when Annie realized what was happening, she got this terrified, defeated look and said, "I think it's time for you to move up to big boy board shorts, Ryan Dean."

"No. Really," I insisted.

*Big boy board shorts. What a bunch of crap.*

The only cool part about the whole experience was that every time they'd look at a new pair of trunks, Doc Mom would hold them up to my waist, pinning them with her thumbs to my hips so she and Annie could imagine how I'd look in them.

Yeah, I'll admit I didn't get too tired of that routine.

And the shopping went on and on until Doc Dad said he had to pee really bad. So Annie and Doc Mom settled on a pair of plain red lifeguard baggies that were exactly the ones I would have chosen for myself about an hour and a half earlier.

While they were waiting to pay, Doc Dad leaned close to me and whispered, "I don't really have to pee, Ryan Dean, but I've found that the need to pee is about the only force that sufficiently shrinks Rachel's universe to the point where she'll cut short a shopping experience."

Now here was a guy I totally understood.

I bet he could fake-cry, too.

# CHAPTER FIFTY-THREE

GREEN.

That's Bainbridge Island.

It's one of the most intensely green places I've ever seen. And I never for a moment imagined the kind of home Annie's family lived in.

The house was set right up against the shore, facing Puget Sound and, across it, Seattle. We drove up a long driveway through trees to the garage, and then walked a pathway through gardens that had been decorated with strange and beautiful metal and enamel sculptures of fish, animals, and native totems.

"Annie made all of these sculptures herself," Doc Mom said, "in her studio."

They were incredible. I looked at Annie. I always knew she was creative and brilliant, but I never realized she could do something as amazing as this.

"You're incredible," I said to her.

"Thank you," she said.

Where the gardens opened up, we stepped out onto a wide grass lawn in front of the house, which was mostly made of stone and had tall windows all along the front, looking out across the water. There was a broad wooden deck on the edge of the lawn, right where the grass gave way to a slope of black lava rocks that lined the shore. You couldn't see any other house from there; the property was surrounded by forest.

And just as we got to the front door, the sun hit the perfect angle in the west behind us, and it looked like the entire city of Seattle turned rust hued, and the peak of Mount Rainier seemed to float, salmon colored, in the sky.

"Hey," I said, "you can see the Space Needle from your front yard."

Annie rolled her eyes.

"If you get changed out of your strip-search clothes, we can walk on the beach before dinner," she said.

I will admit that my inside-out sock was bothering me, but all I had besides school clothes were running shorts, sweats, and my new swim trunks.

"Okay," I said.

Doc Dad led the way into the entry hall and said, "Annie, why don't you take Ryan Dean to the guest room."

Damn.

"Oh, he doesn't want to be that far away, all alone," she said.

*Oh my God. Will it actually happen?*

Annie continued, "I'll put him in the little room across from mine."

Next thing I knew, I heard the clicking of manicured dog nails on the wood floor, followed by the chirplike shriek of repetitive barking, and then this smash-faced little dog appeared and immediately came after my leg in a hump ambush.

"Pedro!" Annie scolded.

"Just kick him," Doc Mom said. "He never quits, otherwise."

You know, when someone tells you to kick their dog—the same dog who is currently in a breeding frenzy with your nicest pair of dorky school pants—it's a difficult thing to judge exactly how hard the dog should be kicked. So I decided I'd give Pedro a conservative three out of five Cossack dancers on the Ryan Dean West How-Far-to-Kick-a-Gay-Pug Spectrum.

"That's mean!" Annie said, but she did kind of laugh as Pedro skittered like a hockey puck toward the sunken living room.

"Good man, Ryan Dean," Doc Dad said. "I don't know why we haven't cut his balls off yet."

And why is it, I thought, that whenever boys consider such measures—despite their justifiability—we always get a bit scared, morose, and angsty?

Oh, well.

"Come on," Annie said. Then she grabbed my hand to lead me down the hallway to our right. She stopped suddenly.

Annie must have realized what she was doing (unlike Pedro, she could control the involuntary impulse to conjugate with Ryan Dean West), because she immediately let go like my hand was a red-hot thing that gets . . . red . . . hot.

Or something.

I followed her, lugging my suitcase and the bag from the sporting goods store.

"The door on the right is your room," she said. "Just across the hall from mine."

I opened my door and set my bags down on the floor.

It's amazing how much a guy can appreciate a non-bunk-bed bed and a bathroom that doesn't have at least two other guys in it at all times. The window was uncovered and looked out at the beach and tall dark pines, and I had my own television and a huge bathroom with an ice-block shower cubicle.

"How do you like it?" Annie said.

"Please adopt me," I said. Then I added, "No. On second thought, that could get a little weird. Let's just hop across the border to Canada and get married."

Annie laughed. I kicked my shoes off and said, "I'll get changed."

"Okay. Meet me in the hall in, like, thirty seconds," she said.

*Hmmm . . .* I thought, thirty seconds meant I'd have time to get *out* of my clothes but not into them. Oh, well, wishful thinking. Docs Mom and Dad would probably disapprove of the clothing-optional houseguest, and that dog was out there waiting for me, anyway.

"Okay," I said, and Annie left me alone.

Whenever I get off an airplane, I feel like I've been deep fried, dripping in oil. And I probably smelled like booze from drunk-bald-fat-guy slobbering on my shoulder. So it felt really good to tear all my clothes off (without a couple security guards pawing through them), and even better to just throw them onto the floor, something I hadn't been able to do all year.

Now, with all the scattered, discarded articles of boy-clothes, this looked like a real guy's room.

All I needed to do was mess up the perfectly smoothed bedcovers, which I did with a jump.

I put on the red trunks they bought me, as well as a gray Pine Mountain RFC (which means Rugby Football Club) sweatshirt, some clean, inside-in socks, and my running shoes, and I was out my door and in the hall in under a minute.

Annie opened her door.

No matter what she wore, Annie Altman always looked perfect. She had changed into faded jeans that were just wearing through at the knees and along the bottoms of the pockets, with a pale blue sweater that really made her black hair and blue eyes stand out, even in the dim light of the hallway.

I had never seen her dressed in "home clothes" before, and I couldn't take my eyes off her.

And, I am such a loser, I couldn't even speak when she asked, "Want to see my room?"

Her room was so . . . Annie. The walls were covered with paintings, and sculptures of fish and birds that she'd made. Her windows looked out into the forest, and she had French doors that opened to a stepping-stone path.

Next to her bed was a Wonder Horse, one of those spring-mounted things kids used to play on, like, a hundred years ago.

"Wow," I said, but my voice cracked like a kid who suddenly realized he was alone inside the bedroom of the girl he loved, which made sense, considering the oppressive reality of my surrounding conditions. "Do you still ride?"

Annie laughed. "Come on."

She opened the paned doors and led me onto the path outside her room.

# CHAPTER FIFTY-FOUR

WE WALKED ALONG THE ROCKY
beach in the sunset.

The water in the sound was so black and rolling, jagged and alive. Everything smelled like the sea and trees. Between the cracks in the rocks, I could see the claws of wedged-in crabs, spitting bubbles, sometimes moving slightly like they wanted to keep an eye on us, like they were spying on us.

"Tomorrow morning we can go run out past that point." Annie's hand indicated a distant and darkening stand of trees.

"This is so nice," I said. My shoes were wet from walking too close to the water. "Thanks so much for asking me, Annie."

"I knew you'd like it."

"I never knew you were such an artist," I said.

"Just like you," she said.

"Crud. You are so much more. I draw stick figures. You make stuff that's *real*."

"I can tell my mom and dad really like you."

I pulled out the leg of my trunks. "I got the trunks on."

"They look good."

We stopped and turned back toward the house. It was beginning to get dark.

I was convinced she was playing the same game with me that I was playing with her, but I wasn't going to fall for it. Not for a second. There was still that sensible and pathetic part of my mind that kept telling me Annie Altman only thought I was a little kid and nothing else.

But we did stand there for a minute, and I could smell her, and feel the warmth like a static charge coming from her. And she looked at my face, and we were so close when she said, "Your stitches look like they're getting better."

I leaned closer to her. Damn, she looked so nice, and I was so impressed by how she lived and the beautiful things she'd created there with her own hands, and I wanted to . . .

*Do not kiss her, Ryan Dean West.*

*Ugh.*

I am such a loser. She knew exactly what she was doing.

She started back to the house and said over her shoulder in her singing voice, the voice that knew everything and made nothing matter, "Don't even tell me that you didn't almost do it just now, Ryan Dean."

Damn.

I couldn't say anything.

Annie stopped and looked back. "So there. We're even. Admit it."

"I don't know what you're talking about," I said. I followed after her, and when I caught up beside her, I held her hand.

"I bet JP would be jealous," I said.

"Don't even go there, West. You said we shouldn't talk about JP to each other."

"Okay."

I sighed. In the fading light, we hadn't noticed that her mother and father had been standing just down the beach, watching us. But we didn't let go of our hands.

Her father's arm was around her mother's shoulders. Doc Mom smiled and said, "You look so nice walking on the beach together."

After dinner, Annie and I went out to the pool house to go for a swim.

Unfortunately, her parents came along. They just sat there reading in lounge chairs, but they were keeping an eye on us too, and I think they enjoyed doing it. But when we sat in the hot tub, I started playing with Annie's feet and rubbing her legs with mine. It was the best feeling I could ever have dreamed up, and I could tell Annie liked it too, but it was really making me crazy. So I leaned my head back on the deck and closed my eyes because I wasn't about to let her think I wanted to kiss her. Or something else. But I will say that all Annie would have had to do was whisper, "Let's go skinny-dipping," and those goddamned red lifeguard trunks would have been hanging from the rafters.

# CHAPTER FIFTY-FIVE

IT FELT SO COMFORTABLE SLEEP-
ing in that bed that I guess I must not have wanted to wake up. When
I did, the sun was already pouring through my window and someone
was knocking on my door.

"Ryan Dean. Are you still sleeping?"

It was Annie.

"I was. Until maybe two seconds ago."

"Sorry."

I rubbed my eyes.

"You can come in," I said.

The door cracked open, and she cautiously peeked her head into
my room. I could see she was dressed for a run.

I folded my hands on the pillow beneath my head. This was like a
dream come true: Annie Altman waking me up in the morning after
we practically took a bath together the night before.

"Come get some breakfast, and let's go for our run. It's beautiful
out there."

It's not so bad in here, either, I thought.

"Okay." I sat up and rubbed my chin. "I'll be right there after I get
ready. I think I need to shave."

Annie laughed. "Yeah, right."

"Hey. I have *one whisker*. Right here under my chin. Just one. I'm thinking of giving it a name, but I don't know if I should let it grow out or chop its head off." I tilted my head back and put my finger on my jaw. "See it?"

"No."

"Well, you can't see it from way over there. You have to get close."

She moved to the edge of the bed.

Score.

"Look," I said. "It's even dark and everything."

I kept my chin up, and Annie leaned over me.

"Oh, yeah," she said. "I can see it."

She was so close.

She said, "It looks so lonely and lost, maybe you shouldn't shave it. And maybe you should name it 'Ryan Dean.'"

I looked into her eyes.

"I better get out of here," Annie said, straightening. Then she spun around and went to the door.

"We're not even anymore, Annie."

Then I heard her call "Pedro," and that little disgusting animal came nail-tapping-panting-slobbering-excited-grunting into my room. Annie left, shutting the door just as Pedro sailed up onto my bed and began frantically mounting my foot. I scooped him up by his little sweaty armpits, his hips still pumping at the air, opened the door with my elbow, and scooted him like a shuffleboarded puck-puppy to the opposite end of the hallway.

Annie was smiling, standing there, watching me.

I looked at her and said, "So, are you going to give me time to get dressed, or is it okay if I come to breakfast in my underwear?"

She laughed, and I said, "And, no, we are not even. Ryan Dean West has officially pulled into the lead."

"It's not fair if you count getting Pedro to think about kissing you."

"Good one, Annie. In that case I'm *way* ahead of you."

I went back inside my room and got into my running gear.

# CHAPTER FIFTY-SIX

DOC MOM FED US BAGELS WITH butter and sweet tomato jam she'd made from her own summer garden, and we drank black coffee and orange juice. And throughout the meal, the doc parents were both trying to talk to us, but our feet were twitching and we needed to get outside.

"I'm sorry, Doc Mom," I said. "I don't usually sleep this late, but this place sure is a beautiful spot for resting."

"Thank you, Ryan Dean. *Doc Mom*—I like that. Poor boy, you sleep as late as you want. You can do whatever you feel like when you're in our house," she said.

I fired a quick and perverted, arched-eyebrow-(it hurt my stitches)-remember-the-Jacuzzi look at Annie, who rolled her eyes.

We ran so far that morning.

I'd almost forgotten that Annie's being on the cross country team meant that anything under ten miles was a warm-up for her. I followed Annie along trails and streets, heading south along the shore of the island, and we came to a park where a stream cut a V-shaped harbor. The place was deserted, too; I saw just one small fishing boat rocking like a lazy walrus off the shore. We stopped running, and walked through wide fields of knee-high grass that made our legs wet.

The park was the site of an old sawmill, now abandoned, but the outer walls of the mill building still stood, square, like a fort, in the middle of the field. And you could tell from the outline of the perimeter of the open space, and how the forest butted up against it, that there had been tall trees there at one time, before the mill was operational.

"Come on," Annie said. "I want you to see inside the building."

I followed her.

It was kind of a surreal place. What was left of the old mill—the floor and side walls—had been entirely constructed of concrete. Huge openings in the sides and in the roof were the gutted remains of former doors and skylights. And just about every available surface inside was painted with bizarre and colorful graffiti, some of it very artistic, and a lot of it just nasty and drugged out. There was even a tree growing from a hole in the floor, all the way up through one of the open skylights, about twenty feet over our heads.

"Who did all this?" I said, turning in my place and scanning all the images.

"Just kids. They get bored living here."

"They do?" I couldn't believe anyone would ever get bored here.

"I remembered seeing something here one time," Annie said. "And I wanted to see if I could find it again, if it hasn't been painted over."

She moved past one of the thick steel girders that supported the roof.

"Come here," she said. "Look. I thought about you when I saw this last time I was here."

Annie pointed down to the base of one of the walls, and there, beneath a big red word that spelled out SOMEDAY, in interlocking letters, was a painting of two overlapping black circles.

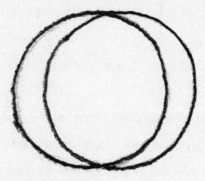

"You remember that?" I said.

"It was about your wish, that last time we were at Stonehenge," Annie said. "And I thought about it a lot. I felt bad because I'd been so mean to you that week, and I realized that I was pretty unfair to you too. I mean about the 'little boy' stuff."

"Oh?" I knew we were standing too close again. I was practically sweating on her, and I didn't want her to just be playing. But she was. I backed away, but just a bit, and I looked at the circles. "So, did you get over it? The outside-the-overlap part of me, I mean?"

She looked at me. Her eyes had that relaxed, smiling look in them. She didn't say anything. We just looked.

Then she stepped closer to me and touched my hand.

I said, "Okay. I don't care. I lose."

And then I kissed Annie Altman.

For, like, twenty straight minutes.

And there was no interruption from the visually abrasive Mrs. Singer; there was nothing in the entire universe except for me and Annie finally getting something over with that had been making us both crazy for so long.

I didn't care that she'd won our little game, because for those incredible minutes, pinning her body between mine and the coolness of the painted concrete wall in that old mill, my hands holding the back of her neck, feeling the softness of her hair falling across the sweat of my arms, I finally didn't feel like such a loser.

I was shaking.

I said, "I told you I'd do it when I wanted to. And I decided I wanted to."

We got back to her house at lunchtime, and her father said, "Wow, you two must have gone pretty far."

Annie smiled at me, and I know she was thinking about the perverted comment I'd normally be tempted to make at such a statement, but this was not a normal time for Ryan Dean West, and she said, "Oh, it was the perfect run, Dad."

And I said, "Yeah. Completely perfect."

# CHAPTER FIFTY-SEVEN

THAT AFTERNOON, ANNIE KEPT HER promise to fix my school pants, but her mom helped. So I stood there in the "sewing room" in my socks and underwear doing the on-off routine with my pants while hot Annie pinned and her hot mother worked the sewing machine.

You know, it's easy to play all cool and stuff about how hot certain females are, but it's another thing entirely to then find yourself actually standing in front of them in your underwear. I'm not really sure if I was handling the opportunity in the most advantageous manner.

I wondered if there were many guys out there who actually could.

I was so red and embarrassed, and Doc Mom tried to make small talk about how nice it was to have a boy in the house, but it was like my tongue had been bee-stung, and I couldn't say anything because I just wanted to keep hearing both of them tell me to take my pants off again.

I am such a loser.

All I could think about was how I'd actually kissed Annie that day, and I wondered if we would ever have the guts to say anything about it, or if we'd even have the guts to make it happen again.

Then I had to stand there, waiting in my boxers while Doc Mom ironed the old hems out and made me try on every pair of slacks one last time before she was satisfied they were perfect. All I knew was that I wished I'd grow another two inches by the next morning so we'd be required to do it over again, and maybe next go-round, I'd be all suave and debonair and stuff, and make witty comments instead of just gurgling like a goldfish on a linoleum floor.

"There," Doc Mom said. "I think you look very handsome."

"Thanks, Doc Mom," I said, and unbuttoned my pants and began pulling them down.

"Uh, Ryan Dean, you can leave them on now. We're finished," she said.

I am *such* a loser.

"He got strip-searched at the airport, Mom," Annie said. "I think he's traumatized by it."

"Really?" Doc Mom said.

Oh, yeah. She's a psychologist. So now she needed to hear the whole story about what happened, and how poor Ryan Dean had been mentally abused. I gave Annie an ultraterrified, oh-my-God-please-don't-tell-your-mom-about-the-Band-Aid-on-my-balls look, but it was too late for that. Annie launched into the entire story, going all the way back to Wednesday when Sean Russell Flaherty stepped on my nuts at rugby practice and I went to the doctor for it.

And Doc Mom, being the compassionate therapist that she is, laughed until she had tears in her eyes (just like Annie does) and said that was one of the funniest stories she'd ever heard.

When Annie was finished with the getting-on-the-airplane-as-Ryan-Dean's-pants-fell-down-again part, I excused myself to return to my room so I could kill myself.

I probably would have, too, except just as I stepped out into the hallway, three things happened at once:

1. Pedro hump-ambushed me, and I almost fell down.

2. I realized that *both* Annie *and* her five-out-of-five-leather-couches-on-the-Ryan-Dean-West-Hot-Therapist-Ink-Blot-Test mom had just had a conversation about my balls.

3. Doc Mom said to Annie, "I just love Ryan Dean." And I swear to God, but then again, this is coming from the same boy who's heard all kinds of twisted things coming from Mrs. Singer's mouth, but I swear to *God* that Annie said, "So do I."

Of course, I can't be absolutely certain, because of the noise of anguished and love-starved grunts coming from that goddamned gay pug.

# CHAPTER FIFTY-EIGHT

WE DIDN'T TALK ABOUT WHAT
happened in the abandoned sawmill, and we didn't kiss again, either,
for that whole endlessly long Saturday. And the next morning when
I woke up, it was drizzling rain, and I was so depressed about having
to leave Bainbridge Island and fly back to Oregon later that day that
I seriously felt like I could cry.

So I stayed in bed until I heard Annie's door open across the hall.
Then she knocked.

"Come in."

This time, she just walked right in.

"Good morning," she said.

"Hi."

"Are you okay?"

I pulled the covers over my face and hid. "I don't want to go back
to school, Annie. Make it be yesterday again."

"Do you want to run?"

"I love running in the rain. Meet me in the kitchen in, like, thirty
seconds."

"Okay," she said. "Let's just run in the woods today."

We sat down to breakfast with the doc parents. We had oatmeal
and black coffee. I love coffee. I hate oatmeal, but I'll be honest, I'd

eat anything at the Altmans' table. I wore my black running shorts and Pine Mountain RFC sweatshirt with a blue cap that I started to take off when I sat down, but Doc Mom told me to keep it on, that I didn't have to be like that in their house.

"Next time you come up, Ryan Dean," Doc Dad said, "do you think you could bring me one of those sweatshirts? I don't have any rugby stuff anymore."

"No problem," I said.

"And I fully intend on coming down and seeing you play a match this season too," he said. "It's been a long time since I've seen the game. Too long."

"That would be really cool," I said.

Doc Mom looked sad. I could tell it was hard for her to always say good-bye to her daughter, but Annie told me they saw each other more often now that she was at Pine Mountain than they ever did when they all lived together full-time.

I guess things work out like that sometimes.

"I'm sure going to miss having you here, Ryan Dean," Doc Mom said. "I want to see you back before Thanksgiving, if your folks will let you."

"If it's okay with Annie," I said. "This was the best weekend I ever had in my life, I think."

Annie tipped her coffee cup empty and said, "Let's go, West, if you're done."

We went out into the gray, wet morning.

Running through the woods north of her house, it amazed me how green things grew on top of green things that were still green and growing. Trees were covered with ferns and vines and mosses, and everywhere it looked as if nothing had been dry in centuries. And in the dark woods as we ran, I could smell that living-ocean scent of the island, and I heard nothing but the sounds of our feet on the wet ground, our breathing, and the static-spark sizzle of rain dripping through the forest cover.

She was running fast, trying to push me, or trying to get somewhere that I didn't know about.

"Hey!" I said. "Stop for a minute, Annie."

Where a tree branch arched across the trail, black, and covered with hair of brilliant moss, Annie stopped and turned around to wait for me. I was panting. Dark rings of sweat made circles under my arms and a V that pointed at my belly, down from my neck. My cap was soaked dark with the drizzling rain.

"Don't kiss me, Ryan Dean."

Now, that was like getting kicked in the balls again.

"Okay."

I bent forward and put my hands on my knees. I spit between my feet.

"Did I do something wrong, Annie?"

"No. I just think we shouldn't do that again."

*Ugh.*

"Okay with me," I said.

I tried to sound like Annie would if she'd said it, all nonchalant and singsongy, but my voice cracked and I felt like a fucking idiot. "I just wanted to say thanks again for having me here. And how much I like your mom and dad."

"You're welcome, Ryan Dean," she said. "Do you want to turn around?"

"No. I want you to make it be yesterday again."

"Stop it, Ryan Dean."

"Okay, Annie. I know what's up. Okay."

"I can't be in love with you, Ryan Dean."

I turned around and started running back to her house. Maybe, I thought, if I ran fast enough, like those fucking stupid old science fiction movies, I could go back in time.

I ran faster than I ever had in my pathetic life.

But it didn't work.

I am such a loser.

What a bunch of crap.

# CHAPTER FIFTY-NINE

I JUST RAN.

The woods were dark; the clouds were getting thicker.

I took off my cap and tossed it into the blackberry vines that grew everywhere in these woods. Then I pulled my sweatshirt off, soaked and inside out, and dropped it in the mud of the trail.

I kept running.

I kicked my foot out of one shoe and threw it as far as I could into the woods to the right. And I whispered, "Fuck you, shoe" when I chucked it. I listened to it hit, falling like a dead bird somewhere out in the dark green. Then I kicked off the other shoe and threw it in the opposite direction. I threw it so hard, it hurt my arm.

My socks were black with mud.

I guess I was kind of insane.

No, I'll be honest. What Annie was doing to me made me completely insane, and I couldn't stand myself anymore. I pulled my socks off and left them in the trail.

Part of me wanted to strip completely naked and just run out into the woods and be some kind of free and wild boy who never had to do anything for anyone except run around naked in the forest and kill things when he got hungry. But just feeling the nylon of my running shorts against my shriveling skin, I guess, somehow reminded me that

I had a plane to catch later that day, and Calculus homework, and I was supposed to be reading *In Our Time*; and I'd been neglecting all that stuff because I was too busy thinking I was some kind of free and wild boy ever since Friday afternoon. So now it was time again to be Ryan Dean West, the fucking loser kid who's fourteen and in eleventh grade.

I sat on the wet concrete outside their front door, shivering.

I think my skin was as gray as the sky and I was hugging my knees to try and get warm when she came up to the house, holding my soaked and muddy sweatshirt and socks at her side.

"What are you doing, Ryan Dean?"

"N-nothing." I was stuttering, I was so cold. "I told you I like running in the rain. I wanted to get wet."

"I'm sorry, Ryan Dean."

"It's no big deal, Annie. Really."

"Stay there," she said, dropping my clothes on the step beside me. "I'm going to get you a towel."

# CHAPTER SIXTY

WE DIDN'T SAY THINGS LIKE WE usually do on the drive to the airport. Doc Mom asked if I had a good time and if I wanted to come back. I gave the polite one-word answers that would have been written down in a script about some other kid.

And the truth is, yeah, I had a *great* time, and, yeah, I wanted to come back so bad, it felt like I was getting stabbed in my skinny-bitch-ass chest, but just wanting that and feeling that wasn't going to change my universe.

I sat at the window on the plane.

I read "Indian Camp" and held Annie's hand for the whole flight, but I didn't say anything to her. I just looked out the window or read.

# CHAPTER SIXTY-ONE

WE WERE THE FIRST ONES BACK, so we had to wait in the airport for Joey.

And then it wouldn't be until Megan and suspended-license Chas arrived from LA that we'd take the achingly quiet and long drive back to Pine Mountain.

So we sat, silently, next to each other on the black vinyl seats in the arrivals lounge, waiting for Joey's flight from San Francisco.

It was ironic that I'd read "The Doctor and the Doctor's Wife," the second story in the Hemingway book, because I thought it was all about how guys and girls don't understand each other at all. And I was already guessing what kinds of ridiculous things Mr. Wellins would say about those first stories, but, still, I thought they were probably some of the best writing I'd ever read. Maybe it was just my mood, I don't know.

I closed the book when Annie said, "Do you want to get something to drink, or something?"

What a choice. I could have something or something.

I wondered if "something" to Annie included all the possible somethings that existed to me, and then I got mad at myself for drawing a diagram of those somethings in my head.

"I'll take some of the second something," I said.

Annie smiled.

"Are you going to talk to me?" she said.

"The Wild Boy of Bainbridge Island doesn't talk," I said. "He grunts."

She laughed. But her eyes looked sadder than they usually did.

"What do you want to talk about, Annie?"

"About how we can't be, like, in love with each other. It would be ridiculous, Ryan Dean."

I leaned my head sideways on the seat back. I think they make those things so uncomfortable just to remind you there could always be something worse than a seat on an airplane, or an eternity in hell.

Our shoulders were touching.

"Oh, I totally agree with you, Annie."

I didn't blink. I just looked right at her.

"So don't be sad, Ryan Dean."

We were so close.

"That would be ridiculous," I said.

She just watched me. I wondered if she thought I was playing, because I wasn't. I was serious then, and I had pretty much given up on everything.

I even thought that once we got back to Pine Mountain, I was going to call my dad and tell him I wanted to go home.

I needed to go home.

I was giving up.

"Did you start reading this yet?" I held the Hemingway up in front of her.

"No."

"It's really good."

"Really?"

And then she leaned even closer to me. I wondered if she noticed I'd shaved that one whisker off.

"Or something," I said.

And then I thought, *Oh my God, she's acting like she's going to kiss me. How can she be doing that? This is absolute bullshit.*

*Please kiss me, Annie.*

She closed her eyes, and very softly, she put her lips on mine. And I closed my eyes too, because I didn't know if I was madder than hell or if I wanted to cry, but why was she doing this? And it felt nicer than anything, and she tasted like the air smelled on the island, full of life and energy.

When she pulled away, we both opened our eyes.

I said, "You are going to make me completely insane, Annie."

"Me too."

We didn't even notice that Joey had been standing right there, watching us the whole time.

"Well, it's about fucking time," Joey said.

I'll say.

And Annie kind of stammered, "Uh. We were *not* just doing that, Joey."

"Yeah. That would be ridiculous," I said. "You must have been drinking on the plane if you thought you saw us kissing."

"Okay," Joey said. "I timed it and everything. It was at least a minute and a half. That's not kissing. You're right. It's *making out*. It's practically having sex in public."

I wanted to high-five Joey so bad, my hand was twitching.

What a fucking awesome thing to say, especially coming from a gay guy.

"Ugh," Annie said, "I need to go get a bottle of water."

When she left, I stood up and said, "Hell, yeah!" and, yes, a new decibel-level record was officially established for the loudest-ever, airborne (since I jumped), gay-straight high-five. Unfortunately, it was a little too loud, and Annie wasn't out of earshot on her water-shopping trip, so she gave me the patented-Annie-Altman-that-will-never-happen-again look.

"What's up with her?" Joey said.

"Dude, she is being really weird about it. She's making me crazy. I don't think she knows *what* she wants."

"Maybe she's afraid she'll get hurt," Joey said. "Because of the way you objectify every girl in the fucking world."

"Dude, Joey. Are you telling me off again?"

"No, Ryan Dean. I'm just saying. You think every girl you ever see is 'hot,' right? Maybe Annie wants to be more than that. That's what I'd think about, if I was you."

"I don't think *every* girl is hot," I said. There was, after all, Mrs. Singer downstairs. "And, anyway, if you were me, I'd be gay, in which case every girl would look exactly like Mary Todd Lincoln."

Joey laughed.

"But I think I know what you're saying," I said.

I envied Joey. He hadn't shaved since Friday morning, and he had some pretty impressive stubble going. I mourned that one whisker I'd shaved off, because I would have shown him. At Pine Mountain, if a boy showed up to class with facial hair like Joey had, they'd take him into the bathroom and make him shave on the spot with a nasty old, used razor. But on weekends, guys like Joey and Chas could just skip the whole grooming thing entirely.

I sighed.

"I shaved this morning, Joey. I had one whisker. Here. Can you see it?"

I held my chin up and pointed.

Joey leaned close and laughed.

"Yeah. Sure." And then he asked, "How was her place?"

"Incredible. I am so in love with her, Joe."

"I can see that, Ryan Dean. More than I can see that nonwhisker, that's for sure."

# CHAPTER SIXTY-TWO

I CALLED MY MOTHER FROM THE AIRPORT.

Well, to be honest, I called home hoping I'd be able to talk to my dad, but no such luck.

RYAN DEAN WEST: Hi, Mom. It's me, Ryan Dean.

I know. I'm an idiot.

MOM: Hi, sweetie! Are you back from Seattle?

RYAN DEAN WEST: I'm at the airport in Portland.

MOM: Did you have a good time, Ryan Dean?

RYAN DEAN WEST: It was the best weekend ever, Mom.

MOM: Oh.

I thought she sounded . . . sad? Awkward pause. *Very* awkward pause.

MOM (*cont.*): Is everything . . . okay, Ryan Dean? You sound different.

I can't believe it. Is she actually *crying*?

RYAN DEAN WEST: Are you *crying*, Mom?

MOM: I'm sorry, baby. You just sound so grown up all of a sudden. Did you and your girlfriend, you know . . .

*Please, someone, kill me now.*

RYAN DEAN WEST: No!

MOM: Well, did you get the package I sent? Did everything work the way the booklet said it would?

*Sniff.*

Why is it a guy can have an entire conversation with a girl and it's like she's hearing something entirely different from what is coming out of his mouth?

RYAN DEAN WEST: Mom. I am *not* calling to talk about sex.

This was so creepily disgusting. Here was the *one* person in the world with whom I would *never* want to talk about the *one* thing I think about constantly.

RYAN DEAN WEST (*cont.*): I'm calling to ask you to FedEx me a new pair of running shoes. I lost mine on the island.

MOM: Oh. I'm so sorry, sweetie.

She sounded crushed.

RYAN DEAN WEST: It's okay, Mom. They were getting too small anyway. I gained ten pounds and I'm two inches taller now than when you saw me in September. I need size ten-and-a-half. Nikes or Asics, okay?

MOM: Ten-and-a-half? *Ten-and-a-half?*

She started crying again.

Crap.

# CHAPTER SIXTY-THREE

TWO THINGS KIND OF HIT ME WHEN I saw Chas and Megan get off the flight from Los Angeles together.

First, they looked like they were tired of each other, like an old married couple who'd gone on too long of a vacation together and did not have fun; and, second, I was kind of jealous that Chas got to spend the weekend with Megan.

I know that's stupid.

Does that make me a bad person? No matter what Joey said, I wasn't ever going to be able to stop thinking of Megan Renshaw as smoking hot, and in some ways she was more accessible to me than Annie.

I'll be honest. Seeing her coming off the plane and realizing I was jealous of Chas did make me feel terrible about the whole situation. And I thought, maybe I just felt that way because in some ways I was convinced that Annie was going to throw me away again. Maybe Joey was right that Annie didn't want to get hurt, but, goddamnit, neither did I. So maybe I just looked at Megan as some type of five-out-of-five-sizzling-white-hot-crescent-wrenches on the Ryan Dean West Safety Net Tool Chart.

I still felt bad, though, and I grabbed Joey by the collar while we were waiting at baggage claim and whispered, "Joey, tell me to grow up again."

And he said, "Ryan Dean, grow the fuck up."

'Cause he saw how I'd been looking at Megan.

You know, there's this lesson in cheesy stories that says be careful what you wish for, but I was never one for cheesy stories, much less morally condescending messages, so it was kind of like dying and going to that special place with Great-Grandma and that two-dimensional Chihuahua of mine when pissed-off-at-Megan Chas grumbled that he wanted to sit in front so "Asswing can sit in the back with the other two girls."

Yeah. Whatever, Betch. Call me a girl. Call me Asswing. But, for a two-hour car ride, my legs would be simultaneously touching the legs of Megan Renshaw *and* Annie Altman, and I fully believed that would precipitate the all-time lowest blood-pressure reading north of Ryan Dean Westworld's metal-detector-tripping equator.

And then again, there was still that unopened bottle of piss, too, so call me whatever you want.

Do things like that explode? I wondered, since I'd never actually kept a bottle of piss around for more than three days—tops—before.

And I was also fully aware of how incredibly stupid I can be at times like this, so I told myself (or, Ryan Dean West said it to the Wild Boy of Bainbridge Island) that I'd better just shut up, keep my eyes forward, and not cop any obvious feels.

Yeah, right. Okay, to be honest, I can abide by the limitation of obviousness, but the "feels" part was a done deal as far as the Wild

Boy of Bainbridge Island was concerned. Oh . . . and eyes forward? Are you kidding me? So that meant shutting up. Hmm . . . That was probably out too.

We got all our stuff loaded into the SUV and piled in.

The back windows immediately fogged up. I felt myself beginning to sweat. I slipped my shoes off and kicked them under the seat, quietly contemplating the beauty of that hump in the floor, which allowed me to touch Annie's foot with my left and Megan's foot with my right.

Suddenly, I found myself in a battle of epic proportions, pitting good and pure Ryan Dean West against the crazed urges of the Humping Wild Boy of Bainbridge Island, who, undoubtedly, had been somehow infected from the saliva of that sex-starved gay pug dog and, as a result, felt a helpless compulsion to hump anything with a pulse.

I am such a loser.

I didn't even make it out of the goddamned parking lot.

RYAN DEAN WEST: Stop trying to play footsie with two girls at the same time. You're getting mud on my socks.

WILD BOY OF BAINBRIDGE ISLAND: I can take them off if you want. You know how I feel about wearing clothes, anyway.

RYAN DEAN WEST: Oh my God. You wouldn't.

(*Wild Boy of Bainbridge Island loosens his tie and begins unbuttoning his shirt.*)

●●●

"It's really hot in here," I said.

Megan smiled at me. She'd slipped off her shoe and was playing with my foot right under Chas's seat, where no one could see what was going on. I felt like I was melting. I had to do something to pull myself back away from the Wild Boy urges.

I fought.

I slipped my hand into Annie's, interlocking our fingers. I squeezed tight, our hands resting on the soft fabric of her skirt where it draped over her thigh.

God! I think I actually began hyperventilating, creating my own microclimate in the backseat, where it was as humid as a rain forest in the Amazon. Worse. It actually started *raining* in the goddamned backseat.

Megan saw that I was holding hands with Annie. She didn't look happy. She pulled her foot away and slipped it back inside her shoe. She turned her face toward the window and put her hand down on the seat between us. That's when . . . she . . . touched . . . my butt.

That gave the Wild Boy renewed strength, and good, pure, and kind Ryan Dean deflated to a wasted and wimpy 152-pound sack of crap. So in a last-ditch effort, I squeaked "I had a really great weekend" to Annie, but I sounded like a third grader on helium.

I cleared my throat. I don't know where this new Ryan Dean West came from, but I realized that everything Joey had been cussing me out about was totally true; and, worse, that Megan Renshaw was every bit as evil as Mrs. Singer.

"And, Annie, I never told you this, well, at least not the right way, but the things you make at your house—everything: the sculptures, and how your room is, your Wonder Horse, and the sounds and smells and everything—is so beautiful. It makes me feel lucky just to know you."

Score.

I rallied my strength and pulled my right foot over the hump, away from Megan, so both of my feet could be tangled up around Annie's. I leaned my head back and looked at her. Megan pinched my butt really hard, but I stifled my jerk reflex, and since it hurt so bad it made tears well in my eyes, it was a potential grand slam as far as Annie was concerned.

But the play in the outfield didn't quite unfold the way I'd imagined.

Chas said, "I just threw up in my mouth, Pussboy."

Pussboy.

Another new one.

Nice.

Megan said, "I think Ryan Dean is one of the sweetest, hottest boys I know."

Okay, I'll be honest. She actually *did* say that. And her hand was still under my butt.

Chas gave me an over-the-shoulder, "You're fucking dead, Pussboy" look.

And Annie gave me the it-was-vacation-craziness-we-are-not-ever-*ever*-going-to-kiss-again look.

Crap.

I was hosed and I knew it.

I sneezed. I suddenly felt terrible. Not terrible because of how much of a loser I was, but terrible because it dawned on me exactly why I was so sweaty and my voice wasn't working.

"Are you okay, Ryan Dean?" Annie asked. She was leaning forward in her seat, looking square at my face, so close.

"I feel like I'm getting sick," I said.

Then, as happens in my reality, all these things occurred at once:

1. (Fight or Flight) Chas turned around and said, "If you fucking puke in my car, Pussboy, I'll make you lick it up." This made me feel a little queasier.

2. (Nice) Annie gave a sympathetic "aww." She put her hand across my forehead (Bliss) to see if I had a fever and said, "Well, you shouldn't have been running around naked in the woods in the rain this morning."

3. (Hot) Megan's hand warmed up considerably, her fingers played inside my back pocket, and she said, "You were running naked in the woods? That's so incredibly sexy."

4. (Kind of thing the Wild Boy of Bainbridge Island lives to hear) Annie said, "You are really hot, Ryan Dean."

Okay, I'll be honest. I know she was talking about my having a fever. But with Megan cupping her hand under my butt cheek and cooing on one side of me, and Annie touching my face and looking so compassionately Florence-Nightingale-hot on the other, a guy can hallucinate, can't he?

# CHAPTER SIXTY-FOUR

BY THE TIME WE GOT BACK TO PINE Mountain, I had been sleeping with my head on Annie's shoulder for over an hour. I woke up when the cold air rushed in on me from the open doors.

I felt Annie let go of my hand.

"We're back," she said.

I felt sick.

"Make it be yesterday again."

Annie smiled.

The others were already around back, pulling their bags out of the SUV. Chas and Megan weren't talking to each other. Megan didn't seem to mind. She wheeled her bag away in the direction of the girls' dorm and said, "I hope you feel better, Ryan Dean."

Then I knew Chas was going to do something to get even with me.

Probably something painful, but at the very least humiliating.

Annie helped me out of the car. I put my feet down in a puddle of rainwater, then realized my shoes were still sitting on the floor beneath the backseat, where I'd left them.

I am such a loser.

"Oh my God! I'm so sorry, Ryan Dean," Annie said. But she was laughing about it too.

Of course it was funny. I just felt like crap.

I slipped my soggy socks back into my shoes and wiped the sweat from my forehead.

"You need to take a hot shower and get into bed," Annie said.

I wasn't so sick I couldn't say, "I might need some help doing that, Annie."

"You are such a pervert." She smiled, and those eyes almost made me feel better.

Joey put my bag over his shoulder and said, "Come on, I'll take this back for you."

We walked through the main gates to the campus together, and just as Annie was turning off toward her dorm, I saw Seanie and JP coming up from the lake path. I turned to Annie and grabbed her hand.

"I'll see you tomorrow, okay?"

"Yeah."

I moved a little closer. I really felt like we were supposed to kiss or something, but I didn't know. I mean, isn't that the normal thing to do after people go away for a weekend together?

"I really did have a great time, Annie. Sorry I got mad about things this morning. You know, I just feel like . . ." I looked down at my sloshing feet and said, "Whatever." I didn't want her to go.

"It's okay, Ryan Dean. Get better, okay?"

Then she let go of my hand and turned away. I sighed. I really wanted to grab her and turn her around right there in front of everyone and just kiss her, the same way we kissed in the sawmill, but I knew Annie wasn't like that, and that no matter how I felt, it wouldn't be the right thing to do. So I slumped my shoulders and followed Joey toward O-Hall, my feet slosh-slosh-sloshing behind him as he carried both of our bags.

"Hey, Nutsack, welcome back." Seanie jogged up to me. "How was the trip?"

Of course, JP stayed back on the path, away from me. And when I turned around to talk to Seanie, I saw that JP was saying something to Annie. And I saw her smile at him, and I wondered if we had that same kind of tired-of-each-other look that Chas and Megan did.

No. I knew we didn't.

"Dude, did you even hear what I've been saying?" Seanie said.

I wasn't really listening to him. I was watching Annie give JP a hug. And then JP looked right at me. It felt like getting kicked in the balls by both of them. I turned away. God, I hated him.

"Huh?" I said. "Oh. I had a great time, Seanie. It was great."

He followed along as we walked to O-Hall, and we talked about things, but I wasn't paying attention at all. I know I told him I'd gotten sick, and I know Seanie was laughing about something he'd done to someone on the Internet over the weekend, and it was probably me and probably had something to do with a Band-Aid, but it was all fogged through the filter of my sickness and how much I wanted to kill John-Paul Tureau at that moment.

# CHAPTER SIXTY-FIVE

AT MIDNIGHT, SOME ASSHOLE PULLED the sheets off my head and beamed a flashlight on my face.

"Get up, Pussboy, we're playing poker."

*Ugh.*

"Let me sleep, Chas. I'm sick. I don't mind if you guys go ahead and play."

My throat felt like I had swallowed a handful of sewing needles. Sideways.

Sheets.

Off.

On the floor.

Gravity.

Hands grabbing my legs. Being pulled over the edge.

My feet slapped down onto the cool of the floor, and someone held me up by my armpits to stop me from recracking my head open.

Crap.

I really hate Chas Becker.

I yawned, and when the fluid cleared from my eyes, I could see Joey, Casey Palmer (of all people—why'd Chas ask that dickhead to play?), and Kevin Cantrell, standing there in front of me with his right arm folded inside a black cloth sling.

"Kevin. Wow. Are you okay?" Awkwardly, I shook his left hand.

There is something really weird about being cornered into shaking a guy's left hand. It felt creepy and dirty. Standing there in my boxers didn't do anything special to make it feel closer to normal either.

I picked my sheet up from the floor where Chas had thrown it and wrapped it around me. I was shivering a little, and sweating, but I wasn't going to get dressed. I refused to.

I fully planned on going back to bed.

Chas began setting up the game, and the guys sat in a circle on the floor. I stayed on my feet.

"I'll be okay," Kevin said. "They have to see if there's going to be nerve damage. The season's over for me, though."

"That's fucked up," Chas said. "I don't know who we're going to get to lock with me now."

In rugby, locks came in pairs, like training wheels. Like balls. Chas and Kevin were arguably the most important guys in the forward pack.

Chas began shuffling.

"Get your twenty dollars out and sit down, Pussboy."

I guess he'd gotten used to my new name.

It did have a lyrical sound to it.

I said, "Pussboy's going back to bed." I looked at Casey and started to climb back up to the top bunk. I still couldn't believe *he* was there in *my* room.

Then Chas said, "Sit the fuck down and get your fucking foot off my bed."

And he sounded seriously dangerous. I knew he was pissed off about Megan. I knew we were going to have to settle it.

Joey said, "Leave him alone, Chas. He doesn't want to play."

Chas started to say something, and I could tell it was going to be horrible, too. You know how you just kind of get that oh-here-comes-Chas-Becker's-fucked-up-comment-about-me-and-Joey-being-gay-together-when-he-knows-goddamn-well-his-smoking-hot-girlfriend-loves-to-make-out-with-me feeling? So before he even fully got the first word out of his mouth, I rasped, "No big deal, Joey. I'm in."

At least, I figured, with five players instead of four, my odds were 5 percent better of not receiving *the consequence*. I grabbed a twenty from my desk and tossed it down to the Bank of Chas.

"Here," I said. "And screw you, Chas."

That's not cussing, is it?

Then Casey tried to be funny and said, "Is it just me, or is someone here about to get his ass kicked?"

"Well, if you're scared, Casey, you could go back to your room and get your pads on, you fucking human tampon," Kevin said.

That was cool. I would have high-fived Kevin, but I felt sorry for his arm.

Casey glared at Kevin. I watched him. Joey was right about Casey

Palmer. There was something cruel and cold in that kid's eyes. Casey Palmer really did know what hate was.

"Hey, come on," Joey said. Damn, Joey always stuck up for everyone. Even tools like Casey Palmer.

I sat, cross-legged, shirtless, and barefoot, with my sheet wrapped around my waist. I probably looked like Gandhi or something, so I put my hands together and said, *"Namaste."*

But Joey was the only one who got it. He laughed, while Kevin looked politely confused, and Casey looked like he was still pissed off about being called a human tampon, and Chas said, "Whatever, you fucking puss. Let's have a drink."

God.

I looked at Joey's feet. He and Kevin were wearing our rugby socks again. But this time, Kevin pulled his sweats up and showed he had a full bottle of whiskey tucked inside the top of one of his socks, and a Maxine's House of Spirits in Atlanta shot glass in the other. I rolled my eyes, but I still had to wonder if Maxine was hot, and if she lived in a haunted house, or was that just made up, and if it was a haunted house, were there any girl ghosts, and can a ghost be hot?

Yeah . . . I just knew someone was going to die tonight.

# CHAPTER SIXTY-SIX

I DECIDED THAT WHISKEY FROM A Maxine's House of Spirits in Atlanta shot glass tasted a hell of a lot better than beer from a can, even if I did notice one of Kevin Cantrell's leg hairs floating in it.

Oh, well, drinking another guy's leg hair can't kill you, can it? But it did make me feel kind of like a zombie. I mean the leg-hair thing—you know, consuming the flesh of the living—not the whiskey, because that made me feel like the Wild Boy of Bainbridge Island.

And then, too, I had to wonder what Gandhi would have thought about the whole leg-hair thing, him being a vegetarian and all.

So, yeah, I did have a drink of whiskey.

Well, to be honest, maybe two.

I know . . . I'm such a loser.

And I'm not going to feel sorry for myself or try to defend my stupidity, which had been elevated to a kind of Wild-Boy-Meets-Gandhi religion, but the whiskey did wash those sewing needles out of my throat, and I was so pissed off about JP and Annie hugging that I honestly believe I was trying to hurt myself.

I had a feeling I wouldn't be going to my classes in the morning anyway.

Eventually, the Wild Boy had just about taken over my entire consciousness, and after two tips from Maxine's shot glass, he was ready to fight Chas and Casey at the same time to settle anything left unfinished between us.

But then the Gandhi part of me said I should just let them both beat the living crap out of me until they got tired of it.

So it was a real ethical dilemma.

Kevin and Joey looked quiet and steady, like they always did. I don't think they drank as much as the other two guys while we played. Casey and Chas were pretty drunk. I thought it was a miracle that they didn't start yelling and breaking things and wake up Mr. Farrow.

After about half an hour, Chas and I were both losing badly, so it became a kind of race between us to see which of us would lose out first and get the consequence, even if the Wild Boy of Bainbridge Island kind of hoped it had something to do with running around in the woods naked in the rain and killing something with my bare hands and eating it raw.

That's when Chas said to Casey, "So what's up with all that shit on your MySite? Now you've got a picture of *his* nutsack . . ."

Chas hitchhiked his thumb at me.

Oh, great. Now everyone thinks they're my balls.

". . . with a Band-Aid on it . . ."

Of course.

Sean Russell Flaherty's creative touch, no doubt.

". . . and all this shit about how much you love *Ryan Dean West*, and there must be about fifty pictures of Pussboy on it too."

It kind of choked me up that Chas actually knew my name, and also that Seanie had that many pictures of me.

I hoped they were good ones.

"I don't know who the fuck has been doing that," Casey said.

I looked at Joey.

"You don't *really* love me, do you, Palmer?" I said.

"Do you want me to kill you now or later?" he answered.

Chas bumped Kevin's good arm and said, "Give me another shot, Maxine."

Chas downed the drink in one swallow and said, "Damn that stuff tastes terrible."

Okay, that was the precise moment the Wild Boy took complete charge of my sensibilities as the pacifist was sleeping off a binge.

I said, "You should try it with a splash of Gatorade in it, Chas."

Well, to be honest, I actually did say "Gatorade," but I was thinking "warm-four-day-old-fermented-Pussboy-piss."

He said, "You have Gatorade?"

"Only just a little."

"I'll try it. Thanks, Pusswing."

Wow. It was just like Christmas. I got another new hate-name from Chas *and* I was about to watch him drink my pee. What could be better than that?

*Dear Pussboy Ryan Dean:*

*Note to self: After I watch Chas drink my piss, it would be a good time to fully commit to NEVER kissing Megan Renshaw again.*

*Ever.*

Kevin began pouring.

"Leave some room on the arrp," I said.

"What?" Kevin asked.

I realized I had grunted.

Wild Boy had so taken control that I was losing the ability to express myself with the conventions of spoken language.

"Room. Leave some."

I took the shot glass from Kevin and chimped up to my bunk. I dug around for my Ryan Dean West Emergency Gatorade Bottle Nighttime Urinal and carefully uncapped it.

In the name of all things holy that piss stunk! I could almost feel the fetid gas cloud escaping from the mouth of the bottle and wafting like a moist cadaver's hand across my face. A quick splash, a speedy recapping, and I was back down on the floor, sweating in my loin-cloth, presenting Chas with his drink.

"Gunga Din to the rescue," I said.

"Does anyone *ever* know what the fuck you're talking about?" Chas said, and took the glass from me.

I watched.

My sheet came unraveled and fell to my feet.

I sat.

Chas drank.

*Oh, yeah. Take that, Betch.*

He squinted, cocked his head, smacked his lips, and said, "I think I like it better straight."

I looked at Joey. His mouth hung open. He looked like he was witnessing a beheading, or something even grosser, like a beheading where the victim is forced to drink some other guy's four-day-old fermented piss first. Because it dawned on me that I had told Joey about the Gatorade bottle when we were on the bus coming back to Pine Mountain from Salem.

"Fuck," Joey said. And I know he would have high-fived me, but he was too deeply repulsed, and he was probably afraid I had some piss on my hand, besides.

"What?" Chas asked.

"Nothing."

And then Christmas came twice in the same day, because Casey said, "Let me try some with Gatorade in it too."

And that's when Joey honestly looked at me like I was a depraved serial killer, or I was going to die or something, but I didn't care because I was the grunting, piss-in-your-drink Wild Boy of Bainbridge Island.

I played it unintelligibly cool.

"I only have enough *Grrrrade* left for one shot. I was going to have it—me."

I had become an ape.

Looking back, I am actually fairly surprised I didn't begin wildly sprouting hair from the vast acreage of hairlessness on my skinny-bitch-ass body.

"Fuck you, then," Casey said. "I'm going all-in."

I hadn't really been paying attention to the game, what with my jubilation over feeding Chas some piss, but I figured I had a pair of fives, which in my two-shots-in-a-152-pound-sack-of-crap perspective looked pretty good. I called. And I also said, "Well, okay, I'll give it to you, Palmer."

I monkeyed back up to my pissatorium and splashed a heavier dose for Casey.

I heard Chas say, "I call," which meant that both of us had our entire stack in play and one of us was definitely going to lose out and get the consequence, but not before that dickhead who busted my nose got his.

I climbed down and handed Casey his drink.

"No more Gatorade. Sorry, guys," I said. "Casey got the last."

I was on top of the world as I watched Casey down that shot.

Then he said, "That's pretty good."

And as he finished his shot of piss-whiskey with a satisfied piss-glistening smirk on his lips, the final card was turned. Casey busted us; and both Chas and I lost out at exactly the same moment.

PART THREE:

the consequence

# CHAPTER SIXTY-SEVEN

THAT NIGHT BECAME THE STUFF of legends.

I didn't mind losing, because I had already kicked ass on a monumental level.

It was just like T-ball: Everyone got a trophy that night.

The adrenaline surge that resulted from watching Chas and Casey both fall victim to my depravity was nearly enough to counteract the effects of the whiskey, and even though I could tell I was feverish and sick, I felt like I could take on the world.

I felt like hunting down JP Tureau and crushing him. Slowly and painfully.

And I was happy that the whiskey bottle was empty. Joey knew better than to take another drink from the Maxine's House of Spirits in Atlanta shot glass-slash-bedpan, but Kevin had no idea what was going on, so it did present me with a kind of moral dilemma that I happily avoided, because even the Wild Boy of Bainbridge Island didn't want to see an okay guy like Kevin Cantrell get piss in his mouth the same week he'd been stabbed by a punk in a street brawl.

By one in the morning, the game was over, and Casey won the hundred dollars in the bank. But in his victory, there was an understated loss that only Joey and I knew about (at least right at that moment), and history was made because it was the first time ever that *two* guys lost out at the same time, which meant Chas and I were going to suffer the crucible of the consequence together.

This was a sobering thought, too, because the Wild Boy part of me began imagining the most horrible and disgusting things that Casey would dream up involving me and a guy I hated as much as Chas.

But Casey was such an unskilled and unimaginative rookie at doling out consequences, and what he came up with hardly seemed that humiliating to me, although it did sound pretty risky.

The flashlight turned off. The only light in our room came from the gray squares cut by the moon on the floor through our windowpanes. Casey tossed the five twenties down on the cracked linoleum by my legs.

"Halloween costumes," he said.

But I was already dressed up as Gandhi-slash-Wild Boy of Bainbridge Island, I thought. Well, I would be, once I found where my sheet had gone off to in the dark.

"What?" Chas said.

"I want you guys to go into town and get Halloween costumes for all of us. Before school starts in the morning," Casey explained.

I gathered up the money. "Fun!" I said.

Yeah, I was pretty damned stupid. "But it's twenty-five miles. That's a long walk," I said. "Can I at least put some clothes on first?"

"You're an idiot," Casey said.

*Oh yeah? You drank my piss.*

I laughed out loud, then Joey cupped his hand over my mouth and whispered, "Shut the fuck up, Ryan Dean."

"Chas has a car. You have to sneak out and take his car. I don't care where you get them from, but you have to come back with costumes for all of us before first class in the morning," Casey said.

"You can't make him do that," Joey said. "Chas is too drunk to drive. They'll get killed."

*Aww, Joey. Always sticking up for idiots like Chas and losers like me.*

"I'm not too drunk," Chas said. (Idiot.)

I knew I should have fought to stay in bed that night. I dug some sweatpants out from the closet and pulled them on. They had holes in them. (Loser.)

"I'm driving, then," Joey said. He was sober. "There's nothing that says I can't go along to keep them out of trouble."

"And they better be good ones, too," Casey said.

I opened the window. There was no way I was going to try to sneak downstairs with Mrs. Singer on that floor. I sensed her Ryan-Dean-West radar was going strong.

I put one leg out over the windowsill, and Chas said, "Hey, Pussboy. Don't you think you should get on some socks and shoes, and possibly a shirt?"

Wow. All Wild Boy had on were sweatpants with holes in the crotch. No wonder I was covered in goose bumps.

"Oh."

"You are the most fucked-up useless drunk I've ever known," Chas said.

*Whatever, piss-breath.*

# CHAPTER SIXTY-EIGHT

WE SCRAMBLED OUT INTO THE DARK
and cold.

Joey led the way along the trail by the lake to the mess hall, and then we turned up the path that cut between the dorms.

I wore a black hooded sweatshirt that covered my head against the cold, but my hole-pocked, ventilated sweatpants had become too short for me and rode up past my ankles, which made my socks look like bouncing, glow-in-the-dark . . . uh . . . socks. Or something.

When we passed the dorms, I looked up at the windows on the girls' building.

"Aww," I whispered, "Annie's up there. And Megan. And Isabel. And . . ."

Yeah, I was going to list every girl I could possibly remember, hundreds of them, all so incredibly hot in their own ways. I pictured them all dressed differently in special sleeping outfits, at a big massive slumber party where the Wild Boy of Bainbridge Island was the only guest present equipped with a set of XYs, but then Chas said, "Shut up, dipshit."

We made it to Chas's car.

Luckily, nobody paid much attention to cars coming or leaving on a Sunday night, and technically, we wouldn't be considered AWOL until tomorrow morning, anyway.

But when Joey clicked the doors unlocked, Chas looked across at me and said, "Leave the dipshit here, Joey. We can take care of this by ourselves."

And I thought that was a pretty goddamned good idea, considering Chas thought it up.

But then Joey said, "I'm not going if Ryan Dean doesn't go."

Crap.

Chas said, "Crap."

For the briefest of moments, Chas Becker and I were of like mind.

I opened the back door and crawled in. At least I could stretch my legs out across the seat. I kicked my shoes off. I wished Annie could come. That would be awesome.

Just when we were about five miles away from the lights of Bannock, which was the only town close to Pine Mountain, and I was almost falling asleep, reclining sideways across the seats with my back against the car door, Chas reached over from the front and grabbed my leg so hard, he tore the inseam on my pants open all the way from my crotch to my knee.

He said, "Now you're going to tell me everything about what's going on with you and Megan."

He must have been stewing about it for days now.

And I can't say I didn't know this was coming.

I'd seen how Megan and Chas looked, getting off that plane. I witnessed firsthand Megan's subtle teases about me in the backseat of that same car as we all drove back to school from our weekends. And, honestly, my back was still bruised from when Chas slammed me up against the soap dispenser the day he caught Megan rubbing her hand on my leg in the mess hall.

But knowing all that still didn't lessen the adrenaline jolt of fear that shot through me.

No matter how smart I thought I could be at a moment like that, I couldn't think of anything to tell him except the truth.

Joey joked, "Don't make me pull this car over, boys."

Chas wasn't loosening his grip.

He wasn't smiling, either.

I swallowed. The pins came back to my throat. My voice cracked as I said, "What do you want to know, Chas?"

Joey tried changing the subject. "I'm going to stop and get some coffee at the gas station here. You guys want some?"

"Yeah," I said. "And I need to pee."

"Me too," Joey said.

Chas let go of my leg. Joey pulled the car in to a minimart gas station. It was really quiet when he turned off the engine.

Nobody moved.

Awkward.

"We've kind of been fooling around," I said.

There. I said it. Finally.

I noticed that Joey had been just about to shoulder his door open, but he froze as soon as he heard my confession.

It echoed like an empty church in that car. I don't think anyone so much as took a breath after I said it. And I know Joey was thinking about what he should do if Chas jumped into the backseat and began murdering me on the spot.

"We just kissed a few times. That's all."

Well, actually, it was exactly twenty-four times, but I felt justified in using the generic "few," realizing that any number greater than "never" was as good as saying "twenty-four."

I could see Joey's eyes in the rearview mirror.

Then Chas did something that nobody would ever have expected. He turned away from me and sighed. He actually looked like it hurt him to hear what I'd said.

"That's what she told me yesterday," he said. "I didn't believe her. I thought she was just screwing around with me. You know how Megan is. Why the fuck would you do something like that to a guy on your own team, Winger?"

"I don't know."

Okay, why do teenagers use that answer so often, especially when we really *do* know? Of course I knew why I did it, and so did Chas, and so would anyone else who ever looked one time at Megan Renshaw.

Then I said, "We're not doing it anymore."

I put my shoes on and opened my door.

"I'm going to pee," I said.

I heard Joey get out of the car behind me. Chas stayed in the passenger seat. As I was rounding the corner to the men's room, Joey caught up to me.

"Damn, Ryan Dean. I think Chas is crying," he said.

"Why am I such a punk, Joe?"

"I tried telling you," Joey said. "You want coffee?"

"Yeah. Black."

Joey went inside the minimart, and I went around back and peed in the bushes. I can't stand gas station men's rooms. I met Joey around front again, and he handed me two cups in paper sleeves. He held an elastic keychain, wrapped around his wrist.

"You need a key for the toilets," he said.

"I peed in the trees."

Joey said, "Oh. I'll be right back."

He went around the corner, and when I got back to the car, Chas was gone.

# CHAPTER SIXTY-NINE

WE SPENT THE NEXT FIFTEEN MIN-
utes looking for Chas around the gas station, even walking both directions away from it along the road, but we couldn't find any trace of
him.

It started raining again, so Joey and I went back to the car and sat.

"I don't know where he'd go," Joey said.

I had a good idea Chas was probably running around in the
woods naked, looking for something to kill. Probably something that
weighed exactly 152 pounds.

I sighed.

"You really did make him drink pee tonight, on top of everything
else, didn't you?"

"Casey, too," I said.

"Damn. Well, he's probably not heading back to PM. It's way too
far." Joey looked at his wristwatch. "It's a little after two. We can finish
this costume hunt, and maybe we'll find him on the way back. I'm
sure we will. He's gotta be around here somewhere, just sitting alone,
cooling off. We might get back in time to sleep a couple hours, at
least, that way."

I didn't really feel bad about anything I'd done, but I did feel
sorry that Chas was hurting over Megan, because I knew that feeling

firsthand. But I tried to remind myself how stupid it was for me to feel sorry for a guy like Chas. Still, the whole thing made me think about how crazy I was for Annie, and how JP was trying to do the same thing to me that I'd been doing to Chas all along.

"Okay." I yawned.

Joey started the car and we drove into Bannock.

"You don't need to say it, Joey. I know this is all my fault."

"It's not *totally* your fault, Ryan Dean," he said. "But you did let it go a little too far."

"Yeah." My eyes scanned ahead. I saw the lights of an all-night grocery store. What grocery store *wouldn't* have costumes for sale just four days before Halloween?

"Hey, Joey," I said. "Why don't you have a boyfriend or anything?"

"What makes you think I don't?"

"Well, no one ever sees you with anyone at school. I mean, not like that," I said.

"I wouldn't do that at school. It would be too much trouble for both of us."

"Oh. So you do have a boyfriend?"

"Of course."

"Well I'm glad for you, then. It sucks being alone. Believe me, I know. Let's try this store," I said, and pointed to the supermarket. I really didn't want to find out too much about Joey's boyfriend, because it made me feel really awkward. I just wanted to know if Joey was okay in his life, because, like I said, I really liked Joey. But I do mean that in a totally non-gay way.

Joey pulled in to the parking lot. It was nearly empty, dark, and rain slicked, with a few scattered shopping carts reflecting the headlights from Chas's car.

"Are there even any other gay guys at Pine Mountain?" I asked.

Joey laughed. "Oh my God, Ryan Dean, why do you care? You're not *curious*, are you? Did Chas completely scare you off girls or something? 'Cause I wouldn't believe that could ever happen."

I shrugged. "No. I was just wondering. 'Cause I can't tell. I mean, I would have never even thought you were gay except you told me. But I do know *exactly* how many fourteen-year-old juniors there are at Pine Mountain. One. And he's a skinny-ass-loser. But he's not gay."

"Well, there are a lot of gay kids at Pine Mountain."

"Hopefully, JP Tureau?" I said.

That would be awesome. Then I wouldn't have to worry about anything.

Joey laughed out loud. "You know? You and Kevin are, like, the only straight guys who've ever talked to me about *me*, about this stuff, who weren't trying to play some kind of fucked-up game, Ryan Dean."

"Well, why not? You're my friend. You're probably the best guy friend I have. But I don't think I could ever be gay."

"Everyone knows you're not gay," Joey said, and I thought, *Phew! That's a relief*, just in case Joey was wondering if I was gay and trying to make, well, gay small talk, and then I thought, damn, that was a screwed-up thing to think about my best friend.

"But you want to know something crazy? And you can't say anything to anyone about this, Ryan Dean. You know who's been seriously trying to hit on me ever since school ended last year? Ever since I came out to everyone?" And then Joey paused to see if I would make a guess (which, I would have said Sean Russell Flaherty just because he's so, well, not like other guys), but Joey said, "Casey Palmer. Can you believe it? Casey Fucking Palmer is gay. That's why he begged Chas to get in the game with us tonight. He won't leave me alone. He fucking scares me, he's so hopped up about getting with me."

Wow. That was a monumental secret, a career-builder for a guy like Seanie Flaherty. If Seanie kept such records, he would easily call that piece of info five out of five J. Edgar Hoovers in off the shoulder sundresses on the Sean Russell Flaherty Ruin Your Life Rating Scale.

"Casey Palmer is *gay*?"

"I'm pretty sure he wasn't hitting on me because he thought I was a girl," Joey said.

"Casey Palmer is *gay*?" I said again. Then I doubled over, laughing.

"Remember," Joey said, "you are *not* going to say anything, okay? You know, football and everything. He's a piece of shit, but leave him alone about it."

"I pissed in his drink," I said. "A lot. And the idiot thought it tasted good too."

"Yeah. You've got balls, Ryan Dean. Except for when it comes to girls."

"Well, he deserved it. He busted my nose."

Then Joey stepped out of the car and said, "Come on. Let's get some Halloween crap and get the fuck out of here."

And as I followed Joey into the store, I kept asking him, "What do you mean, 'except for when it comes to girls'?"

But he just said, "Never mind."

# CHAPTER SEVENTY

IN LESS THAN THIRTY MINUTES, we paid for five Halloween costumes, two tall cans of energy soda (I believed one of us was going to puke before we got back, and I hoped it would end up on Chas's leather upholstery), and some cold medicine and throat lozenges for me.

I opened the box of cold pills before we were out of the store and popped three of them into my mouth. I washed them down with the energy drink.

So, yeah . . . between the whiskey, the cold pills, the energy drink, cherry-menthol (is there anything that tastes more unnaturally disgusting?) throat lozenges, and the pumped-up rushed feeling from completely ruining Chas Becker's life, I was pretty much prepared to have some kind of seventies-Grateful-Dead-flashback-only-it-was-twenty-years-before-I-was-born experience.

We found some passable costumes for the five of us who played the game that night, too, even though I tried to convince Joey not to get one for Chas; and that way he could be the Invisible Man. But Joey said that wasn't funny, because if we didn't find Chas and he got into trouble or something, it would look like we'd stolen his car and ditched him.

Here's what we ended up with (in alphabetical order):

*Becker, Charles:* Well, we found Chas a Superman cape, but there was nothing to go with it. Fortunately, the supermarket sold kids' underwear and we bought him a three-pack of boys' size XL briefs with Pokémon characters on them. Then we also got him some red women's pantyhose to go underneath the briefs. So, basically, Chas's most horrible night in his life had just gotten worse. Oh, well, that's what he gets for leaving me and Joey alone and trusting us to be in charge of his future.

*Cantrell, Kevin:* Kevin would be the token pirate. We found him a hat, an eye patch, and a plastic hook we thought would look perfect sticking out from his black arm sling.

*Cosentino, Joseph:* Joey got the cool costume: prison stripes from Alcatraz, a fitting outfit for someone who was spending his senior year in O-Hall.

*Palmer, Casey:* Casey lucked out in a big way. We chose one of those plastic face masks of Wonder Woman and a golden lasso rope accessory for the guy with the serious case of the hots for Joey. We could have been much, much crueler, and even Joey admitted that he thought Casey would be jealous because Chas's costume was so much gayer. Of course, I had to laugh about that.

*West, Ryan Dean:* A discovery of true Zen-like perfection, I got a leopard-spotted caveman-loincloth kind of thing that had one suspender strap that tied in a knot over the shoulder. The Wild Boy of Bainbridge Island would be in full effect on Thursday night in O-Hall.

Score.

The O-Hall boys were not allowed to go to the dance with Pine Mountain's good boys and girls, but that would not stop us from dressing up and having our own Halloween.

We left the store with our bags of goods, determined to seek out Chas's hiding place and get back to Pine Mountain in time to scrounge at least three hours of sleep before class, but it wasn't going to turn out to be that easy.

Just as Joey opened his door, a voice came from the darkness in the lot behind the car.

"Can I talk to you boys a minute?"

And my juvenile-delinquent-from-Boston self instantly thought, great, it's a cop. A man cop, no less, to make things even worse. But when I turned around, I realized that unless the Bannock Police Department hired hundred-year-old officers who got around with walkers, we were pretty safe. And even if they did, I thought, I knew it would be easy enough to talk Joey into making a run for it.

Or a brisk walk for that matter.

The old man came out of the rain at the speed of a newborn glacier, taking two steps, then lifting the walker, then setting it down, then two steps, lift, set. I rubbed my chin to see how much that one whisker had grown in the time it took for him to get to Joey's side of the car.

And why does Joey always have to be so goddamned nice and understanding?

Joey said, "Leave us alone and go to hell, fucking crusty old man."

Well, um . . . to be honest, Joey didn't actually *say* that. I think I was wishing it so hard, I actually imagined it, which was the girliest thing I've probably ever done in my life. He actually just said, "Sure."

Two steps. Lift. Set.

I needed a shave.

And the poor guy looked terrible. He had a dirty white beard and just kept his eyes fixed ahead, staring at me and Joey as he two-stepped-lifted-set inch by inch, wearing what looked like rain-soaked and food-stained pajamas.

"Can you boys please give me a ride home? I'll pay you," he said.

*Please, for once in your life, don't be nice, Joey.*

"What are you doing out here?" Joey said.

"I just went for a walk," he said.

And I thought, he either lives about twelve feet away from here or he started his walk during the Reagan Administration.

"And then I got caught in this damned rain."

"Where do you live?" Joey asked.

No!

But it was too late. I knew Joey and I were both helplessly being sucked into a black hole of Joey Cosentino's niceness.

"I live in a residential group home for child molesters who kill teenage boys with hatchets," he said.

Okay, I'll be honest. I think the whiskey-cold-medicine-energy-soda-disgusting-cherry-menthol-throat-lozenge-lack-of-sleep effect was taking its toll on me. What he *really* said was something like, "I live in Bannock on Battle Point Lane. It's about two miles from here."

"We could call you a cab," I said. I held the remainder of the poker bank out in my hand. "We'll even pay for it."

"Naw," Joey said. "Come on. We'll take you home."

Good old perfect Joey.

Goddamnit.

"Thank you," he said. "Thank you boys so much."

I just hoped he killed Joey first.

We loaded the old man's walker and our bags into the back of Chas's SUV, then helped him up into the passenger seat beside Joey. I sat in the back and hunted around for something that could be used as a weapon.

"Joey?" I said from the backseat as he started the car.

"What?"

"Why are my pants ripped all the way down and my underwear hanging out?"

"Remember? Chas?"

"Um. No."

That cold medicine was the shit.

"Maybe you should go to sleep, Ryan Dean."

"Why are we driving Chas's car without him?"

"I'll tell you about it tomorrow."

"You're the best, Joey."

Joey shook his head. When we came to the entrance to the parking lot, the old man pointed him to turn right. Then he patted Joey on the shoulder and said, "Thanks again. You're going to take a right up here at Haley Street. By the way, my name is Ned."

And then Ned dug around in his pocket and said, "How much do you want for the cab ride, boys?"

"You don't need to pay us," Joey said.

I closed my eyes and lay down across the seat. Then I felt the car turn right and begin lurching forward along a bumpy, unpaved road.

"This is Battle Point," Joey said. "How far up here do you live?"

Then I knew we were completely hosed.

Ned said, "Where?"

It began pouring.

Joey said, "Is this your street?"

And Ned said, "I live in Waterloo, Iowa."

Oh, yeah. Me and Joey. Both total losers.

So I said, "Ned? Will you please kill Joey first? He really, really deserves it."

# CHAPTER SEVENTY-ONE

SO THERE WE WERE, IN THE MIDDLE
of the fucking night, in the rain, on an unlighted dirt—make that
"mud"—road somewhere between Oregon and Bolgia Nine in the Eighth
Circle of Hell with an ax-wielding sodomist in a walker who thought he
was in Waterloo goddamned Iowa.

Good times.

Ned stared blankly out the windshield. "I don't remember any of
this in Waterloo."

"Oh, *that* Waterloo," I said. "So, Ned, was Napoleon really as short
as everyone says?"

"What?" Ned said. Then he pointed out the window in front of
Joey. "I think you took a wrong turn, son. Where's the Cedar River
from here?"

"We're in the middle of it, Ned," I said.

Joey stopped the car, right there in the middle of the river of mud
that used to be a road. Not that we were running the risk of blocking
any traffic, that is, unless salmon used this fucking road to spawn on.

Spawning salmon . . . *awww* . . . made me think of Annie. God!
I'd never see her again! I felt like I would start crying, but I became
determined that I had to live so I could stop JP from depositing his
genetically inferior milt all over her.

"But you remembered this road and how to get here," Joey said. "And how far it was. Are you sure you didn't want to come to Battle Point Lane?"

"Is this Battle Point Lane?" Ned asked.

"Yes," Joey said.

"Are we in Waterloo?" Ned asked. "My son lives there."

"Catch and release, Joey," I said. "Let's put him back where we found him."

"Maybe he'll recognize his house if we find one up there." Joey nodded his chin in the direction of the road-torrent.

I didn't see any houses up there.

"Maybe he'll remember the spot where he hid all the bodies of the other kids he tricked into taking him here," I said.

"What?" Ned said.

"Ryan Dean"—Joey looked over his shoulder at me—"I really think you should try to go to sleep."

He sounded a little stressed.

Joey started the car forward slowly.

I said, "Here, Joe. Do you want a cough drop?"

I dropped one of the paper-wrapped lozenges in his hand.

"Thanks," he said.

"Don't thank me. They taste like crap. But they keep you awake."

"Then stop eating them."

"I think it's just up ahead," Ned said.

That's exactly when the driver's side of the car lurched downward sharply and the axle struck against something hard, with a grating, metallic clang. We were in a hole up to the top of the car's wheels. Joey tried backing the SUV out, but we were stuck.

Oh, yeah, and that's when the water started coming in through the bottom of Joey's door, too.

"Fuck!" Joey said.

"Don't give him any ideas," I warned.

"This isn't the place," Ned said. "I'm sure of it."

And that's probably about the time that Joey seriously considered throwing the old man out too. If it wasn't precisely at that moment, I'm sure he felt like it when Ned started screaming insanely in wild terror.

You know, there is something especially frightening when you're stuck in the darkest depths of hell, in the middle of a raging torrent of mud, and the insane old lost guy in the front seat starts screaming like he's going to die. I mean, I figured Ned had probably stared Death in the face more than a few times in just the past four or five hours, let alone since the discovery of fire, so when you hear a guy who you know has gone through as much shit as Ned has—in a lifetime that was undoubtedly measured by geologic periods as opposed to calendars—screaming like that, well . . . you just know you're going to die too.

"Fuck!" Joey said again.

"Aaaaaaahhhhhhh!!!!!!!!" Ned shrieked.

Oh, yeah.

Fun times.

Honestly, though, I have to admit to the selfish pleasure I took in the fact that the water was pouring in on the two fuckers in the front seat and not on the guy in the back who never would have come up to Ned's abattoir for adolescent boys if Joey wasn't so goddamned nice all the time.

Then Ned added something extra special to his scream. It kind of went like this: "BBBLLLLLAAAAARRRRRHHHHHHHHHH-HAAAAAAAAAGG!!!!!!!"

Which, I think, was probably Mrs. Singer's first name.

But, anyway, the bloodcurdling sound was so unnerving that I screamed too, and just like a girl, which didn't make Joey very happy.

"Fuck!" Joey said.

And when I screamed, it made Ned scream even more insanely.

I began laughing so hard, I was actually crying, which probably had something to do with the fact that I knew we were going to die and now I decided I didn't want Ned to kill Joey first, because watching him do it would scare the shit out of me.

Ned shrieked again. It was a good one, too. Probably a solid fifteen seconds. And it was so high pitched that I'm pretty sure a pod or two of migrating gray whales in the Pacific veered off course for a minute, paused and looked landward, and knew exactly where that hundred-and-fifty-year-old asshole was, even if Joey and I didn't have a fucking clue.

I laughed so hard, I thought I was going to throw up.

"What's so fucking funny?" Joey said.

I could hear the wheels spinning uselessly in the muddy water outside, and the splashy-soothing-fountain sounds of Joey's and the insane guy's feet up front.

Then all I could hear was another scream. If I wasn't laughing so hard, I probably would have beat Ned with his walker.

"I'm sorry, Joey." I laughed. "Now I can finally say I told you so." I paused. "Bitch."

That's technically not cussing.

I laughed.

Ned shrieked and wailed.

Joey said, "Fuck!"

"Okay, Joe. I'll get out and see if there's anything I can put under the wheels to get some grip."

"But you're sick, Ryan Dean."

"Dude, Joey," I said (scream). "Believe me, there's nothing I want more than to get out of this car right now."

I opened my door and looked down. The water rushed past the car's running boards so fast, it looked like we were in a motorboat or something. I could see how the back wheels were spinning uselessly, kicking back rooster tails of mud in the dark.

I knew I'd end up getting soaked, which wasn't a good idea, so I slipped off my socks and shoes and left them on the car seat. Then I pulled up the legs of my sweatpants as high as I could and stepped out into the cold and muddy flow.

Ned screamed again.

Damn, he had quite a set of pipes for an old guy.

I waded around to the back of the SUV, already wet up to my waist.

I yelled up to Joey, "Stop gunning it. I'm going to look for something to wedge under the wheels."

Ned gave me an approving "EEEEEYYYYAAAAAAAAAGGGGH-HHH!!!"

I paused.

I slogged up to Joey's window and knocked on it. The water was streaming into the rip in my sweats, pulling them away like a drift net. I hoped salmon didn't bite.

I knocked on Joey's window again.

He lowered it halfway.

"Joey," I said.

Ned screamed, and Joey tensed and closed his eyes like it physically hurt him.

"Suppose I had a gun. With only one bullet in it. And I gave it to you. Would you shoot Ned, me, or yourself?" I laughed. Life doesn't present a guy with too many the-lady-or-the-tiger kinds of lessons.

Joey flipped me off and raised his window.

Ned wailed.

Through the open back door, I heard Joey say, "Fuck!" It sounded kind of nice. It lifted my spirits.

I waded away. I actually considered, momentarily, just leaving Joey and Screaming Ned there, so I could become the Wild Boy of the Eighth Circle of Hell, but I did want to get back to Pine Mountain and Annie and a certain kid of French descent whose dreams still needed some serious crushing.

And, besides, we had another rugby game coming up that week, and the team would never be able to get by without Kevin, our winger, and our starting fly half.

When I got out of the creek we were stuck in, I found enough fallen tree bark and rocks to begin making sufficient braces all around the rear wheels. On the first trip back to the car, though, I fell down in the river, so I took my hoodie off and tossed it onto the backseat with my shoes and socks. No sense getting everything I owned soaked and muddy. I knew it was stupid, because I was sick, but I figured I'd be able to scrounge up something dry to wear among our new Halloween costumes.

Everything looked ready to go. I waded to the car and told Joey to try backing out, and that I'd stand away and watch. Before I closed my door, Ned screamed again, and then I said, "And, Joey? We are either going back to the store or I'm not getting in this car ever again. It'll be you and Ned. Alone."

Joey didn't say anything.

I closed the back door and walked over to the side of the mud road.

The rain slowed to a drizzle, but the level of the creek didn't change at all.

The SUV's reverse lights came on.

Slowly, shakily, Joey got Chas's car unstuck. He backed it up to the side of the road, where I was waiting for him. I got in the backseat, dripping and shivering.

It was three in the morning.

# CHAPTER SEVENTY-TWO

NED STOPPED SCREAMING WHEN WE got back to the store.

Joey didn't say a word the whole way there. And I just sat in the backseat with my arms hugged across my bare chest, smiling all the time because of how stupid we were for trying to do a good deed for a lunatic like Ned.

The worst part of the whole experience—no, wait . . . it wasn't the worst part, because being stuck in the car with Screaming Ned was worse, and something even worse than that, still, was going to happen to me before the night was over.

So, okay, a pretty screwed-up part of the whole experience happened when we took Ned back to the store. I guess I truly did look like the Wild Boy of the Eighth Circle of Hell, because I was soaked and covered in mud, barefoot and shirtless, with my boxers hanging out from a gaping hole in my torn sweatpants that were pulled up past my bony kneecaps; and the store manager laughed at us when we offered to pay for a cab for the old fucker. He asked us if "Screaming Ned" had played his old funny trick again where he'd take foolish do-gooders out to the middle of the forest and scare the living shit out of them.

And we said . . . uh . . . um . . . no?

Oh, yeah. He said Screaming Ned was a regular fucking celebrity in Bannock.

And the manager laughed at us and walked Ned (Two steps. Lift. Set. Two steps. Lift. Set.) next door, to the donut shop owned by Screaming Ned's fucking alcoholic son, who had been sleeping behind the counter while Ned did his performance art on me and Joey.

Yeah, I don't think Joey would have even batted an eye if I told him I was going to throw a shopping cart through the window of that goddamned donut shop.

When we left, I got into the backseat again.

Joey said, "The water's all gone from up front, Ryan Dean. You can sit up here."

"I need to get some dry clothes on, Joey. And there was no way I was about to get undressed in front of Screaming Ned. I'm going to break down and do it, Joey. I'm freezing, and I'm going to put on some of those Pokémon briefs."

Now, *that* was the worst part of the whole Screaming Ned episode.

Anyway, it was a three-pack, and I was pretty sure Chas wouldn't count to see if one was missing.

"Joey," I said as he started the car (finally!) along on its way out of the parking lot. "Please turn up the heater. And, by the way, I've never been completely naked in a car alone with a gay guy before."

There was this raw-meat sucking sound as I tore my sweats and boxers down over my feet.

Joey laughed. "Neither have I. But, Ryan Dean, don't try on the pantyhose."

"Uh. Joey? Wasn't going to. Ass."

Joey laughed.

I pulled on my dry socks.

It was really weird. Those Pokémon briefs were surprisingly comfortable, and I hadn't worn briefs since I was in, like, third grade. I put on Joey's convict pants, pulled on my hoodie, and climbed up into the front seat beside Joey, just as we came to the gas station where we'd lost Chas earlier.

"I feel a lot better," I said. "I swear I won't wreck your prison pants."

"I swear to God I won't pick up any more psychos."

"Does that mean we *aren't* going to look for Chas?"


We found Chas Becker walking back along the road toward Pine Mountain. He was wearing one of those big plastic yard-leaf bags. He must have gotten it from a sympathetic gas station clerk; and he kind of looked like a big, reflective, black ghost when we passed him.

Joey slammed on the brakes and backed the car up right on the highway until Chas lifted his down-turned head and saw it was us. I started to climb over to the backseat, but Joey grabbed my hood and pulled me back, saying, "No way. I do *not* want to sit by him, Ryan Dean. Let him sit there."

The next thing I knew, Chas was tearing off his garbage-bag rain slicker and getting into the backseat.

"You guys are assholes," Chas said. "I was almost going to call the cops and say you stole my fucking car. Pricks."

"We tried to find you, Chas," Joey said. "You took off; it wasn't our fault."

I was staying out of it entirely, but after a few seconds, Chas said, "Well, fuck you anyway, Winger. I still don't think we're settled about this."

I just looked at Joey, but I didn't say anything.

But at that moment, I knew I was going to stay away from Megan Renshaw, even if I also knew how difficult she could make keeping that commitment. And, hell, I knew how weak I was too, and I don't mind admitting it.

I sighed.

I just had to think about Annie.

It had been such an incredibly long day that started way back when she came into my room while I was still in bed and we went running in the rain together on Bainbridge Island.

Then, all of a sudden, Chas threw my soggy sweatpants and boxers onto the dashboard in front of me, which kind of made Joey swerve the car because it startled him. It sounded like a rump roast being dropped onto a basketball court.

Chas leaned over from the backseat and looked at me.

"Are you naked? What the hell were you two homos doing in my car back here?"

Then we had to tell him the whole story. Well, to be honest, Joey told it to him, because I was shutting up for the rest of the night. And it wasn't really the whole story, either. Joey told him about the costumes, and then how we picked up Screaming Ned, but he wisely left out the part about getting Chas's car stuck in a fucking flash flood. He just said I fell in a creek when I was helping Ned get to his house.

So Chas said, "What a total do-gooder dipshit."

And I left it at that.

But I made him drink pee.

And I made out with his smoking-hot girlfriend too.

Somehow, miraculously, we made it back to O-Hall, and I was finally in bed (although I was sharing my accommodations with a now-lighter bottle of urine—which made me think, as far as a bottle of piss is concerned, are you more of an optimist if you think it's half-empty?—and a still-unopened FedEx mailer of condoms and porn from my mom).

I was completely, irreversibly, asleep by five o'clock.

# CHAPTER SEVENTY-THREE

YOU KNOW, THERE IS SOMETHING tragically disappointing in two hours' sleep after an epic night like that.

So, when the alarm went off at seven, I dreamed I was back in that car, stuck in the river, sitting behind Screaming Ned as he sharpened his meat cleavers.

Chas wasn't in too much of a hurry to get up and hit the snooze button either, and when I did finally stumble down from the top bunk, I couldn't figure out how to turn the goddamned thing off, so I just yanked the plug from the wall.

But it was one of those clocks with a battery backup, since we lose power so much in that old dorm, and it kept Screaming-Nedding at me.

So I put it under my pillow.

*Think about Annie.*

*Think about Annie.*

I wanted to stay in bed so bad. I knew I was horribly sick from all the crap I'd been through in the past twenty-four hours, but I had to force myself to think about Annie Altman, because I knew I had to get in JP's way as much as I possibly could for the next three days, before Halloween.

So I had to make myself go to school.

I left a groaning Chas Becker and the door open behind me and stumbled down the hallway toward the showers, dragging my towel along the floor at my feet, with my eyes crusted over and half-closed.

I saw Mr. Farrow standing at his doorway. He cocked his head toward me, kind of like a cat who'd been sprayed in the face with a squirt gun. Then I saw a couple guys coming out of the bathroom, and one of them pointed and started laughing at me.

I looked down.

Oh, yeah.

Pokémon.

Briefs.

Crap.

I am such a loser.

What could I do? I looked at the guys straight on. I kept walking toward the showers.

I said, "Oh yeah. Admit it. You know you want some of these bad boys."

# CHAPTER SEVENTY-FOUR

BUT I MISSED ANNIE AT BREAKFAST, and I barely made it to Conditioning class on time, having to run and attempt to tie a necktie with shaking hands the whole way from O-Hall to the athletics complex.

I was a mess.

That day, getting through my world was like trying to swim in a pool of warm mayonnaise while carrying two bowling balls.

I just had to keep telling myself I could do it, but I had a hard time convincing the tired and sick Ryan Dean West.

I knew ahead of time that I wasn't going to say *anything* to Seanie about what I'd done the night before. As great as the story was, I'd have to keep all those things bottled up—how I'd gotten drunk again and made Chas and Casey drink my piss, the drive into Bannock and how Chas started crying and ran away when he found out I'd been making out with his girlfriend, learning about how Casey was gay and had been hitting on Joey, getting our Halloween costumes, and, of course, the lunatic Screaming Ned—and hope I didn't explode from not being able to tell. Because most of it just wasn't the kind of stuff I'd want everyone in the whole world finding out about on some new perverted website designed by our demented scrum half.

I had to run in regular tennis shoes in Conditioning class because of what I'd done with my running flats on Bainbridge Island the day before. God! I could not believe that only twenty-four hours had passed since I tore my clothes off in the rain during that run with Annie. Hopefully, my mom would get those new shoes to me by the afternoon, even if she was probably still crying about my growing up, getting taller, having sex, and whatever else she imagined that wasn't really happening to me.

We were sent out on the three-mile lake run, and this time I decided I was going to stay right there with Seanie and JP. No matter what, I wasn't going to let JP try to get between me and Seanie, too. Even if they were roommates and we did hate each other, I was going to stay friends with Seanie Flaherty.

We ran three across, with Seanie in the middle of us, slowly, in the back of the pack. It stopped raining, and our legs were splattered with mud to our thighs. I thought if I talked to Seanie the whole way, even about stupid stuff, it would shut JP up and make him mad at the same time.

"Hey, Nutsack, did you guys play cards last night?" Seanie asked.

"Yeah."

"Well, did you win? Did you lose? Did you get drunk? What happened?"

"I'm not saying, Seanie."

"Dude, one of these days all you guys are going to get thrown out of school for that shit."

"Oh. Tough break. Throwing me out of O-Hall," I said. "Casey Palmer played with us."

Have you ever noticed how, when you're going into a conversation and you tell yourself ahead of time, do *not* say anything about *X*, your mouth will almost automatically start spilling its guts about *X* before you can do anything to stop it? So I kind of felt my stupid-hungover-cherry-menthol mouth beginning to say, "And Casey Palmer is gay and won't stop chasing after Joey," but just in the nick of time steered clear of it and said, "And Casey Palmer . . . *won*."

"Why'd you play with *that* asshole?"

I shrugged.

*Shut up, Ryan Dean.*

"Hey, by the way," Seanie said, "did I tell you? I'm taking Isabel to the dance."

"Nice," I said. Why the hell did he have to bring that up? "Isabel's hot."

(If you happen to have a thing for girls with faint moustaches.)

"You think every girl is hot. Didn't you get any of that pent-up sexual frustration out of your system at Annie's house over the weekend?"

(If anything, the weekend made it worse.)

I sighed, picturing Annie and me pressed up against that painted wall in the sawmill. Then I took a dig at JP.

"I sure did."

Seanie high-fived me.

But that was all I was going to say, because if I said anything about fooling around with her in the hot tub, or making out at the sawmill and in the airport, or how she woke me up both mornings—God!

Just thinking about it was making me crazy—I knew they'd both go straight to Annie and tell her what I'd said.

I coughed.

Seanie said, "I saw Annie this morning. She said you got sick from running in the woods naked in the rain. Did you really do that?"

(Well, I wasn't completely naked, but I'd take another shot over JP's bow.)

I laughed. "Yeah."

"Damn."

"I'm not going to be at practice today," I said. "I'm going to get my stitches out this afternoon."

I could feel JP peering around Seanie to look at me.

Seanie said, "Go in there extra muddy and maybe that hottie nurse will give you another sponge bath."

"My luck, Doctor No-gloves will want to check out my nuts again."

"Just tell him all he has to do is look at Casey Palmer's website." Seanie laughed.

"Yeah. Very funny, Seanie. I heard about that. Trouble is, he's seen mine in real life, so he'd know that those baby ones in your picture are so small, they could only belong to Sean Russell Flaherty." I shoved him, and he came within a hair's breadth of crashing into JP.

"Ouch. Good one," Seanie said.

"Watch it, fucker." JP almost tripped avoiding Seanie. I had no doubt he was pissed off at me now.

I was pretty sure the whole class had passed us by that time; I saw them all running back from the turnaround in the opposite direction. I stopped at the turn and folded my hands together on top of my head, then gave JP a dirty look.

I'll admit it. I felt like fighting him.

"Something wrong?" I said to him.

"You almost knocked Seanie into me," JP said. "Fuck you, Ryan Dean. I know what you're trying to do."

I kept my hands on my head, but I stepped right up to him. I know that was stupid. JP could kill me. He was a good four inches taller. And, yeah, I did cuss. But there is nothing else a guy can do at a time like that.

"No. Fuck *you*, JP." I know. Not a very good comeback. Then I said, "What the hell do you think you're doing asking Annie out? Aren't there enough girls here who'd go out with you so you wouldn't have to fuck over one of your former best friends?"

I'd been saving that up for about a week, and it sure felt good to get it out. Just like it was going to feel to get those stitches out, I thought. If I lived until the afternoon.

Seanie said, "Hey, come on. Stop it. Let's just run, guys."

Too late. I let go of my hands and dropped them in front of my chest and shoved JP back toward the water's edge.

He came right back at me and threw a hellacious punch with his right fist, but his foot slipped away in the mud beneath him, so what would probably have knocked me out cold ended up glancing off my left rib cage. It hurt bad enough, though. In fact, I was pretty sure it cracked a rib. But I turned with JP's punch and cocked a straight right fist and fired it square into his nose.

JP's head snapped back, and purple blood sprayed from beneath my knuckles as he lost his balance and fell backward—right into the muddy shallows of the lake.

On the Ryan Dean West Stimulus-Satisfaction scale of things, it was without a doubt one of the best physical sensations of my entire, pathetic life. In fact, as I thought about it, punching that bastard was right up there in the top three:

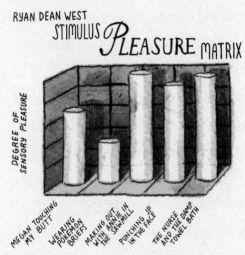

RYAN DEAN WEST
STIMULUS *PLEASURE* MATRIX

DEGREE OF SENSORY PLEASURE

MEGAN TOUCHING MY BUTT
WEARING POKEMON BRIEFS
MAKING OUT WITH ANNIE IN THE SAWMILL
PUNCHING JP IN THE FACE
THE NURSE AND THE DAMP TOWEL BATH

SOURCE OF STIMULATION

And hearing and seeing him splash down in all that cold black mud was almost as pleasing as punching him. Unfortunately, I knew, he was going to get right back up.

"What the fuck are you guys doing?" And the next thing I knew,

Seanie, who was definitely not famous for his tackling ability, took me right down with a diving side tackle. He wrapped his hands around the collar of my sweatshirt, pinning my shoulders into the mud.

"What the fuck, Ryan Dean!"

I thought Seanie was going to hit me too. In the years I'd known him, I never saw Seanie so serious or mad about anything. From where I was pinned, I could look up and see JP stumbling out of the lake. He was soaked and filthy, and a mouth-wide streak of blood painted a line from his nose down across his shirt, to the top of his shorts. He came over to Seanie's side and tried to kick me, but Seanie dove at JP's foot and took the force of his kick in his own collarbone.

"Stop it, you fucking assholes!" Seanie yelled.

That kick had to hurt him, and I felt bad that he took it for me.

Seanie screamed at us, "You're going to get thrown off the team. You're going to get your asses thrown out of school!"

When JP realized he'd kicked Seanie, he backed away and turned around, pulling the bottom of his shirt up to stop the blood that streamed from his nose.

Seanie got off me, and I stood up, but he stayed between me and JP, who bent forward and kept his back to me.

"Okay, Seanie," I said. "Okay. I'm sorry, Seanie. I didn't mean to get you in the middle of this crap. I'm a fucking idiot."

Yeah, I was mad.

Then I turned around and ran back to the locker room.

# CHAPTER SEVENTY-FIVE

IT WAS SO AWKWARD SPENDING THE
next two hours in classes with Megan.

She and Joey tried talking to me, but I didn't say anything. Joey looked
tired too. He understood. In Calculus, I drew Joey a cartoon of Screaming
Ned, and he started to laugh so hard, I thought he was going to pee his pants.

Then, during Econ, I started coughing pretty bad and excused
myself so I could leave to get a drink.

That's when Megan followed me out.

And I didn't even know it until I was bent over the drinking fountain and I felt her cool hand rubbing the back of my neck.

I'm not going to lie. It felt pretty goddamned nice.

*Think about Annie.*

*Think about Annie.*

"Are you okay, Ryan Dean?"

I stood up and turned around. I wiped my mouth with my shirtsleeve.

"I don't know," I said. "Me and JP got in a pretty bad fight this morning. I think I'm going to get in big trouble. I busted his face. And to top it off, I'm pretty sick."

She just looked at me with those half-scolding-half-sympathetic-totally-hot Megan Renshaw eyes and brushed my hair back with her hand. I knew she was going to kiss me, too.

*Think about Annie.*

*Think about Annie.*

I turned my face away.

"I can't do this anymore, Megan. We have to quit doing this."

I walked back to class. I felt even worse.

And then I felt like dying when Megan came in.

She was crying.

I put my head down on my desk. Joey knew what was going on.

I am such a loser.

# CHAPTER SEVENTY-SIX

OKAY. BEING IN CLASS WITH MEGAN was pretty awkward.

But it was nothing like how I felt when I saw JP walk in to American Literature.

I'd practically run there so I could see Annie before anything happened. I was convinced that JP wouldn't show up, that someone would come in to escort me to the headmaster's office for what I'd done.

So I wanted to at least see Annie one more time before getting arrested or kicked out of Pine Mountain.

She was already sitting down when I got there. I dropped my bag onto the floor beside my desk and practically collapsed in the seat beside her.

"Hey," she said. Her eyes looked so warm and happy. "I thought you'd stay home today. How are you, Ryan Dean?"

"I'll be honest, Annie," I said. "I am terrible. But I just needed to see you today."

"I'm glad." And she leaned over, just slightly, into the space between us, like we were playing that game that got us both so frustrated over the weekend. So I leaned a little closer too.

"You look amazing," I said. "And this is the first morning since Friday I can look at you and not have to keep one eye out for a horny gay pug."

She laughed.

We squeezed hands in the space between our desks. That's when I knew everything was okay. And that's when JP walked in and saw us.

He looked terrible. The bridge of his nose was swollen and red all the way across from eye to eye. His left eye had a big black bruise that slashed down toward his cheek, and his upper lip puffed out like he'd been stung by a bee.

I wanted to look away when he came in, because of the way he was glaring at me, but I thought that would seem too much like backing down, so I kept my eyes fixed right on his. I'll admit that I was pretty scared. It really felt like we were going to fight again right then and there in front of Mr. Wellins. Then the old pervert would be even more convinced that everything just boils down to sex, I guess.

"JP, what happened to you?" Annie was surprised, but her voice still had that tone to it like nothing bad could ever happen.

I started coughing, and JP stared at me as he sat down on the other side of Annie.

"Nothing," he said. "Rugby. Just playing too hard with *the boys*."

He said it without blinking, looking past Annie. And I knew exactly what JP meant by the "boys" comment.

"Hey. Now you won't need a mask for Halloween," I said.

Annie gave me a scolding look. But those eyes, they were always smiling when she looked at me.

I knew I was going a little too far with JP, but I didn't feel bad about it. I wanted him to know that I wasn't going to give up—that he'd have to first. So then I really messed with him. I said, "Sorry about that, JP," and I held my hand out to shake, right in front of Annie's face, and I looked at JP like nothing in the world had ever happened out there at the turnaround by the lake.

I held my hand there, open.

JP wouldn't take it.

I shrugged and pulled it back.

Score.

*I just kicked your ass for the second time today, buddy.*

Then Mr. Wellins began with his blah-blah-blah-Nick-Adams's-father-brutalizes-the-Indian-woman-almost-like-he's-having-sex-in-front-of-his-son-and-to-humiliate-and-castrate-the-woman's-husband. So it was note-passing time.

Annie—

Did you see that? What JP did? Whatever.

Love,

Ryan Dean

*Yeah. Don't talk about it, remember?????*
*Love,*
*AA*

I get my stitches out today.

*Nice. I think they look sexy.*

You never said that to me before.

*Oh, well. They'll be gone tomorrow, and so will the sexy. Ha ha ha.*

I bet he'd be happy to split my head open again. Ha ha.

*Stop it.*

Okay. Sorry. Sawmill.

*What's that supposed to mean?*

Nothing. Will you meet me at Stonehenge today after I get my stitches out? That way you can see if it really is possible for Ryan Dean West to lose the sexy.

*You are perverted.*

Will you? Please?

*Okay.*

Even if it's raining?

*You shouldn't go out in the rain. You're sick.*

Say you will.

*Okay.*

OKay. See you there. Promise. RD

# CHAPTER SEVENTY-SEVEN

I COULD NOT BELIEVE IT: HER NAME
was Hickey.

She leaned over me, so close her breath tickled the hairs on my
eyebrow as she looked at the stitches there. My eyes just kind of naturally fixed straight ahead to the points of her boobs, which is when I
noticed her name tag: D. L. HICKEY, R.N.

And I thought, what an awesome name. Of course, I also tried
to make up as many perverted words beginning with D and L that I
could stick before a hickey:

Does Love

Delivers Luscious

Daringly Lewd

Delightfully Located

And I was on about the seventeenth set, sweating in my collar,
when she said, "Are you hot, Ryan Dean?"

Which almost made me start hiccupping again.

"Just a little."

"Here." Nurse Hickey loosened my tie and unfastened my shirt's
top buttons. Any more of that treatment and those stitches would
have popped out by themselves. "Why don't you lie back here, and
I'll get those right out."

I put my head down on the paper-covered pillow on the bed and stared up as she snipped and pulled those stitches from my head, one by one.

"There," she said. "All perfectly handsome again."

Then she brushed her fingertip across the line over my eyebrow.

Whew. It was official. I could have asked her to write a note for Annie: *Ryan Dean West did not lose the sexy.*

I couldn't move. Something behind my zipper would definitely have broken if I did.

When she finished, she put her scissors and tweezers-things down on a metal tray beside the bed and began scribbling something on my patient chart.

Then she got this puzzled look and she turned toward me, half smiling.

"You were in here two days in a row last week?"

"Uh, I was?"

She said, "Your chart says you came in with a laceration on your . . . scrotum."

Oh, God.

They actually write stuff like that down?

*Scrotum?*

What a ridiculous word. If I ever became a doctor, I swore to myself then and there, I would legitimize the use of the word "ballsack."

"Oh." I cleared my throat. I felt like I was going to pass out. "Um. Yes."

"From rugby?"

"Uh."

And then I realized . . . score! I was getting Nurse Hickey to talk about my balls. What could be better than that?

"Have you ever thought about going out for the tennis team instead?"

"I love rugby. Nurse Hic . . . Hickey."

Goddamnit. Hiccups.

"And how's that healing up?"

*Whoa.*

Opportunity of a pathetic lifetime.

So I said, "I think it's kind of buh . . . bothering me."

"Here." She set my chart down on the tray. "Stand up and drop your pants."

I love America. Dreams do come true here.

Okay. I'll be honest. She actually *did* tell me to stand up and drop my pants, which made it a milestone in my life, being that Nurse Hickey was a smoking five-out-of-five-toothless-one-eyed-hillbillies on the Ryan Dean West Drop-Yer-Pants-Boy Tote Board. Better still, she was now the *third* female with such a rating to make that demand of me in the past few days (counting Annie and Doc Mom, when they were fixing my trousers).

Well, needless to say, standing was a bit . . . uh . . . problematic for a couple reasons, probably the least of which was the woozy head rush

I got when my feet hit the floor. But I bravely did as Nurse Hickey asked. Unbuckled and unzipped, my pants went to my shoes, and then she laughed and said, "Are those *Pokémon*?"

Ooops. I forgot.

Well, they were comfy.

"How cute."

I felt myself turning red.

What a loser.

I lifted up my shirttails, stuck my thumbs in my waistband, pulled, and . . .

"Hold on there, hotshot," Nurse Hickey said. "Keep them up for just a minute. Doctor Norris will be right in."

Then she turned around and walked out of the examination room.

NO!!!!!!!

I knew I deserved it, but come on!

I am such a pathetic loser.

# CHAPTER SEVENTY-EIGHT

OKAY.

I need to vent.

So, after the lengthy and serious talk Doctor No-gloves gave me about how it's perfectly normal for boys to get overly scared when they receive a catastrophic fucking penis injury, but that everything would be *just fine* and I should try to think of it in the same way I'd think about getting a cut on my elbow, which most boys normally don't even think twice about (but my elbow isn't my penis, you moron)—so just stop worrying, Ryan Dean, there is nothing wrong (except Doctor No-gloves got it ALL wrong about how the setup to the ballsack exam that Nurse D. L. Hickey was *supposed* to do happened in the first place); and, oh, I should probably start wearing boxer shorts instead of little-boy tighty Pokémon fucking briefs because my body was "changing," and I would begin to appreciate the "growing space" and if I ever needed to talk to him about these kinds of things since my dad lived in fucking Boston, he'd be there for me, bare hands and all—I took my embarrassed, skinny (but now up to 157 pounds after Doctor No-gloves insisted on weighing me since I was fucking naked anyway) bitch-assed self out of that innermost circle of hell as fast as possible so I could take a quick shower to wash that bastard's Old Spice smell off my *scrotum* and wait for Annie at Stonehenge.

*Ugh.*

Okay, I'm breathing again.

# CHAPTER SEVENTY-NINE

IT WAS ACTUALLY NICE TO BE IN O-Hall when it was so quiet. All the guys were at either rugby or football practice.

I laughed to myself, thinking about Casey Palmer being gay. But, then, I didn't think it was funny that Joey was gay. I guess it was because Casey was such a poser with his sexuality. But probably a lot of guys were. Who knew?

There was another FedEx package sitting on my bunk when I got to my room. My mom came through. I was a little worried about opening the box, though, because at this point, I didn't know what to expect from her.

Nice.

She'd sent the size ten-and-a-half Nikes that I asked for, and in the box with them, she'd added a can of shaving cream, a razor, and some Chanel aftershave cologne. I guess she had a mother's intuition about that one whisker on my chin. I found an index card in there too. On one side, my mother wrote:

Ryan Dean,
I hope I recognize you next time I see you.
I love you and miss you.
—Mom

And on the other side, in my dad's writing:

Son,
You're growing up, my man. I know you've
seen me do this enough times that you won't
cut the shit out of your face (Mom would be
pissed at me for not sending you a book called
"How to Shave for the First Time.") Ha ha.
Love,
Dad

Yeah, my dad talked like that.

So I showered, and I actually shaved, too, and put on some of that cologne. I gelled my hair. Oh, I also switched out of the Pokémon briefs, and I did realize there was a lot to be said for having that "growing room" down there, like Doctor No-gloves told me, but I still intended to wear them on Halloween under my Wild Boy of Bainbridge Island loincloth, growing room or not, just to keep things, uh . . . put away.

I put on those brand new Nikes and my nicest black and blue sideline warm-up suit from my rugby team gear, then headed downstairs before any of the other guys even made it back from practice.

But, in the stairwell, I ran right into something even worse than Doctor No-gloves's nutsack exam and puberty pep talk, if there could be such a degree of miserableness.

Just as I opened the door from the boys' floor, I stumbled onto Mr. Farrow and that freakishly unhot witch from downstairs, Mrs. Singer.

Together.

Standing at the landing on the tenantless girls' floor. They were kissing, and it wasn't one of those innocent oh-hello-you-frosty-and-cadaverous-old-hag-from-downstairs-so-nice-to-see-you-this-afternoon pecks on the cheek, either. It was all tonguing and moaning and noisy, and Mrs. Singer was wearing only a bathrobe, and it burns my eyes even now to admit that I noticed it, but she didn't have anything on underneath it; and it sears the very depth of my soul to confess it, but I knew they must have *just had sex.*

Or something.

I think I screamed.

Like Ned.

Okay, I'll be honest. I didn't scream, but, for whatever reason, they both instantly radared in on me standing above them.

"Oh. Uh . . . Ryan Dean!" Mr. Farrow said, pushing himself away from the creature and nonchalantly combing a trembling hand through his wild, just-had-sex hair. I noticed the fresh shine of saliva in the corner of his mouth, and his glasses were crooked.

Apparently, they weren't in on the doctor's-appointment-early-return-day for Ryan Dean West, and I'm going to get a little side-tracked here, but I was always totally convinced that Mr. Farrow was completely gay.

Go figure.

I guess he was attracted to corpses and decay and not just to boys.

Then Mrs. Singer looked up at me, but I was too crafty for her. I kept my eyes fixed straight down on the floor until she left and I heard the door close behind her. So it was just me and Mr. Farrow.

Like, superawkward.

I kind of wanted to laugh. I wondered if he had a mom who'd sent him a "How to Have Sex the First Time with a Cadaverous Hag from Hell" leaflet.

Farrow began coming up the stairs toward me.

There was no way out.

"Did you skip practice today, Ryan Dean?" he asked. And he moved and talked all calm and slow, like a murderer. A murderer who had just had sex with a cadaverous hag from hell.

I pointed to my eye.

"I was at the doctor's. Got my stitches out today."

"Oh." He leaned close. He didn't need to—he could see perfectly fine from where he was. He smelled like sweat. "It looks good."

"Thanks. Well. Uh. Bye."

I started to slip past him.

"Ryan Dean."

I froze.

"Please don't say anything about this."

What a creepy child-molester thing to say.

Then Mr. Farrow said, "I can transfer you back into the boys' dorm at the ten-week grade report. In two weeks."

I didn't say anything. The door off the mudroom opened, and Joey and Kevin came in.

"Hey," Joey said. He stopped and looked at me, then he high-fived me. Not a record breaker, but a solid one nevertheless. "Nice job on the stitches. And, damn, Ryan Dean. You look about two inches taller than yesterday." And he laughed. "My ears are still ringing from Screaming Ned."

"That was *almost* the worst thing I ever had to put up with," I said.

But, I thought, not even close to what I just saw about a minute ago.

"Hey," Kevin said. He had a rugby ball tucked inside his sling. "Nice hair, Winger. Let me guess . . . Annie?" And Kevin leaned close to my face and sniffed, then said, "Oooooh."

I said, "Yeah," and they kept going upstairs.

I lowered my voice. "I don't know what you're talking about, Mr. Farrow. Say something about *what?*"

Then Mr. Farrow nodded like we were striking some kind of deal, but we weren't. Because I thought about it right then. Yeah, I didn't like Chas Becker. I hated him, in fact. And some of the other guys in O-Hall were real dipshits, and the communal bathroom was always nasty and crowded, and bunk beds are for prisons.

But I knew I couldn't go back to the boys' dorm.

"Please don't transfer me out of O-Hall, Mr. Farrow," I said. "I'd get in too much trouble. If I went back to my old room, I'd be kicked out of school the first day, and I'm not going to say why, but you just have to believe me. Please?"

And, yeah, I was doing the think-about-peeing face on him.

"Well, then," he said.

The door opened. Casey and Chas came up the stairs toward us. Chas was saying something to Casey about how "she's been crying all goddamn day long," but I avoided looking at them.

I knew what he was talking about, anyway.

Still, I had to wonder what Chas would say if he knew he was pouring his lovesick heart out to a gay guy with the serious hots for the fly half on our rugby team.

I passed them on my way down. And when I glanced back over my shoulder, Mr. Farrow was gone and the stairwell was empty.

At the bottom, I saw Mrs. Singer watching me through the window on the door to the girls' floor. Then she turned away and the window was empty. It actually made me shudder. I stopped just before going outside and pressed myself up against the girls' door.

"My name is Ryan Dean West," I said.

My voice cracked. Loser. "I'm the boy you caught down here in the bathroom that first night before school started. I just wanted to say I'm sorry and ask you to please stop doing all these horrible things to me."

The door cracked open, and I could see just a bit of her so-unhot-she-looked-like-Screaming-Ned-after-a-close-shave face. Mrs. Singer said, "I'm going to cook you and eat you on Halloween, Ryan Dean West."

Then I ran.

Okay. To be perfectly honest, she probably said, "Nice to meet you, Ryan Dean West," but I did my duty by apologizing, and I wasn't about to stick around and have my soul sucked, receive a cascade of ice shards pouring through the fly of my boxers, come down with diarrhea, suffer a spontaneous bloody nose, or have her lay another ungodly curse on my as-yet-untested reproductive appliances, either.

# CHAPTER EIGHTY

ANNIE WAS ALREADY AT STONE-
henge when I got there.

She walked along the wishing-circle path, and I stood back at the edge of the trees and watched her.

"The nurse said for me to tell you that I did *not* lose the sexy. She said there's way too much of it going on there."

She looked at me and laughed.

"Let me see it," she said.

Hmmm . . . another Ryan Dean West would have undoubtedly made a perverted comeback to that, but, somehow, I just felt different standing there.

She walked over to me, and I could see her eyeing me up and down, but I watched her face. I leaned close.

Game on, Annie.

She put her thumb on the small scar.

"Well?" I asked.

"Okay," she said. "You look good dressed like that, and the way you fixed your hair, Ryan Dean. You look taller."

That's when I realized that Annie had completely stopped calling me West. I thought it meant something. And I liked it.

"You're the second person to say that, Annie. I think I'm going to have to come over and have you and your mom fix my pants again."

"Do you want to come back?"

"Oh my God, Annie, I'd leave right now if I could. I'd start walking."

Annie said, "Maybe you can come for the four days over Thanksgiving."

"That would be awesome," I said, even though I knew it would make my mom and dad unhappy that I wasn't going home. I held her hand, and we walked under the trees. It was beginning to rain again, but none of it fell through.

"What were you wishing for?" I said.

"Not going to tell you."

"Okay." I inhaled. On the walk out here, I'd thought about what I needed to tell her. It was important, and I knew I had to stop acting like such a . . . uh, Wild Boy.

"I need to tell you something, though, Annie. Me and JP got in another fight today. That's why his eye was black. I punched him. I'm sorry. I'm not going to do it again. I don't want you to get mad about it, so I told you before you heard it from Seanie or someone else. I don't know why I've been acting so stupid."

Annie sighed. "Ryan Dean."

"I know. I'm sorry. And I decided I can't be upset about you going to the dance with him either. I'm just going to have to forget about it. I'm really sorry, Annie. Will you forgive me for being such a jerk?"

She stood right in front of me, so close we were practically touching. We just looked at each other's eyes, and I knew we were going to kiss, but she pulled back and said, "I can't be in love with you, Ryan Dean."

Yeah. I heard that before. And this time I wasn't going to be a baby about it and run away. So I said, "Yes you can be."

For the longest time, it seemed like there was no sound at all except the rain dripping through the trees above us.

I said it again. "Yes, you can be, Annie."

And she said, "I know."

"I know, too, because I've never said this to anyone, but I am so in love with you, Annie, that I almost can't stand it, and it's making me insane."

Then I don't know if she laughed or was going to cry, but she kind of shook and she put both of her hands on my shoulders and said, "I *do* love you, Ryan Dean," and then we just about collapsed into each other's arms.

I felt so relieved. I closed my eyes and inhaled, and we kissed like we did that other day in the sawmill, and neither of us would let go. It was better than every wish I ever made coming true all at the same time.

"You smell nice," she said.

"I shaved."

She laughed. "Why?"

"Hey, now."

We walked through the forest, heading back toward O-Hall along the trail by the lake. It was getting late, and I needed to change back into my dress clothes or they wouldn't let me have dinner.

I didn't care, though. Everything was perfect, and I just wanted to sleep.

But it was so exciting to think about sitting down to dinner with Annie for the first time as a real, honest-to-God couple. I wanted so badly to be alone with her.

Annie said, "Oh my God. I am in love with a fourteen-year-old boy."

"Get over it, old hag. When you're ninety, I'll be eighty-eight."

# CHAPTER EIGHTY-ONE

EVERYTHING IN MY UNIVERSE CHANGED that day.

Annie left me at O-Hall. We promised to meet for dinner in half an hour. I watched her walk away, and after every few steps, she'd turn around and see me following her with my eyes, and she'd say, "Go on, Ryan Dean. Get dressed."

But I watched her until I couldn't see her anymore.

I went inside. I could hear the guys upstairs noisily getting ready to storm the mess hall. I paused beside the girls' door and looked through the window to see if Mrs. Singer was there. For some stupid reason, I wanted to say thanks to her, like she'd lifted the curse or cast some love spell over Annie.

I know. That was dumb.

I pushed the door open and stuck my head inside. The hallway was dark, but I saw Mrs. Singer standing at the far end, just staring at me. She looked like Mary Todd Lincoln . . . and not just because she had the big-black-dress thing going on; I mean, she *really* looked like someone dug up the corpse of Mary Todd Lincoln fifteen minutes ago and propped her up at the end of the O-Hall girls' floor hallway.

I said, "Thanks," and slipped back upstairs.

# CHAPTER EIGHTY-TWO

SEANIE AND JP DIDN'T SIT NEAR US at dinner that night.

It didn't matter to me.

Annie and I played "feet" under the table. We hardly ate anything at all because we just stared at each other, and I could tell it started to annoy Joey and Isabel that we were so focused in our own thing—it was like the rest of our friends didn't exist.

The next couple of days were kind of like that: Mine and Annie's universe got smaller and quieter.

Seanie didn't say much to me.

I know he was mad about my starting that fight with JP at the lake, and how Seanie had to take some punches himself when he got between us. JP had long since stopped talking to me, and Megan just moped around like she was so depressed.

Yeah, she didn't talk to me either.

Oh. And neither did Chas—ever since last Sunday night and the consequence and Screaming Ned, and me making Chas cry when I confessed that Megan and I had been fooling around.

He didn't even put forth the effort to call me Pussboy or Asswing anymore.

Nothing.

Joey told me that Megan had broken up with Chas and it was all because of me. So, if I threw in the fact that I'd caught Mrs. Singer and Mr. Farrow practically copulating right there in the O-Hall stairwell, I figured all I'd need to do was publicly out Casey Palmer, then the entire state of Oregon, minus Annie Altman and Joey Cosentino, would want me dead.

I was on thin ice, but I didn't care.

# CHAPTER EIGHTY-THREE

THE DAY BEFORE HALLOWEEN, WE had another rugby match.

We played at our own field, on Wednesday after classes, so Annie got to be there.

Our opposition was a club team from Southern California called the Pumas that had come up on tour to play against teams in the Pacific Northwest, where everyone knows we play a tougher game. None of us really liked playing against club teams; they were notorious cheaters as far as things like player eligibility were concerned, and most club coaches' only priority was winning, so they'd do anything unethical to get there. Coach M knew it too, but it was preseason and we all wanted to play anyway.

Besides that, Southern California? Give me a break. Saying you play rugby in Southern California is like saying you surf in Colorado. Dude.

But they were tough, and that's probably because, to me, it looked like they had some players who had been out of high school for a couple years and were married and had mortgages and tattoos and children of their own.

We ended up beating them pretty badly, though, 42–12, and the coolest thing was that Coach M said he wasn't going to let anyone wear Kevin's number for the rest of the season.

Kevin stayed on the sidelines wearing the number four jersey with his arm in a sling. That's probably what pumped us up the most for the game, even though I knew half the guys on the team didn't want to talk to me, much less give me the ball.

Joey did, though, and I scored one time. But Joey was on fire that day and put in three tries by himself.

The boys on the other team got pretty hotheaded, and a couple times it looked like they were going to try to start fighting, but we kept it under control and had a good game of it. Their coach ended up in such a bad mood, though, that he made them leave the social early and get back on their bus to head up to Seattle. That was fine with me, because we all got out of there early enough to give me hope that I'd catch up to Annie in the mess hall before we had to check in at our dorms.

It was dark, and I was afraid she'd already gone home for the night, so as soon as I could, I took off running for the mess hall. And JP was right behind me.

"Hey, fucker," JP said.

I knew he was there.

I stopped and turned around. It was so quiet and cold. There was no one else around, and I could just barely hear the sounds of the students who were still having dinner in the mess hall.

"I'm not going to fight about it anymore, JP," I said. "It doesn't matter."

"Screw you, Ryan Dean."

"Look. I didn't mean it when I said I was sorry the other day. But I do now. I'm sorry, JP."

JP didn't answer.

"We might as well just find some other way to waste our time, because, trust me, it's over," I said.

"Fuck you."

This would have been a perfect time and place for him to absolutely kill me, and I knew it.

Trouble is, I'm pretty sure he did, too.

Oh, well, I thought, I'd gotten my shots in on JP enough in the past week, and I was way ahead on the scorecard. Worst of all, I knew I deserved it.

"You want to punch me, JP?" I put my hands out. "Go ahead. I told you I'm not going to fight you anymore, and I meant it."

Just then, Seanie came up from behind, totally out of the dark.

He was out of breath from running after us. "What are you guys doing?"

JP walked off without answering, straight for the boys' dorm.

"What the fuck, Ryan Dean? We used to all be friends. *What the fuck?*" Seanie was pissed again. He turned away, following JP.

"Seanie," I said. "I didn't do anything this time. I swear to God." I followed after him. "Seanie, listen to me. Just a second."

But he wouldn't stop, so I just let him go.

# CHAPTER EIGHTY-FOUR

I COULDN'T SLEEP THAT NIGHT.

I just lay there on the top bunk and stared up at the emptiness between me and the ceiling, thinking about what Seanie had said, how we all used to be friends, and how his voice had a tone in it like he blamed me for doing something that I don't think was entirely under my control.

This time.

I listened to Chas sleeping and wondered how I'd managed to live this long sharing a room with him. I wanted to ask him about Megan, but I knew those would likely be the final words spoken on this earth by Ryan Dean West.

For three days, Chas hadn't said one word to me, but Megan looked so sad and it made me feel terrible, because deep down I didn't see her as just some hot girl. I really did like her. I really did think she was a great person. I just knew better than to get too close to her again.

RYAN DEAN WEST 2: Did you actually just say that to yourself—that you don't see Megan Renshaw as just some hot girl?

RYAN DEAN WEST 1: I can't help it. Something's changing in me.

RYAN DEAN WEST 2: Oh . . . so you finally *did* decide to join Team Joey.

RYAN DEAN WEST 1: That's a shitty thing to say.

RYAN DEAN WEST 2: How about Isabel? Isn't she fuzzy-hot?

RYAN DEAN WEST 1: Shut up.

RYAN DEAN WEST 2: Doc Mom? Mrs. Kurtz? Aren't they my-best-friend's-kinky-mom hot?

RYAN DEAN WEST 1: Ugh.

RYAN DEAN WEST 2: How about Annie?

RYAN DEAN WEST 1: If you weren't me, I'd punch you in the face.

RYAN DEAN WEST 2: Nurse Hickey?

RYAN DEAN WEST 1: Okay. I'll give you that. Nurse Hickey is a hissing five out of five leaky air-conditioning units on the Ryan Dean West Global Hotness Scale.

RYAN DEAN WEST 2: My man. There is hope for you after all.

(*RYAN DEAN WEST 1 wipes the sweat from his forehead.*)

RYAN DEAN WEST 2: Loser.


I couldn't stand it anymore. I had to get my wimpy, feeling-sorry-for-myself ass out of bed.

I slipped on my warm-ups and carried my shoes in one hand so I wouldn't squeak on the floor, and I left.

In the dark hallway, I ran into Joey as he was coming out of the bathroom.

He whispered, "Are you leaving or something?"

"I have to go outside. I can't sleep."

"Dude, I am so beat up from the game, I can't even lie down. Let me get dressed, and I'll meet you out there in a minute."

"Okay."


I didn't feel awkward talking to Joey, or being in a situation where we were alone together, and I know that's a crappy thing for me to even point out in the first place, like I have to defend myself to myself for being best friends with a guy who happens to be gay.

But most guys just got all tense around Joey in normal social situations, like any time when we weren't out on the pitch and bashing each others' brains in playing rugby.

You could just see it in the way guys' shoulders would tighten up, and you could hear it in the way they'd talk—like they never really talked directly *to* Joey, even if they were asking him something, it always looked like they were talking past him, or to the ground or something, and in really short sentences.

It's weird, but I noticed it, and I'm sure Joey did too.

I saw him come out from the mudroom, and he let the door close slowly behind him so it didn't make the slightest sound. Then he sat down on the steps and slipped his shoes on.

"Where are you going?" he said.

I shrugged.

"That witch downstairs didn't see you, did she?" I said.

"Why are you so scared of her?"

We talked low until we were far enough away from O-Hall.

"Dude, Joey, she does horrible things to me. Trust me. I know she's a witch or something."

Joey laughed. "Whatever." Then he said, "I asked Kevin to come, but once he's in bed, forget it. It hurts him too much to get in and out of bed, anyway."

Joey walked slowly and carefully. He limped.

There really isn't too much in the world that hurts worse than a guy's body does the night after a rugby game, and the fly half almost always takes more shots than any other player on the field.

I threw a rock out into the lake.

"I caught Mr. Farrow having sex with Mrs. Singer on Monday, when I came back from having my stitches out. How nasty is that?"

Joey laughed. "No fucking way."

"Dude, don't tell anyone. At least, that's what Mr. Farrow begged me. That's why we were talking on the stairs when you and Kevin came in that day. He even said he'd get me out of O-Hall if I kept quiet about it."

"Are you going to do it?"

"I asked him not to," I said. "I wouldn't last in the boys' dorm. JP hates me. I think Seanie does now too. It sucks."

"You push things too far, sometimes, Ryan Dean. Just your luck."

"I know."

"But, shit, everyone knows you're a fighter. You're not afraid to take on anyone," Joey said.

"Oh, I'm afraid. But when you have to fight, you have to fight. There's nothing else you can do." I threw another rock. "Annie finally told me she's in love with me."

"Did you tell her first?"

"Yeah."

"Damn. You've got some guts, Ryan Dean."

"So, sorry if it seems like we've been ignoring everyone else."

"Dude. It's pretty obvious."

Then Joey high-fived me, but it was weak, so we had to do it again. Not a record breaker, but it was solid.

"At least there's one thing I haven't totally screwed up," I said.

"Yeah."

*Damn,* I thought. Joey didn't *have* to agree with that. But then again, Joey wasn't the kind of guy who'd ever lie about things just to make someone feel better.

I sighed. "Yeah. I feel terrible about JP and Seanie. We used to be such good friends. But I couldn't handle him chasing after Annie like he's been doing. I should have known she didn't really care about him. Well, not like that, anyway. God! I am such an idiot. I wish I could just do it all over again. I wish I never got put in O-Hall in the first place, and now it's like I can't ever get out."

Joey threw a rock too.

"Yep," he said. "You know, nothing ever goes back exactly the way it was. Things just expand and contract. Like the universe, like breathing. But you'll never fill your lungs up with the same air twice. Some-times, it would be cool if you could pause and rewind and do over. But I think anyone would get tired of that after one or two times."

"Sometimes, don't you just ever feel like screaming, like Screaming Ned?" I asked.

Joey laughed out loud, "Sometimes I feel like driving back to Ban-nock and finding him at that donut shop just so I can kick the shit out of him."

Then I laughed too. "That was one of the most amazing nights ever."

"Yeah."

I felt better.

We walked back to O-Hall and kicked off our shoes before open-ing the door and climbing upstairs. I was afraid we'd run into Mrs. Singer, but then I thought she just had this certain thing for zeroing in on me, so Joey was like a protective charm against her.

I said good night and thanks, and we hugged—a guy hug, okay? with the patting on the back and stuff—and Joey slipped into his room.

And as I was walking down the hallway to my room, I saw that Casey Palmer had been watching me, just standing in front of his door with his arms folded, like he was pissed off and wanted to fight.

He whispered, "That explains it. What were you guys out doing tonight, little fucking faggot?"

*Man*, I thought, *you have some balls saying shit like that to anyone.*

I walked past where Casey was standing.

Then I stopped and said, "Don't be stupid, Palmer."

"I fucking hate you queers. I'm sick of all the shit Joey pulls around here. Someone needs to straighten his shit out."

Nick Matthews opened the door to their room and stepped out into the hallway, shirtless and wearing only his boxers. Nick was a fat offensive lineman with a tattoo of a skull on his hairy shoulder.

"We should fuck these little queers up, like you said, Case."

I glanced back toward Joey's door. I wished he'd been there to hear what Nick and Casey said, but I was also glad he wasn't. It would have been a terrible fight, right then and there.

And I can't even explain how much I wanted to rip into Casey about what I knew, and out him in front of his hairy, tattooed roommate, but I literally bit down on my tongue and went to bed without saying another word.

# CHAPTER EIGHTY-FIVE

SEANIE AVOIDED ME THE WHOLE NEXT day. He wouldn't talk to me in Conditioning or even at our team meeting at the end of the day.

We didn't have practice on Halloween. Coach let us out early. Most of the guys on the team didn't live in O-Hall. That meant they were all going to the dinner party, while the O-Hall boys would be the only twelve kids eating in the mess hall and then going home.

Alone.

At least some of us had costumes. And I knew that Joey and Kevin were going to do whatever they could to make sure we all had something to laugh about that night. So I just tried to not think about what Annie was going to be doing without me.

But, of course, that was like trying to not think about getting kicked in the balls right as you're watching that foot make contact.

Things like this were really the worst part of being assigned to O-Hall, because as Joey, Kevin, and I left the mess hall after our quiet dinner, we could all hear the sound of the music coming from the activities center.

And I'm not going to lie about it, but even though Annie and I had made our commitment to each other, the sound of that music was eating me up on the walk back to my room.

I didn't say anything to Joey about running into Casey the night before.

I probably should have, now that I think about it, but at the time, I just thought it would make Joey want to fight him. But when we got back to O-Hall and we saw the painfully unhot Mary-Todd-Mrs.-Singer standing on the stairs (which was the first time I'd ever seen Mrs. Singer in the presence of any of the other guys, so I was a little relieved to finally know she was *real*), I found out something that was almost unbelievable.

"Mr. Farrow is not here this evening," she said. "He's left me in charge."

Which, I thought, meant she actually *was* going to cook me and eat me.

"I don't care what you boys do. Just stay off my floor and keep the noise down, and none of us will get into trouble. Correct?"

I looked at Kevin and Joey.

They heard it too.

So, to me, the "I don't care what you boys do" part was as good as a permission slip for us to go to the dance.

The Wild Boy of Bainbridge Island was ready to break free.

We ran upstairs to dig out the costumes.

"I think she killed Mr. Farrow," I said. "Or she's got him chained to her bed."

Then Kevin said, "Maybe we should have stalled her a little longer to give him a chance to finish chewing off his arm, then."

# CHAPTER EIGHTY-SIX

SO THERE I WAS, STANDING IN THE middle of the floor, wearing absolutely nothing but those Pokémon briefs, when the door pushed opened and Chas and Casey walked in.

Chas just stared at me and shook his head.

"What?" I said.

But it really did creep me out the way that Casey looked at me, especially considering what I knew about him, and what he obviously thought about me and Joey, too.

God! That was all I needed after the crap I'd been through that week, to have some angry, horny, gay football player chasing after me, or jealously thinking I'd been having sex with the guy he was attracted to.

Casey Palmer was a dangerous psychopath.

"Your costumes are there in the cubby," I said. "Have fun. You're going to like what we got."

Joey and I had left a bag marked CHAS, and one marked PALMER, inside my closet after we separated out the goods.

I didn't really want to be alone with them when they opened the bags and saw what we got for them to wear, so I was glad when the convict-striped Joey appeared down the hallway, walking toward my open door.

"Joey!" I called, and he came over.

"You're not going like *that*, are you, Ryan Dean?" he said.

I just gave Joey a dirty look, but I noticed as Casey eyed him, then looked back at me, back and forth, like he was watching a tennis match or something. And I wanted to say, *Dude, you have it so fucking wrong about me and Joey, you stupid moron*, but it was so obvious what he was thinking.

He was burning up. I could see him turning red, how his hands shook.

Like he was actually *jealous* of me, and in a totally, obviously gay way, too. I couldn't decide whether it was funny, scary, or what.

I pulled the Wild Boy leopard skin up over my legs and tied the single strap on my shoulder. I had to tie it pretty loose, because the fake-jagged-cut bottom barely covered my nuts.

I thought it was perfect.

"Oh, yeah, Annie will dig this," I said, hoping that Casey was paying attention to the fact that I *wasn't* talking about a guy.

I slipped my bare feet into my running shoes and walked past Joey. "I'm going to go get some hair gel from Kevin."

And, as I left, I heard Chas saying, "I'm not putting that shit on," and Casey complaining, "Is that all you fucking got me?"

So I guess they weren't totally satisfied with their outfits.

But they put them on anyway. And I don't know why Casey Palmer had to tag along with us, either. He could have gone out with Nick or any of the other assholes from O-Hall, but he was making it so obvious—to Joey and me, at least—that he had some kind of perverted interest in hanging around us.

Casey Palmer was after something.

What a fucking dolt.

Chas looked especially ridiculous.

We didn't really think about it that night in Bannock, but not too many women come in size six foot four, so he had to cut the feet out of the pantyhose just to get the crotch past his knees.

Then he had his own pair of Pokémon briefs on top of the red nylons.

I said, "Oh! Twinsies!" And I lifted up my loincloth.

Chas flipped me off.

He wore our blue rugby socks to cover the holes at his feet, then a white T-shirt we had marked up with a big blue C, and, finally, the cape, which, since it was for a kid, went down to just the top of his ass.

Yeah, Joey confirmed what I sensed all along: You couldn't get much gayer looking than that.

Kevin looked great. He was all in black, with that hook-hand sticking out from his sling. Of course, he had an eye patch, and he'd tied his hair down under a doo rag made from an old black T-shirt.

It was a big deal for Kevin to do that, because his perfect blond hair was always, well . . . perfect. Kevin Cantrell had magic hair. It never even got messed up playing rugby, and he hated wearing anything that would put one strand out of place. Then he had a three-pointed pirate hat on top of the doo rag, and he'd even taken a black Sharpie and drawn a moustache (that was about half as thick as Isabel's) across his lip.

Kevin was a great sport. He would do anything, even if it meant permanent marker to the face.

He even offered to draw chest and leg hairs on the Wild Boy of Bainbridge Island, but the whole permanent-ink thing was a deal breaker as far as I was concerned.

Casey Palmer just moped along with us, stung and angry, wearing that cheesy elastic-band-highly-flammable-carcinogenic-plastic Wonder Woman mask and dangling about a yard-and-a-half-long cord of gold lamé from his right hand.

And on that long walk across campus from O-Hall to the dance, I kept wondering the same few things over and over.

First, why the hell is Casey tagging along with us, and who is going to be the one to orchestrate the ditching of his ass? Second, it is really, *really* cold walking around practically naked. And, oh, by the way, third, it feels like my balls have turned into frozen raisins and the skin on my one exposed nipple has shriveled to the size of . . . uh . . . something . . . that's really small and round. And hard.

Or something.

*Brrrrrr.*

And I didn't even think, the whole way over there, that they weren't going to let the O-Hall boys into the dance once we got there, but that's exactly what was going to happen.

"Ryan Dean West? What are you doing out?"

The old pervert, Mr. Wellins, was working the door.

He added, "Fantastic costume, by the way."

*Yeah. Whatever. Stop staring at my shrunken nipple.*

But I knew Mr. Wellins liked me. I could lay it on so thick when I wrote essays for him, and, of course, I had the highest grade in his Lit class. I knew exactly what he wanted to hear: *duh*, sex.

Why don't other kids get that?

It's never about what *you* think, it's about what the professor *wants* you to think.

No-brainer.

"But you boys are going to get into trouble for being out of Opportunity Hall."

I knew I had to work my magic.

Anyway, my eyes were watering already. I really did need to pee, even though I thought it would probably come out in sharp yellow ice cubes.

Ouch. Thinking about that made my eyes water even more.

"They gave us permission at O-Hall to come out tonight," I said. "Because we've been very good, Mr. Wellins. You could call over and ask Mrs. Singer, and she'll confirm it."

Mr. Wellins looked like a judge weighing character-reference testimony.

I was shivering.

I said, "Oh. And I have my final essay for you on *In Our Time*."

And I knew this was a kill shot: "I wrote it on the sexual tension between Nick and Bill in 'The Three-Day Blow.'"

Yeah, I know. Too easy with a title like that, but I wasn't going to go there.

I continued, "I mean, how they get drunk together, alone in the cabin, and Nick puts on a pair of Bill's socks, and Bill tells Nick how he's glad Nick didn't get married. Very thick with the taboo of forbidden, unacted upon, and unrequited homosexual curiosity, I think."

I swear to God, Mr. Wellins looked so emotionally moved, I thought he was going to start sobbing. "You are brilliant, Ryan Dean."

I just made that shit up on the spot because of how much I had to pee, and how much I wanted in to the dance.

*Ugh.* Now I knew I'd have to go hammer out that crappy essay before Lit class.

Sorry, Hemingway, but this old guy murdered some of your best chops for a generation of students.

Mr. Wellins said, "Well, it does sound to me as though you boys have been applying yourselves. Have a good time at the dance, Ryan Dean, and I'll look forward to seeing that essay tomorrow."

Crap.

Forbidden and unacted upon.

Sometimes, I surprise myself by how much of an idiot I am.

# CHAPTER EIGHTY-SEVEN

IN THE DOOR, HIGH FIVES FROM JOEY
and Kevin for playing Mr. Wellins like one of those balsa-wood-paddle-and-a-red-bouncy-ball-attached-on-a-long-rubber-band-with-a-staple-in-it-that-I-don't-know-what-the-hell-they're-called-things, and . . .

First stop: urinals.

So, I'm standing there, thinking, *Hey, wearing a miniskirt really does save a lot of time and trouble when a guy needs to pee. Convenient.*

When I came out into the dance hall, I found Joey and Kevin, but Casey and Chas were gone, thankfully.

It was hard to recognize anyone else, because I didn't know what kids were wearing what costumes, and the place was so dark and crowded. I decided I'd have to do my duty and fully check out every single girl there—and, potentially, every cross-dresser—until I found Annie.

I swung past Joey and Kevin and said, "I'm going to look for Annie. I'll see you guys later. Whatever you do, try to ditch Palmer for good."

Joey smiled and nodded.

Kevin leaned to my ear and said, "Oh, I don't think Palmer's going to be around us after what Joey just said to him."

I looked at Joey. "What did you say to him?"

"Nothing," Joey said. "Don't worry about it. Go find your girlfriend."

Later, I found out from Kevin that Joey told Casey Palmer straight out that there were plenty of gay kids at Pine Mountain and that Casey needed to stop hitting on him, and that Joey would be happy to introduce him to some of the other gay boys around school.

He said it loud enough that people heard it. Chas Becker, in his permanent state of cluelessness, didn't realize that Joey Cosentino was not joking.

A girl from the soccer team, wearing a grass skirt, glided up to Kevin and started cooing over his stab wound. Yeah—it was the whole stitches thing with some of these girls. Next thing I saw, Kevin had his hook looped into the top of her skirt and she was leading him out to dance.

The dance floor was crowded with kids dressed in every imaginable disguise. A few of them wore school clothes, which, I guess, was a kind of costume in itself, because there wasn't much sense in bothering to pack a Halloween costume for incarceration at Pine Mountain. Still, I was glad for mine, especially when I'd get the incidental brush-up from a girl. It was by far the best costume there.

The air in the room was thick and humid.

I waded out through the pulsing, vibrating crowd.

I saw Seanie sitting down on a giant L-shaped sofa next to Isabel. They were drinking sodas. I knew I'd never find him dancing, he was so uptight about stuff like that. And, of course, Seanie was dressed like a flasher, wearing a long yellow raincoat with what looked like nothing on underneath it. Isabel seemed more than a little uncomfortable next to him and kept an obvious gap between them open on the couch. I figured Seanie had already played the want-to-see-what-I-have-on-underneath-my-raincoat game with her.

Isabel was dressed like an octopus or something. I didn't really get it, but she had a lot of arms. Oh, and a moustache, which I still found kind of hot.

"Hey, Seanie."

Seanie practically jumped when he saw me.

"Hi, Ryan Dean," Isabel said. "Awesome costume."

"Thanks." I gave her a little flex and showed some thigh.

"How'd you get in?" Seanie asked.

"They let us out of O-Hall. Hey, can I sit down for a second?"

Seanie, always uncoordinated with things like that, scooted over to give me space between him and his date.

Whatever.

I sat.

One of Isabel's stuffed arms brushed up along my bare leg.

I looked at her, then at Seanie.

"I came to apologize to you again, Seanie. And I'm going to apologize to JP, too. I know we're probably never going to be friends again, not like we were, but I'm sorry for starting a fight and then getting you caught in the middle of it."

I held out my hand, and Seanie shook it. I could tell by the way he squeezed that everything was okay with him. Guys can just tell things about other guys with the pressure of a handshake. Too tight, and you're a competitive asshole. Not tight enough, or cold and moist, you probably spend a lot of time looking at porn sites.

It's a science.

"We'll always be friends, Ryan Dean."

"Thanks."

Then Seanie said, "Why do I suddenly feel like we should go back to your place and make out or something?"

Isabel coughed.

She didn't get Seanie at all. I don't even know why she came out with him in the first place.

Seanie said, "JP isn't here. He didn't come. He stayed at home, pouting."

"That sucks," I said. "'Cause of me. Is Annie here?"

Seanie looked around. "She's here somewhere. She's kind of pouty too."

"What's she dressed like?"

"A doctor."

Oh. Score.

"Hi, Ryan Dean!" Mrs. Kurtz appeared before us, obviously surprised to see an O-Hall boy at the dance.

Then she leaned over to Seanie and whispered something to him, which I thought was pretty weird, and he laughed.

Mrs. Kurtz straightened up and gave me a wink, then disappeared into the crowd of dancers.

"What was that all about?" I said.

Seanie said, "She told me to tell you, Pokémon, if you're going to sit on the couch, maybe you should cross your legs or something." Then Seanie leaned forward, looked up my loincloth, and said, "Yep. You want to know how come I know you're gay?"

"Because guys who check out other guys' balls just kind of *do* know that stuff?" I guessed.

Yeah, it was back to normal with Seanie, but I still didn't cross my legs. Whatever.

What guy crosses his legs?

I saw Megan in the crowd, dancing by herself, or, at least it looked like she was dancing by herself. She could have been dancing with a hundred people, for all I knew.

And, damn, she looked good. She was dressed like a stewardess, complete with that little angel-food-cake-shaped hat, pinned at a tilt in her fluttering hair. She had been watching me.

I stood up.

"We'll have to make out later, Seanie," I said. "I'm going to cruise around and try to find Annie."

Of course, that wasn't completely a lie. Well . . . the making-out part was.

Seanie said, "It's a date."

So I moved out into the dancers, watching Megan, who was looking right at me.

I reasoned that Halloween was going to turn out to be some kind of a Ryan Dean West twelve-step-and-apologize-to-everyone-whose-feelings-I've-hurt night.

Seanie made one down.

Now I had the rest of the fucking planet to go.

Then Mrs. Kurtz hip-bumped me, the way people did when they danced at discos in the seventies.

Two things: (1) Are you kidding me? And (2) That was incredibly hot. *Plus*, she had just been looking at my underwear, which made me feel warm and . . . um . . . kind of springy.

So I leaned closer to her ear, since the music was blaring, and I said, "I apologize for how I was sitting over there, Mrs. Kurtz. It was rude. I've never worn a skirt before."

And she high-fived me and said, "Ryan Dean, you are adorable."

Eh . . . the jury's still out on that word.

I really don't think I like it much.

Mrs. Kurtz danced off, and I snaked through the flailing bodies.

But, there. I had apologized to *two* people now, and I hadn't even been out of the urinal for ten minutes.

Megan wasn't going to be as easy as those first two, though, because, deep down, I still knew she could get anything she wanted from me.

Anything.

And that was pretty scary.

I got right next to her. It was so hot there in the middle of all those people. And I mean hot, not necessarily "hot," even though

Megan, the naughty stewardess, scored an unarguable five out of five depressurization-air-masks-plus-a-bonus-chicken-potpie on the Ryan Dean West Frequent-Flyer-in-Flight emergency survey.

That's, like, off-the-scale hot.

"Hey," I said.

"Dance," she said.

I've never been shy about dancing.

Boys who are shy about dancing look like uncoordinated morons, and girls definitely get turned off by that. So I danced. We got real close, and I held on to Megan's hips, which, now that I think about it, was a huge mistake, because I suddenly forgot everything in the world except for how incredibly hot (and I don't mean thermally hot) she was.

"Megan?"

"What, Ryan Dean?"

"Huh?"

She rubbed her hips square into mine. She began hiking up my little leopard-skin loincloth with the curve of her butt. God! Good thing we were out in the middle of the crowd, 'cause this was the kind of dancing you read about in the papers where schools get burned down by angry crowds of torch-carrying, moonshine-cooking, toothless, one-eyed hillbillies.

"I said, 'What, Ryan Dean?'"


RYAN DEAN WEST 2: Think about baseball.

RYAN DEAN WEST 1: Crap. I don't know a goddamned thing about baseball.

RYAN DEAN WEST 2: It's just a figure of speech. Think about a place in the universe where there is no such thing as sex.

RYAN DEAN WEST 1: Okay, you're going to have to give me a hint. Is it Bannock?

RYAN DEAN WEST 2: You're a fucking idiot. Think about your middle name.

RYAN DEAN WEST 1: Okay. I hate my middle name.

RYAN DEAN WEST 2: So do I.

RYAN DEAN WEST 1: What's my middle name, anyway?

I couldn't even remember my middle name.

"Do you know what my middle name is, Megan?"

"No. What is it?"

Then I said it. "Mario."

I'll be honest. That actually *is* my middle name. And saying it helped snap me out of the fact that I was beginning to act like Pedro-the-humping-pug-dog right there in front of half the goddamned school.

And she said, "That is the hottest middle name ever!"

Which didn't do anything to help slow the boy-to-dog transformation.

"I needed to tell you something," I said. "Stop dancing for a second."

Then she looked serious.

We stopped.

I pulled my loincloth, which was up over my belly, down. Nobody even noticed. That's how high school dances are these days, in case you didn't know.

"I wanted to say I'm sorry, Megan."

"Okay, Ryan Dean."

"I really like you, Megan. You're honestly the first girl I ever kissed. I really like you. But I'm in love with Annie. You know that, don't you?"

"I broke up with Chas."

"I know," I said. "And if it's my fault, I'm sorry for that, too."

"Don't be."

"You are a better person for it, Megan. You are beautiful and brilliant, and nobody who sees that in you ever stopped for a minute to consider how you had beaten all the other girls at Pine Mountain to win the dubious prize of Chas Becker."

I sounded like William Jennings Bryan giving a speech about crosses and gold and shit.

Megan said, "You should be a lawyer, Ryan Dean."

"Are we okay, then? Or do you hate me?" I asked.

"We're okay," she said. But she looked sad. Then she said, "I'm in love with you anyway, Ryan Dean."

*Ugh.* I did *not* see that coming. I swear I almost fell down.

"Start dancing," I said. My voice cracked, but she couldn't hear over the music anyway, so I just *felt* like a loser, I didn't actually *sound* like one.

"I'm going to take a little walk. I need to think about things before I screw them up worse than they are."

Megan started dancing.

"Ryan Dean?"

"What?"

"Annie sure is lucky," she said. "You're the best person I know."

I didn't know what to say to that. It felt terrible and amazingly wonderful all at the same time.

It sure sounded nicer than "adorable."

She kept her eyes on me. I felt embarrassed and stupid as I backed away through all the dressed-up dancers.

Someone tugged at me from behind. Kevin had switched his hook into his good hand and caught my shoulder strap with it. He was dancing with about six girls, and he pulled me into the middle of the circle.

"Isn't this awesome?" he said.

"Have you seen Annie?"

He shrugged.

I was dripping with sweat.

"I need to find her," I said.

# CHAPTER EIGHTY-EIGHT

IT TOOK ME A WHILE TO BREAK OUT from Kevin's girl-circle.

It was kind of like playing Red Rover, only against six hot girls who I didn't mind bumping into over and over until I finally made my way through.

As soon as I cleared a path, I ran face-first directly into a big blue *C*.

"Watch it, Pussboy."

For just a second, I was almost touched that Chas Becker was speaking to me again.

I gulped.

I had to do it. I was on a mission.

I put my hand on his shoulder and pulled his Tyrannosaurus Rex head down to my skinny-bitch-ass-size-snack-morsel face.

"Chas, can I talk to you for a second?"

*Before you finally kill me.*

God! He looked so ridiculous in that outfit.

"What about?"

"I . . . uh . . ."

Yeah, Pussboy forgot what he was doing.

*Okay, snap out of it.*

"I'm sorry for what I did, Chas. I apologize. A guy should never do the kind of crap I did to you."

I figured this could officially count as an apology for making him drink my pee, too, if I worded it vaguely enough.

"I guess I let things get out of control, and so I apologize. I also said I'm sorry to Megan, and I promise you both it won't happen again. So, sorry, Chas. I know you're probably still going to kill me, but at least I got it off my chest."

Then I put out my hand for him, and he shook it.

"You have balls, Winger. But I still fucking hate you."

Fair enough.

"I hate you, too, Chas," I said, and smiled.

Then, beyond Chas's shoulder, at the edge of the dance floor, I caught a glimpse of green surgical scrubs and soft black hair draping over the glint of a stethoscope.

It was Annie. She hadn't seen me yet.

I moved behind her, stalking her. I put my chin right over her shoulder and whispered, "I know you're probably booked up, but do you think you could squeeze me in for a quick physical?"

She turned around suddenly.

At first, I thought she was going to slap me, but then she looked shocked and surprised at seeing me, and she gave me that awesome smile where her eyes tear up, and I hate to say it, but just looking at her there kind of made my eyes tear up too.

"Oh my God!" she said.

Then she threw her arms around me, and we hugged like we

hadn't seen each other in years. That felt so good, because I was practically naked anyway, and all sweaty, and here I was hugging an out-of-control physician.

What could be better than that? Well, except for the quick kiss we stole. Kids get in trouble for kissing at Pine Mountain, so you have to be discreet. And the best place to be discreet was out there in the middle of the dance floor, so the Wild Boy of Bainbridge Island took a tight squeeze on Annie's hand, so we wouldn't get separated, and I pulled her out through the crowd and into the deepest, darkest, wildest kiss we ever had.

"How did you get in?" she said.

"They let us out of O-Hall, and I dirty-talked Mr. Wellins into letting us come in."

Annie laughed.

She put her hands in my hair, and we danced.

"I love what you're wearing," she said.

"I am the Wild Boy of Bainbridge Island," I said. I lifted up my loincloth. "With Pokémon undies."

She laughed and pretended to cover her eyes (but not very convincingly, I noticed), and I said, "Okay. I showed you mine, now you have to show me yours."

"You are such a pervert, Ryan Dean."

"I think your pug infected me."

We danced until we were both exhausted.

When I led her off the floor to get something to drink, I finally remembered that there was one more important thing I had to do, and it *wasn't* apologizing to Casey Palmer. I would *never* do that, no matter how many times I made him drink pee.

"I bet Seanie and Isabel haven't moved from that couch all night," I said. "Let's go see."

Annie's cheeks were red from dancing.

I watched her as she drank lemonade tea.

"Wait a second," I said.

I pulled her back so we were face to face. She looked at my eyes, and I knew she was playing that game we have between us. She knew I was doing it, too.

I whispered, "You *can* be in love with me."

She hugged me and put her mouth to my ear and said, "I know."

And I looked at her and said, "Oh. Now, about that physical, doctor. . . ."

She pushed my shoulder back. "Shut up."

We held hands, and I led her over to the sofa, where I found the Seanie-gap-Isabel arrangement had not changed since I left. Annie and I sat down on the small side of the L, so I could sit facing Seanie with my legs uncrossed.

Seanie nonchalantly flipped me off.

"Annie, can you wait here for a few minutes? There's one last thing I have to take care of," I said.

"What?"

"I want to go get JP and make him come to the dance before it's over."

"I don't know if you should. He's pretty pissed, Ryan Dean," Seanie said.

"It's okay," I said. "One more try."

I rubbed Annie's knee and kissed her cheek, quick, so no one would notice. "And don't let Seanie try to get you to play the want-to-see-what's-under-the-raincoat game."

"Oh. He already did that," she said, and rolled her eyes.

# CHAPTER EIGHTY-NINE

THE COLD AIR FELT GOOD ON MY sweating skin, but only for about half a minute.

That's when I started shivering.

Then I decided I should run to the boys' dorm.

In the dark, I saw the black and white stripes of what could only have been Joey, walking down the trail ahead of me, like he was going home to O-Hall. And I could just tell by the way he was moving that he was pissed off about something.

I called out, "Hey Joe."

He stopped and turned. I could see his shoulders relax a bit.

"What's up?" I said.

"I'm going home."

I walked over to where he stood.

"I found Annie in there," I said.

"I saw you dancing. You guys look great together, and it's about fucking time, Ryan Dean."

"Is everything okay?"

Joey said, "I'll tell you about it later."

"Oh. Okay."

Yeah. Something happened.

I knew Joey would tell me about it later and that it was probably something ridiculous, too. Casey Palmer was on a tirade, no doubt. The asshole just wasn't going to let things go.

"Where are *you* going?" he asked.

"I'm going to try to get JP to come out to the dance before they send us home," I said. "He's in his room, pouting. I can try, at least."

"Well, I'll see you later, then," Joey said.

"You sure everything's okay?"

He sighed.

Something was wrong.

"Ryan Dean? I figure that between you, Kevin, and Annie, I have about three real friends here. So, thanks for that."

"You're my best friend, Joe," I said, and he smiled. "Hey. Do you ever listen to the Who?"

"Um, do I look like I'm fifty?"

"My dad loves them. Sometimes he walks around with his shirt off, singing, acting like he's Roger Daltrey, but he's so *my dad*, and he looks like a scrawny lawyer from Boston," I said. "Anyway, they have this song he always sings, 'How Many Friends.' Ever hear it?"

"No."

"I have an iPod. Want to listen to it?"

"*You* have an iPod?" Joey said. He looked intrigued, but at the same time he kind of knew I was playing a joke on him.

"Yep."

"Okay."

I put my hand inside my loincloth. Man! It felt like a frozen leg of lamb going down there against my skin. I dug around, then pulled my hand up and held my closed fist out for Joey.

"Here," I said.

He held out his hand and I put (of course) nothing in it. Then I said, "Here, you need the earbuds," and I proceeded to put nothing into each one of his ears with the tips of my freezing thumbs.

"Is it loud enough?" I said.

"Um. No?"

"Retard. You didn't even touch play. Don't you even know how to use a fucking iPod?"

And, yes, I apologize. I really did say that. Joey looked kind of shocked, too, but I knew he needed a little magic.

Joey pressed his index finger down into his empty palm. I windmilled my arm like I was Pete Townshend slashing a guitar. And, yeah, I'm a rugby player. We sing and we're not uptight about it. So I jumped up in the air and gave my best howling impersonation of my scrawny-Boston-lawyer dad imitating Roger Daltrey.

Joey squinted a cautious look at me and shrugged.

And I sang, "'How many friends have I really got? That love me, that want me, that'll take me as I am?'"

I heard someone, out in the dark, scream, "Shut the fuck up, Ryan Dean!"

"Okay, that's it. I'm not singing anymore," I said. "Now give me back my iPod before we get in trouble."

Joey smiled and shook his head.

I said, "Dude. High five."

We slapped hands. Truly our all-time gay-straight high five record setter.

"Oh. One more thing." I said, "Chest bumps."

Then we jumped up and bumped chests, and I started laughing so hard.

"Joey, that was the gayest thing I ever did. Well, except for the time I wrote a poem to Seanie."

That made Joey laugh.

Just a little, though.

"Damn," I said. "I'm freezing my nuts off. I better go get JP before they shut it down."

"I'll see you later," Joey said. We shook hands, and Joey put his hand on my shoulder. "Thanks, Ryan Dean."

"I mean this in such a completely and totally non-gay way, Joey, but I love you," I said.

"Shut the fuck up, Ryan Dean."

I laughed.

Joey went off to O-Hall, and I ran on frozen bare legs for the boys' dorm, where I used to live.

# CHAPTER NINETY

IT WAS WEIRD BEING BACK IN THE boys' dorm after so long.

It all looked so nice and normal, like a resort hotel compared with the linoleum-cement-rough-wood-lack-of-heating of O-Hall. But it was kind of the same way I felt that night when I sat down with the freshmen having dinner—I could make a case that I belonged here, but I knew I really didn't.

Not much of an overlap anymore, I guess.

Seanie and JP's room was on the second floor. There was an elevator, too. Weird.

I knocked.

"JP?"

I knocked again.

I heard his voice through the door. "Come in."

I opened the door.

He knew it was me. I guess he recognized my voice. He didn't even move his eyes when I came in.

JP was lying down on the couch, watching television. That's how these dorm rooms were: Everyone had his own—private—bedroom, and two or three of them would connect to a common living room and a bathroom, so it was a lot more private and a lot more like living at home than the prisonlike atmosphere of O-Hall's barracks.

He was alone, but he had taken the time to put a costume on, which meant he was at least thinking about going out.

Typical JP: His face was blacked, which was a good cover for the massive purple bruise around his eye, and he was dressed in combat fatigues with a camouflaged bucket hat that shaded his eyes.

"Hey." I sat down on a red chair across from him. "They let O-Hall go to the dance."

"You look like a gay caveman," JP said.

"Well, that wasn't quite the effect I was going for."

"Dude. You have Pokémon underwear on."

Damn that crossing-the-legs requirement!

"Cool, huh?"

JP inhaled and raised his eyebrows, a silent "whatever."

"JP, I'm going to say it one more time, and then I'm going to shut up," I said.

"Or you could shut up now," he said.

I swallowed. "No. I'm sorry for being such a dick. I'm sorry I started those fights with you. You should have kicked my ass, and I can't blame you if you're still planning on doing it. But I came to take you to the dance."

"You really *are* a gay caveman."

I laughed.

"We're having a lot of fun there."

"Even Seanie and Isabel?"

"Well, okay. I'll be honest. Not them. They're total losers. But everyone else is."

He sort of smiled.

"So, put your shoes on." I stood up and held my hand out to him. He grabbed it, and I pulled him up so he was sitting with his feet on the floor.

"Sorry," I said again.

"Okay," he said. He put his feet into his army boots and began lacing them up. "I'm sorry too, Ryan Dean. I really was going for her, you know? I never thought she'd be interested in you."

Maybe I was still a little sensitive about the whole JP thing, but hearing him say that really did sting a little.

"Why'd you think that?"

JP shrugged. "'Cause you're just a kid."

"Screw that, JP."

I know. I'm such a loser, but I was so sick of that crap, I almost felt myself getting ready to fight him again.

"Hey. You won. It doesn't matter," JP said. "Does it?"

He tied his bootlaces and stood.

I took a deep breath and tried to make myself believe that it didn't really matter.

"I guess not. Come on. Let's go. There's still an hour until ten. Maybe you can at least get Isabel to dance with you."

"Dude, she has more facial hair than Seanie."

"I think she's kind of hot," I said. "And anyway, Seanie never dances, so you'll have to settle for fuzzy Isabel."

We shook hands again before we left, but it was an uneasy kind of peace between JP and me.

He was an intense guy, and I couldn't expect him to just forget about everything. And I even asked him straight out, when we stepped outside into the cold on our walk over to the dance, "JP, do you think we'll be friends again?"

And he said, without even thinking about it, "No."

At least he was honest.

At least I could hope we'd stop fighting.

Mr. Wellins looked drunk, and he waved JP toward the door with an emotional "John-Paul, where have you been?"

JP just shrugged and said, "Homework."

But before we went inside, JP stopped me and said, "Ryan Dean, I'm going to tell you something that I don't really care if you know or not. And it's probably the nicest thing I'll ever do for you. You know the other day when you and Annie came back from Seattle? On Sunday?"

"Yeah."

"You remember how you saw Annie give me a hug?"

I remembered that.

And I thought, *What's he trying to do? Start a fight, right here in front of everyone?*

"Yeah."

"Well, right before that, she'd just told me that she couldn't come to the dance with me. That's why I didn't come tonight. She backed out on me. She felt bad, so she hugged me while you were over there talking to Seanie. She told me that she couldn't come to the dance with me because she was so fucking in love with Ryan Dean West."

"She told you that?" I asked. "On Sunday?"

"She started crying about it."

Then I really felt confused.

That was the same day when she'd told me not to kiss her, when I went crazy on our run.

And then she admitted it to JP before she ever got close to telling me. Maybe she wanted to see if she could fight it. Maybe she wanted to wait for me to break down and say it first, like it wasn't so god-damned obvious anyway. And then, the next day, I got in that fight with JP and busted his face and it was all over nothing, really, now that I heard what Annie had said.

I felt like dog shit.

"Why didn't you tell me? When we were running at the lake, you could have said something," I said.

"You wouldn't shut up," JP said. "All that crap about you and Annie running around naked or whatever the hell you were talking about. It was sickening, and then, when you pushed Seanie, I was ready to go. And I would have fucked you up if my foot didn't slip and Seanie didn't get his dumb ass in between us like that. I would have fucked you up."

I didn't say anything after that.

I felt like such an idiot.

We went into the dance, and I knew John-Paul Tureau and I really weren't ever going to be friends again.

# CHAPTER NINETY-ONE

I MAY NOT HAVE SUCCEEDED, BUT I did what I needed to do.

At least I tried to make things right with the victims of the Wild Boy.

JP came to the dance, and, yeah, it was awkward. He didn't say anything or dance or anything. He just sat on the sofa between Seanie and Isabel while Annie and I danced until the lights came on and they told us all to go home.

I didn't see anyone from O-Hall then, but I volunteered to walk Annie and Isabel back to the girls' dorm, so I let Seanie off a serious hook, because I knew he was dreading how, exactly, to go about saying good night to his "date."

And he had the guts to call me "permavirgin."

I was pretty sure the only female lips Sean Russell Flaherty had ever touched besides his mom's were flickering images on a computer monitor.

Isabel walked about ten feet in front of us, but she'd turn around every few paces to make sure we were still there. Annie had her arm around my shoulders, because I was so cold. But I'm pretty sure that wasn't the only reason.

I put my mouth next to her ear and whispered, "You told JP you were in love with me before I said it to you."

"It doesn't count if you tell someone else." She smiled.

"Yes it does."

"Okay, then, in that case, you told Joey you were in love with me *wayyyy* before I said anything to JP." Then she laughed.

Wow. She just totally kicked my ass.

"Joey told you that?" I said.

She just smiled.

Of course he did.

"Okay. You got me," I said. I kissed her. "I love you, Annie."

"I love you, Ryan Dean."

"Hey, Isabel?" Isabel stopped and turned around, and I said, "When was the very first time Annie told you that she . . ."

But Annie covered my mouth with her hand before I could ask the whole question, so I stuck my tongue out and licked her fingers all over, and she squealed and laughed and ran up to Isabel, whispering something urgent to her roommate.

# CHAPTER NINETY-TWO

WHEN I GOT BACK TO O-HALL, EVERY-
thing seemed weird, like I was walking into the last five minutes of a
horror movie.

That's about the only way to describe it.

It was totally dark and quiet, no lights in any of the windows. I
thought that either everyone had come back and they were all asleep,
or nobody had come back yet and I was there entirely alone.

I walked up the three steps to the landing and slipped my shoes
off. I guess I didn't need to go barefoot, because it wasn't like I was
technically sneaking in, but it was just so eerily quiet that I didn't
want to make any noise on my way upstairs.

Things got stranger inside the mudroom.

The door onto the lower floor was standing wide open, and there
were all kinds of muddy shoeprints going in and out, like the place
had been raided by an army of guys wearing athletic shoes. I could tell
they weren't the kinds of shoes that Mr. Farrow would wear, and definitely not Mrs. Singer, so I knew the tracks had to have been made by
some of the guys from upstairs.

So I was kind of relieved that I was carrying my shoes, because
I could just imagine the morning's shoe investigation from a very
pissed-off pair of resident counselors.

I took a step inside the girls' floor.

My feet sloshed in a puddle of cold water on the linoleum. I was pretty creeped out by this point, and I kept wondering where the hell Mrs. Singer was.

She was gone.

I could tell the bathroom door was open too, and I could just faintly hear the sound of water splashing, like the guys had been in the girls' floor showers and not turned them off all the way.

I decided right then that I was *not* going to take another step further into the hallway, and just then I heard a couple screams like wildcats out in the woods, very distant, but the kind of sound that you just hate to hear in the middle of a quiet and spooky night.

When you're all alone.

That was enough for me. I turned around and went upstairs, without shutting the door and without so much as glancing behind me even one time.

Upstairs was like a tomb.

I walked the length of the hallway, quietly wishing someone would pop out from a room to go to the bathroom or something, even if it was that asshole Casey Palmer.

But there were no sounds at all.

I kicked an empty whiskey bottle, and it clinked along the floor. It sounded like a hundred xylophones inside a stone tomb.

Someone fucked up.

There were footsteps on the staircase. This was it, I thought, I was about to be murdered.

Casey Palmer appeared at the top of the stairwell. He had abandoned the Wonder Woman outfit and was dressed in sweats. His skin was slick with sweat, and his eyes were drunken and glazed.

"What happened, Casey?" I said. I tried to sound as nice as I could, because, I'll be honest, I was afraid of the way Casey Palmer was looking at me.

Casey ignored me. He walked past me, kind of floating like a ghost in the dark. He smelled like sweat and whiskey and puke, all at the same time.

He stopped and swiped his hand at me to grab me, but I slipped away from him. Casey stumbled and nearly fell down.

He said, "I'll fucking kill you if you ever say anything to me again, kid."

Then Casey slipped inside his room and shut the door.

When I got to my room, I actually began *wishing* that Chas would be in there.

I opened the door. At first, all I could see were the red numbers on our alarm clock. I bent forward and looked into the lower bunk. Chas was there, asleep. I actually breathed a relieved gasp at seeing him. I leaned over him, just to make sure he was really there.

"What the fuck are you doing, homo?" he said.

Yeah. Good night to you, too, Betch.

"I'm sorry. I was creeped out. It's like nobody's here, and it looks like someone trashed the girls' floor, or something."

I was shivering, mostly from the cold.

I took off my costume and slipped on some boxer shorts and a sweatshirt. I debated whether or not to go to the bathroom to brush my teeth. I grabbed my toothbrush and stuff, but I was still spooked about the way things felt out there.

"I don't know what the fuck's going on," Chas said. "I've been trying to sleep for a while, and I don't think Farrow or that bitch downstairs is even here, because about an hour ago there was all this running around and slamming shit around until I stuck my head out in the hall and told them to quiet the fuck down."

I decided to skip the dental hygiene.

Something was definitely *not right* out there, and I wasn't going to get caught up in it.

I climbed up in my bunk and lay there, trying to stay awake and see if I would hear that howling again.

But I fell asleep.

PART FOUR:

words

OKAY.

LET'S CALL THIS AN INTERMISSION.

WITH A BIT OF AN APOLOGY, I GUESS.

YOU EVER HEAR OF JOSEPH CONRAD? HE SAID, "ONE WRITES HALF THE BOOK: THE OTHER HALF IS WITH THE READER."

MR. WELLINS MIGHT SAY THAT I HAVE MADE YOU A CONSCRIPTED AUDIENCE; THAT I DIDN'T GIVE YOU A CHOICE AS TO WHETHER OR NOT TO BELIEVE ME, AND, BELIEVE ME, SOMETIMES I CAN'T BELIEVE MYSELF.

OR SOMETHING.

BUT I WROTE THIS ALL DOWN, AND I TRIED TO MAKE EVERYTHING HAPPEN THE EXACT SAME WAY IT DID WHEN I WAS SEEING IT AND FEELING IT - REAL TIME - WITH ALL THE CONFUSION, THE PRESSURE, AND THE WONDER, TOO, EVEN THOUGH I DID GET OFF THE PAGE ONCE IN A WHILE AND MAKE JABS AT THINGS. WHICH IS KIND OF LIKE THE CARTOONIST DRAWING A CARTOON OF HIMSELF WHILE HE'S DRAWING HIMSELF.

BUT YOU CAN'T BLAME A KID FOR WANTING TO DO THAT, CAN YOU?

OH, AND DON'T EVEN ASK ME ABOUT ALL THE STUFF I CROSSED OUT. IT'S REALLY EMBARASSING.

BUT, THROUGH EVERYTHING, I THINK WHAT STRIKES ME MOST IS HOW A GUY CAN BE GOING ALONG, SAILING ON A PARTICULAR COURSE (EVEN IF IT SUCKS), AND HE'LL THINK EVERYTHING IS SO STEADY AND PREDICTABLE, AND THEN *BAM!* SOMEONE STEPS ON HIS BALLS, OR HE GETS INTO AN UNCONTROLLABLE FISTFIGHT WITH ONE OF HIS BEST FRIENDS.

OR EVEN WORSE THINGS THAN THAT.

AND YOU CAN'T SEE AROUND CORNERS, SO YOU JUST HAVE TO DEAL WITH IT AND TRY TO STAY AFLOAT.

AND THINGS GET TOUGH.

AND YOU'RE SUPPOSED TO GROW UP.

AND IT'S ALL A BUNCH OF BULLSHIT.

SORRY.

# after midnight

JUST WORDS.

No more pictures. No charts or plays or poems.

Now it's just about the words.

# friday morning

THE CREEPIEST NIGHTS SEEM TO evaporate into nothing once the sun comes up and you can hear the sounds of guys out in the hallway talking crap to each other and play fighting while they get ready for school.

So I hardly gave another thought to how scared I had been when I came home from the dance; and I didn't really even want to ask any of the other boys what had gone on in the dorm before I got back to O-Hall.

Routine has a way of making you feel like an idiot after you've gotten all worked up over things not being in their expected order. So I showered and got into my uniform, just like I'd do on any other morning.

We ran in Conditioning class.

JP still wasn't talking to me, but I had a feeling that things were just okay, and nothing better than that, between us; and when Seanie and I spoke, I was careful to not be such a smart-ass and say things just to pick at JP again.

But Joey didn't show up that day for Calculus.

I remembered how pissed off he seemed the night before, and since it was Friday and all, I just figured he was taking a day off and going home early. Still, I mostly hoped I'd be able to talk to him again before he left, so I could find out what he was so bugged about when I saw him outside the dance.

Then it really sank in that it was Friday.

It meant Annie and just about everyone else would be leaving for home too, and I wished I didn't feel so goddamned scared and alone without my friends around.

When Megan saw me in class, she smiled and said, "I like how you dance, Ryan Dean. Pretty hot."

I turned red.

"Sorry about that. We were kind of getting a little nasty, Megan."

She laugh-whispered, "A *little*?"

"Hey, did you see Joey, or hear if he's sick or something?"

"No. I saw Kevin this morning, though," she said. "You should ask him."

"Okay. And thanks for the dance, Megan. I had a lot of fun."

She turned around and rubbed my forearm and winked at me.

*Ugh.*

She made me feel so weak.

# lit class

I DIDN'T NORMALLY RUN INTO KEVIN at school, but I looked for him everywhere that day after Halloween.

Eventually, I just quit trying. I knew I'd see him at lunchtime, when he and the others left for their weekends at home.

Somehow, I'd managed to scrawl out my Nick-and-Bill-are-gay-for-each-other essay for Mr. Wellins, and he practically salivated when I handed it in to him at the start of Lit class.

What a moron.

What a criminal waste of a blue book, too.

I sat down.

Annie smiled, but JP didn't even turn to look at me.

I wished he'd just get up and change seats and leave us both alone.

After all, I did what I could. I screwed up and got into a fight with a guy who was one of my best friends. And I knew JP was going to pout like this for the rest of the year—maybe the rest of high school entirely.

Then Mr. Wellins began talking about Halloween costumes, and how they were manifestations of suppressed sexuality, and he started blah-blah-blahing about every goddamned kid in the class and how he took notes on all of us at the dance last night, and Ryan Dean West was in touch with his atavistic and primal man-drives, and, oh—let's go around the room and talk about our Hemingway essays.

So, yeah, Annie and I pretty much shut it all out, scooted our desks close together, held hands on my lap—score one for atavism!—and whispered and mouthed our own unobserved conversation. And all the while, I was praying that old pervert didn't call on his favorite caveman to out poor Nick Adams and his friend.

"I had so much fun last night," I said.

"So did I. You're a great dancer."

"Shut up." I rolled my eyes and squeezed her fingers. "It's going to be so boring here this weekend. Ask your mom and dad about Thanksgiving. I really want to go."

"I know they'll want you to come. It'll be so great, Ryan Dean. It's just a few weeks away."

"It'll seem like forever. I'm going to go crazy this weekend without you."

She leaned closer and looked right into my eyes with that amazing look she had.

I know we would have kissed if we hadn't been sitting right there in a classroom.

JP coughed and gave us a quick dirty look and scooted his desk farther away from Annie's.

Good.

"Who are you going to the airport with?" I asked.

"Kevin's driving. With one arm. And Megan and Joey." She said,

"Chas isn't coming, so you won't be totally lonely, Ryan Dean. Think of all the fun you two boys will have together."

She laughed quietly.

Crap.

"Have you seen Joey today? He wasn't in Calc or Econ."

"He'll meet us at lunchtime."

"I'll walk you out when you leave."

"Okay."

"Which brings us to young Mr. West," Mr. Wellins announced, snapping Annie and me out of our midclass dream.

He went on, "Ryan Dean has a particularly interesting theory on sexual tension that is quietly hinted at, like an urgent whisper, by Hemingway in 'The Three-Day Blow.'"

*Ugh.*

The class weakly attempted stifling their laughter.

All this crap, just to get into a stupid Halloween dance. And, by the way, what did he mean with that "young Mr. West" comment? I was so sick of that crap, and I even got it from perverted old professors.

"Please elucidate, Ryan Dean," Mr. Wellins said.

"Oh. Please do, young Mr. West," JP whispered mockingly from the other side of Annie's desk, without turning to look at me.

Crap.

# lunchtime

BY THE END OF CLASS, I STARTED getting pretty depressed thinking about Annie going home for the weekend.

When I saw her at the start of lunch, carrying her suitcase out to the parking lot, I imagined myself throwing my body in front of Kevin's car, kicking and screaming, to stop her.

She waited at the gate for me, standing with Kevin and Megan. I couldn't see Joey anywhere.

I grabbed the suitcase from her hand so I could carry it for her. I took Kevin's from him, too.

He said, "Thanks, Ryan Dean."

"Any of you seen Joey?"

The girls both looked at Kevin, who shook his head and said, "He didn't come home last night. I was hoping maybe you'd know what happened."

Kevin looked worried.

That's when I got kind of scared.

"No one knows where he is," Kevin said. "I went and checked at the office, too, because his car's still here."

I looked out at the lot.

Joey's BMW was parked next to Kevin's car, like it always was.

"What?" I said. I couldn't believe it. "I saw him leaving the dance."

"I didn't see him all night," Kevin said. "Once I started dancing, I never saw him after that. They called his parents. They think he ran away or something. He did it before, remember? The cops are going to come."

I did remember the time Joey ran away from school for three days, but he didn't have a car then. Why wouldn't he just *drive* away this time?

We started walking out to Kevin's car.

Kevin said, "He got into a fight or some shit with Casey and Nick. Some of the guys on the team got between them or there would have been a fucking riot at the dance. Nobody even noticed."

"And you're just going to leave anyway?" I said.

"What else can I do? Joey's a big boy. He's almost eighteen, Ryan Dean. He's done this before, and I haven't gone home in three weeks," Kevin said. "Joey'll be okay. He's just pissed about something. Again. No big deal. The boys will cool off, and everything will be back to its old shitty, O-Hall self."

"He looked pissed off last night," I said.

"Nick and Casey got drunk," Kevin said. "Shitfaced. They fucked the place up, and nobody knew anything about it. Those fuckers stayed up all night cleaning the mess up. Farrow and the old woman downstairs never knew shit about what those guys did while they were gone on their little Halloween binge."

"Something's not right," I said.

"You worry too much, Winger."

We loaded the suitcases into Kevin's car, and I walked over to Annie's door. I hugged her, and we kissed before she got in.

"I'm going to miss you," I whispered. "I love you."

She looked like she was about to cry, and in a weird way that made me feel really good.

I closed her door, and Kevin started the car.

He said, "Tell Joey to call my house when he shows up. He'll be back today. I know Joey. Just watch."

"Okay," I said. "Well, I'm going to check with the office again."

"It's going to be okay, Ryan Dean. I'll see you on Sunday."

I looked back at Annie and said, "Bye. See you, Kevin. Megan."

And I stood there beside Joey's car and watched them drive away.

# friday afternoon

IT WASN'T OKAY.

The police came before the end of lunch. I was summoned to the headmaster's office. I had to tell them about seeing Joey when he left the dance, and how he looked upset but he wouldn't say why, and who the guys were from O-Hall that went along with us.

The officers listened.

They wrote it all down.

But I didn't tell them everything. How could I tell them *everything*?

At first, the policeman who talked to me seemed kind of nice and concerned about Joey. And he knew about how Joey had run away before. He told me that if Joey didn't show up, they were going to search the campus and the woods in the morning.

Then the officer who interviewed me asked if I knew Joey was gay. And when I told him yes, he asked flat out if I was gay, or if I knew if Joey had a "lover" or not, and that just pissed me off so bad, I wanted to cuss, but I didn't.

I shut up.

I told him he should go talk to someone else.

Stupid fucking bastard.

# o-hall that night

JOEY NEVER SHOWED UP.

Something was wrong, and I knew it. I could feel it jangling my nerves like the sound of the empty whiskey bottle I'd kicked when I walked the hallway in the dark the night before.

I got back to O-Hall at about four o'clock that afternoon.

The place was quiet and empty, which was typical for a Friday afternoon. Downstairs, everything had been cleaned up from the night before. But I was still sick from that lingering feeling you just can't shake after waking up from a terrible nightmare—remembering the muddy shoeprints, the water on the floor, the shower running in the bathroom, and those weird sounds I'd heard coming from the woods.

But it wasn't a dream. Kevin Cantrell knew that. He knew enough about O-Hall and the boys we lived with, though, so it was no big deal to Kevin.

I could not make it not a big deal.

I was stressed out and in a bad mood from everything that had happened; and I wished I didn't feel so alone, that Annie could be there with me.

As I passed by the downstairs hall door, I decided to go for a run before dinner.

I froze when I saw Mrs. Singer watching me from the other side of the door. I wasn't about to open it, but somehow, she didn't scare me as much as she used to. I still wouldn't look at her face, though.

I just watched the doorknob and listened to see if she was going to come out.

She didn't.

I went up to my room and changed out of my clothes and into my running things.


I didn't go all the way up to Buzzard's Roost. It was getting too dark, and I had to turn back. But I stopped at Stonehenge and sat down for a while on that same fallen tree where I'd sat so many times with Annie Altman.

I missed her so much. Even though she'd only been gone for a few hours, it felt like I'd never see her again.

I walked the wishing circle.


That night, Chas and I watched television with Mr. Farrow. Awkward. It was like sitting in a sauna naked together. We were the only ones left in O-Hall, but we didn't say anything to him, or to each other. I could tell Mr. Farrow was uncomfortable around me, though, and I probably would have thought it was funnier if I could only get rid of the creepy feeling that I hadn't been able to shake since the day before.

So, later, when we were lying in bed, I was so frustrated and sick of the silence that I actually broke down and started talking to Chas Becker.

"So, did you break up with Megan, or was it the other way around?"

I heard Chas exhale and roll over.

He didn't say anything for about a minute, and then, finally, "Why do you fucking care?"

"'Cause I can't stand how quiet it's been."

"She broke up with me. So, go for it, little Pussboy."

"I already told you about that, Chas," I said. "I'm sorry. Me and Megan aren't doing anything." I folded my hands behind my head and sighed. "Did the cops come and talk to you?"

"Yeah."

"What did you say?"

Chas grunted. "What could I say? That we drink booze and play poker and do crazy shit? That maybe Joey's just doing some stupid consequence or something? I don't know anything about Joey. He just ran away."

"Yeah. I hope he's okay. I hope he comes back."

"I always thought you guys seemed a little gay for each other," Chas said.

I wanted to say, ask your girlfriend how gay I am, Betch, but I'd had enough fighting for a while.

"You're an . . ." But I stopped myself because I didn't want to cuss at him. "That's messed up, Chas. Can't Joey have any friends without it being about that? Aren't you his friend too?"

"Me?" Chas said. "I don't have any fucking friends."

Go figure.

At least he was smart enough to know that much.

Chas Becker really was a genius, when it came to knowing how pathetic he was.

# seven in the morning

I WOKE UP AT SEVEN.

When I climbed down from the top bunk, Chas rolled over and said, "What the fuck? It's Saturday, dipshit."

I wanted to kick him in the head so bad.

"I know. I just don't want to stay in bed."

Chas rolled toward the wall and put the pillow over his face.

I pulled on my warm-ups and slipped my feet into my running shoes.

I went outside into a cold drizzle. It felt like it was going to snow, and the clouds hung down so low and white that I couldn't even see the tops of the trees around me. It looked like there was a pillow over the face of the world.

I headed for the mess hall.

Weekends were kind of fend-for-yourself eating arrangements at Pine Mountain. There was always plenty of self-contained microwaveable stuff left in the coolers for the kids who stayed, but there was no real food at PM, and there were no people to serve it, either.

But before I got to eat my breakfast, I saw what looked like about a hundred police officers, park rangers, and school staff, all gathered around the front gates to the school.

Now they were really looking for Joey.

I went back to O-Hall.

●●●

Chas Becker was not pleased when I pulled the covers off his face and actually touched his bare arm, shaking him.

"Wake up, Chas."

"You are a total fag, Pusswing. You do realize you are touching me. Right?"

"They're doing a search for Joey. In the woods. Get your fucking ass out of bed, and let's help look for our captain."

I fought the urge to shut my eyes. I guessed it would hurt just as bad if Chas knocked my teeth in, whether I watched him do it or not.

But he just took a deep breath, rubbed his eyes, and sat up.

When he put his bare feet down on the floor, he looked around our room in the foggy light and said, "It's fucking cold."

"Yeah."

He held his hand out so I could help pull him to his feet.

Chas stripped and got into some thermals and sweats, gloves, and a hat. He looked like he was ready to go snowshoeing, and I have to admit I wished I had more layers on too.

At least I'd stuffed a couple microwave breakfast sandwiches into my pockets. They were still warm, so I kind of hated giving one up for Chas when we stepped outside and into the drizzle.

They tasted nasty, but Chas thanked me for bringing him breakfast in bed, even if, according to his understanding of the universe, it only proved how much of a homo I was.

●●●

We knew the places to look, anyway.

There was a big drainage culvert halfway between O-Hall and the highway to Bannock. It was where O-Hall boys sometimes went to smoke weed or cigarettes with their friends, or, if they were alone, to jerk off to some nasty old porn mags everyone seemed to leave there.

Nobody was there.

Chas took a piss against the side of the drainpipe and asked if I had any cigarettes or chew.

I shook my head.

He said, "Yeah. I didn't think so."

"You really think I'm a pussy, don't you?"

Chas stared at me, unblinking, like a rhino or something equally terrifying, standing three feet away from me while he tucked his dick back inside his thermals, and said, "Fuck. You? You're about the most unpussy sack of shit winger I've ever seen on a rugby pitch in my fucking life. I think half your scrawny-ass weight must be taken up by balls. Winger."

I nodded.

I wished I had a cigarette to give him after that.


We followed the lake around toward Stonehenge.

It started to snow, a wet, Pacific Northwest snow that fell in clumps, soaking and unpleasant. We ran into two Forest Service rangers near Stonehenge. They got excited when they saw us, and took out the photocopied pictures they'd been carrying of Joey's school ID, holding the images between their eyes and us like they were some kind of prism that could sort out and break up the bullshit from the truth.

Nothing.

But we kept looking.

# saturday afternoon

THEY FOUND JOEY IN THE WOODS, not far from O-Hall, at about three o'clock that afternoon.

He was tied to a tree, stripped naked, and had been beaten to death.

# later

I NEED TO VENT.

But I can't.

The words won't come.

# playing the game

I'LL BE HONEST. I DIDN'T CRY.

I didn't even say anything at all.

Because I didn't want to hear it, so I just didn't talk to anyone anymore.

Annie and I would walk together. Sometimes, we would go to the wishing circle, and I'd always hold her hand. When I needed to, I would whisper to her. She was the only one.

But I stopped talking after Joey died. I was too afraid.

My parents tried to take me out of Pine Mountain. They said I needed help.

I sent them a letter so they'd know I would be okay, and in it, I wrote that taking me away from Annie would kill me. So, after two weeks, Annie's mother and father came to Pine Mountain so they could see me.

Doc Dad watched me play rugby. I gave him the Pine Mountain RFC shirt he wanted, but I didn't talk to him. He shook my hand, and I could tell he was happy to see me, but I couldn't look him in the eyes, because I knew they'd look like hurt, and I wasn't going to cry in front of anyone.


I swear to God, when I played, sometimes I would see Joey out there leading the back line, but it was always someone else.

During our game, I could hear Doc Dad on the sidelines, cheering. He enjoyed the game. It made me feel good. I liked Annie's father.

Doc Mom came to see me, alone, in my room.

We didn't say anything, and it was dark. The window was covered. I sat on my bed, and she sat across from me in a chair.

It was like that for twenty minutes: just dark nothing. Then she stood up and sat beside me on my bed and she put her arm around my shoulders, and I began talking.

I told her about my iPod and how I sang for Joey the last time I ever saw him.

After a while, she said, "Anyone in the world would be so lucky to call you their friend, Ryan Dean."

I told her about how Joey always stuck up for anyone, even people he didn't like. And I told her the story about how Chas made me drink beer the night before school started. I told her about how we drank whiskey, too, before Halloween, and I'd peed in Chas's and Casey's drinks that night when Joey drove us into Bannock to get costumes and we lost Chas but picked up Screaming Ned.

And telling that story made me smile, but it hurt so much.

So when I was finished talking about Joey, Doc Mom said, "Okay, Ryan Dean, I am not a therapist anymore. Now I'm just a mom."

Then she squeezed me so tight and she kissed my head and said, "I am so sorry, baby. I am so sorry," and we both cried for I don't know how long.

Annie waited outside. But when I was finished with my crying, I told Doc Mom that I couldn't go out.

"I don't want anyone to know I was crying," I said.

Doc Mom said, "Okay, Ryan Dean. I'll wait as long as you want me to."

"I'll be okay, Doc Mom."

# in the boys' dorm

ON THE DAY THEY FOUND JOEY, THE police sealed off O-Hall, and we never went back there again.

Never.

They talked to Chas and me for hours, separately. I told them almost everything, but not the stuff I didn't think would matter.

They didn't ask, anyway.

Casey Palmer and Nick Matthews killed Joey that night of the dance. They got drunk. They were mad. They beat him until he stopped being Joey.

I loved Joey Cosentino.

After I told the police what I knew about Casey, they went to his home.

Casey Palmer and Nick Matthews never came back to school. I heard they both confessed right away, and I figured it was because Casey didn't want it coming out in his trial about how he'd been chasing after Joey for so long. That's what I think, but I could be wrong.

Either way, I didn't care about Casey's reasoning.

Pine Mountain closed down O-Hall. None of us ever saw Mr. Farrow or Mrs. Singer again. They were gone, cut loose. Nobody needed them, and nobody needed anything like O-Hall again, either.

I'll be honest. I was actually sad about them closing down O-Hall, as weird as that sounds. I wished I could go back to the noise and the smell, the crowded and dirty bathroom.

They moved me and Kevin and Chas in together at the boys' dorm, each of us with our private bedroom, and the big living room where we'd sometimes fight over what to watch on our television.

We talked about it once, much later, and we decided that we were all better suited to live in O-Hall, so I told Kevin and Chas that I was going to do my best to get them to reopen it and then I'd do something bad so they would have to send me there for my senior year.

Chas said, "You're a fucking idiot, Winger."

Yeah. I know.

Chas Becker and I became friends. He didn't turn me into an asshole, and I didn't teach him how to draw comics. It was a balanced relationship, but a weird one.

Wingers and forwards are not allowed to be friends.

But Chas and I needed each other.

He picked on me. That was to be expected. Kevin Cantrell, like always, was the calming peacemaker in our new three-man family. We played poker on Sundays. We invited Seanie Flaherty and JP Tureau to the games.

There were no more consequences.

How could you top the magnificent shit we had done in O-Hall?

How could you ever make anything worse?

The thing about rugby is this: You can hate a guy off the pitch who will save your fucking balls on the pitch when you play on the same side. There is nothing more glorious than that.

One time, in the boys' dorm, while we were playing a game of Hold 'Em, I made JP Tureau laugh.

I thought, *When we are seniors, me and JP are going to be cool again.*

# thanksgiving

THIS TIME, I REMEMBER TO TAKE off my belt before I walk through the metal detector at the airport, so I avoid the humiliation of a second strip search from Officer Nutgrabber.

What happened to Joey messed me up worse than anything I ever had to recover from. And I'll be honest. It scared me to leave Pine Mountain, even if it did mean spending four days with Annie. I couldn't sleep those nights before Thanksgiving came.

As ridiculous as it sounds, I kept thinking something terrible would happen if I left Kevin and Chas.

But I knew I was being stupid and that I had to do something to make myself get over being afraid, if I was ever going to grow up and get better.

After all, I was supposedly on a mission to do just that—to reinvent Ryan Dean West—in my junior year at Pine Mountain Academy.

Well, fuck that.

We hold hands for the entire flight. I point out the window, grinning, and say, "Remember?" I kiss her when we cross the Columbia River, and Annie smiles and says, "You are such a pervert."

●●●

I imagine that there will never be a moment in my life when I am not in love with Annie Altman. Being back on Bainbridge Island is almost like filling my lungs up with the same air again, the air that smells so green and thick with the ocean.

We walk out on the beach in the freezing and damp cold of the evening. Her parents watch us go, standing in the open doorway. But they leave us alone.

"I'm going to be better, Annie."

"First thing tomorrow, we're going for a run. Even if it's raining. You can tear your clothes off if you feel like it, and we'll jump in the hot tub when we're done."

"You're asking for the Wild Boy to return, you know."

And Annie laughs and takes off, running down the beach. I chase after her, but she lets me catch her too easily, and we kiss right there as her parents watch us.

I know it's kind of ridiculous, but I realize now how wrong that old pervert Mr. Wellins is. Almost nothing at all is ever about sex, unless you never grow up, that is.

It's about love, and, maybe, not having it.

What an old, delusional idiot he is.

But what do I know?

I'm just fourteen.

# quiet time

I'LL SAY IT NOW. I DIDN'T TALK for those weeks because I was afraid of the words.

The words came together and said how Joey died: alone and scared.

And he never did anything bad to anyone.

Ever.

But when I was quiet, I could hold on to Annie's hand, and that was a word that didn't need to be spoken. And Doc Mom, sitting with her arm around me and listening and crying, that made words too.

The same words that make the horrible things come also tell the quieter things about love.

I found out something about words. There are plenty of words I can put on paper, words I can see with my eyes and scribble with my hand, that I never had the guts to say with my mouth.

Sometimes, I used to think I was brave; but I don't believe that anymore.

And then it's always that one word that makes you so different and puts you outside the overlap of everyone else; and that word is so fucking big and loud, it's the only thing anyone ever hears when your name is spoken.

And whenever that happens to us, all the other words that make us the same disappear in its shadow.

Okay. I got it out.

Time to be quiet.

I can breathe again.

Here's a look at
Ryan Dean West's senior year
at Pine Mountain

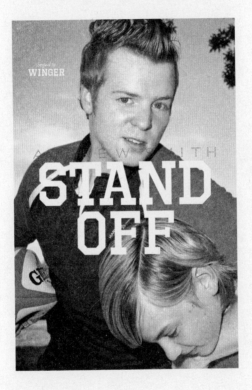

EVERYONE KEPT TELLING ME, "YOU need to draw again, Ryan Dean. You need to draw. . . ."

So I did.

I started drawing again in the summer before Annie and I went back to Pine Mountain for our senior year. The problem is, I'm pretty sure I didn't draw what everyone expected.

Let me explain.

Annie Altman, the most beautiful and together girl on the planet, an undeniable five out of five Swiss Army knives on the Ryan Dean West If-You-Could-Only-Have-One-Thing-When-You're-Stranded-with-Nothing-Not-Even-Your-Clothes-on-a-Deserted-Island-What-Would-It-Be Scale, happened to be on an island with me, but it wasn't deserted, so decency laws required us at the very least to have our swimsuits on. And I didn't have a Swiss Army knife either, which would have come in handy because neither one of us remembered to put any utensils in our picnic basket, so we had to eat my mom's potato salad with our fingers, which—*ugh!*—I thought was kind of sexy when our fingers touched in the cold mayonnaisey mush. But at least I had Annie, and we both had our swimsuits, and it was August, on one of those rare crystal-clear windless afternoons in Boston Harbor.

We spent the day at the beach on Spectacle Island, lying next to each other on a blanket in the sand. Naturally, I couldn't help but think about how there was only one thin article of clothing on my body; and how Annie and I were so close, our hands and feet touched, and I could feel her electricity sending sparks right up through me.

But I couldn't help thinking about a lot of other things too: about going back to Pine Mountain in a week, about how tough last year had been on me, and about the likely impossibility of me surviving my senior year there.

Annie put her hand on my belly and rubbed.

"You have to know how crazy that makes me, Annie."

"I do?"

"In about five seconds, I don't think I'll be held legally responsible for my actions."

Annie laughed. "Calm down, Ryan Dean. I was only trying to get the potato salad smell off my fingers."

"Oh. Nice. Ryan Dean West, fifteen-year-old human napkin."

Annie lived on Bainbridge Island, in Washington. It meant a lot that her parents trusted us enough to let her come to Boston to spend the last whole week of summer vacation with me before we had to report back to Pine Mountain Academy. But it wasn't like anything was going to happen, right? Annie was seventeen, and so beautiful. And I was just a fifteen-year-old napkin-boy who couldn't shake the feeling that something terrible was going to come out of nowhere and ruin everything for me again and again.

Drawing, for me, was like Pine Mountain Academy: I wanted to go back to it, and I also didn't want to go back.

OKAY. YOU KNOW HOW WHEN YOU'RE
a senior in high school, and you officially know absolutely everything about everything and no one can tell you different, but on the
other hand, at the same time, you're dumber than a poorly translated
instruction manual for a spoon?

Yeah. That was pretty much me, all at the same time, the only fifteen-
year-old boy to ever be in twelfth grade at Pine Mountain Academy.

When you're a senior, you're supposed to walk around with your chest out and your shoulders back because it's like you own the place, right? I didn't feel that way. In fact, from the first day I got back to Pine Mountain, I was quietly considering flunking out of all my classes so I wouldn't have to move on with my life and be a sixteen-year-old grown-up.

What a bunch of bullshit that would undoubtedly be.

And, speaking of bullshit, the day I came back to Pine Mountain Academy to check in and register, I learned that I would be rooming—in a double-single room no less—with some random kid I didn't even know. It had somehow failed to sink in to my soiled-napkin brain that my last year's roommates, Chas Becker and Kevin Cantrell, had graduated from Pine Mountain and moved on to the fertile breeding grounds of adulthood, leaving me roommateless, condemned to a single-size room with two beds in it, and matched up with Joe Randomkid, whom I'd already pictured as some bloated, tobacco-chewing, overalls-wearing midwesterner who was missing half a finger from a lawn-mowing or wheat-threshing accident and owned a vast collection of '70s porn mags (since we weren't allowed to access the Internet at PM and look at real porn like most teenagers do).

Not that I look at porn, like most *normal* teenagers. I'm not like that.

But nine-and-a-half-fingered Joe Randomkid would be exactly like that, I decided.

So by the time I turned the key on my all-new, 130-square-foot boys' dorm prison cell with two twin beds, two coffin-size closets, and matching elementary-school-kid-style desks with identical 40-watt desk lamps, I already deeply hated Joe Randomkid and, at the same time, had no idea in the world who he was.

Even before I fully opened the door on our bottom-floor-which-is-usually-only-reserved-for-freshmen dorm room, I had pretty much everything about Joe Randomkid all figured out.

## JOE RANDOMKID RUINS TWELFTH GRADE: A PLAY BY RYAN DEAN WEST

SCENE: *A very small ground-floor room in the boys' dorm at Pine Mountain Academy, a prestigious prep school for future deviants and white-collar criminals, located in the Cascades of Oregon.* JOE RANDOMKID, *a chubby and pale redhead from Nebraska with a stalk of straw pinched between his lips, is lying with his hands behind his head, dressed in overalls (with no shirt underneath the bib) and work boots, on one of the two prison-size twin beds, as* RYAN DEAN WEST, *a skinny, Bostonian, rugby-playing fifteen-year-old upperclassman, enters the room from the outer hallway.*

JOE RANDOMKID: Howdy! The name's Joe. Joe Randomkid. I'm from Nebraska, and my pa's a hog farmer. We have, I reckon, close to twenty-two-hundred hogs on the farm, give or take a few depending on how hungry me and my brothers are. I have ten brothers! And no sisters! Can you imagine that? Ten of them! Their names are Billy, Wayne, Charlie, Alvin, Edmund, Donny, Timothy, Michael, Eugene, and Barry, and then there's me, Joe. How come I ain't ever seen you around? Are you a new kid? I been here every year since ninth grade, but you look like you're just a kid who can't possibly be old enough to be in twelfth grade. What sport do you play? Me? I'm on the bowling team. Got a two-oh-four average, which is number one in the state in Nebraska and Oregon for twelfth-grade boys. I bet being all skinny like that, you're on swim team or maybe gymnastics. Or do you cheer? Are you one of those *boy cheerleaders*? I don't think there's nothing wrong with that at all. Cheerleading's probably more of a sport than NASCAR is anyhow. Who's your favorite driver, by the way?

Are you one of them ones who get to pick up the girls and spin them around over your head like that? If I ever did that, I couldn't help but look up their skirts, am I right? Or do you not like girls and stuff? 'Cause if you don't, that's okay too. I realize it takes all kinds. All kinds. And maybe you're from California, after all.

RYAN DEAN WEST: (*Ryan Dean West walks across the room and looks out the window.*) Now I know why they put me on the ground floor.

The End

Mom and Dad had helped me move in this time. It was weird. All the other times they'd dropped me off at Pine Mountain, it was like they couldn't possibly leave fast enough.

Dad carried in my two plastic totes. One of them contained all my clothes and boy stuff—you know, deodorant and the razor Dad sent me last fall that was still as unnecessary as ever—and the other had school supplies, some brand new bedsheets, and a microwave oven, which I had no idea why they'd insisted I bring along. I lugged in the big canvas duffel bag filled with all my rugby gear that was soon to be packed away in my locker over at the sports complex.

I wanted to play rugby again almost as much as I wanted to see Annie, whom I hadn't seen since she left Boston for Seattle five days before.

And—*ugh!*—Mom cried when she put my new sheets on the exceedingly gross, slept-on-countless-times-before, yellowing boys' dorm twin-size fucking mattress, and I just stood there, helplessly giving my dad a *what-the-fuck* look. He shrugged.

At home in Boston, I had a big bed. I'm not sure where my Boston bed fit in on the hierarchy of royalty—you know, queens and kings and such—but it was easily twice as big as a twin, if this thing even *was* an actual twin. It was probably a preemie or something—the afterbirth of a twin. So we'd had to stop at a department store in this little town called Bannock, which is about twenty minutes from Pine Mountain, to get some sheets, and the only ones they had that would fit my dorm bed following the incoming rush of PM brats were pink flannel and decorated with a winged unicorn who, according to the inscription beneath her glinting hooves, was named *Princess Snugglewarm*.

Yeah. It was going to be a great year, wasn't it?

"Why are you crying, Mom? Don't worry about the unicorns. We can hide them beneath the blanket. I checked. It only has Princess Snugglewarm on one side, so we can flip it over so it only looks a little gay," I said.

Mom sniffled. "Oh, Ryan Dean. It's not that, baby. There's only so many more times left in our lives when I'll be able to put sheets on your bed and tuck you in."

This coming from the woman who wept when she bought me a box of condoms because she actually thought Annie and I were having sex—like that was ever going to happen—when I was fourteen.

It was hopeless.

And not only do horses with big fucking spikes coming out of their heads scare me, but I hate flannel sheets besides.